La Corda d'Oro

11
Story & Art by Yuki Kure

La Corda d'Oro

CONTENTS
Volume 11

Kahoko Hino
(General Education School, 2nd year)

The heroine. She knows nothing about music,
but she finds herself participating in the school music
competition equipped with a magic violin.

Ryotaro Tsuchiura
(General Education School,
2nd year)

A soccer player and talented
pianist who seems to be
looking after Kahoko.

Len Tsukimori
(Music School, 2nd year)

A violin major and a cold
perfectionist from a musical
family of unquestionable talent.

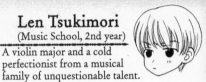

Kazuki Hihara
(Music school, 3rd year)

An energetic and friendly
trumpet major and a fan of
anything fun.

Keiichi Shimizu
(Music school, 1st year)

A cello major who walks to
the beat of his own drum and
is often lost in the world of
music. He is also often asleep.

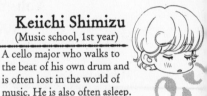

Azuma Yunoki
(Music School, 3rd year)

A flute major from an
ultra-traditional family who's
very popular with girls. Only
Kahoko knows that he has
a dark side!

Hiroto Kanazawa
(Music teacher)

The contest coordinator,
whose lazy demeanor
suggests he is avoiding any
hassle.

The music fairy Lili, who got
Kahoko caught up in this affair. ⤵

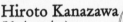

Story

Our story is set at Seisou Academy, which is split
into the General Education School and the Music
School. Kahoko, a Gen Ed student, encounters
a music fairy named Lili who gives her a magic
violin that anyone can play. Suddenly Kahoko
finds herself in the school's music competition,
with good-looking, quirky Music School
students as her fellow contestants! Kahoko comes to accept her
daunting task and discovers a love for music. But near the end of the
school's big music competition the violin loses its power and disappears.
Although Kahoko is discouraged at first, she decides to continue playing
with a normal violin. And now a new semester begins...

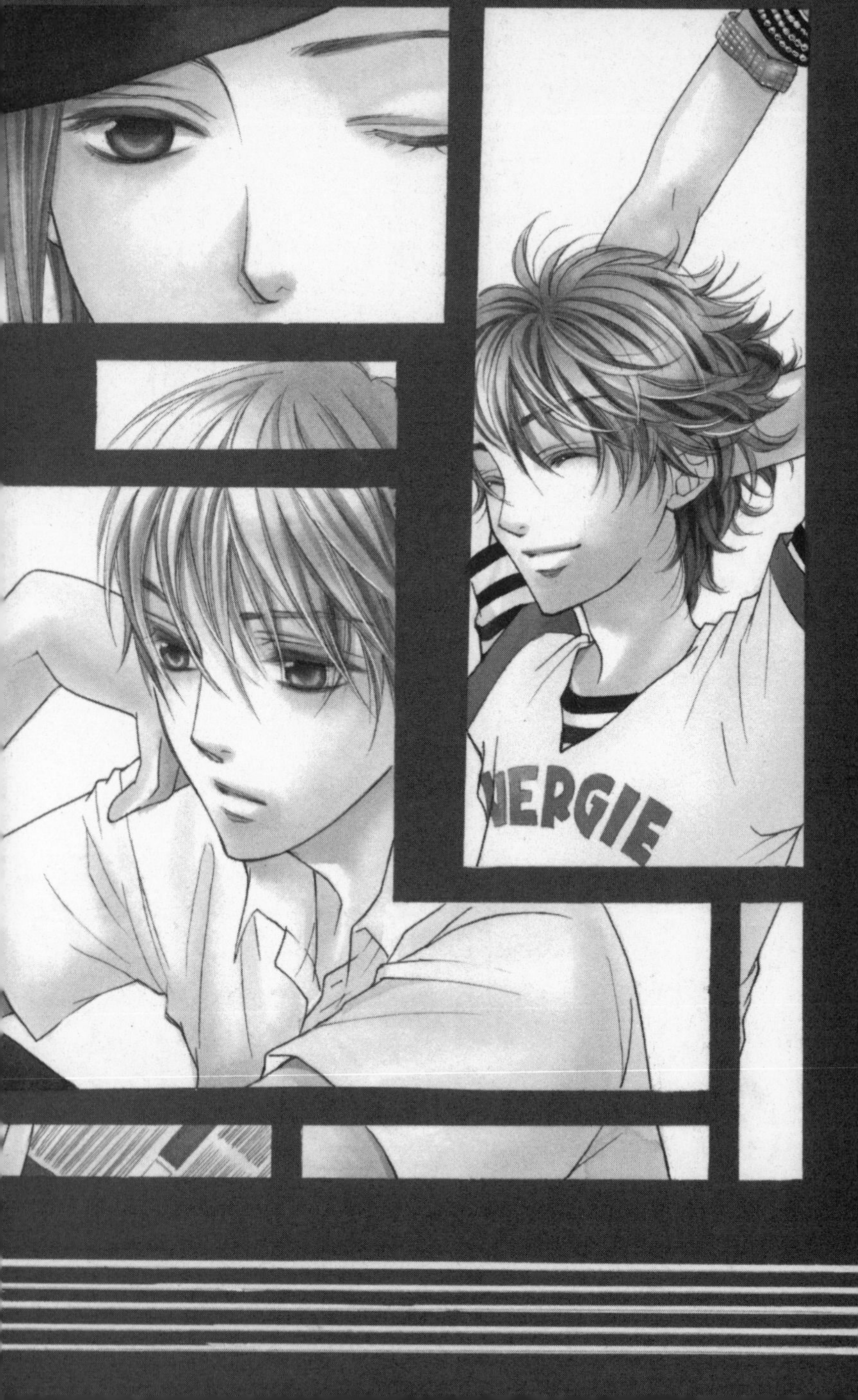
NERGIE

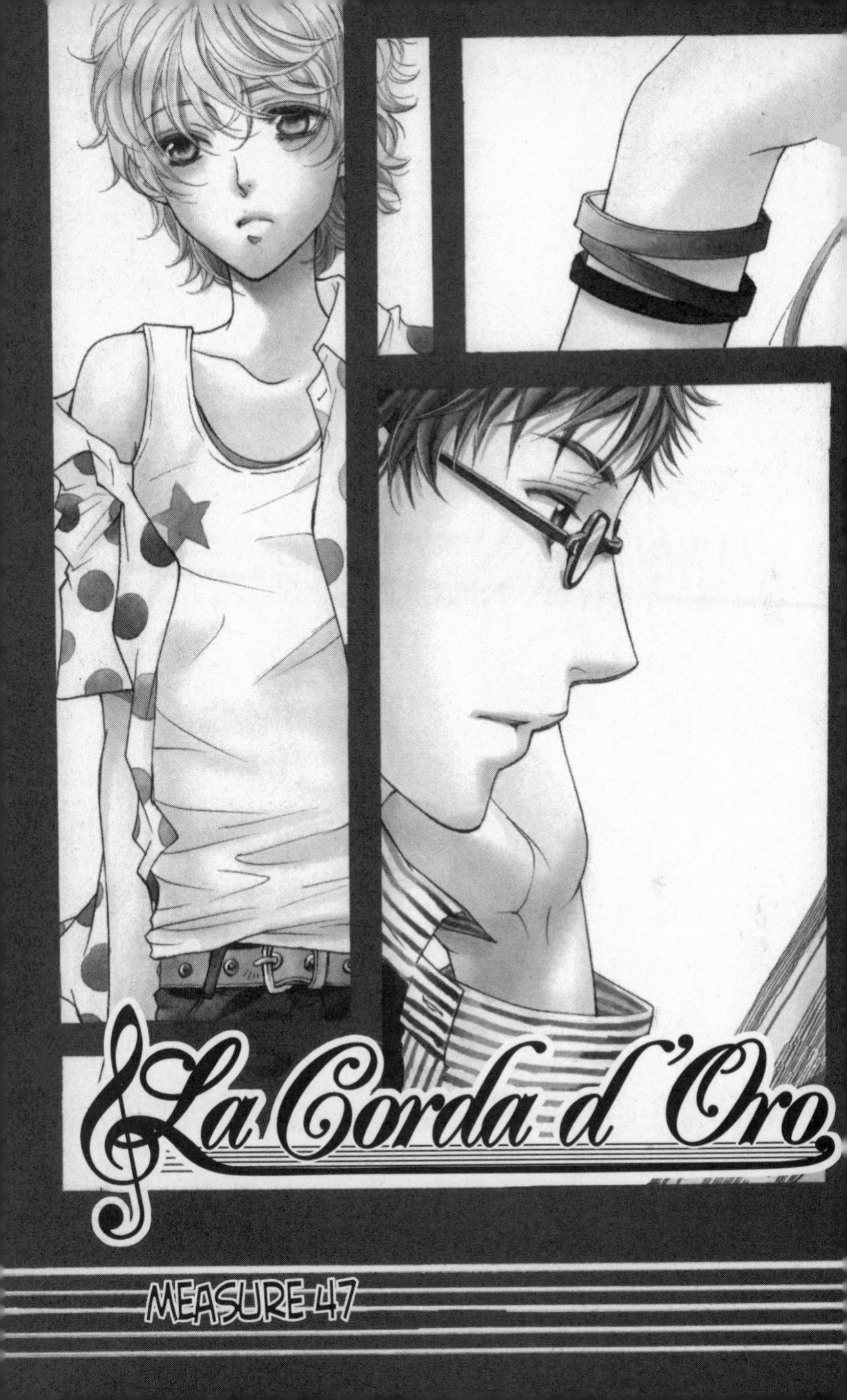
La Corda d'Oro
MEASURE 47

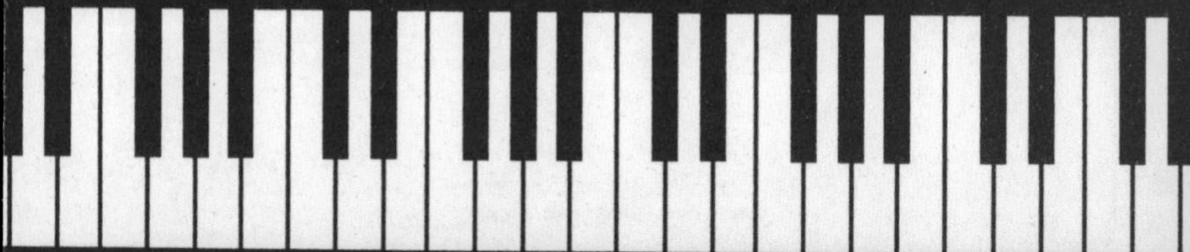

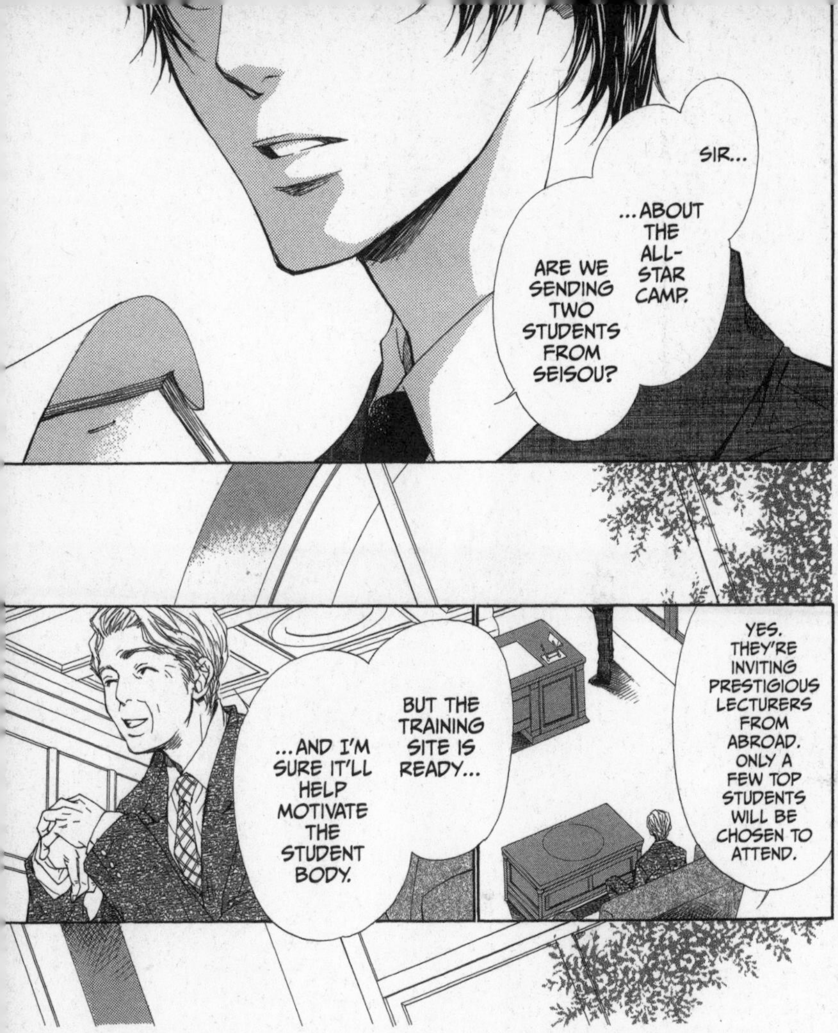
SIR...
...ABOUT THE ALL-STAR CAMP.
ARE WE SENDING TWO STUDENTS FROM SEISOU?
YES. THEY'RE INVITING PRESTIGIOUS LECTURERS FROM ABROAD. ONLY A FEW TOP STUDENTS WILL BE CHOSEN TO ATTEND.
BUT THE TRAINING SITE IS READY...
...AND I'M SURE IT'LL HELP MOTIVATE THE STUDENT BODY.

Daily Happenings 39

Oh really?

One of my assistants recently underwent surgery to fix her vision. To which another assistant, Dame N, responded...

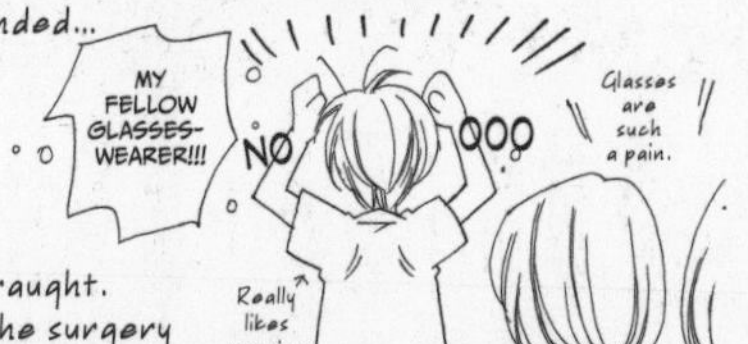
MY FELLOW GLASSES-WEARER!!!
NOOOO
Glasses are such a pain.
Really likes wearing glasses.

She seemed really distraught. The assistant who got the surgery always wore very stylish eyewear.

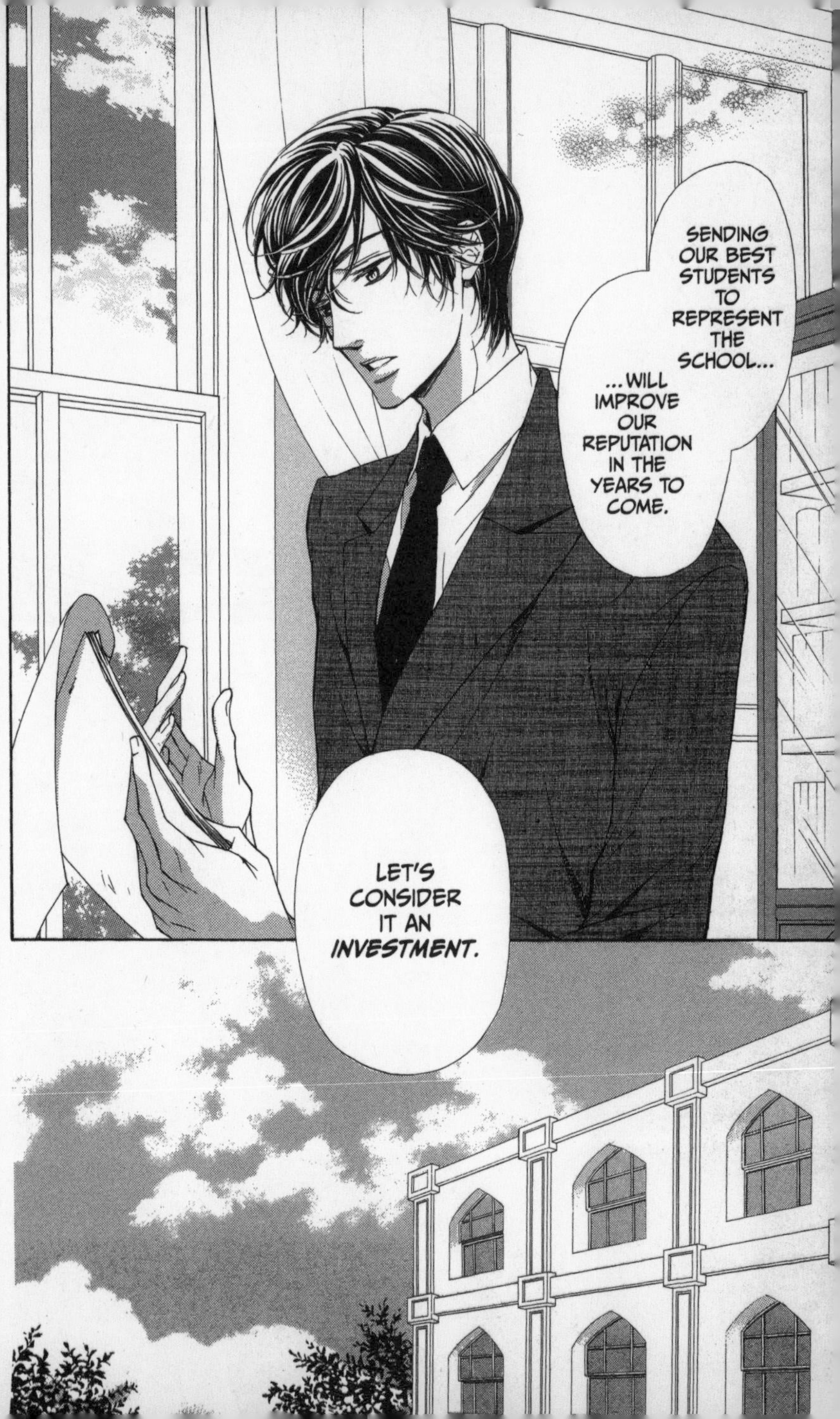
SENDING OUR BEST STUDENTS TO REPRESENT THE SCHOOL...
...WILL IMPROVE OUR REPUTATION IN THE YEARS TO COME.
LET'S CONSIDER IT AN *INVESTMENT*.

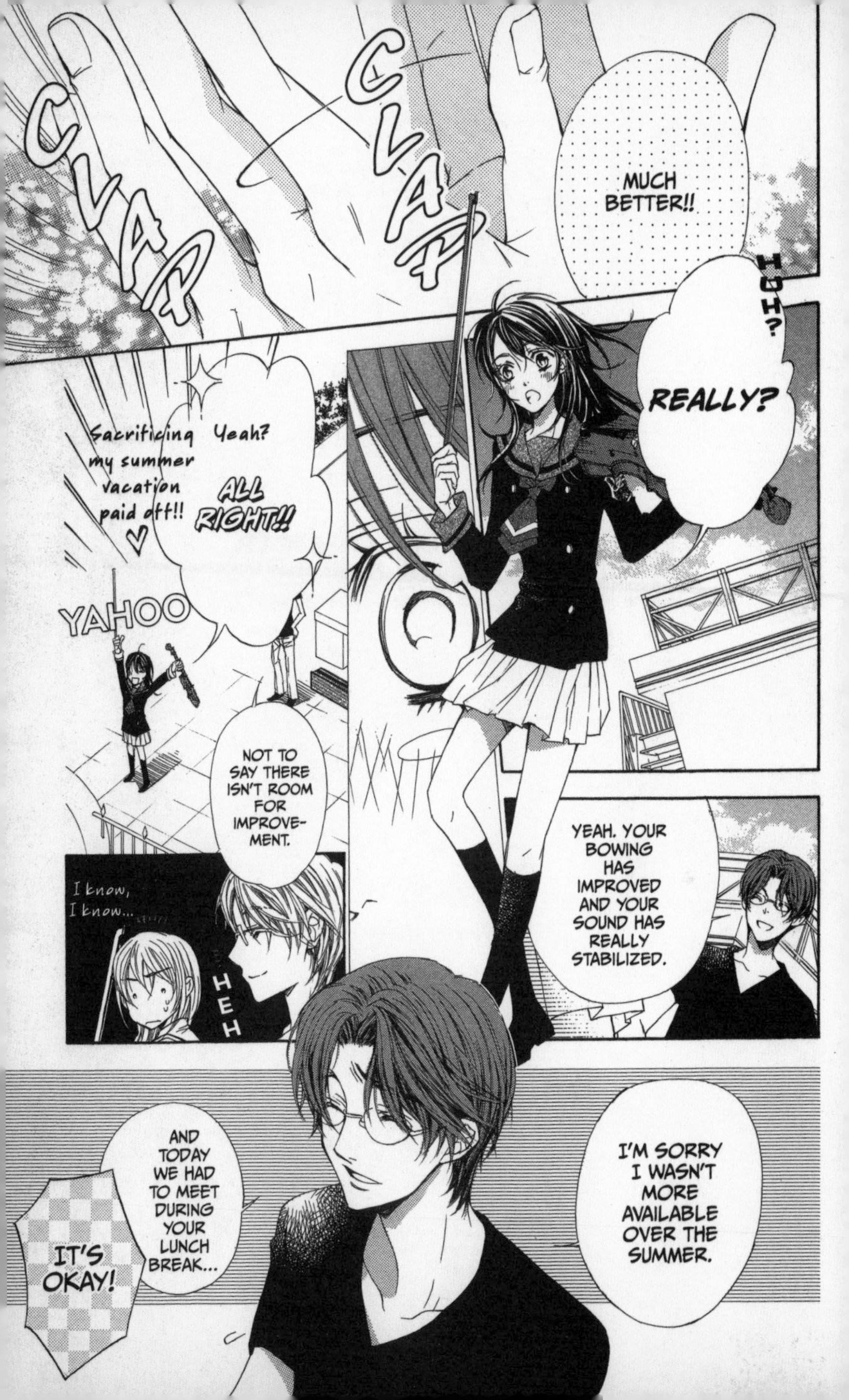
MUCH BETTER!!
CLAP
CLAP
HUH?
REALLY?
Yeah?
ALL RIGHT!!
Sacrificing my summer vacation paid off!! ♡
YAHOO
YEAH. YOUR BOWING HAS IMPROVED AND YOUR SOUND HAS REALLY STABILIZED.
NOT TO SAY THERE ISN'T ROOM FOR IMPROVEMENT.
HEH
I know, I know...
I'M SORRY I WASN'T MORE AVAILABLE OVER THE SUMMER.
AND TODAY WE HAD TO MEET DURING YOUR LUNCH BREAK...
IT'S OKAY!

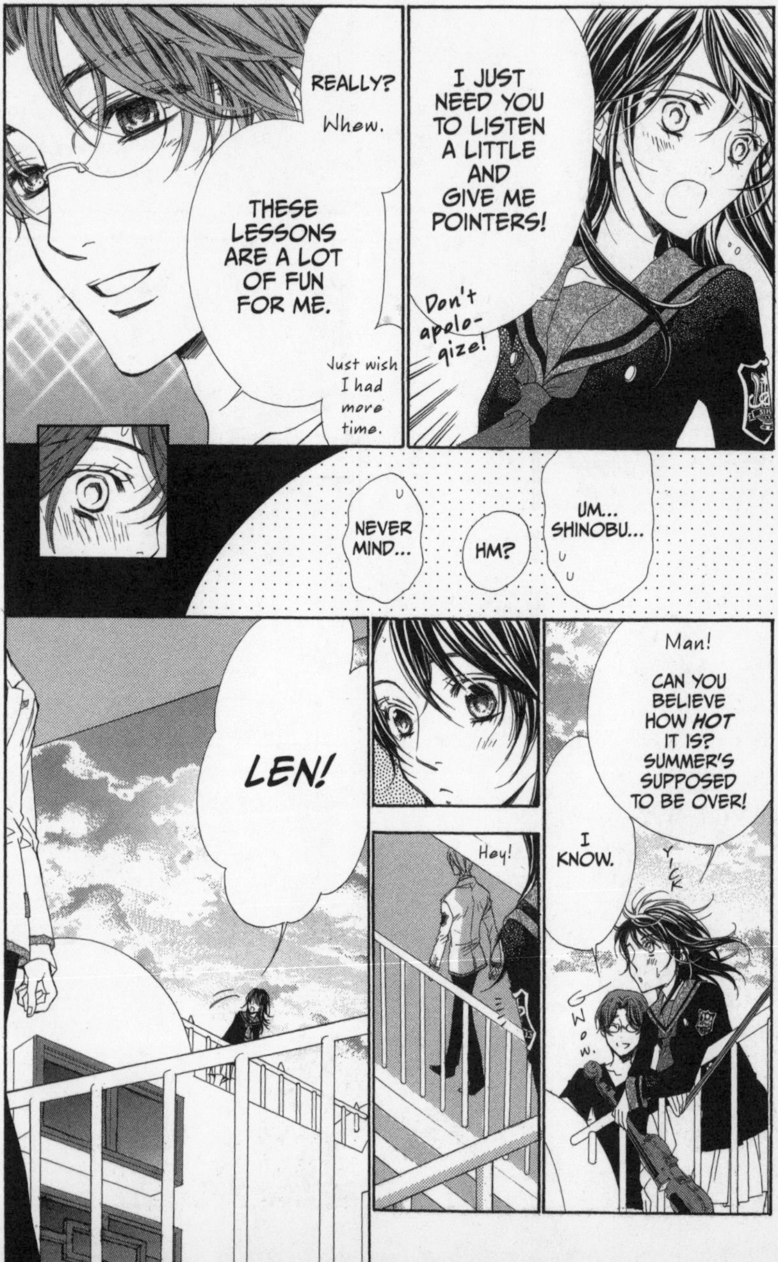
I JUST NEED YOU TO LISTEN A LITTLE AND GIVE ME POINTERS!
Don't apolo-gize!
REALLY?
Whew.
THESE LESSONS ARE A LOT OF FUN FOR ME.
Just wish I had more time.
UM... SHINOBU...
HM?
NEVER MIND...
Man!
CAN YOU BELIEVE HOW HOT IT IS? SUMMER'S SUPPOSED TO BE OVER!
YICK
I KNOW.
Wow.
Hey!
LEN!

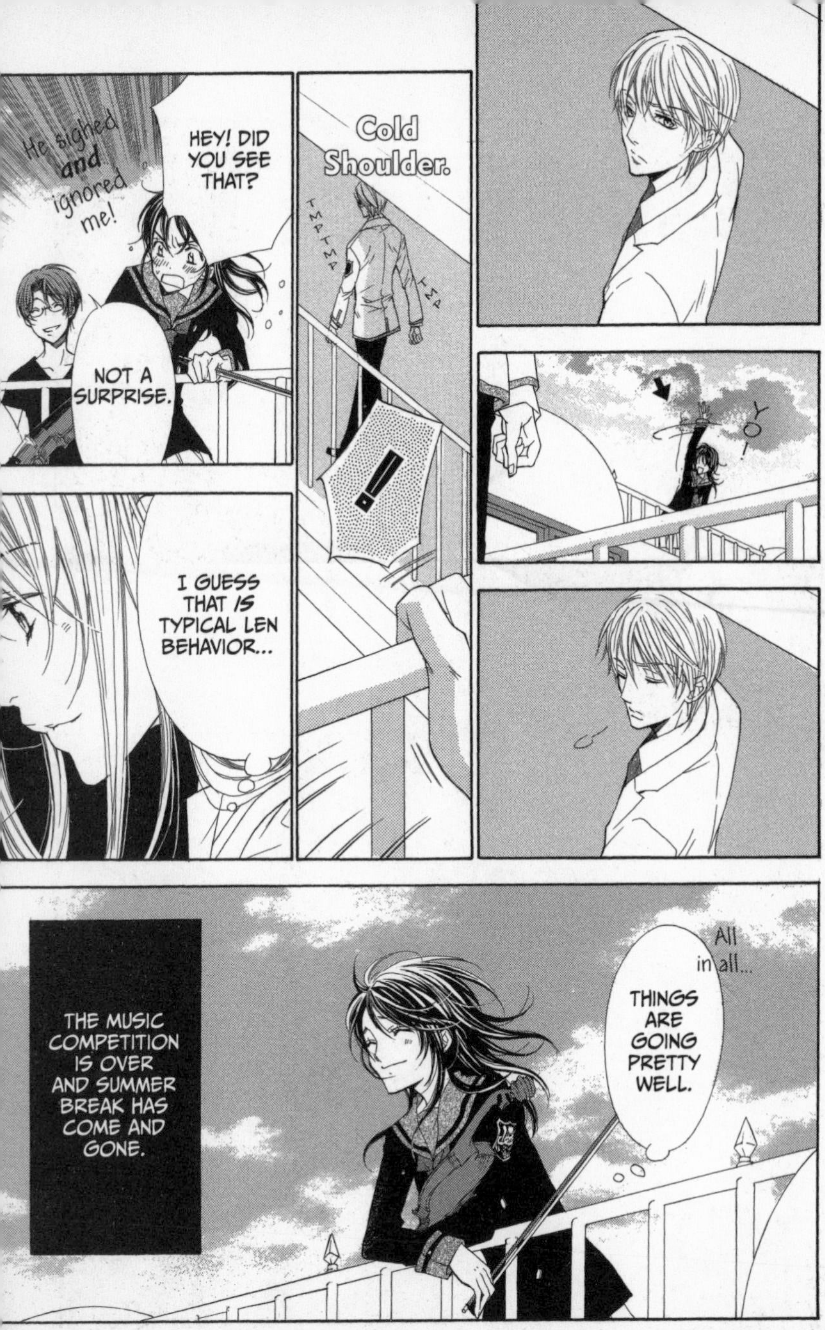
YO!
Cold Shoulder.
!
HEY! DID YOU SEE THAT?
He sighed and ignored me!
NOT A SURPRISE.
I GUESS THAT *IS* TYPICAL LEN BEHAVIOR...
All in all...
THINGS ARE GOING PRETTY WELL.
THE MUSIC COMPETITION IS OVER AND SUMMER BREAK HAS COME AND GONE.

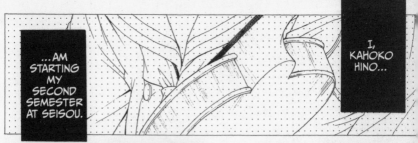

...AM STARTING MY SECOND SEMESTER AT SEISOU.

I, KAHOKO HINO...

3-B

AZUMA?

WHAT'S UP, LEN?

DON'T SEE YOU HERE VERY OFTEN.

12

Thank you so much for picking up *La Corda d'Oro* volume 11!

There are a lot of side stories in this volume. It's supposed to mark the beginning of a new storyline after the big music competition. I hope you enjoy it!

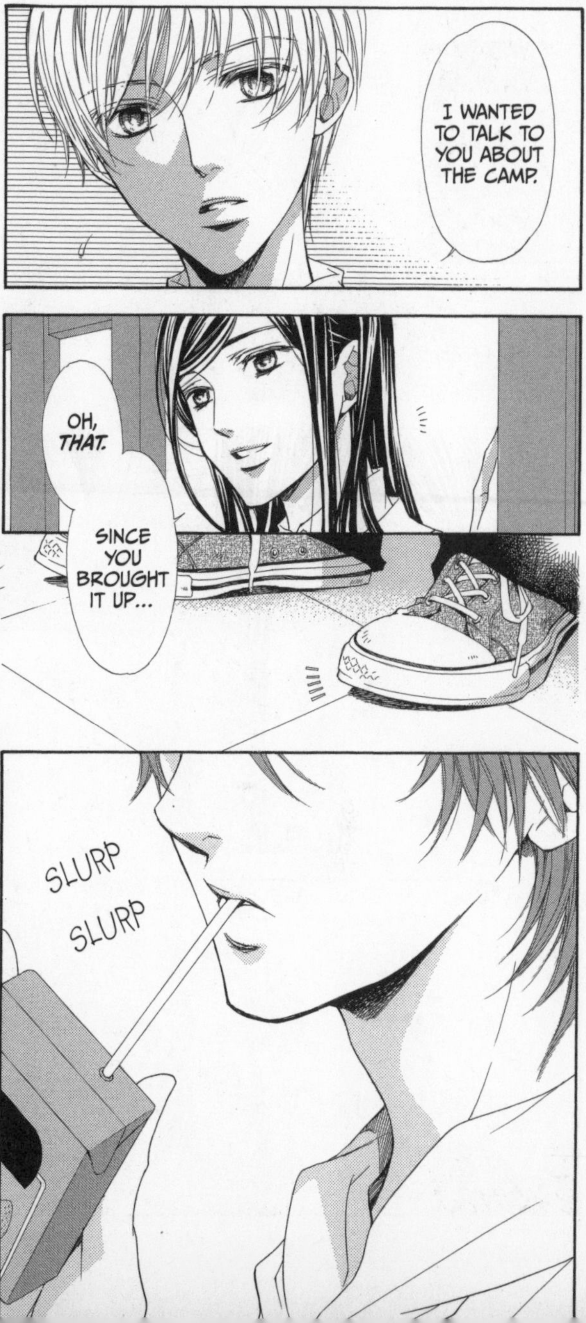
I WANTED TO TALK TO YOU ABOUT THE CAMP.
OH, *THAT.*
SINCE YOU BROUGHT IT UP...
SLURP
SLURP

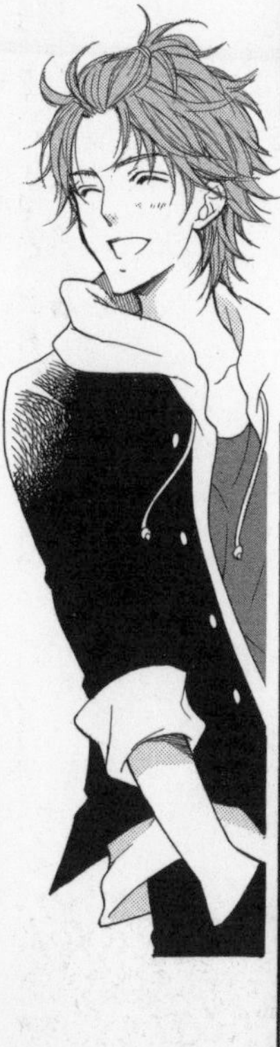

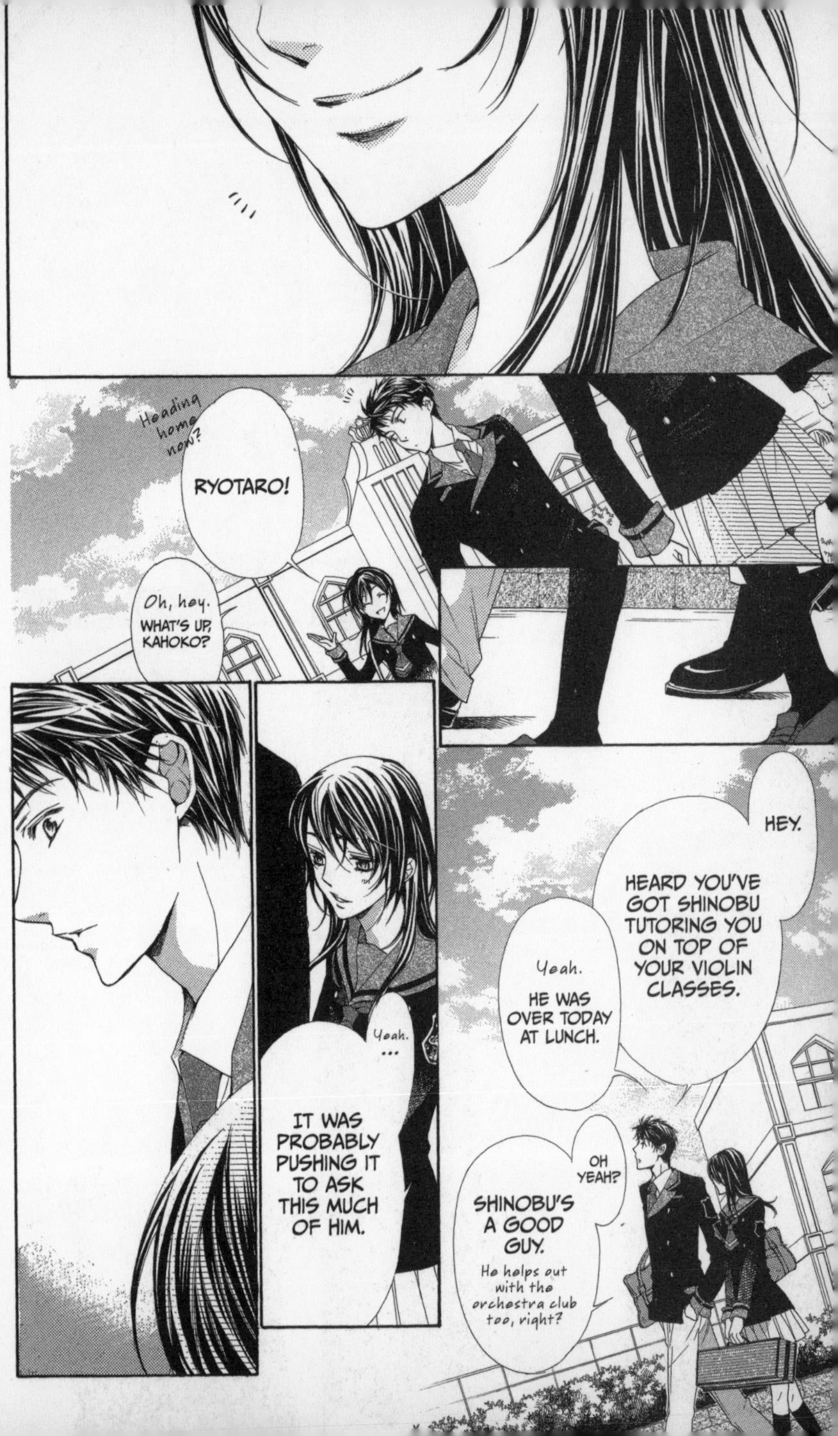
RYOTARO!
Heading home now?
Oh, hey.
WHAT'S UP, KAHOKO?
HEY.
HEARD YOU'VE GOT SHINOBU TUTORING YOU ON TOP OF YOUR VIOLIN CLASSES.
Yeah.
HE WAS OVER TODAY AT LUNCH.
OH YEAH?
SHINOBU'S A GOOD GUY.
He helps out with the orchestra club too, right?
Yeah.
...
IT WAS PROBABLY PUSHING IT TO ASK THIS MUCH OF HIM.

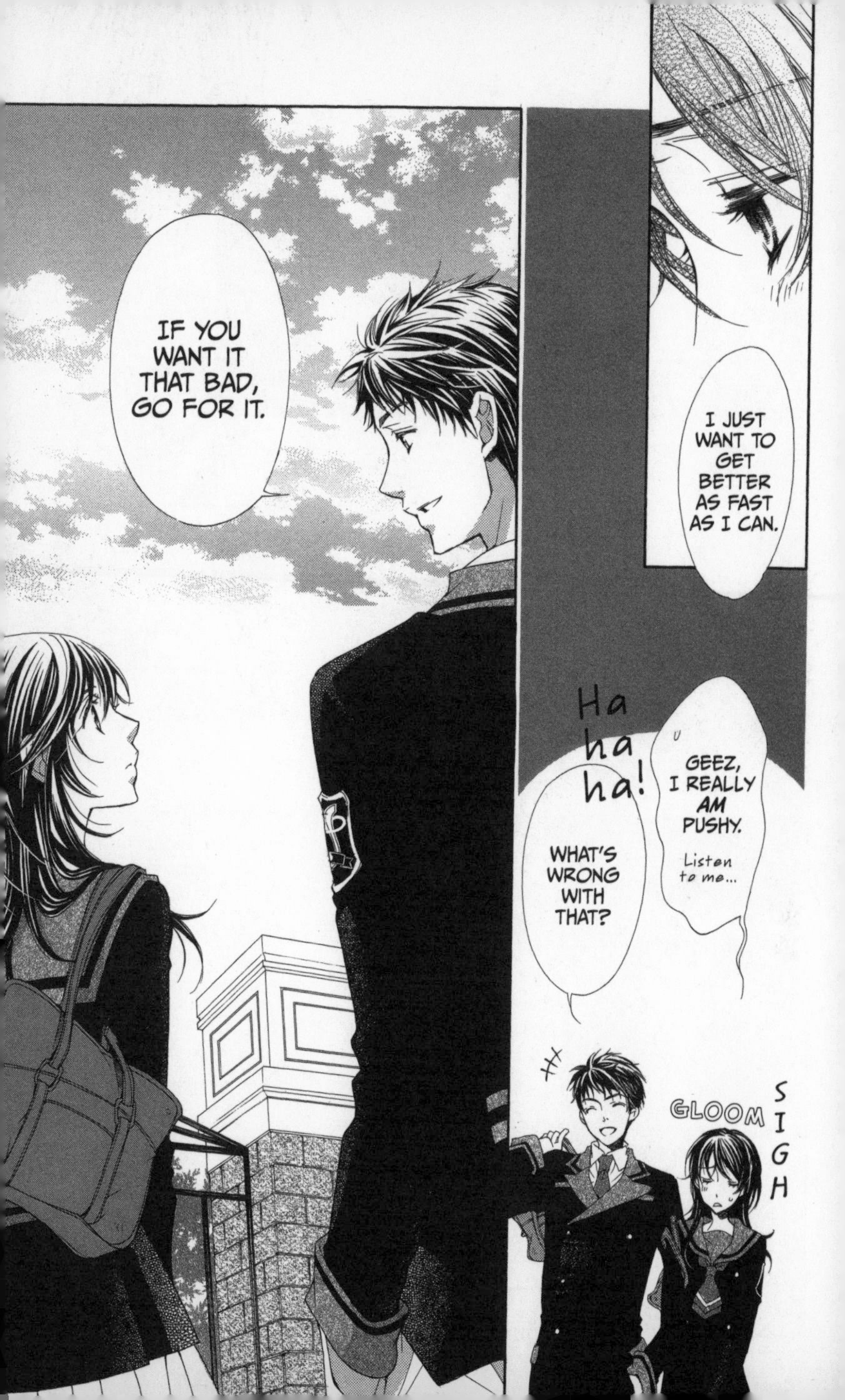
I JUST WANT TO GET BETTER AS FAST AS I CAN.
GEEZ, I REALLY *AM* PUSHY.
Listen to me...
Ha ha ha!
WHAT'S WRONG WITH THAT?
GLOOM
SIGH
IF YOU WANT IT THAT BAD, GO FOR IT.

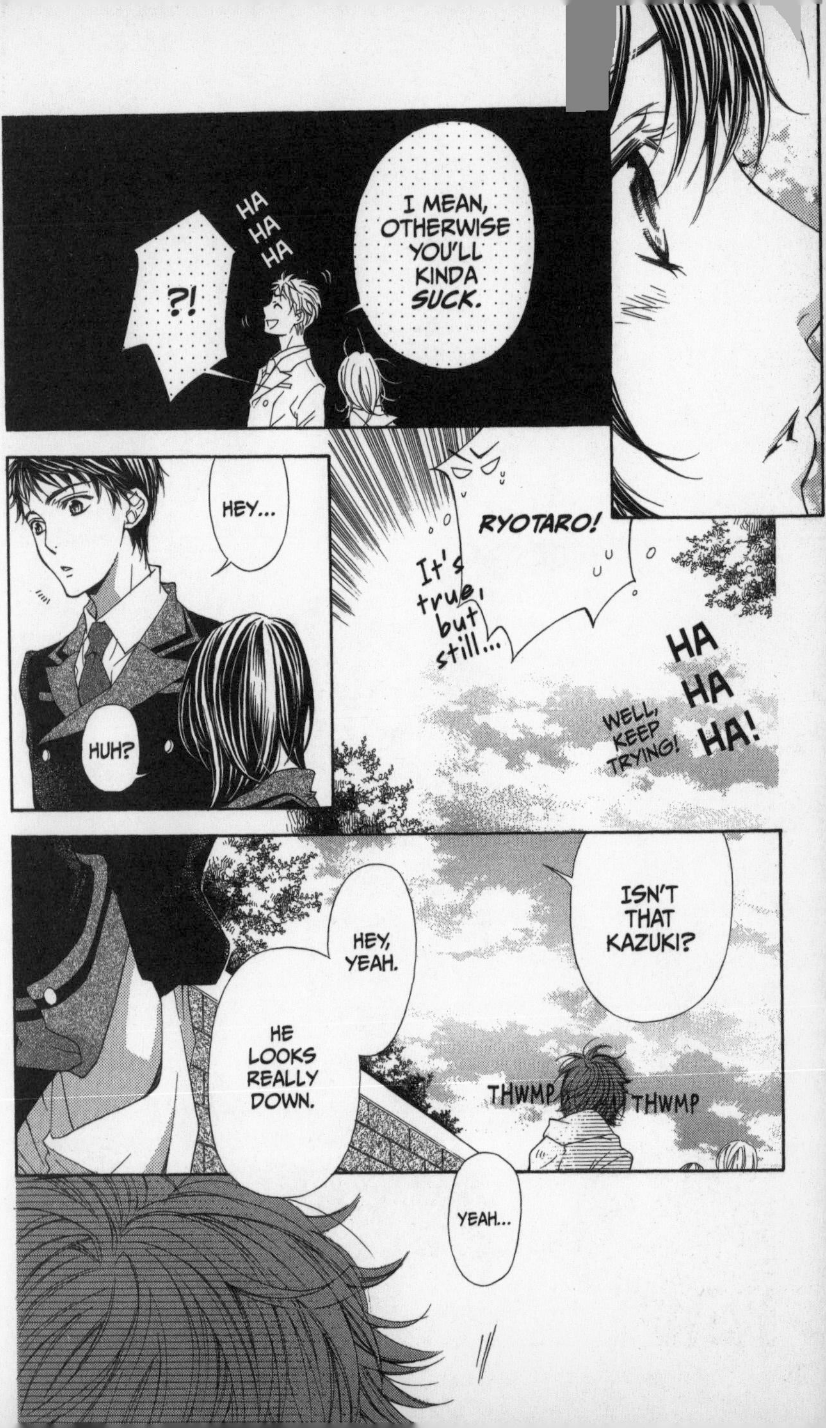
I MEAN, OTHERWISE YOU'LL KINDA SUCK.
HA HA HA
?!
RYOTARO!
It's true, but still...
HA HA HA!
WELL, KEEP TRYING!
HEY...
HUH?
ISN'T THAT KAZUKI?
HEY, YEAH.
THWMP THWMP
HE LOOKS REALLY DOWN.
YEAH...

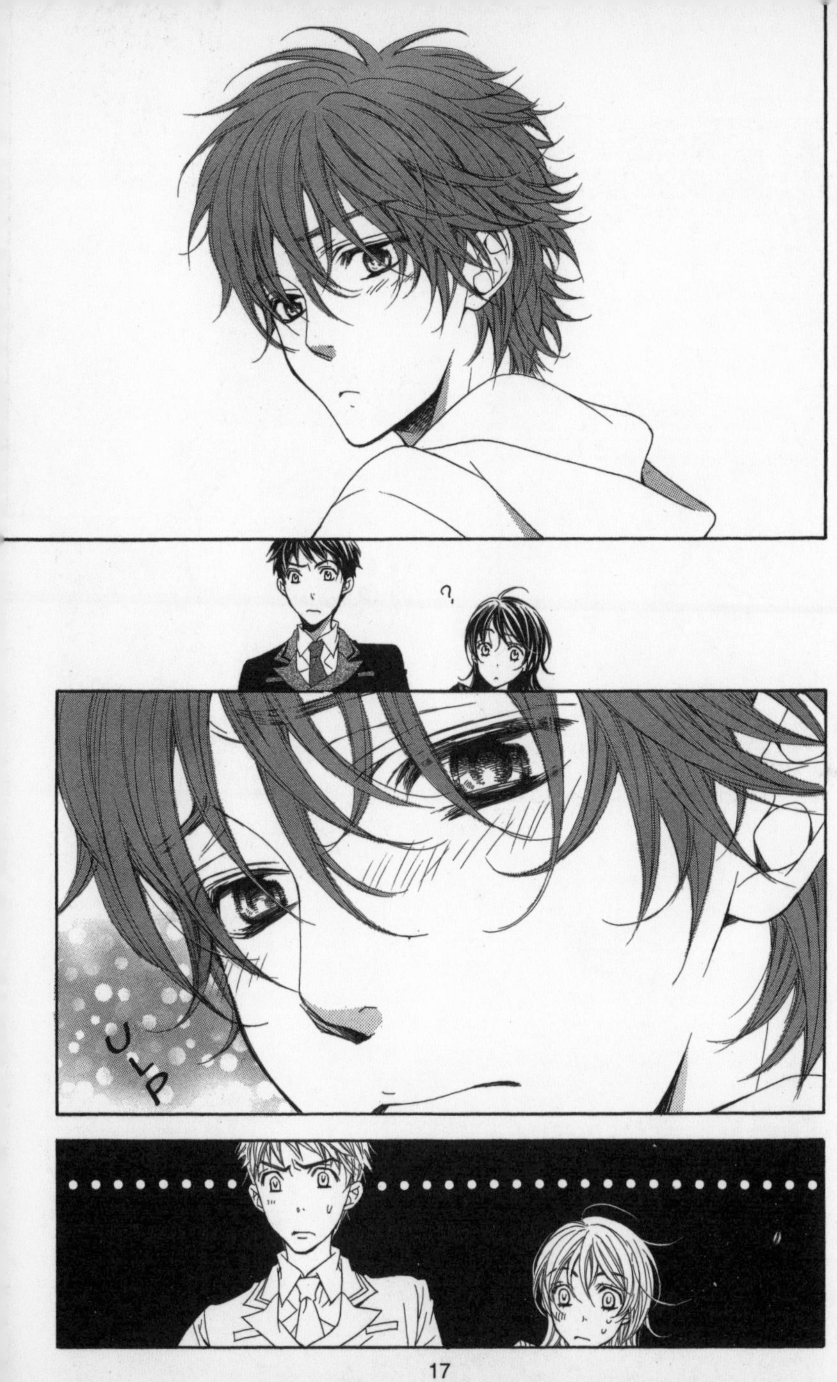
?
ULP

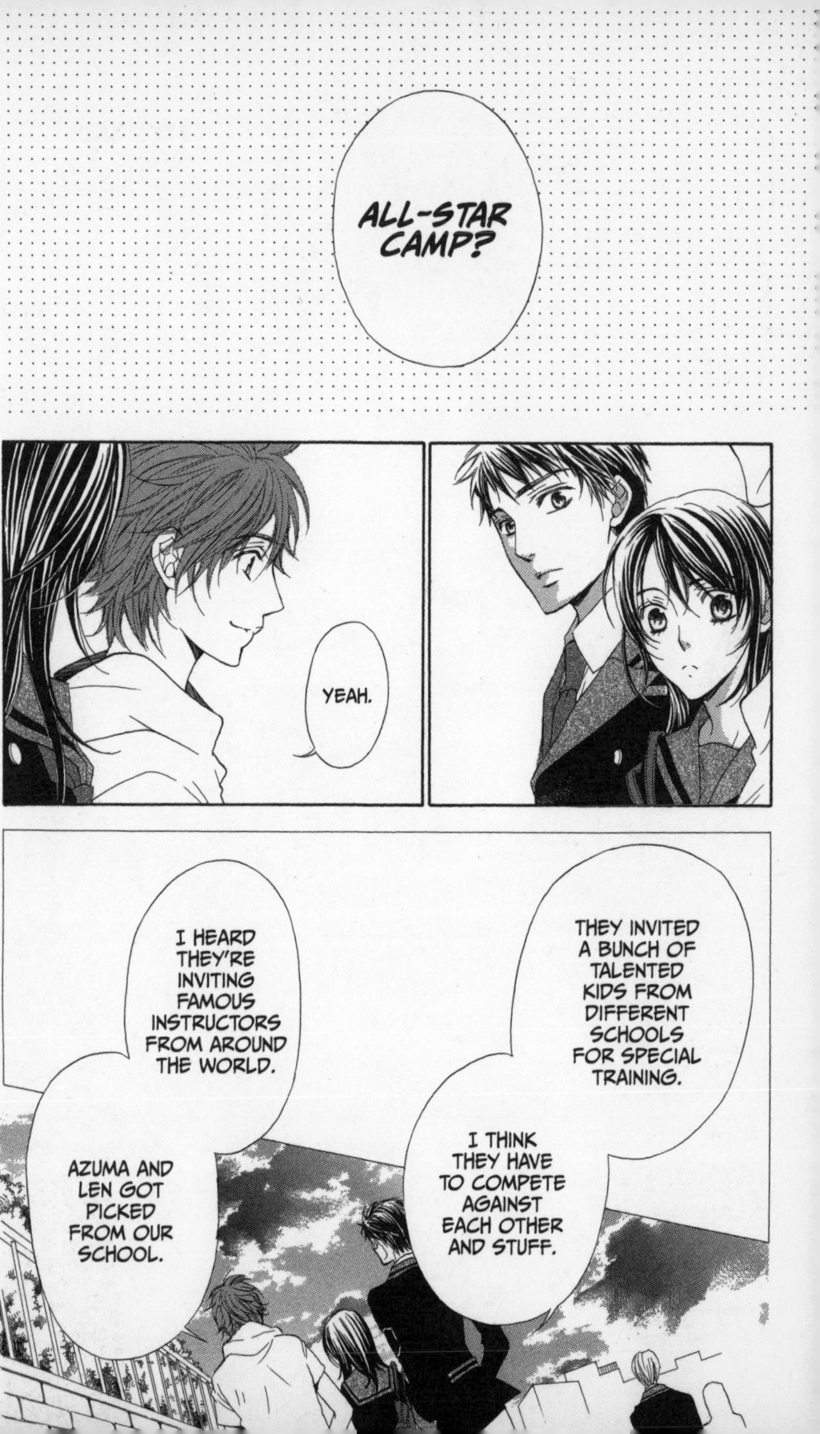
ALL-STAR CAMP?
YEAH.
THEY INVITED A BUNCH OF TALENTED KIDS FROM DIFFERENT SCHOOLS FOR SPECIAL TRAINING.
I THINK THEY HAVE TO COMPETE AGAINST EACH OTHER AND STUFF.
I HEARD THEY'RE INVITING FAMOUS INSTRUCTORS FROM AROUND THE WORLD.
AZUMA AND LEN GOT PICKED FROM OUR SCHOOL.

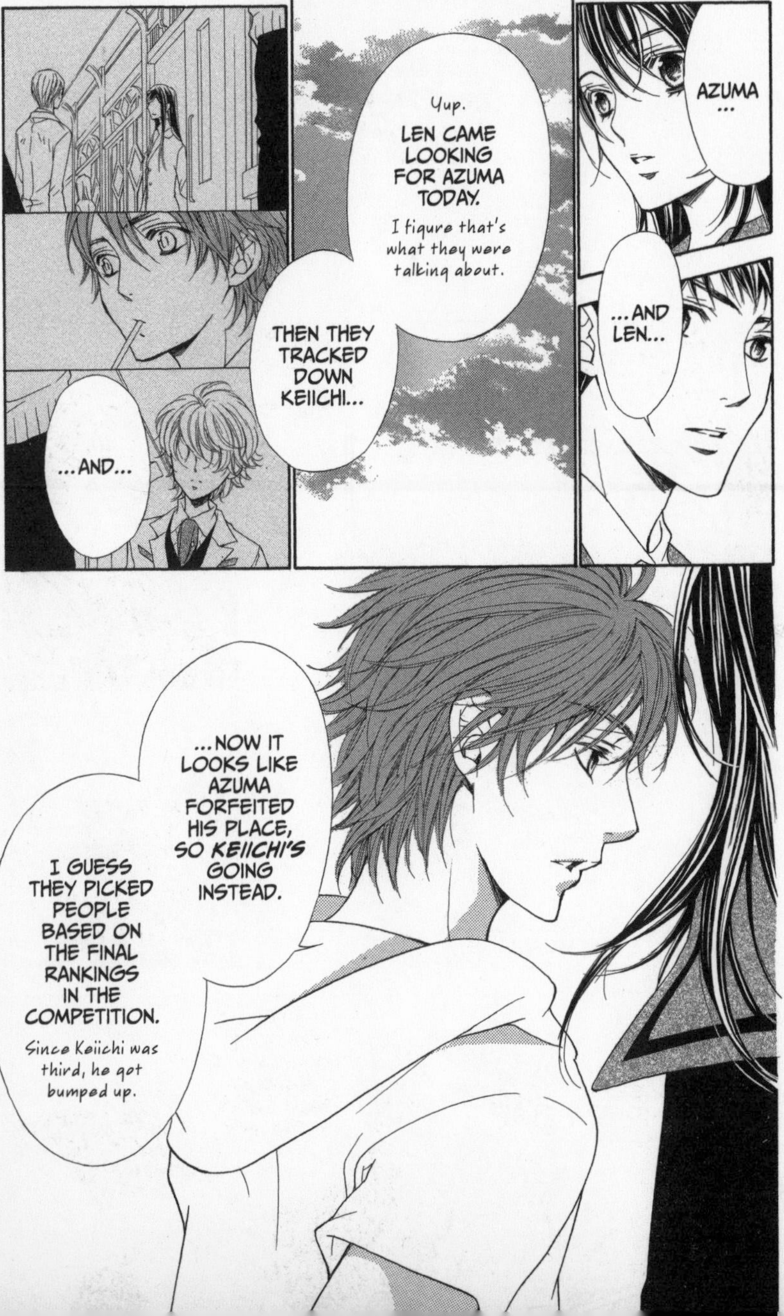
AZUMA ...
...AND LEN...
Yup.
LEN CAME LOOKING FOR AZUMA TODAY.
I figure that's what they were talking about.
THEN THEY TRACKED DOWN KEIICHI...
...AND...
...NOW IT LOOKS LIKE AZUMA FORFEITED HIS PLACE, SO *KEIICHI'S* GOING INSTEAD.
I GUESS THEY PICKED PEOPLE BASED ON THE FINAL RANKINGS IN THE COMPETITION.
Since Keiichi was third, he got bumped up.

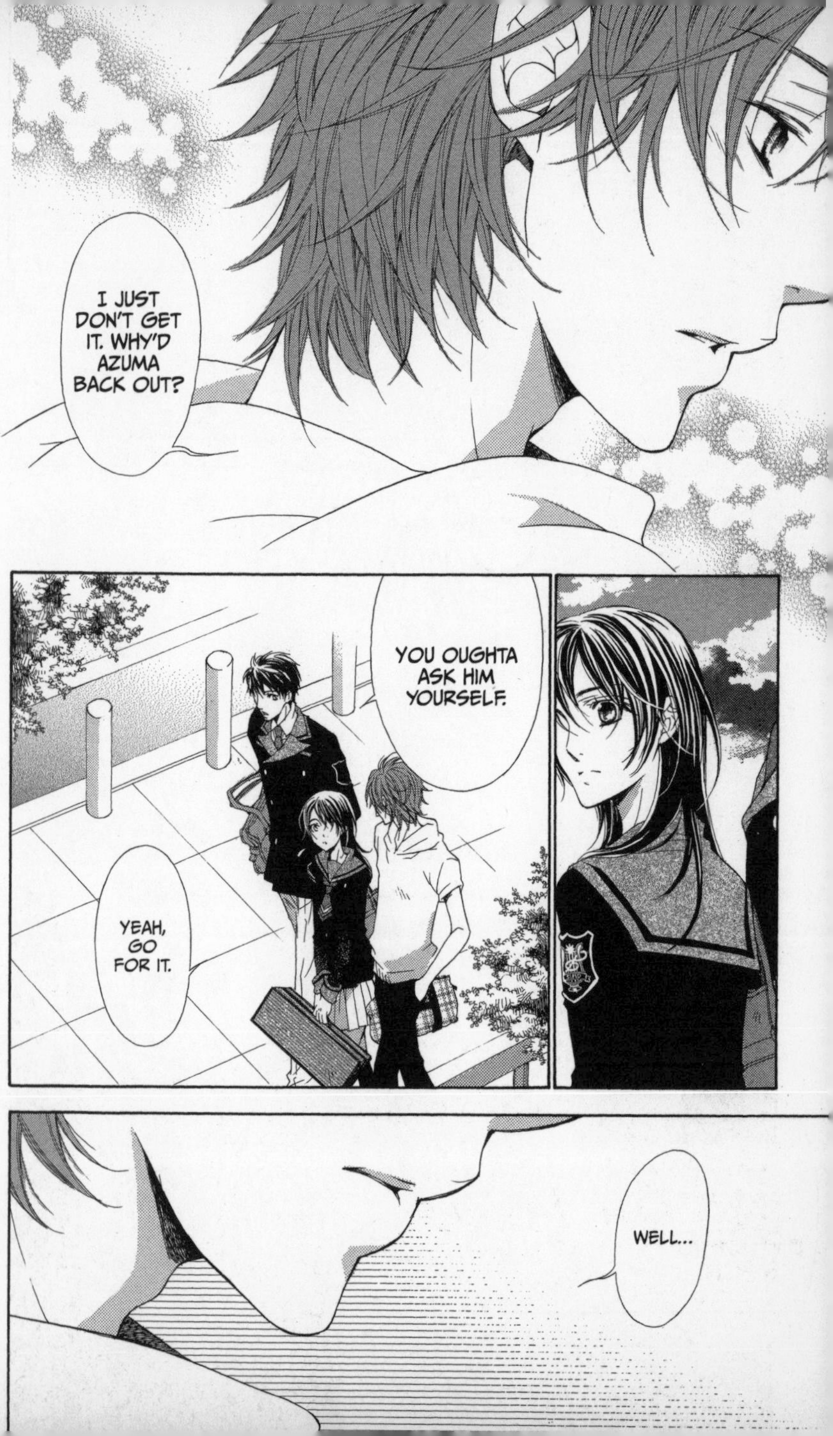
I JUST DON'T GET IT. WHY'D AZUMA BACK OUT?
YOU OUGHTA ASK HIM YOURSELF.
YEAH, GO FOR IT.
WELL...

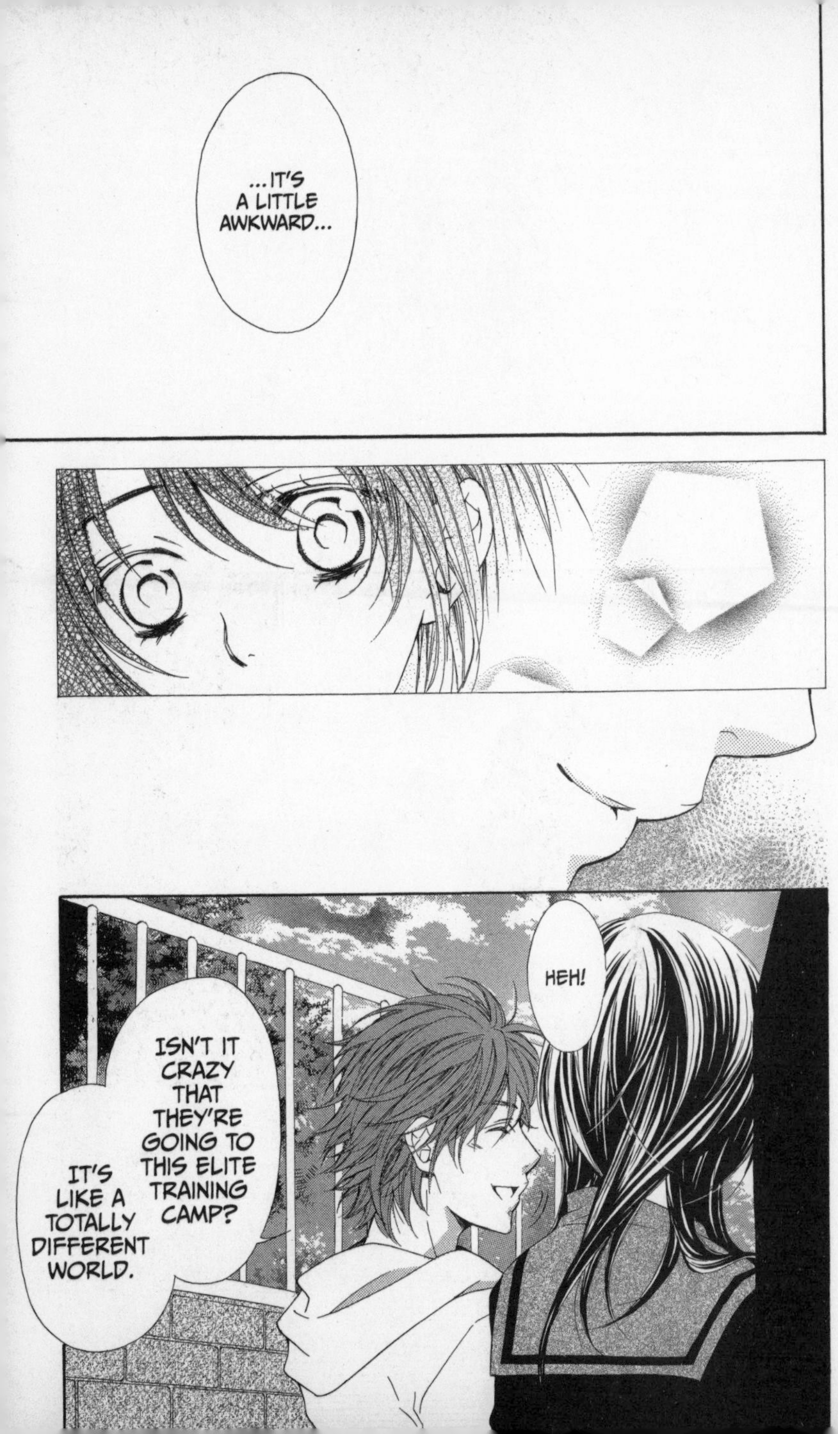
...IT'S A LITTLE AWKWARD...
HEH!
ISN'T IT CRAZY THAT THEY'RE GOING TO THIS ELITE TRAINING CAMP?
IT'S LIKE A TOTALLY DIFFERENT WORLD.

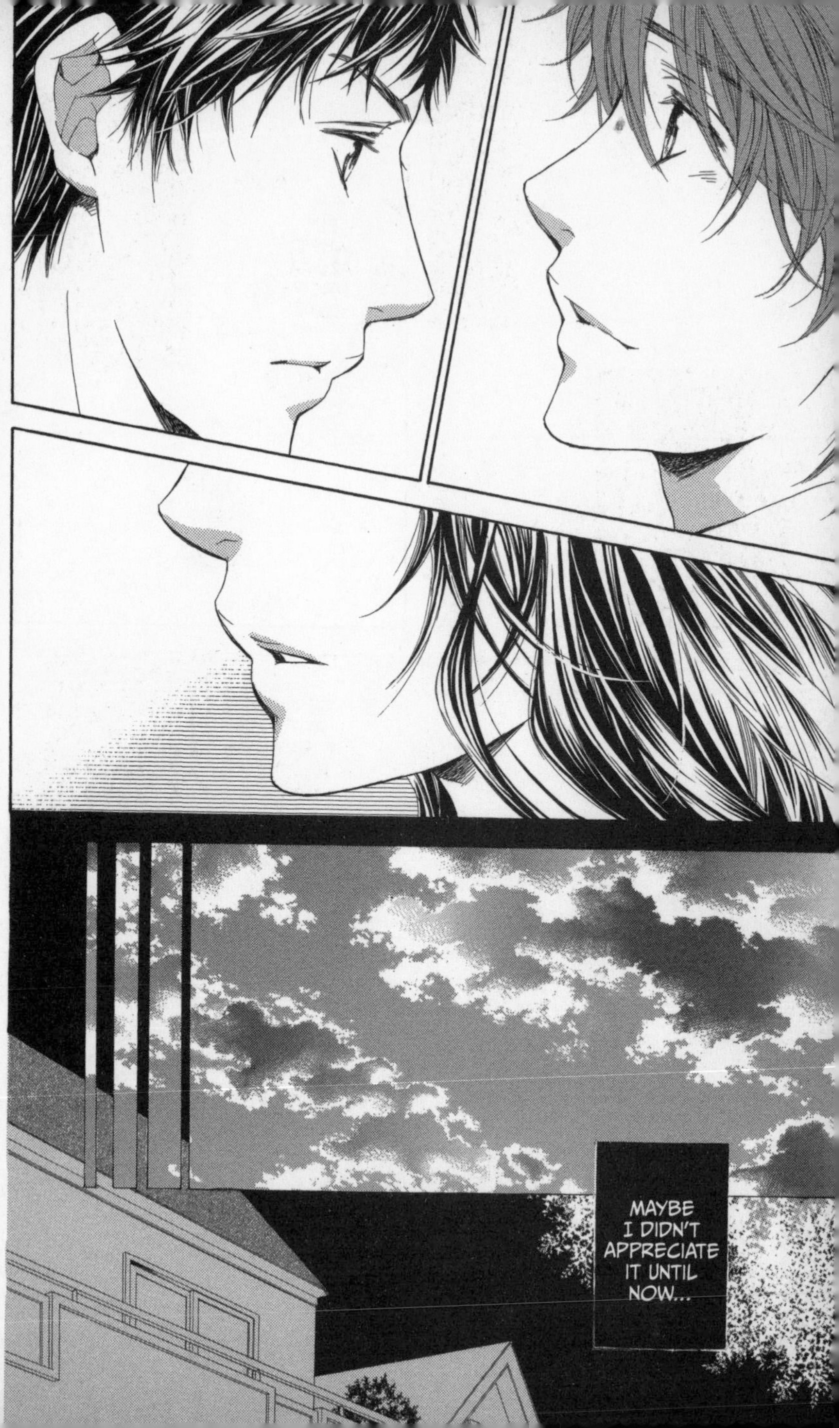
MAYBE I DIDN'T APPRECIATE IT UNTIL NOW...

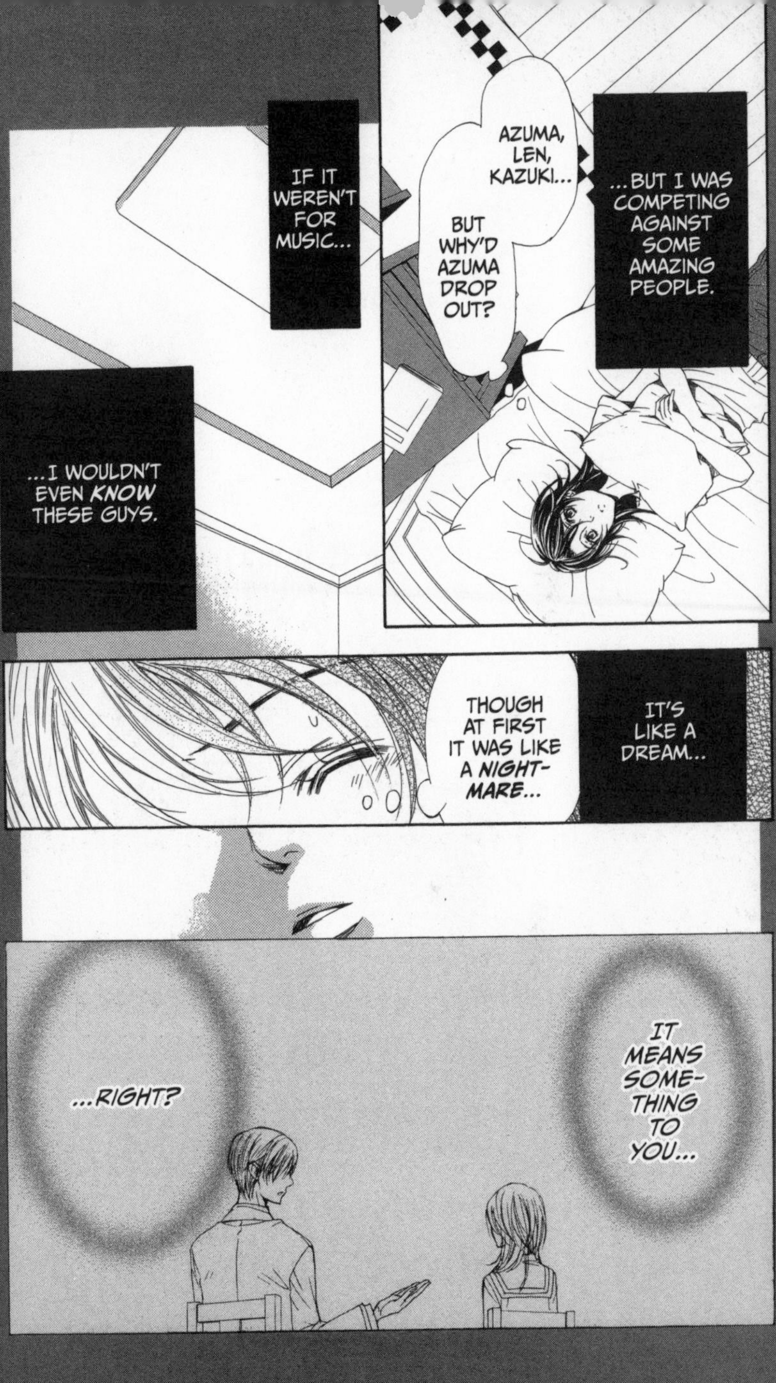
...BUT I WAS COMPETING AGAINST SOME AMAZING PEOPLE.
AZUMA, LEN, KAZUKI...
BUT WHY'D AZUMA DROP OUT?
IF IT WEREN'T FOR MUSIC...
...I WOULDN'T EVEN *KNOW* THESE GUYS.
IT'S LIKE A DREAM...
THOUGH AT FIRST IT WAS LIKE A *NIGHTMARE*...
IT MEANS SOMETHING TO YOU...
...RIGHT?

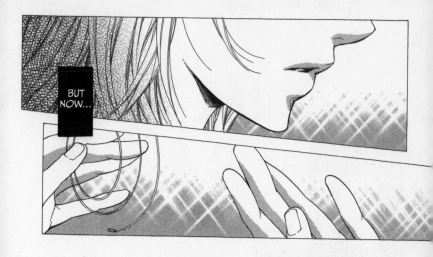

BUT NOW...

...I WANT TO STAND ON THE SAME STAGE AS THEM AGAIN.

I WONDER IF I CAN REALLY AIM THAT HIGH...

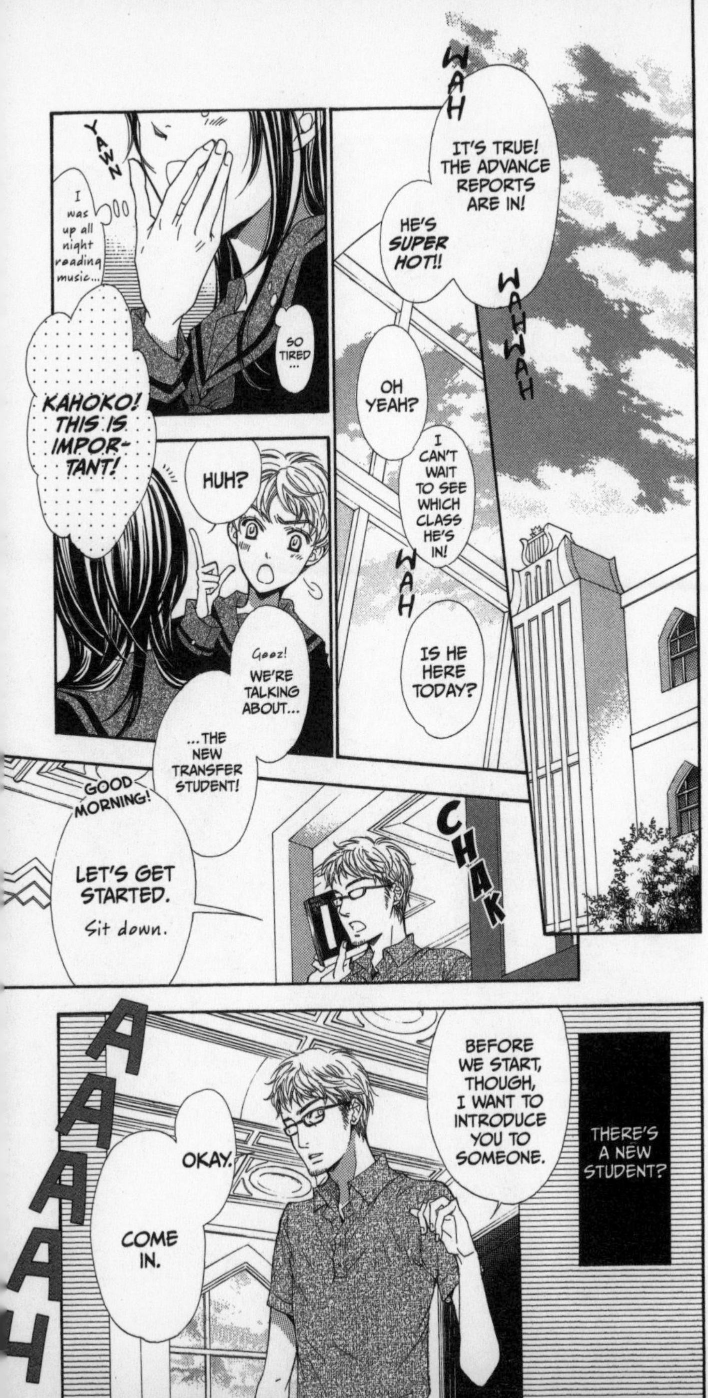
WAH
IT'S TRUE! THE ADVANCE REPORTS ARE IN!
HE'S SUPER HOT!!
WAHWAH
OH YEAH?
I CAN'T WAIT TO SEE WHICH CLASS HE'S IN!
WAH
IS HE HERE TODAY?
YAWN
I was up all night reading music...
SO TIRED...
KAHOKO! THIS IS IMPOR-TANT!
HUH?
Geez! WE'RE TALKING ABOUT...
...THE NEW TRANSFER STUDENT!
CHAK
GOOD MORNING!
LET'S GET STARTED. Sit down.
THERE'S A NEW STUDENT?
BEFORE WE START, THOUGH, I WANT TO INTRODUCE YOU TO SOMEONE.
OKAY.
COME IN.
AAAAAH

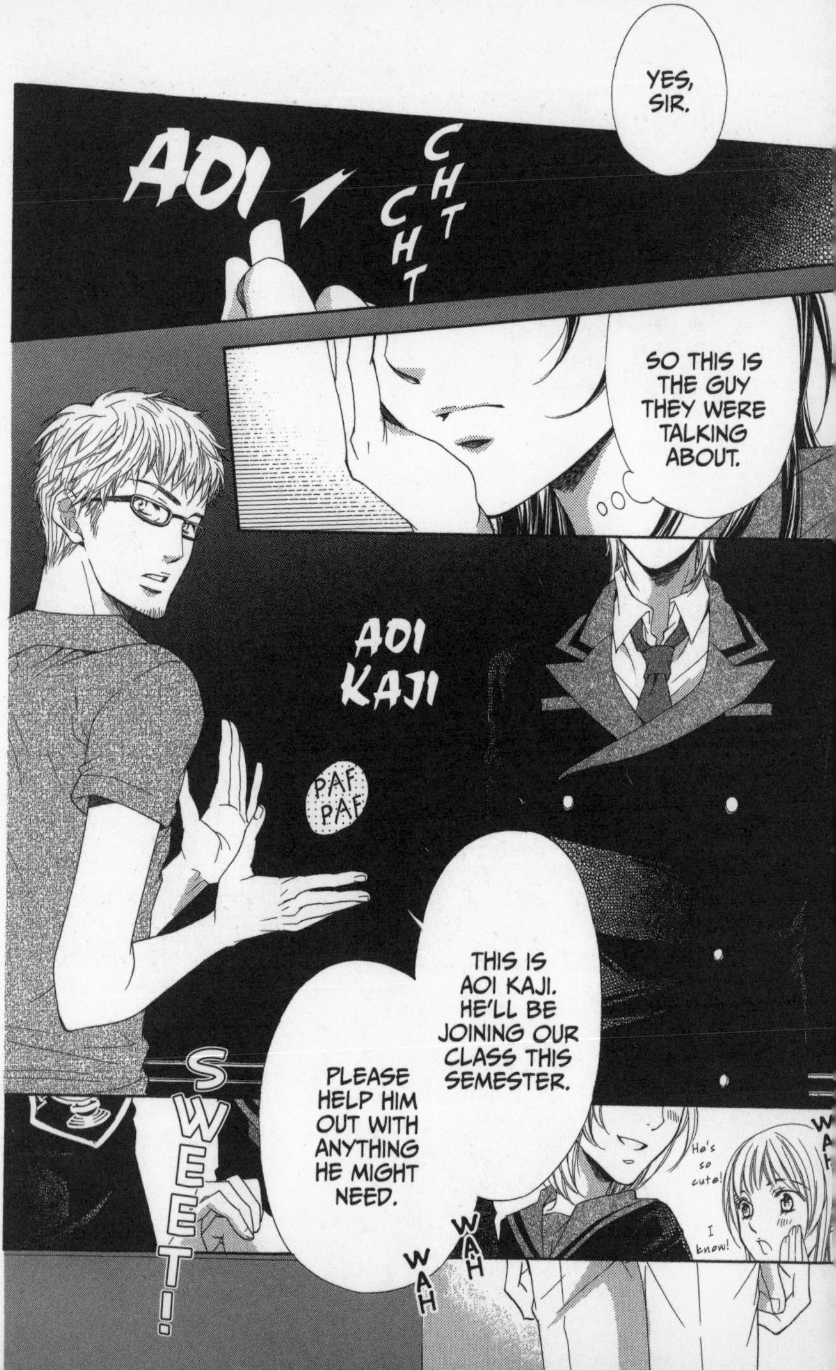
YES, SIR.
AOI
CHT CHT
SO THIS IS THE GUY THEY WERE TALKING ABOUT.
AOI KAJI
PAF PAF
THIS IS AOI KAJI. HE'LL BE JOINING OUR CLASS THIS SEMESTER.
PLEASE HELP HIM OUT WITH ANYTHING HE MIGHT NEED.
SWEET!
WAH
He's so cute!
I know!
WAH
WAH

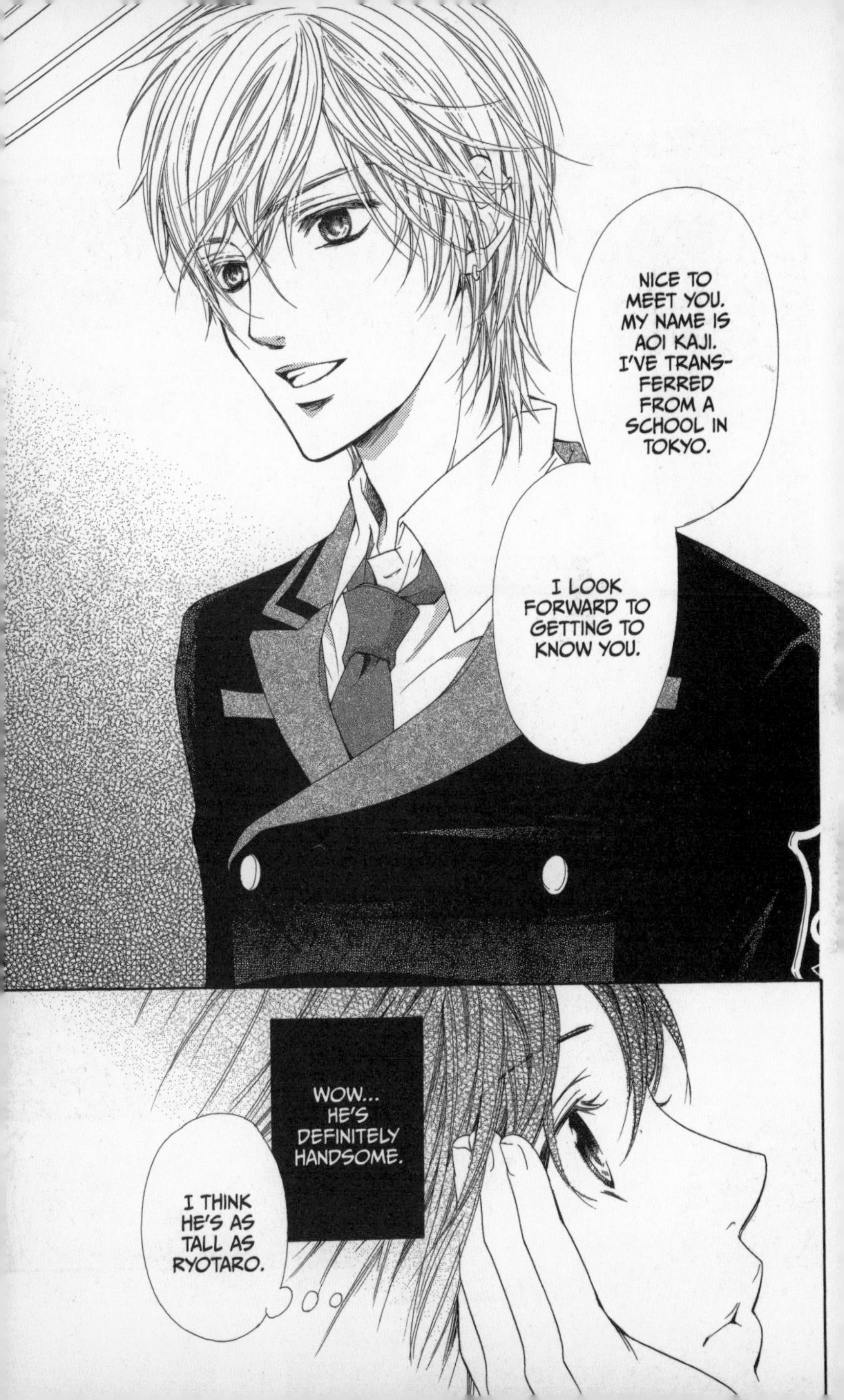
NICE TO MEET YOU. MY NAME IS AOI KAJI. I'VE TRANSFERRED FROM A SCHOOL IN TOKYO.
I LOOK FORWARD TO GETTING TO KNOW YOU.
WOW... HE'S DEFINITELY HANDSOME.
I THINK HE'S AS TALL AS RYOTARO.

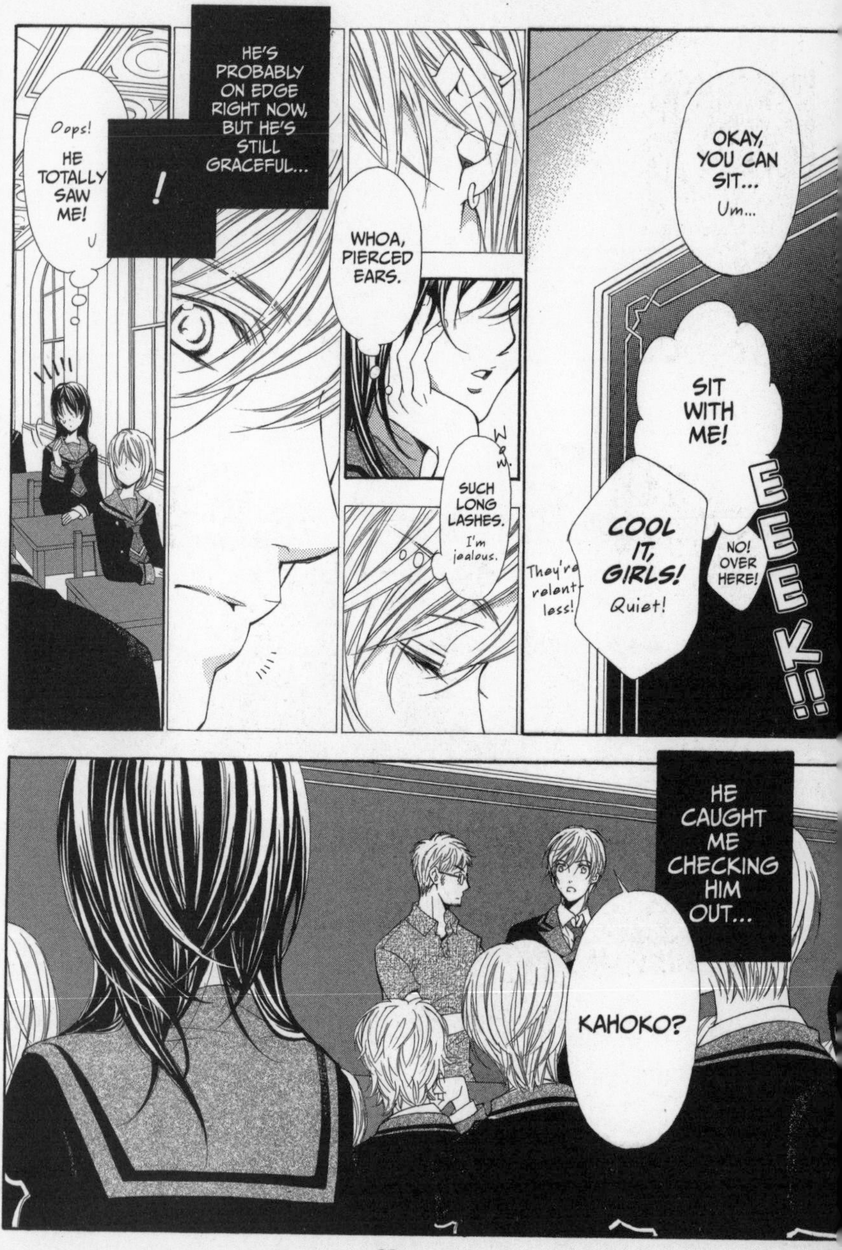
OKAY, YOU CAN SIT... Um...
SIT WITH ME!
EEEK!!
NO! OVER HERE!
COOL IT, GIRLS! Quiet!
They're relentless!
WHOA, PIERCED EARS.
WOW.
SUCH LONG LASHES. I'm jealous.
HE'S PROBABLY ON EDGE RIGHT NOW, BUT HE'S STILL GRACEFUL...
!
Oops! HE TOTALLY SAW ME!
HE CAUGHT ME CHECKING HIM OUT...
KAHOKO?

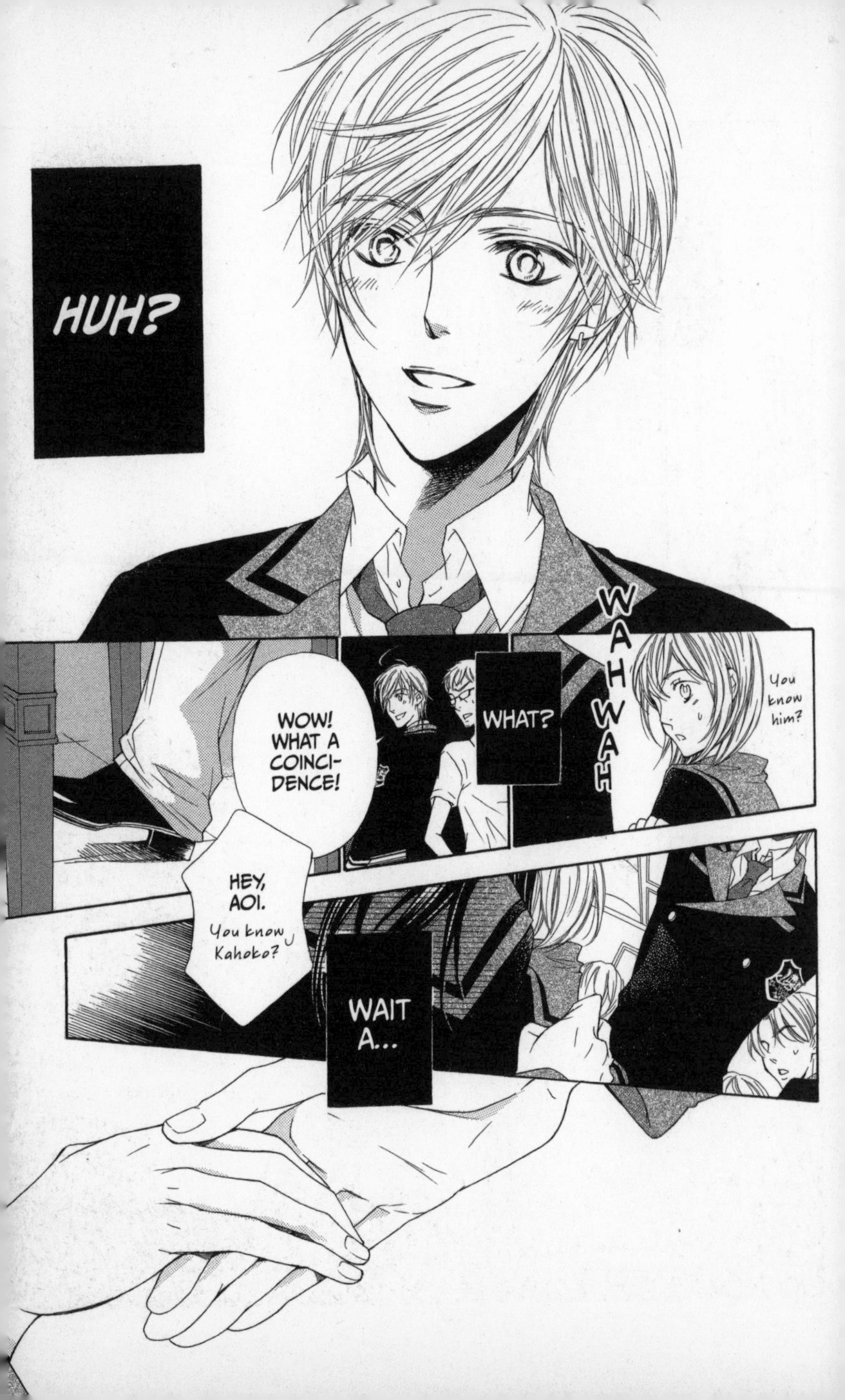
HUH?
WAH WAH
You know him?
WHAT?
WOW! WHAT A COINCIDENCE!
HEY, AOI.
You know Kahoko?
WAIT A...

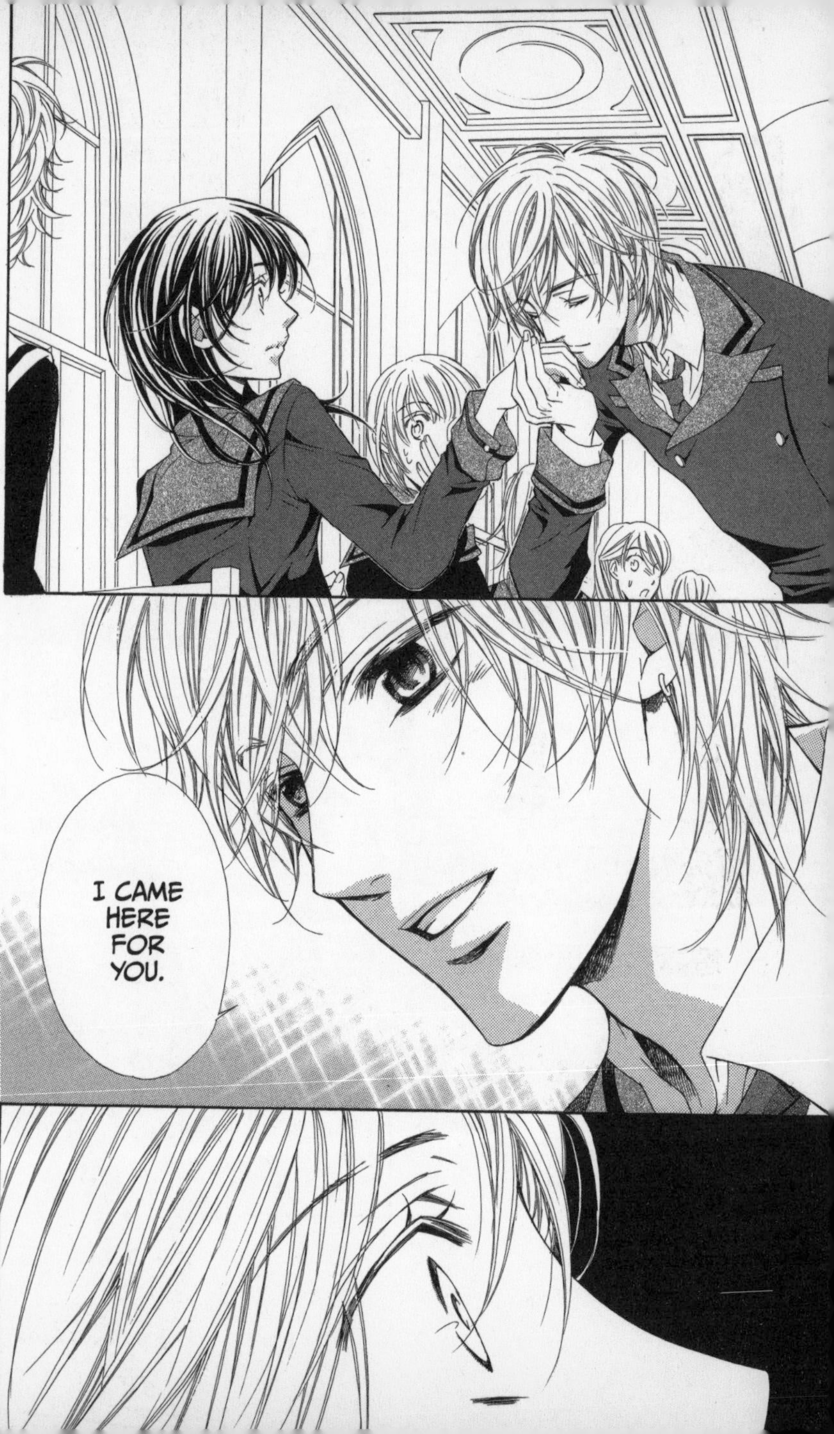
I CAME HERE FOR YOU.

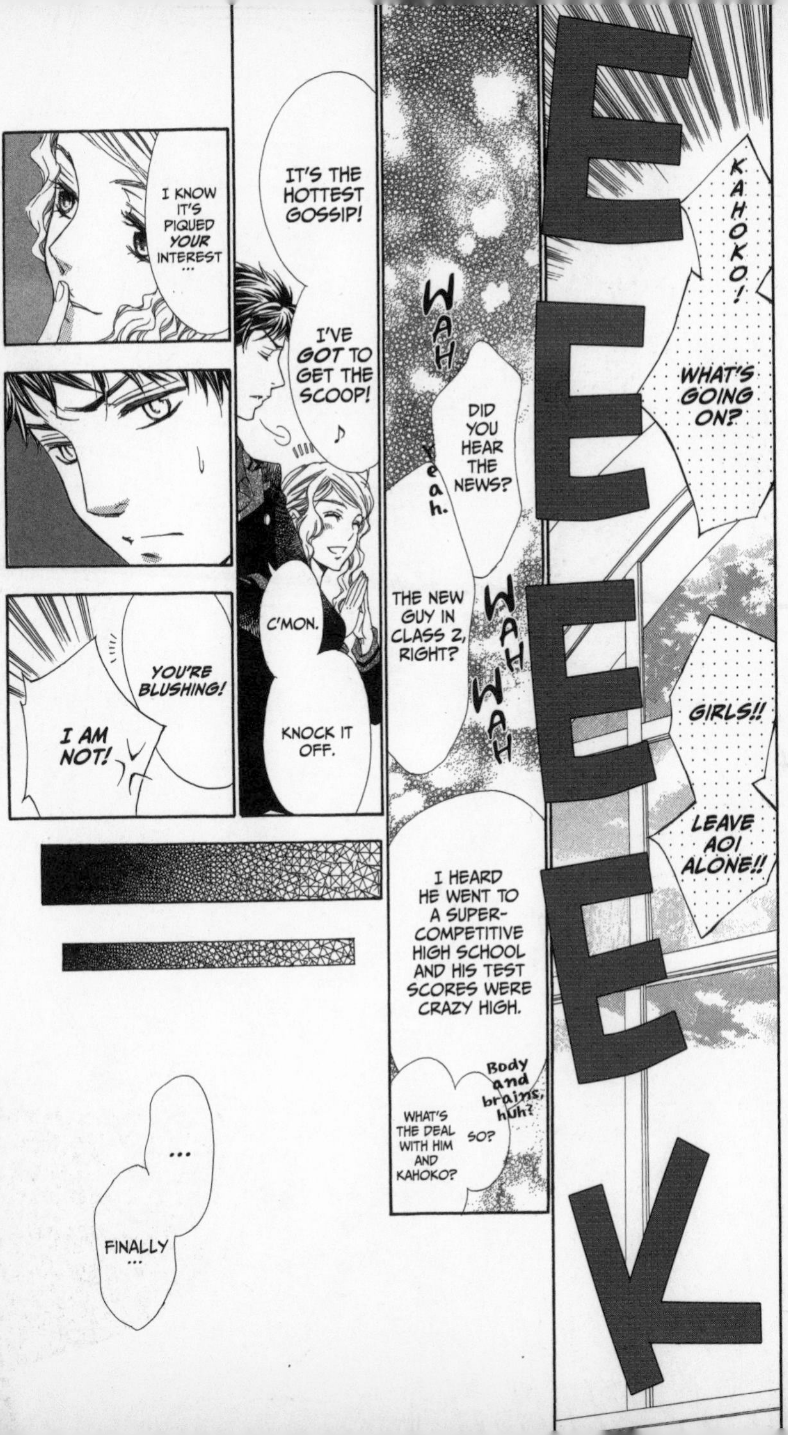
EEEEEK
KAHOKO!
WHAT'S GOING ON?
GIRLS!!
LEAVE AOI ALONE!!
WAH
DID YOU HEAR THE NEWS?
Yeah.
THE NEW GUY IN CLASS 2, RIGHT?
WAH WAH WAH
I HEARD HE WENT TO A SUPER-COMPETITIVE HIGH SCHOOL AND HIS TEST SCORES WERE CRAZY HIGH.
Body and brains, huh?
SO?
WHAT'S THE DEAL WITH HIM AND KAHOKO?
IT'S THE HOTTEST GOSSIP!
I'VE GOT TO GET THE SCOOP! ♪
C'MON.
KNOCK IT OFF.
I KNOW IT'S PIQUED YOUR INTEREST...
YOU'RE BLUSHING!
I AM NOT!
...
FINALLY...

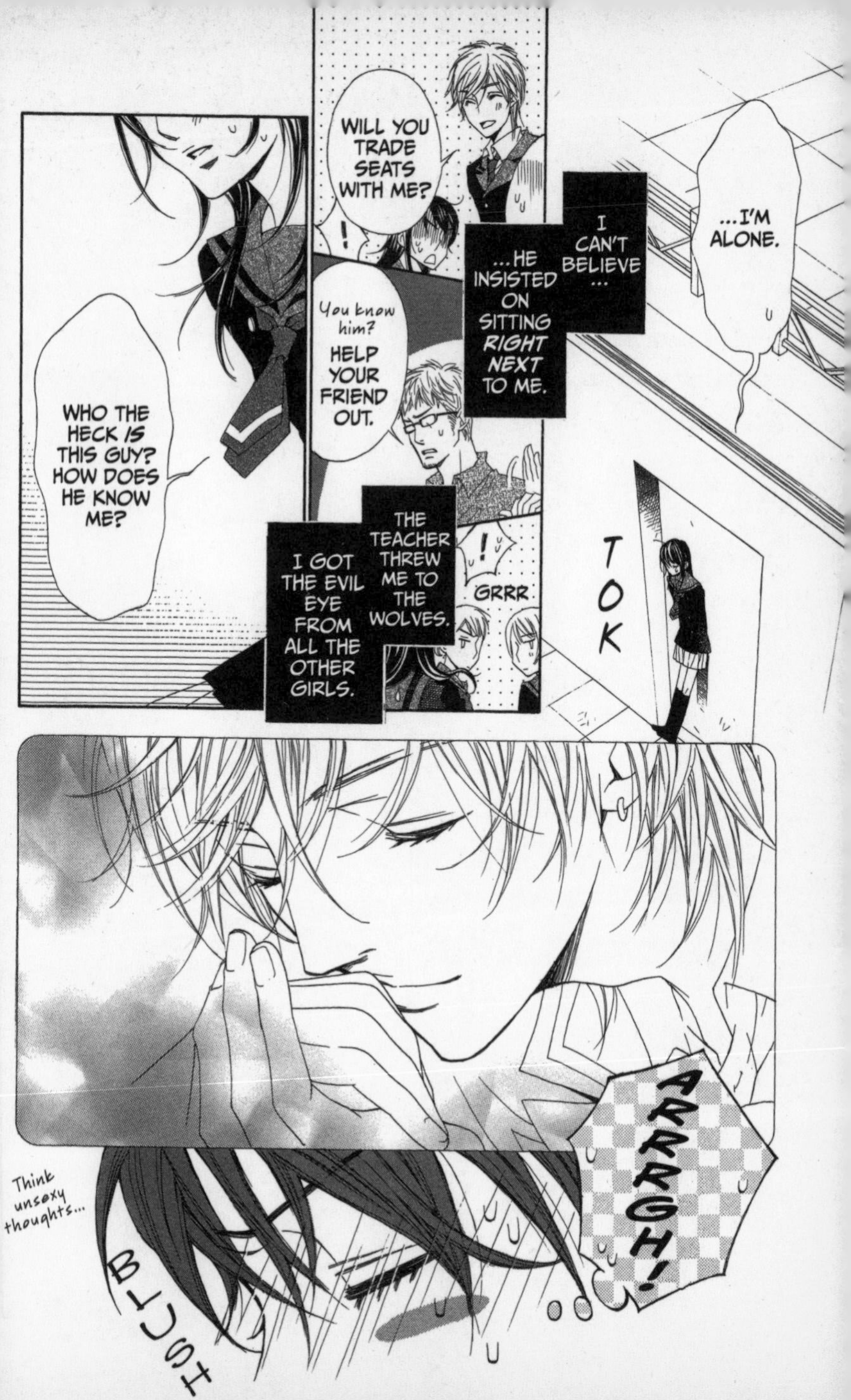
...I'M ALONE.
TOK
I CAN'T BELIEVE ...
...HE INSISTED ON SITTING RIGHT NEXT TO ME.
WILL YOU TRADE SEATS WITH ME?
!
You know him?
HELP YOUR FRIEND OUT.
THE TEACHER THREW ME TO THE WOLVES.
I GOT THE EVIL EYE FROM ALL THE OTHER GIRLS.
!
GRRR
WHO THE HECK IS THIS GUY? HOW DOES HE KNOW ME?
ARRRGH!
BLUSH
Think unsexy thoughts...

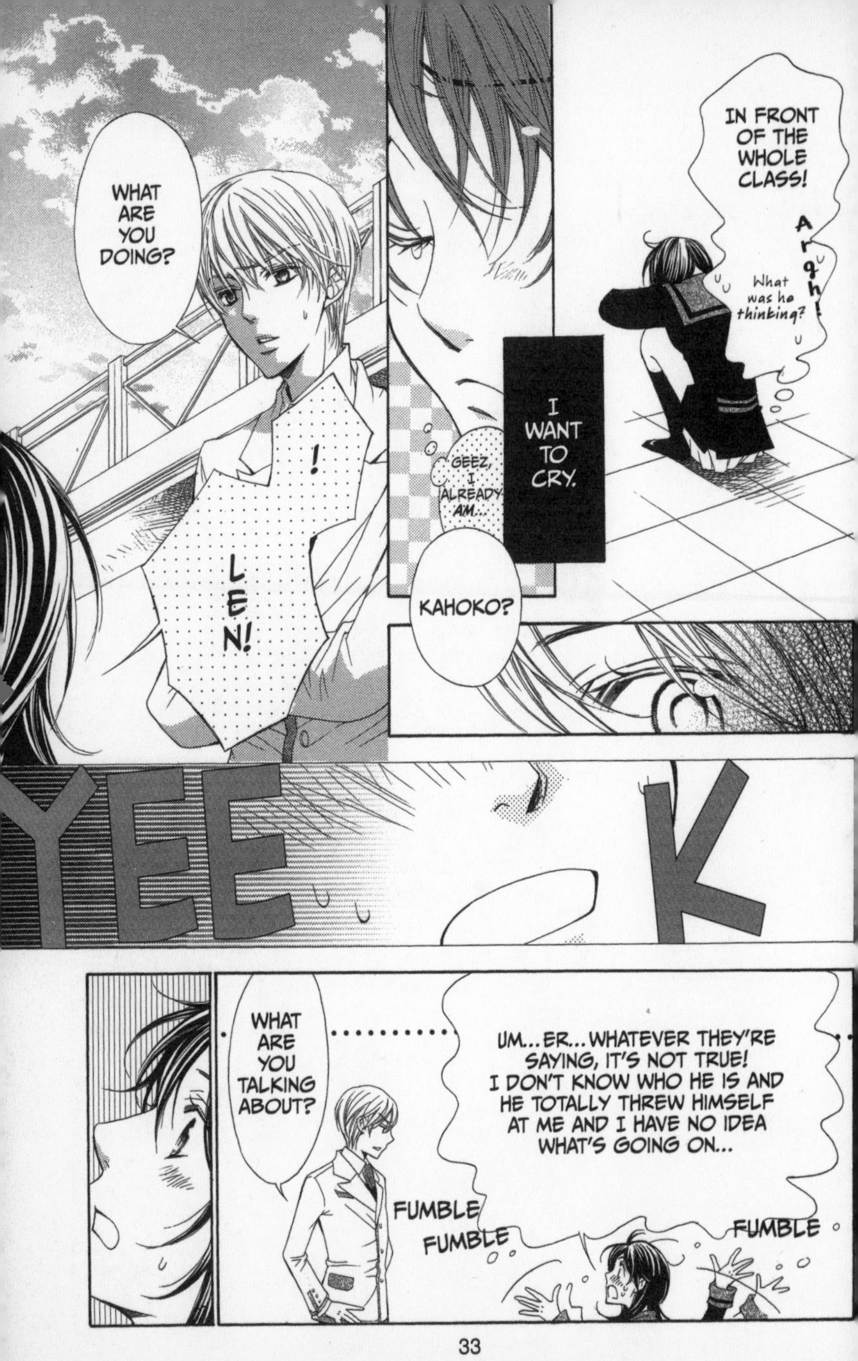

IN FRONT OF THE WHOLE CLASS!
Argh!
What was he thinking?
I WANT TO CRY.
GEEZ, I ALREADY AM...
KAHOKO?
WHAT ARE YOU DOING?
!
LEN!
YEEK
UM...ER...WHATEVER THEY'RE SAYING, IT'S NOT TRUE! I DON'T KNOW WHO HE IS AND HE TOTALLY THREW HIMSELF AT ME AND I HAVE NO IDEA WHAT'S GOING ON...
FUMBLE
FUMBLE
FUMBLE
WHAT ARE YOU TALKING ABOUT?

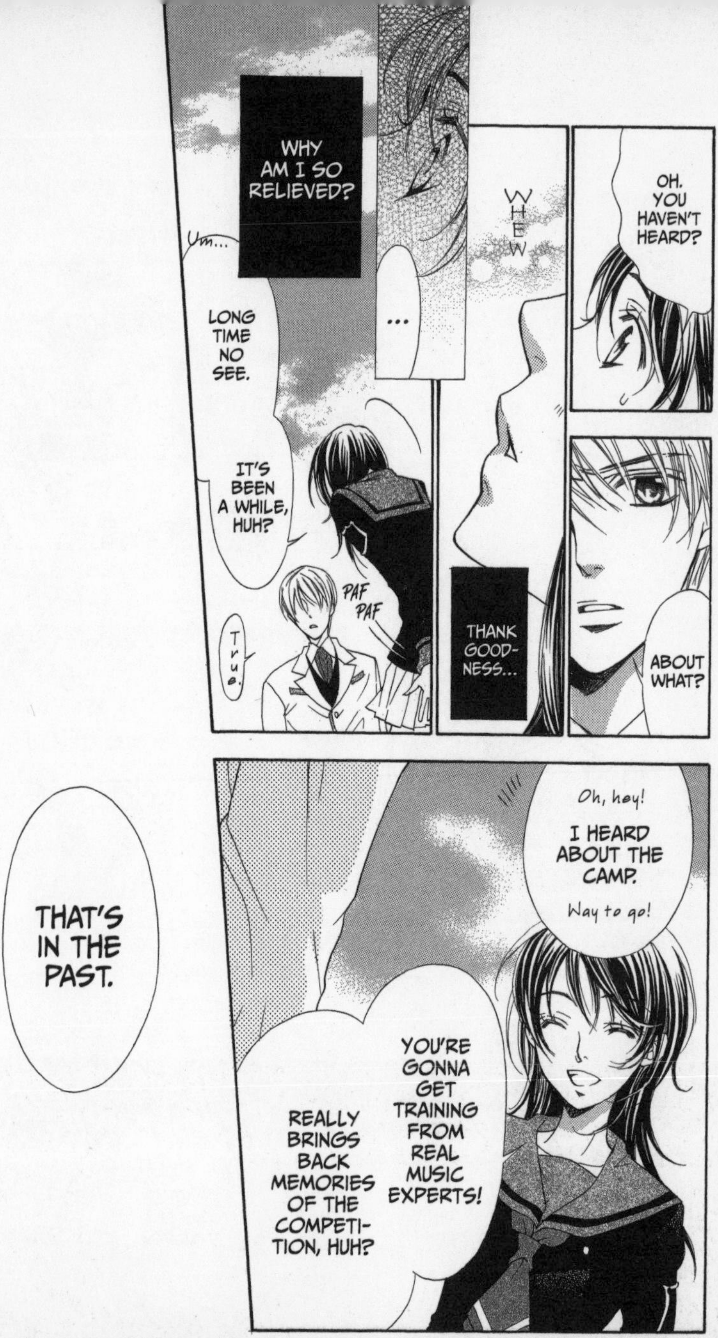
OH. YOU HAVEN'T HEARD?
ABOUT WHAT?
WHEW
THANK GOODNESS...
...
WHY AM I SO RELIEVED?
Um...
LONG TIME NO SEE.
IT'S BEEN A WHILE, HUH?
PAF PAF
True.
Oh, hey! I HEARD ABOUT THE CAMP. Way to go!
YOU'RE GONNA GET TRAINING FROM REAL MUSIC EXPERTS!
REALLY BRINGS BACK MEMORIES OF THE COMPETITION, HUH?
THAT'S IN THE PAST.

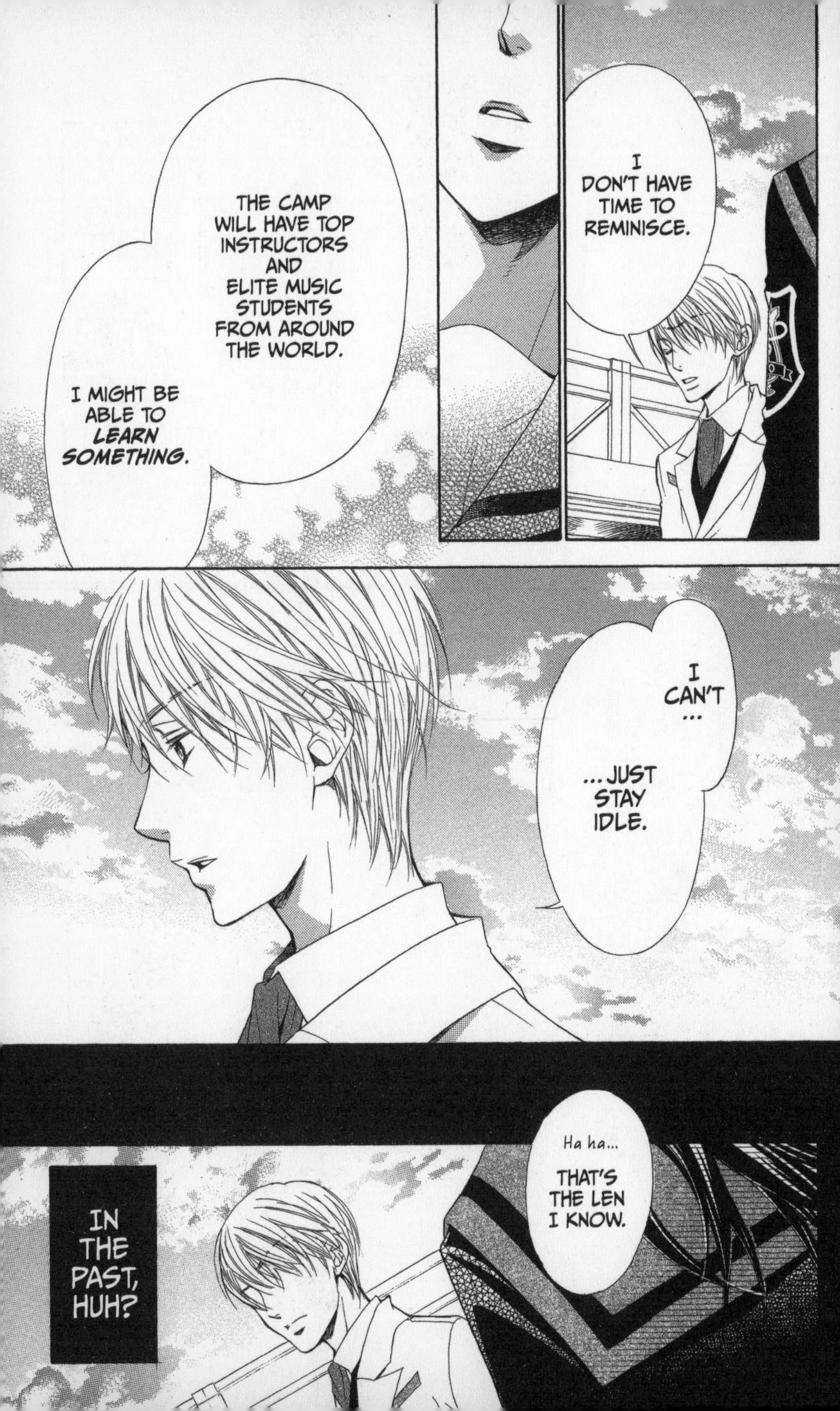
I DON'T HAVE TIME TO REMINISCE.
THE CAMP WILL HAVE TOP INSTRUCTORS AND ELITE MUSIC STUDENTS FROM AROUND THE WORLD.
I MIGHT BE ABLE TO *LEARN SOMETHING.*
I CAN'T ...
... JUST STAY IDLE.
Ha ha...
THAT'S THE LEN I KNOW.
IN THE PAST, HUH?

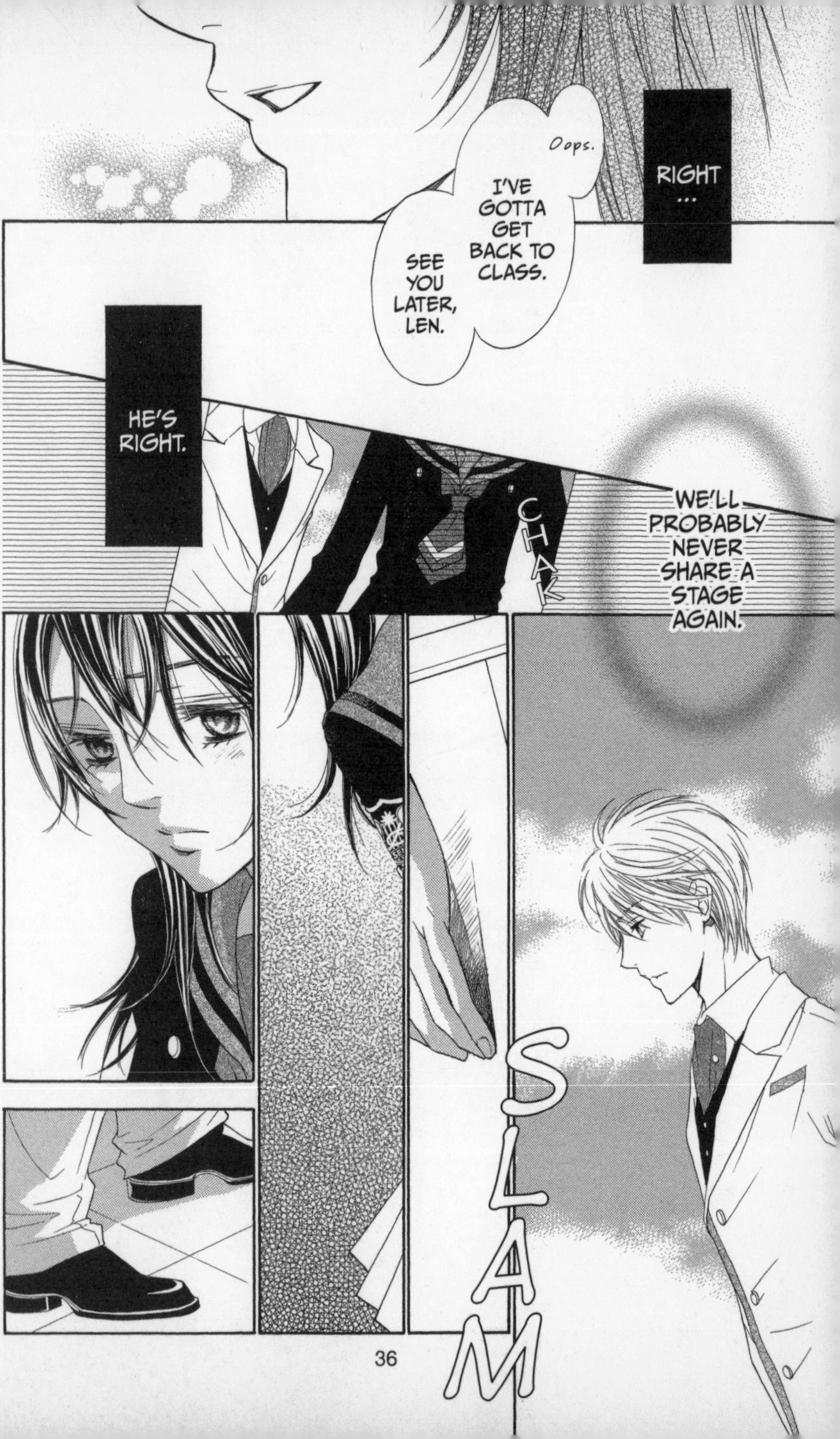
RIGHT ...
Oops.
I'VE GOTTA GET BACK TO CLASS.
SEE YOU LATER, LEN.
CHAK
HE'S RIGHT.
WE'LL PROBABLY NEVER SHARE A STAGE AGAIN.
SLAM

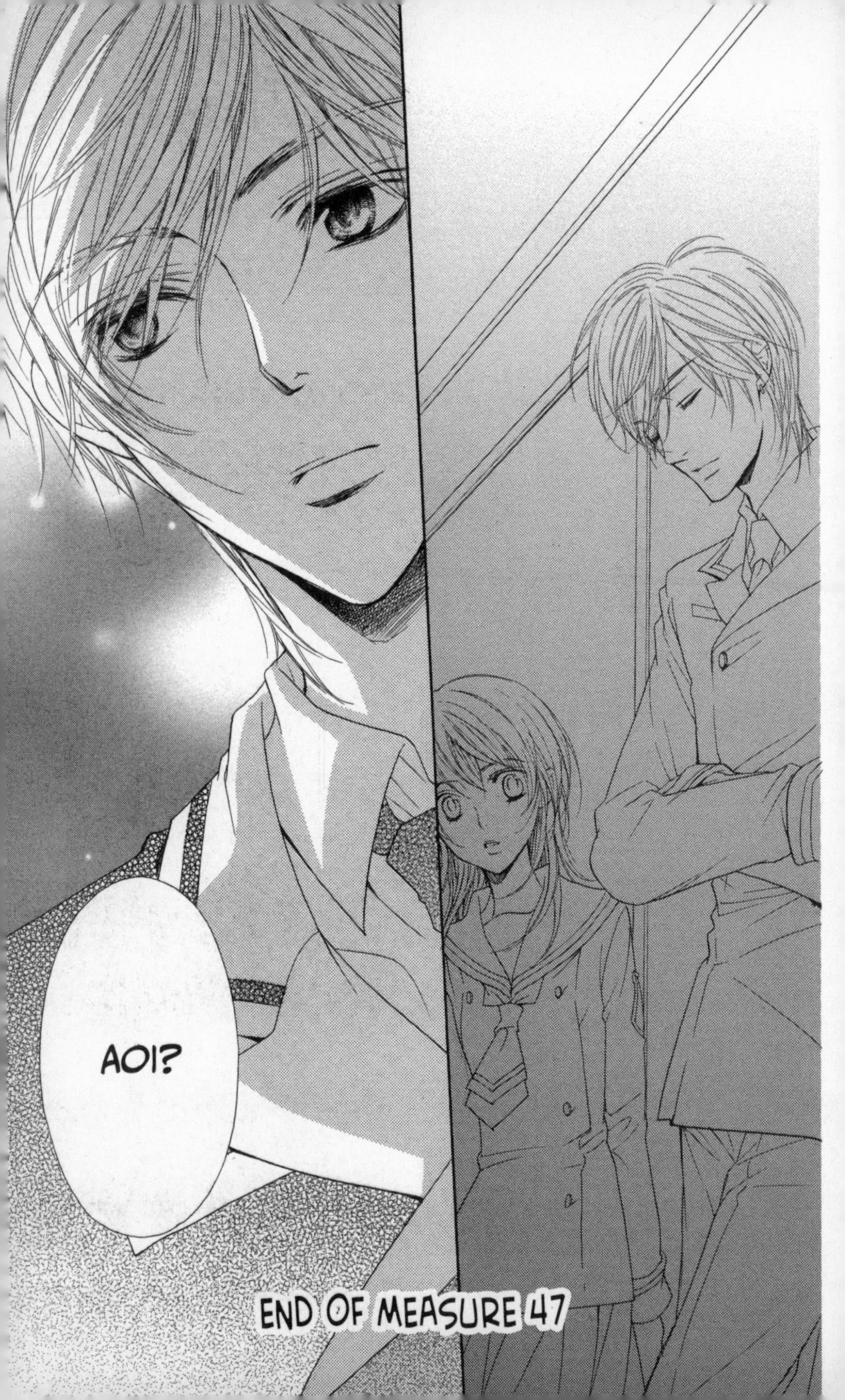
AOI?
END OF MEASURE 47

La Corda d'Oro
PSST
WOW... THAT'S INCREDIBLE...
PSST PSST
YEAH, AND THE CAMP IS SUPPOSED TO BE OWNED BY THIS FAMOUS CONDUCTOR.
PSST
I HEARD THEY'VE GOT A HUGE CONCERT HALL AND DORMS FOR STAYING OVERNIGHT.
PSST
HEY! STOP SHOVING, KAHOKO!
SORRY, RYOTARO!
PSST
I JUST CAN'T GET OVER IT. SHOKO'S HOUSE WAS AMAZING, BUT THIS...
This is like her place on steroids.

Daily Happenings 40

The outbreak...

In the spring, the Benjamin plant in my studio had an aphid infestation. Then, in the rainy season, weird mushrooms I'd never seen before started growing on the windowsill. (The heck...?) Then summer came and I had an ant epidemic.

There are ants on my script.

I admit I considered moving when I saw the mushrooms...

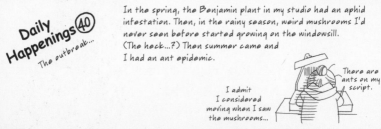

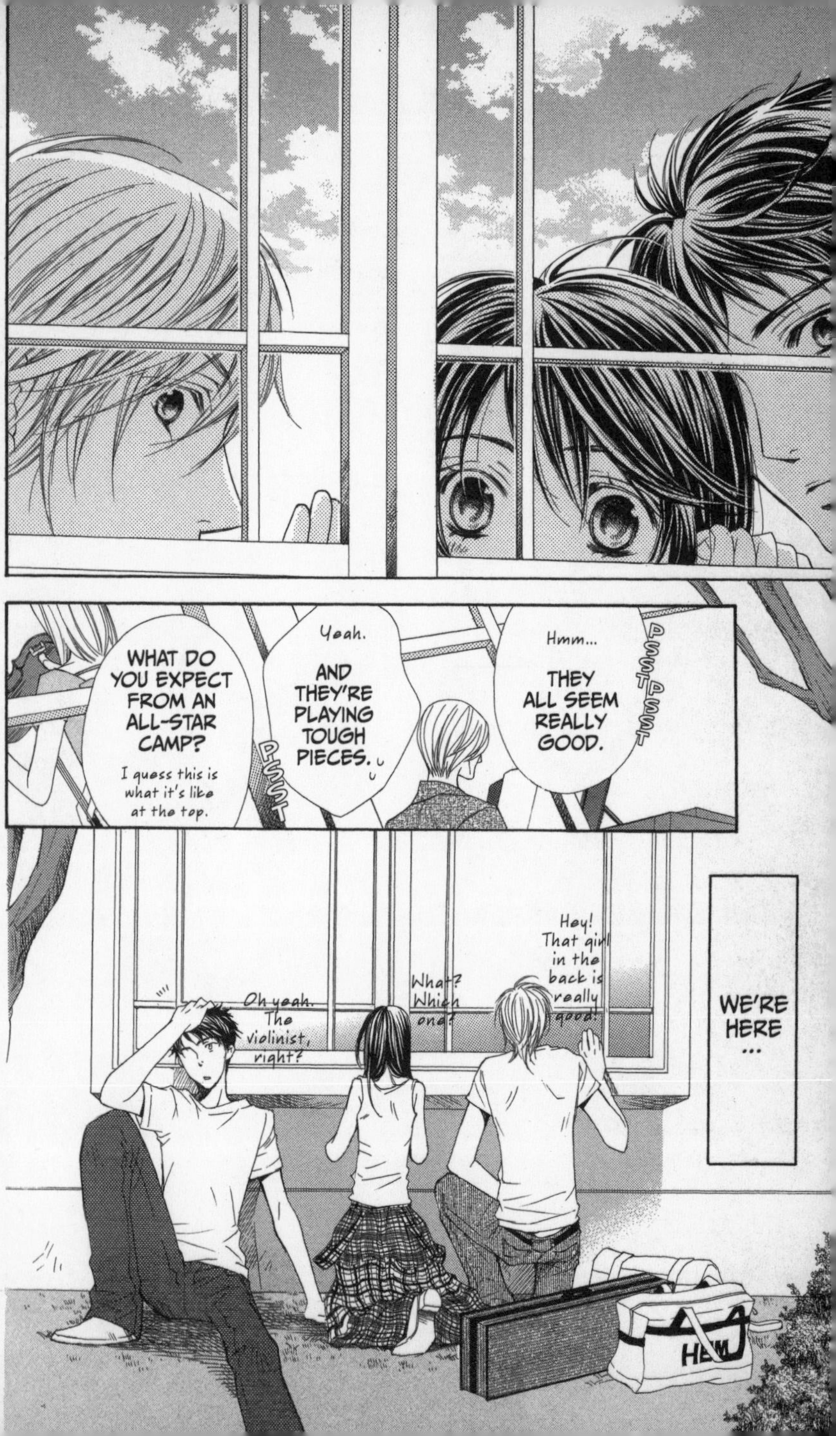
PSST PSST
Hmm... THEY ALL SEEM REALLY GOOD.
Yeah. AND THEY'RE PLAYING TOUGH PIECES.
PSST
WHAT DO YOU EXPECT FROM AN ALL-STAR CAMP? I guess this is what it's like at the top.
WE'RE HERE...
Hey! That girl in the back is really good!
What? Which one?
Oh yeah. The violinist, right?
HEM

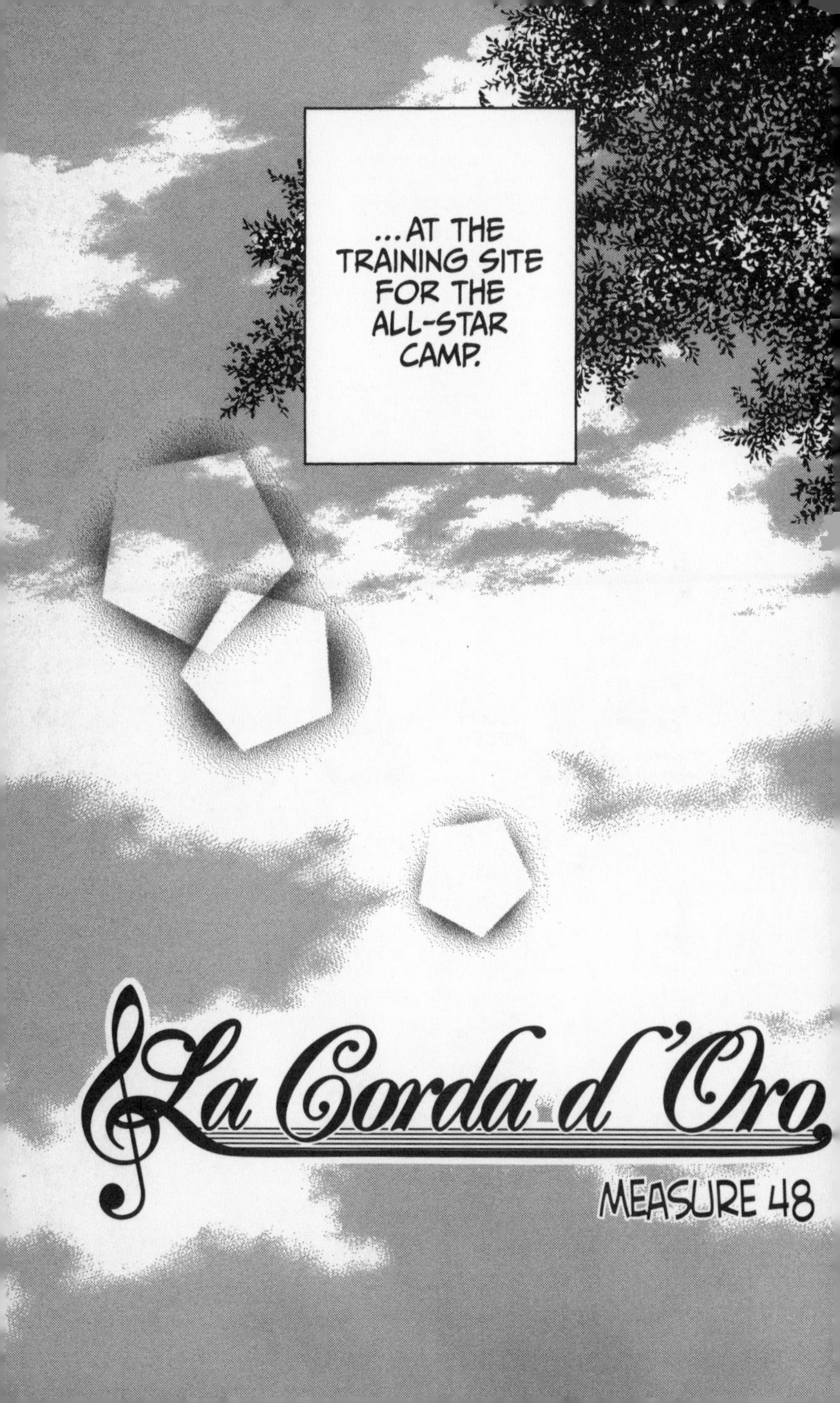
...AT THE TRAINING SITE FOR THE ALL-STAR CAMP.
La Corda d'Oro
MEASURE 48

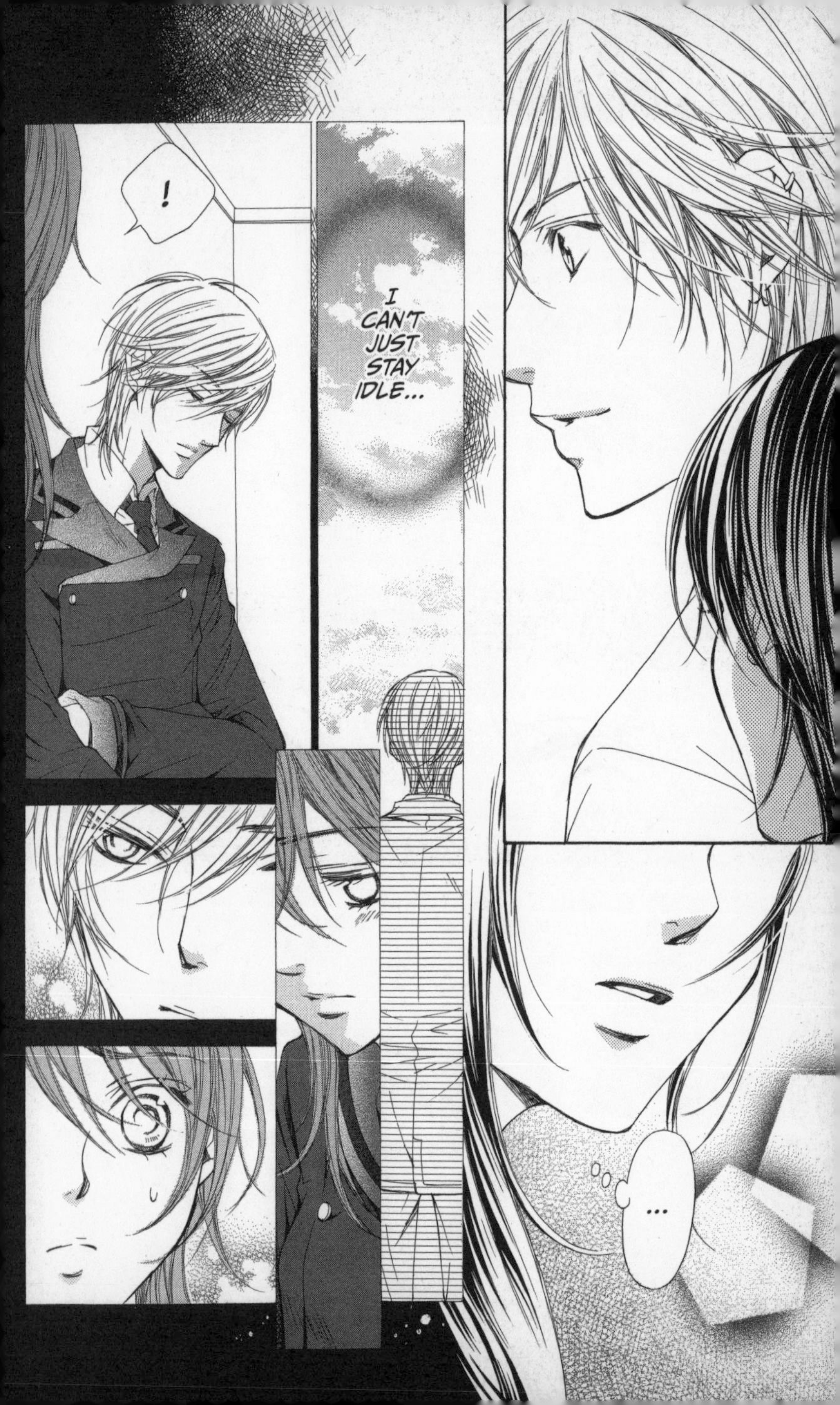
I CAN'T JUST STAY IDLE...
!
...

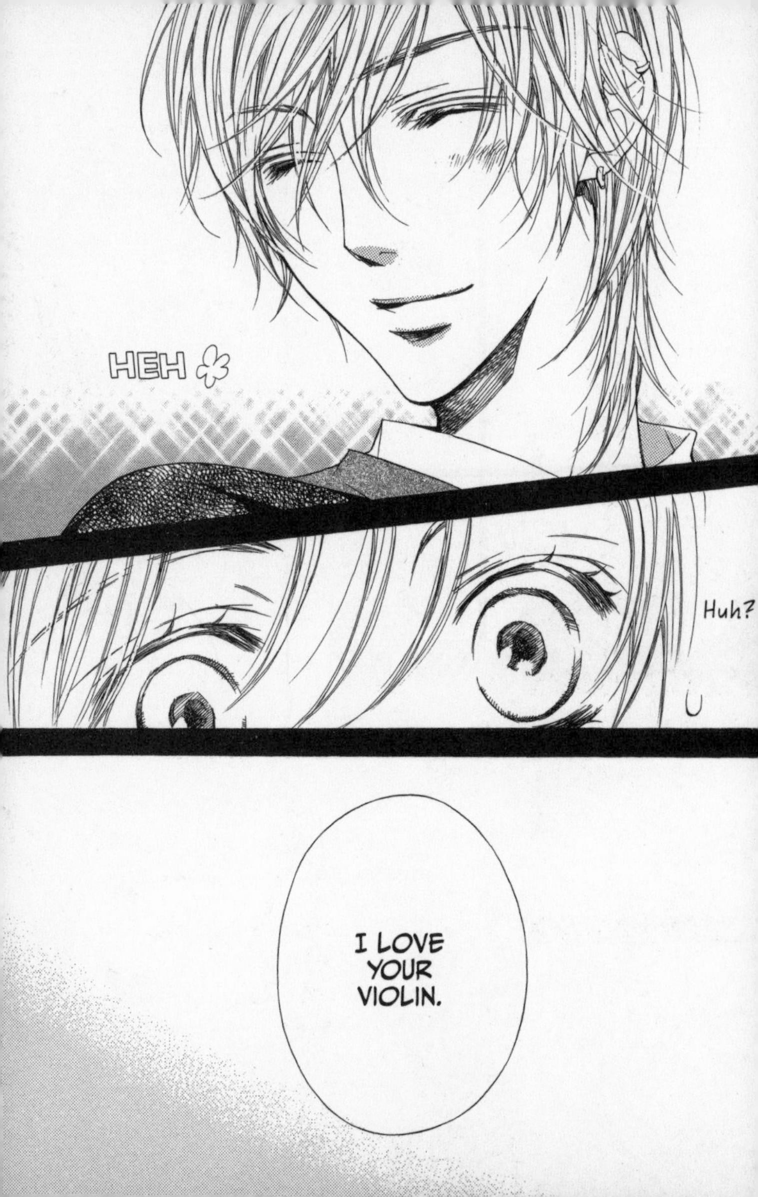
HEH
Huh?
I LOVE YOUR VIOLIN.

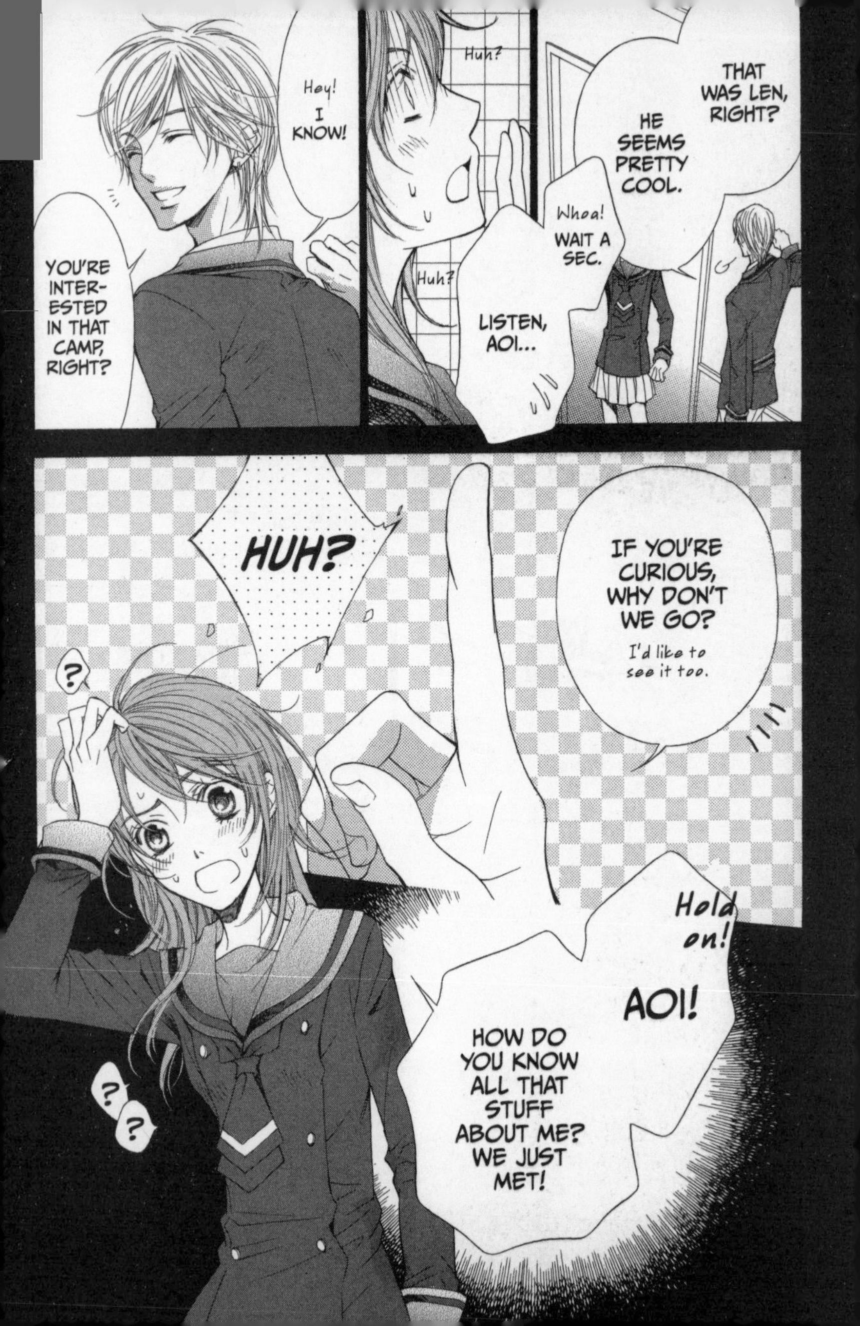
THAT WAS LEN, RIGHT?
HE SEEMS PRETTY COOL.
Whoa!
WAIT A SEC.
Huh?
Huh?
LISTEN, AOI...
Hey! I KNOW!
YOU'RE INTER-ESTED IN THAT CAMP, RIGHT?
IF YOU'RE CURIOUS, WHY DON'T WE GO?
I'd like to see it too.
HUH?
?
Hold on!
AOI!
HOW DO YOU KNOW ALL THAT STUFF ABOUT ME? WE JUST MET!
? ?

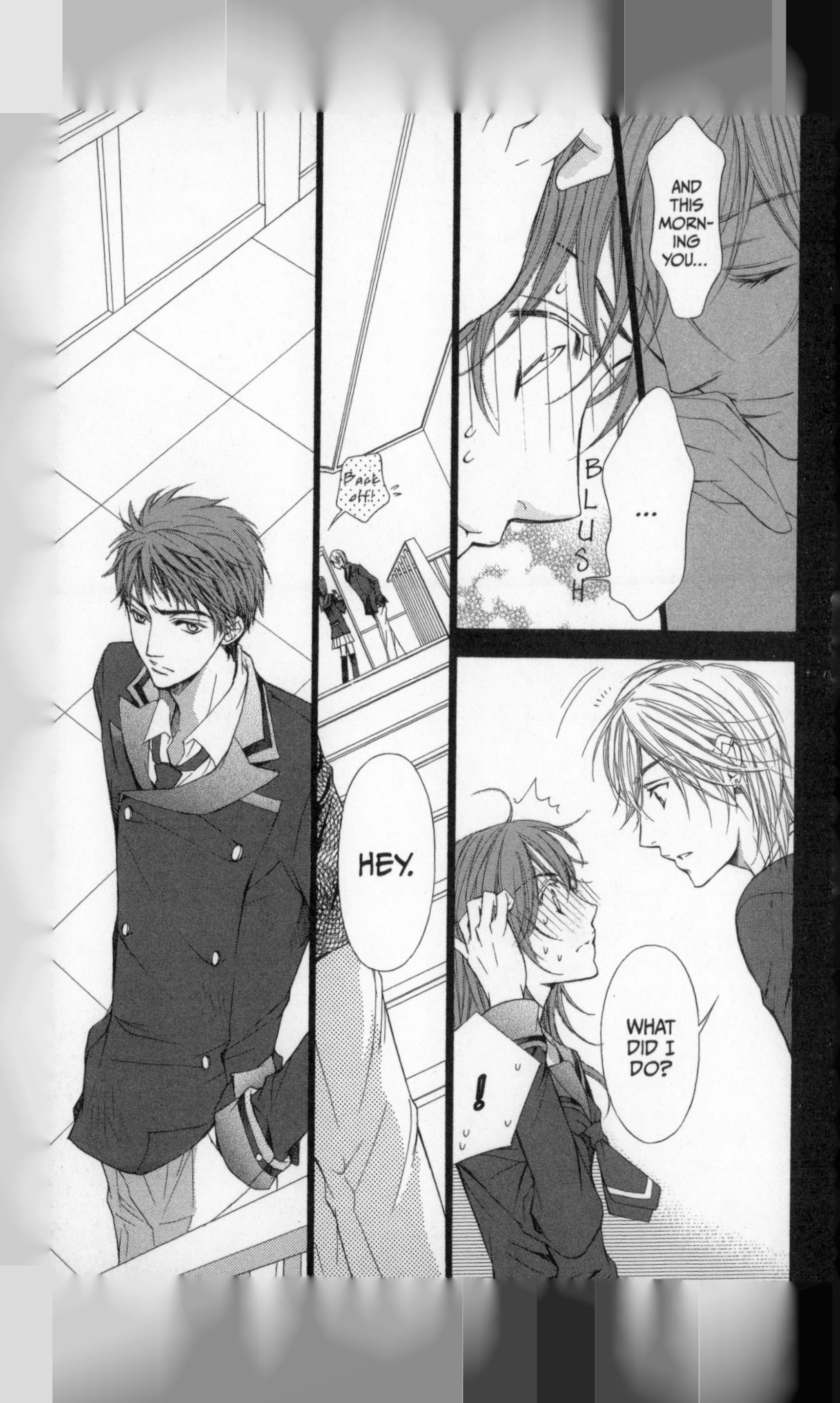
AND THIS MORNING YOU...
...
BLUSH
WHAT DID I DO?
!
Back off!
HEY.

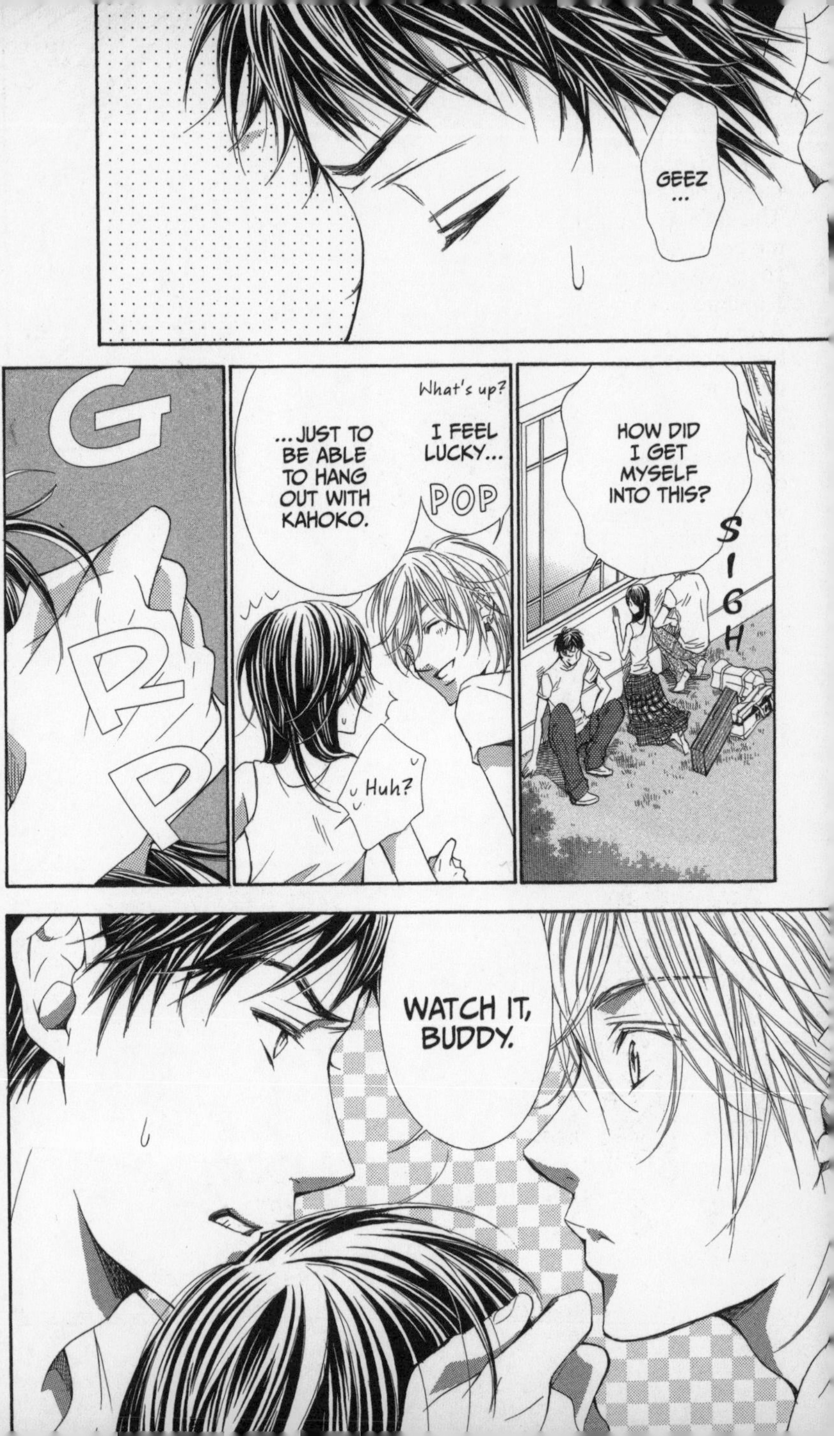
GEEZ
...
HOW DID I GET MYSELF INTO THIS?
SIGH
What's up?
I FEEL LUCKY...
POP
...JUST TO BE ABLE TO HANG OUT WITH KAHOKO.
Huh?
GRP
WATCH IT, BUDDY.

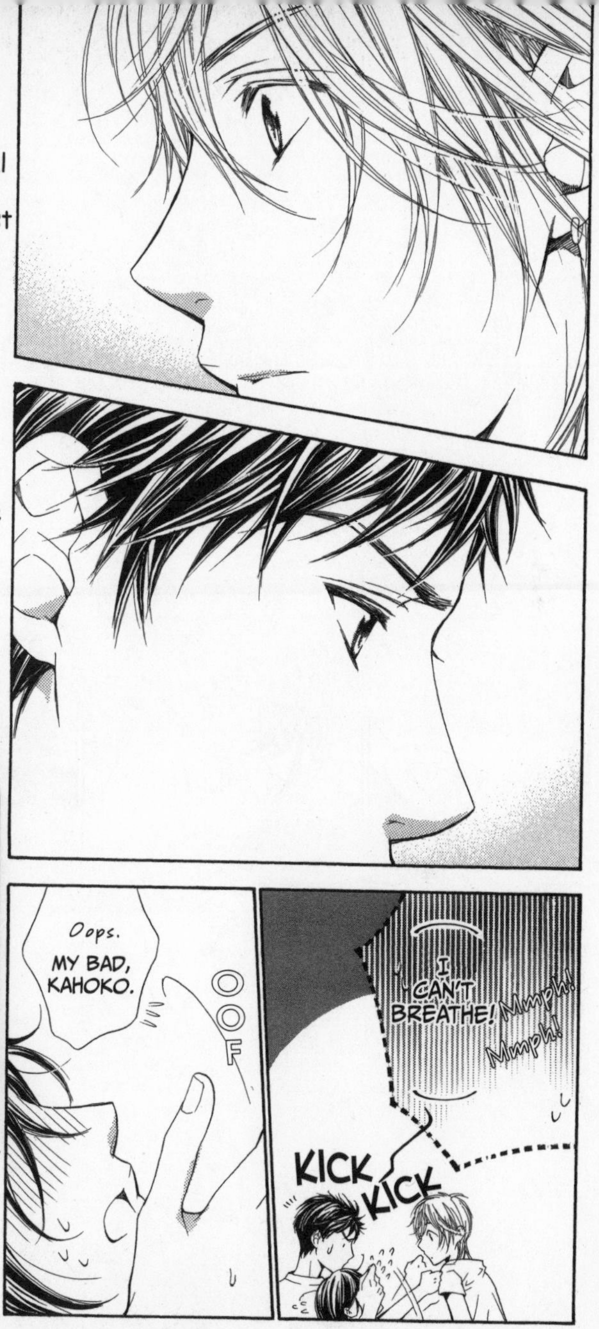
I CAN'T BREATHE!
Mmph! Mmph!
KICK
KICK
Oops.
MY BAD, KAHOKO.
OOF

For this sketch, I decided to go with a traditional boys' uniform. The design is just my personal taste. Maybe I should put Azuma in a bleached white uniform...

Aoi makes his debut in this volume. Please be nice to him.♪

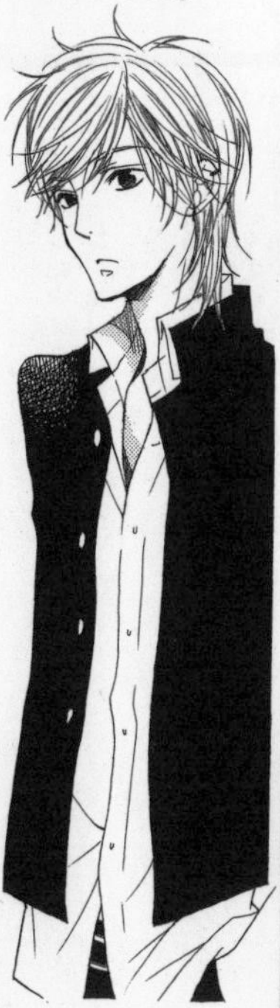

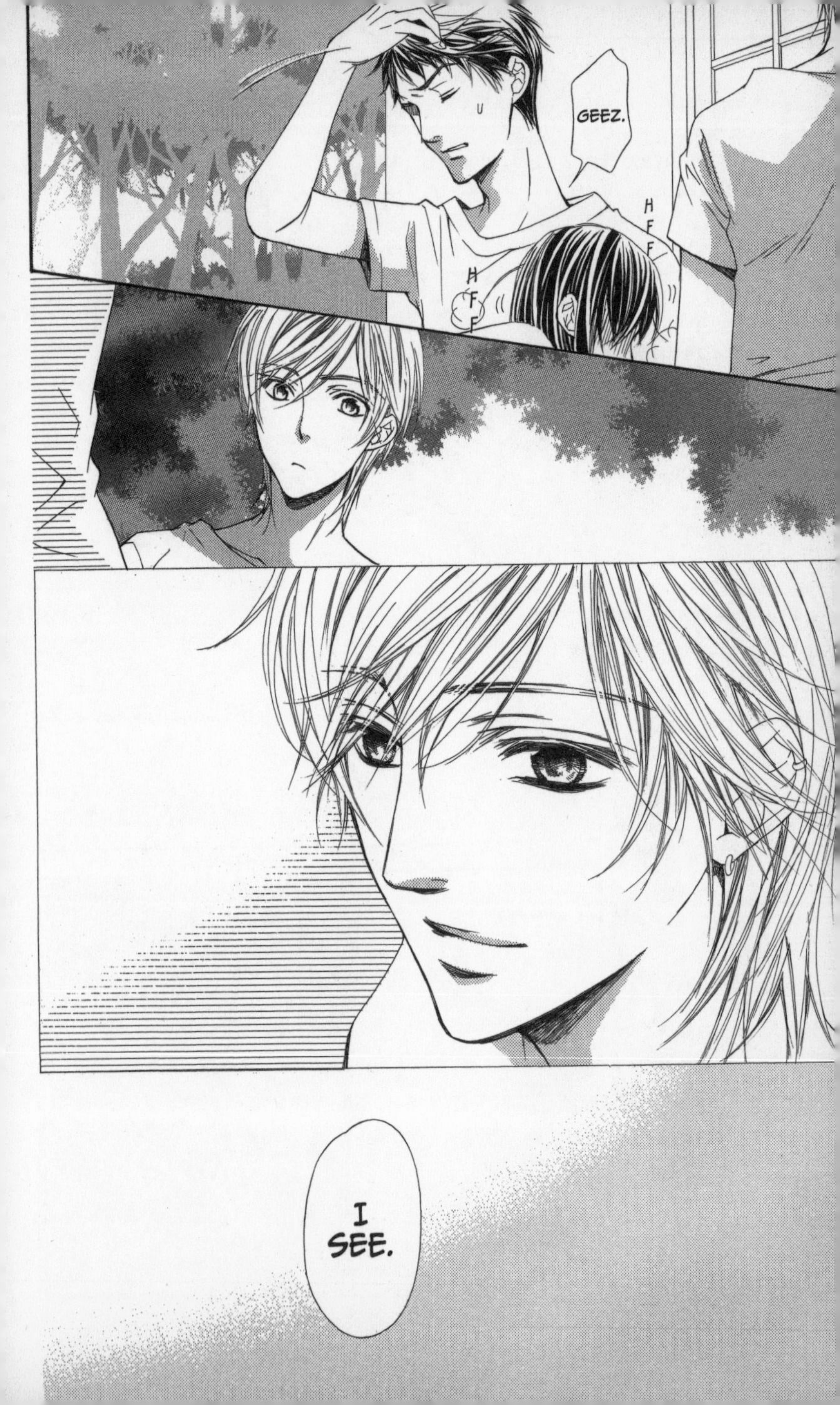
GEEZ.
HFF
HFF
I SEE.

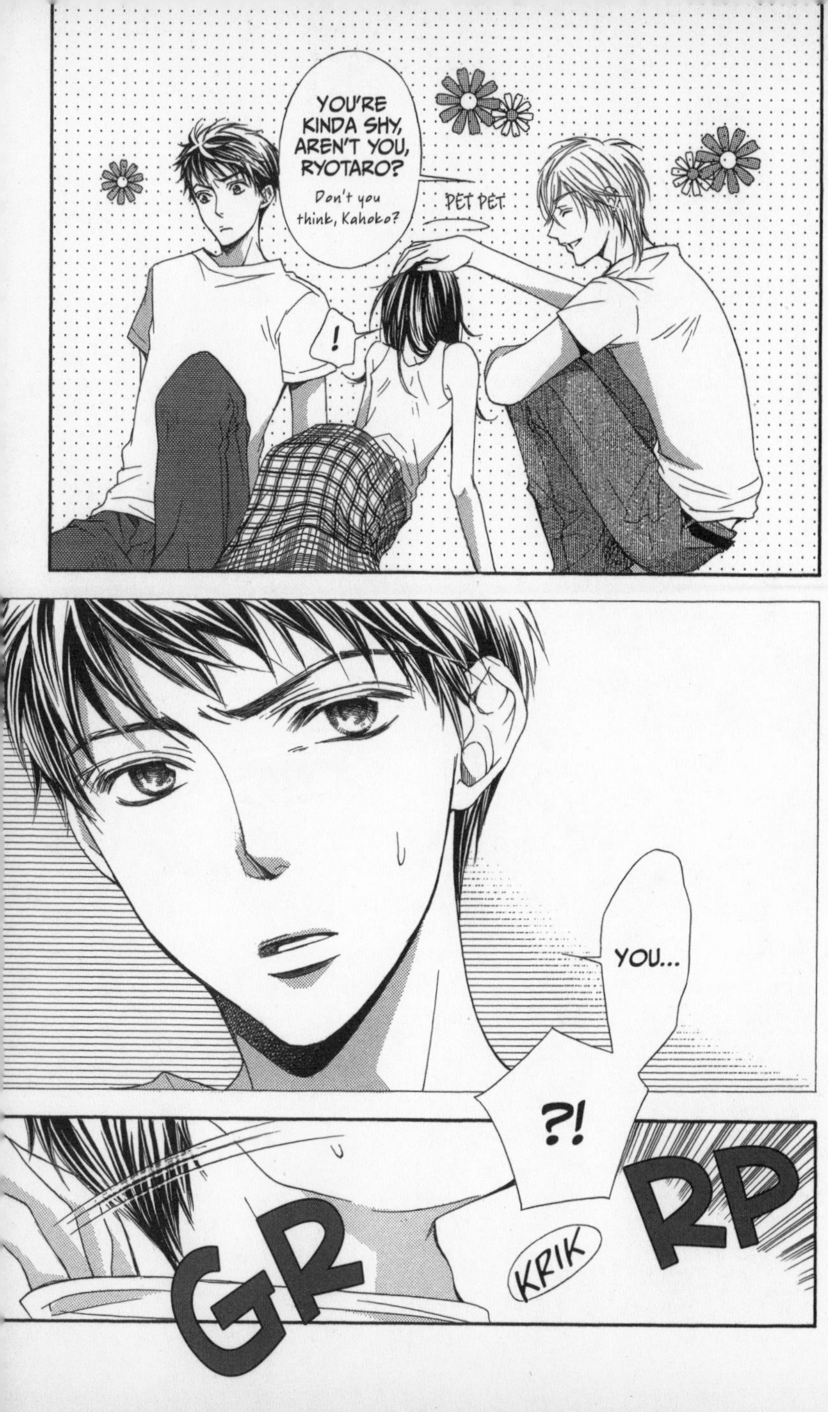
YOU'RE KINDA SHY, AREN'T YOU, RYOTARO?
Don't you think, Kahoko?
PET PET
!
YOU...
?!
GR
RP
KRIK

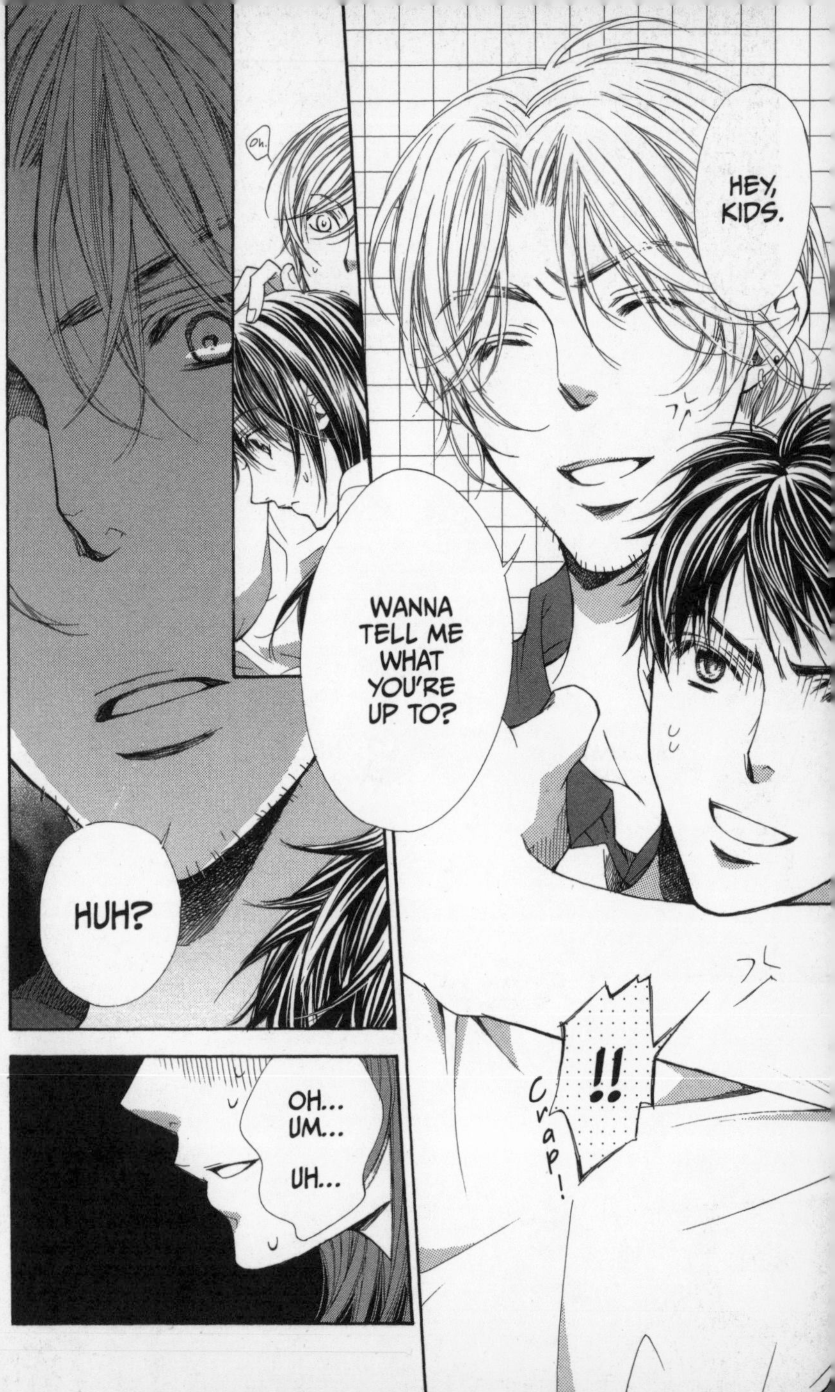
HEY, KIDS.
WANNA TELL ME WHAT YOU'RE UP TO?
Oh.
HUH?
!!
Crap!
OH... UM...
UH...

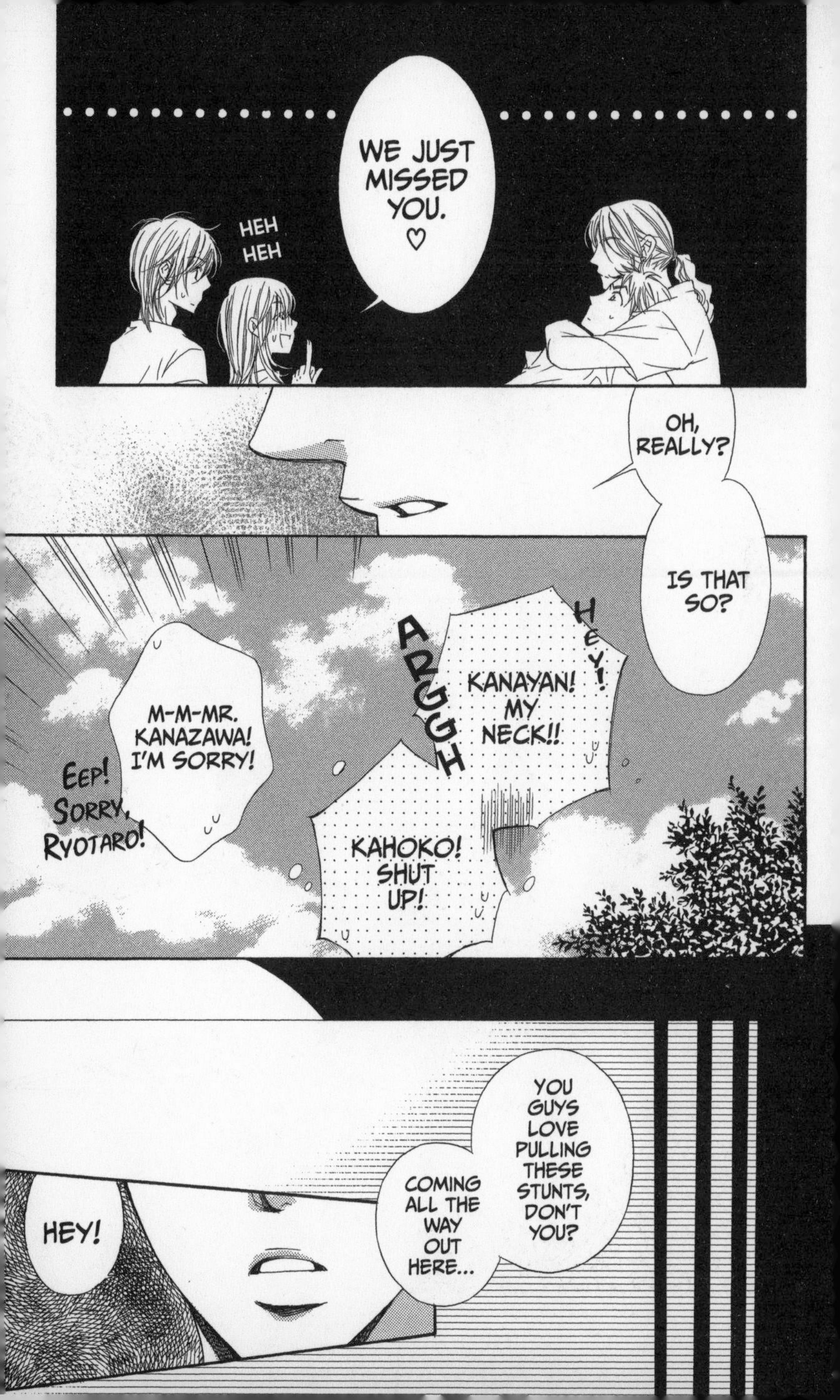
WE JUST MISSED YOU. ♡
HEH HEH
OH, REALLY?
IS THAT SO?
HEY!
KANAYAN! MY NECK!!
ARGGH
KAHOKO! SHUT UP!
M-M-MR. KANAZAWA! I'M SORRY!
EEP! SORRY, RYOTARO!
YOU GUYS LOVE PULLING THESE STUNTS, DON'T YOU?
COMING ALL THE WAY OUT HERE...
HEY!

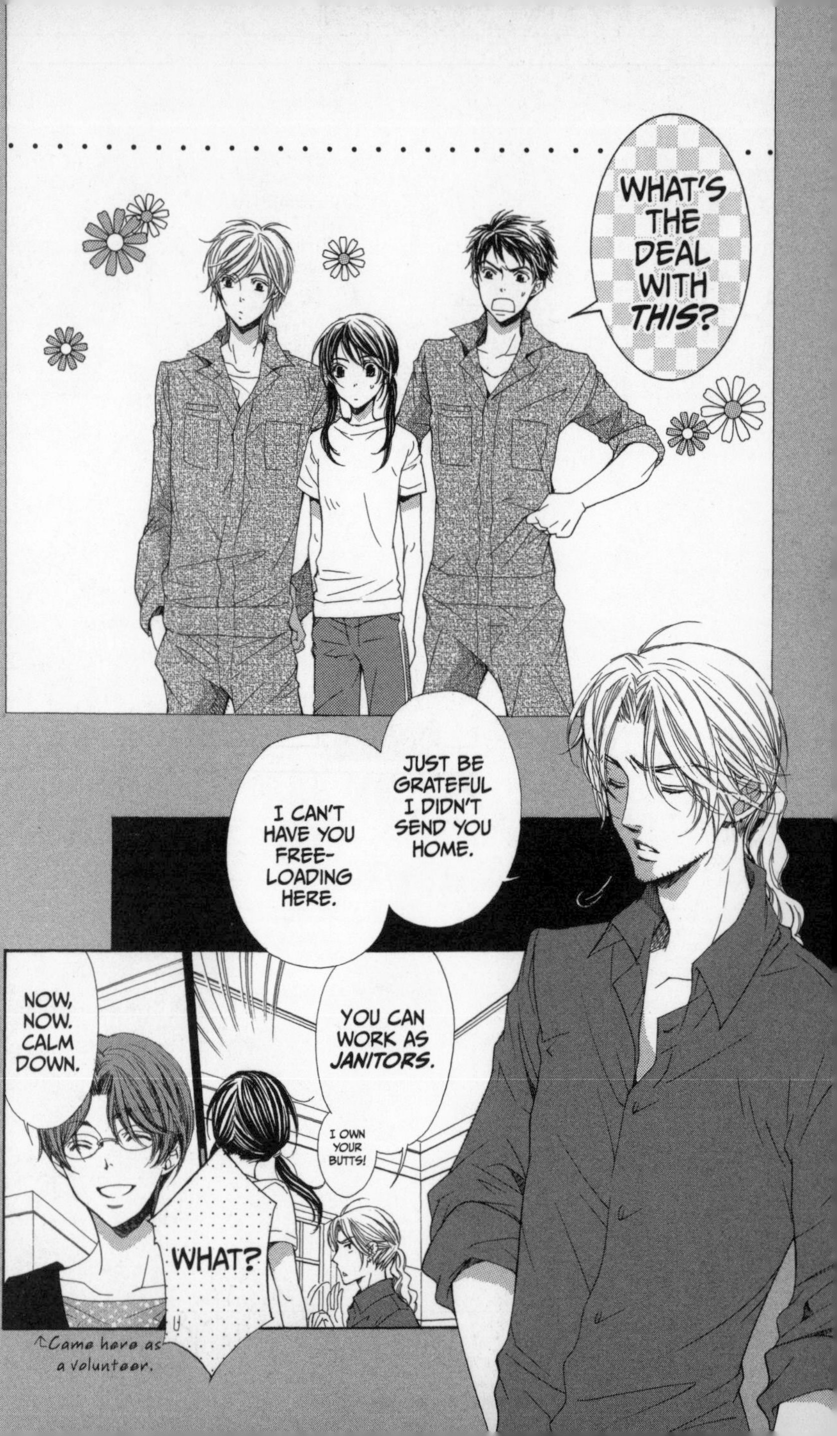
WHAT'S THE DEAL WITH *THIS?*
JUST BE GRATEFUL I DIDN'T SEND YOU HOME.
I CAN'T HAVE YOU FREE-LOADING HERE.
YOU CAN WORK AS *JANITORS.*
I OWN YOUR BUTTS!
NOW, NOW. CALM DOWN.
WHAT?
←Came here as a volunteer.

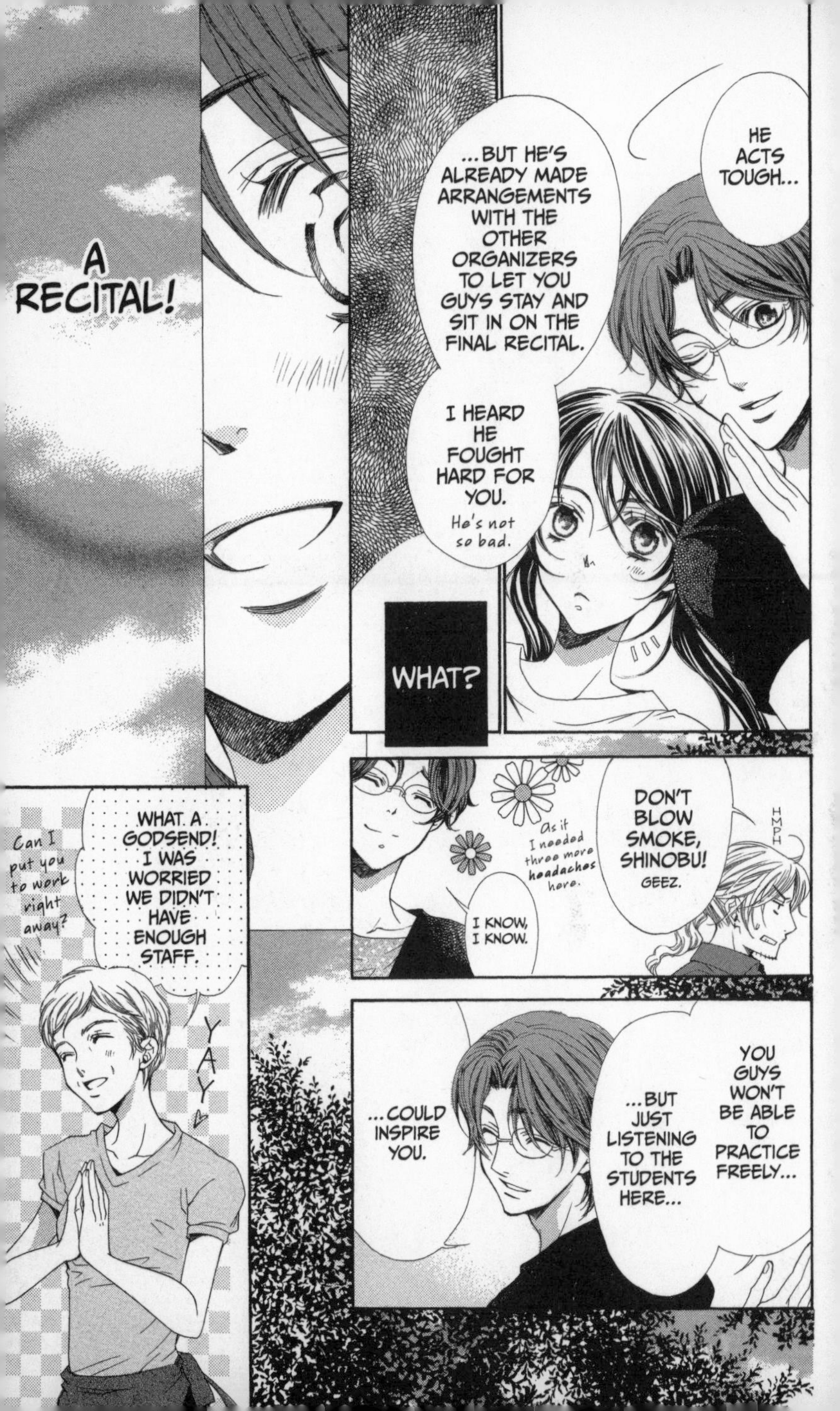
HE ACTS TOUGH...
...BUT HE'S ALREADY MADE ARRANGEMENTS WITH THE OTHER ORGANIZERS TO LET YOU GUYS STAY AND SIT IN ON THE FINAL RECITAL.
I HEARD HE FOUGHT HARD FOR YOU.
He's not so bad.
WHAT?
A RECITAL!
HMPH
DON'T BLOW SMOKE, SHINOBU!
GEEZ.
As if I needed three more headaches here.
I KNOW, I KNOW.
YOU GUYS WON'T BE ABLE TO PRACTICE FREELY...
...BUT JUST LISTENING TO THE STUDENTS HERE...
...COULD INSPIRE YOU.
WHAT. A GODSEND! I WAS WORRIED WE DIDN'T HAVE ENOUGH STAFF.
Can I put you to work right away?
YAY♥

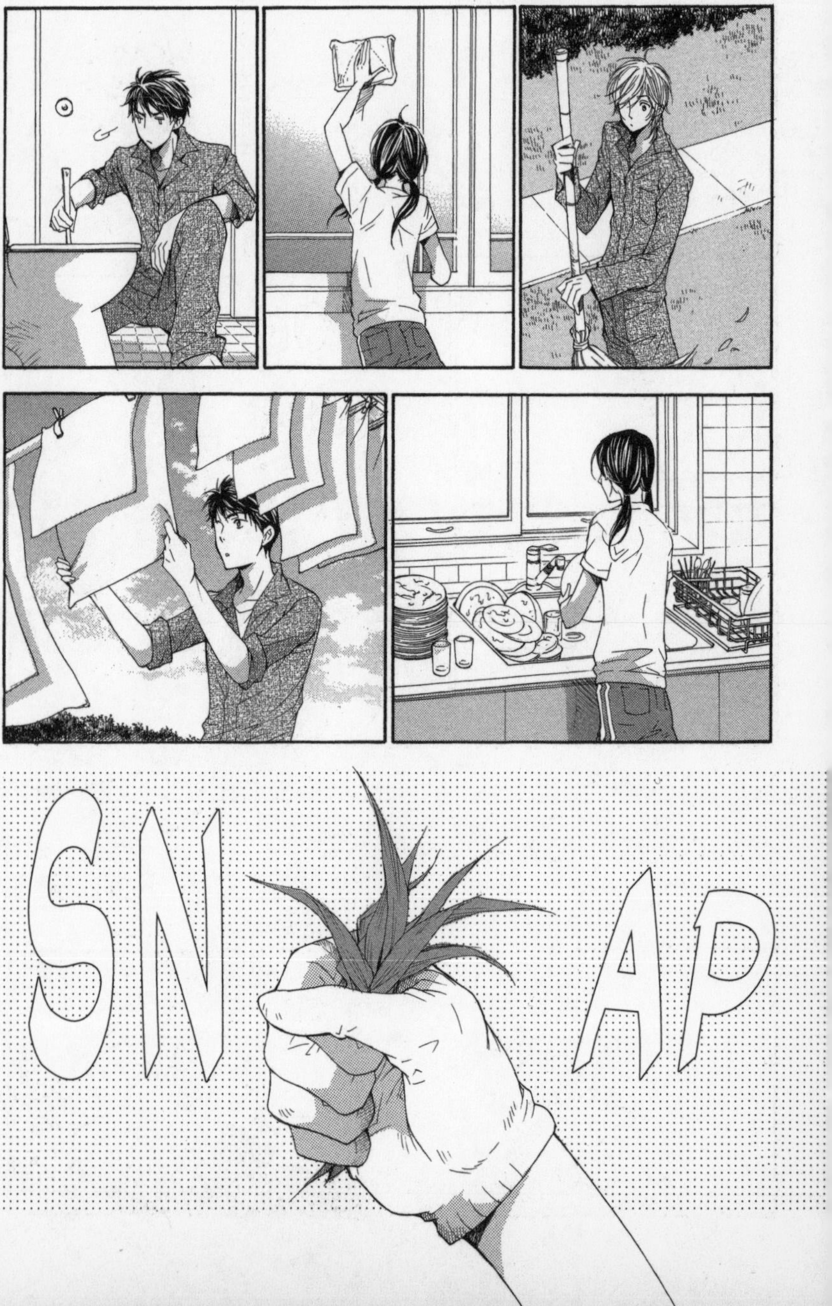
SNAP

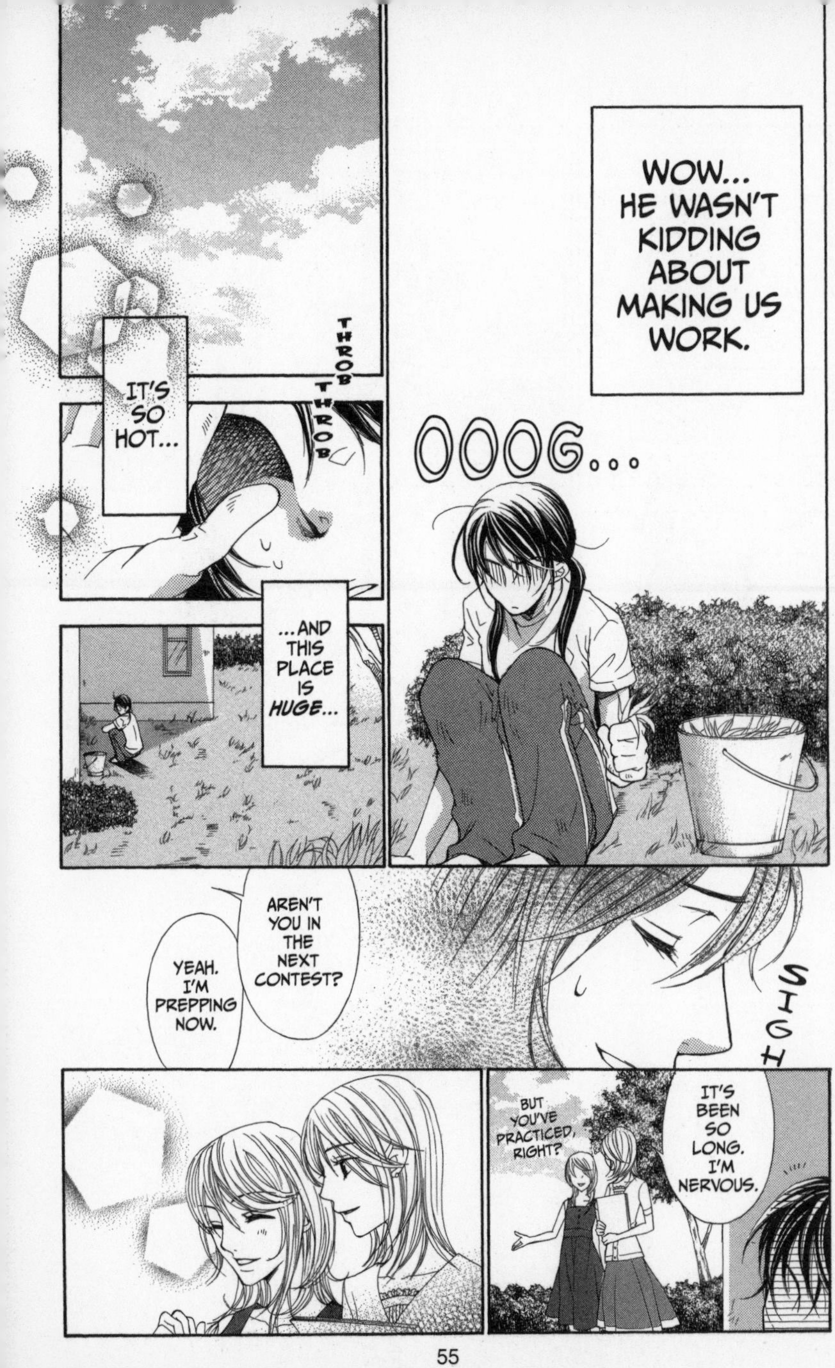
WOW... HE WASN'T KIDDING ABOUT MAKING US WORK.
OOOG...
IT'S SO HOT...
THROB THROB
...AND THIS PLACE IS *HUGE*...
SIGH
AREN'T YOU IN THE NEXT CONTEST?
YEAH. I'M PREPPING NOW.
IT'S BEEN SO LONG. I'M NERVOUS.
BUT YOU'VE PRACTICED, RIGHT?

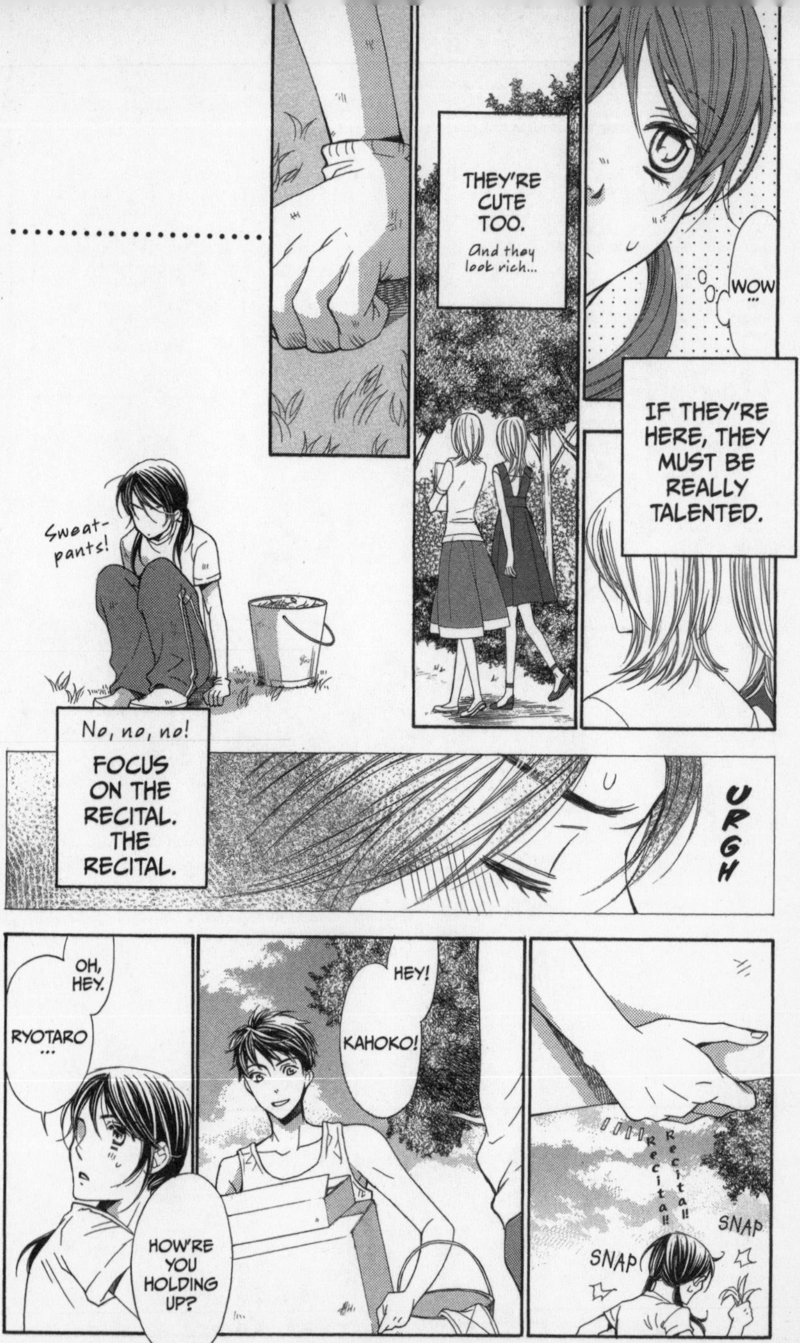
WOW...
IF THEY'RE HERE, THEY MUST BE REALLY TALENTED.
THEY'RE CUTE TOO.
And they look rich...
Sweat-pants!
URGH
No, no, no!
FOCUS ON THE RECITAL. THE RECITAL.
Recital! Recital!
SNAP
SNAP
HEY!
KAHOKO!
OH, HEY.
RYOTARO...
HOW'RE YOU HOLDING UP?

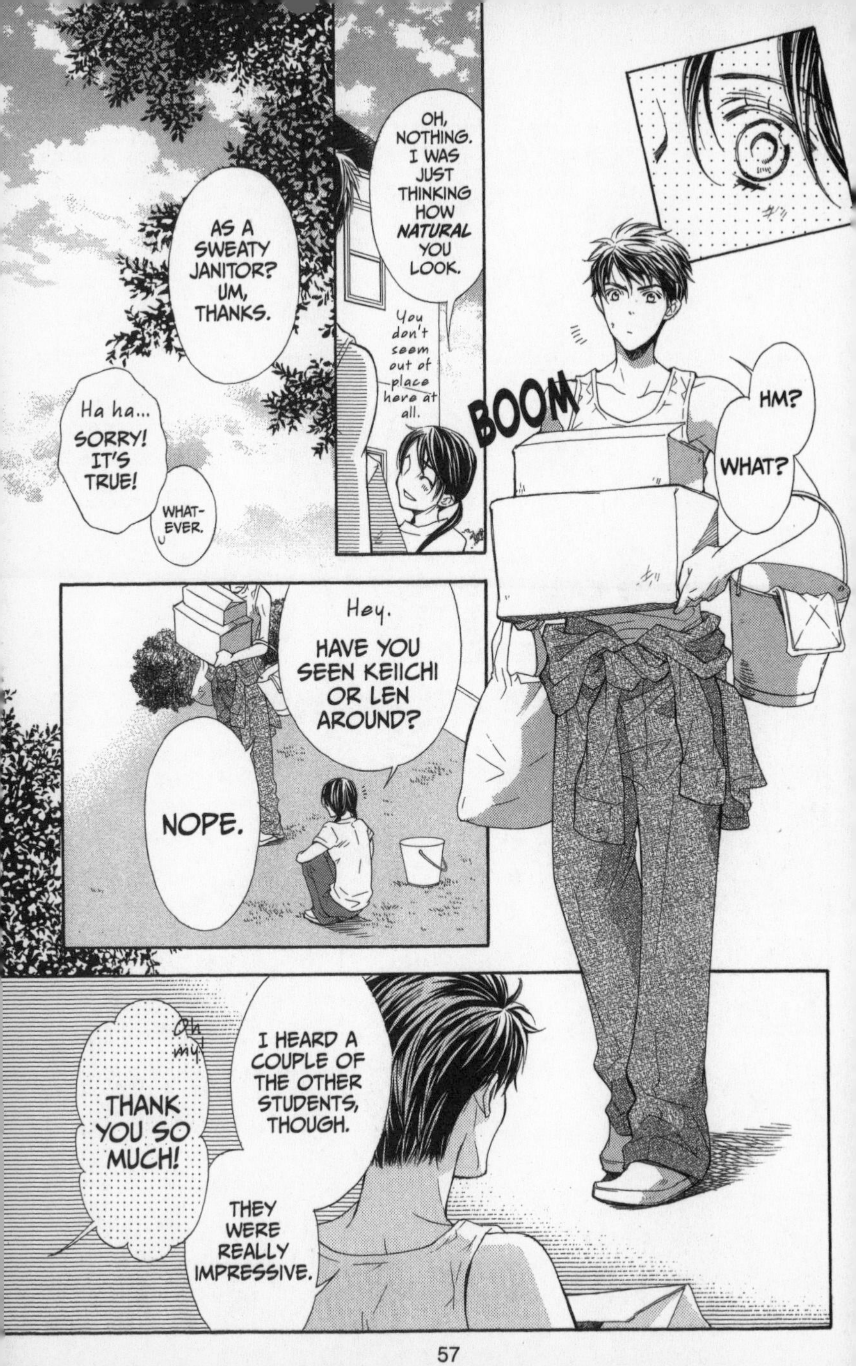
BOOM
HM?
WHAT?
OH, NOTHING. I WAS JUST THINKING HOW ***NATURAL*** YOU LOOK.
You don't seem out of place here at all.
AS A SWEATY JANITOR? UM, THANKS.
Ha ha... SORRY! IT'S TRUE!
WHATEVER.
Hey.
HAVE YOU SEEN KEIICHI OR LEN AROUND?
NOPE.
I HEARD A COUPLE OF THE OTHER STUDENTS, THOUGH.
THEY WERE REALLY IMPRESSIVE.
Oh my.
THANK YOU SO MUCH!

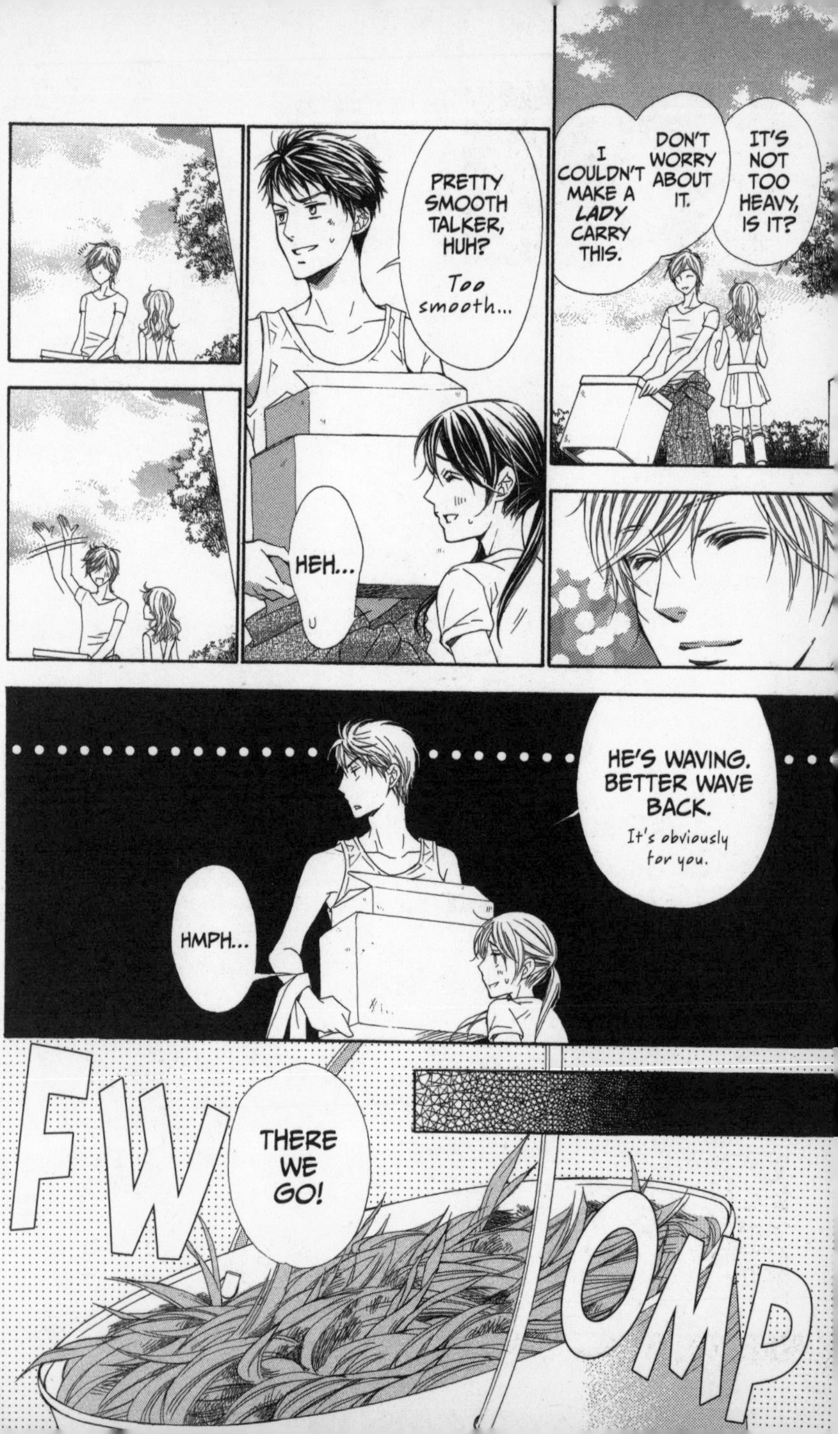
IT'S NOT TOO HEAVY, IS IT?
DON'T WORRY ABOUT IT.
I COULDN'T MAKE A *LADY* CARRY THIS.
PRETTY SMOOTH TALKER, HUH?
Too smooth...
HEH...
HE'S WAVING. BETTER WAVE BACK.
It's obviously for you.
HMPH...
THERE WE GO!
FW...OMP

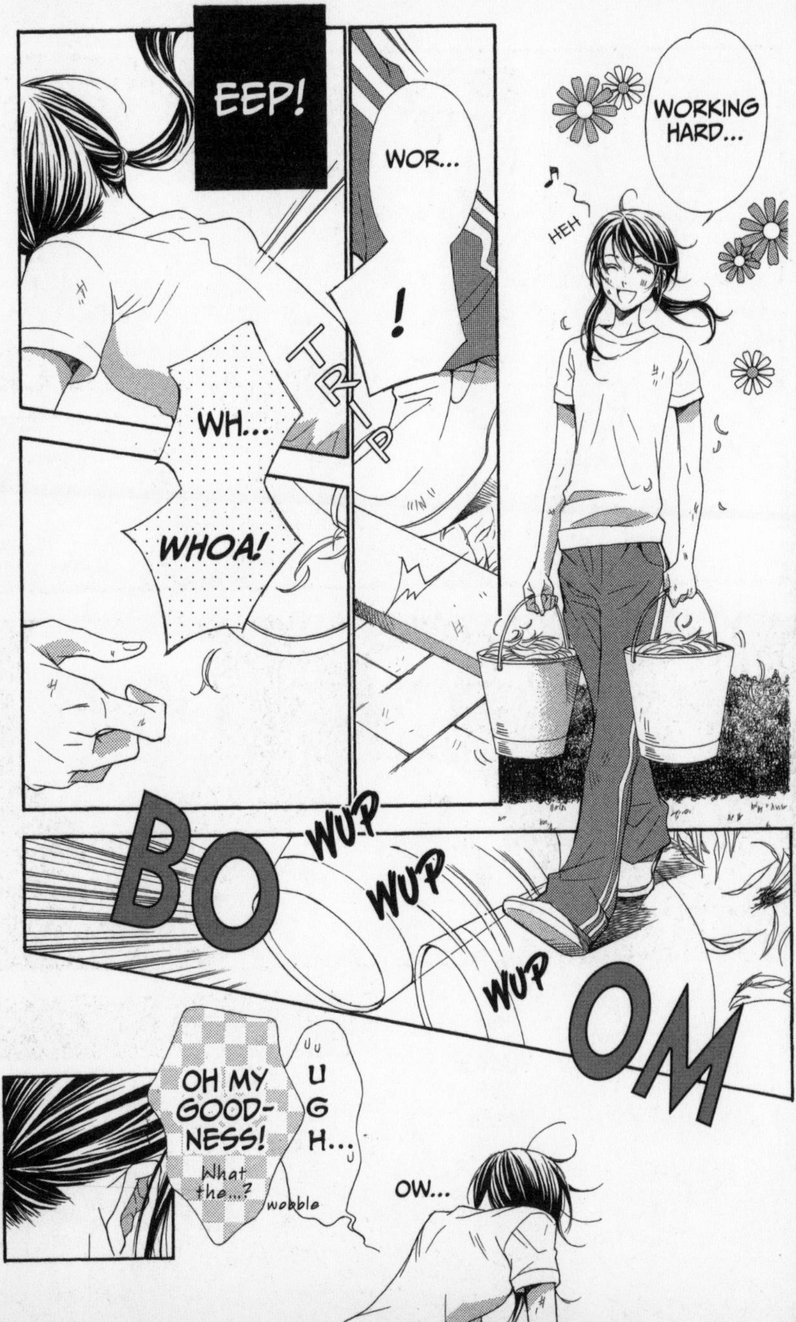
WORKING HARD...
HEH
WOR...
!
TRIP
EEP!
WH...
WHOA!
BO
WUP
WUP
WUP
OM
OW...
UGH...
OH MY GOODNESS!
What the...?
wobble

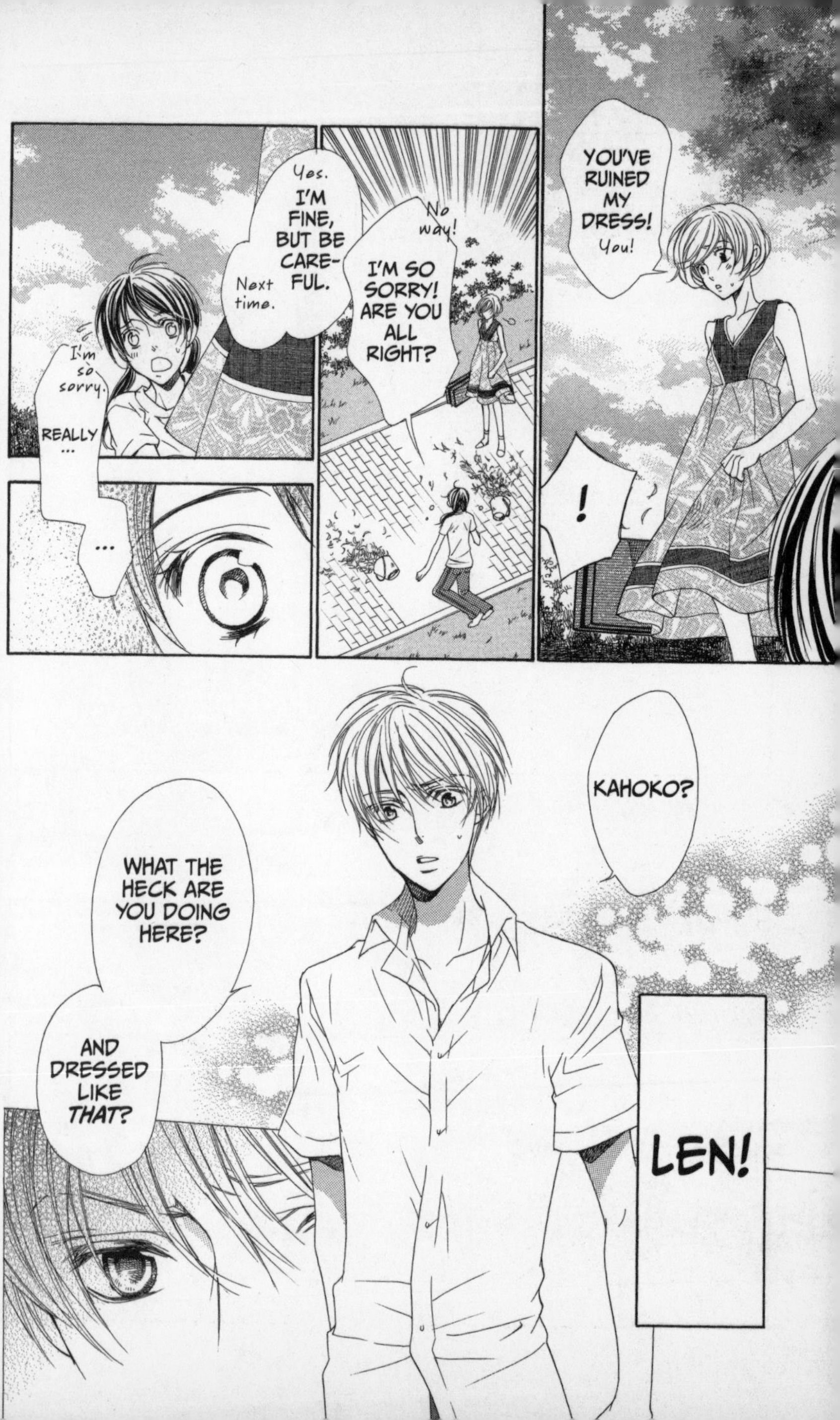
YOU'VE RUINED MY DRESS!
You!
!
No way!
I'M SO SORRY! ARE YOU ALL RIGHT?
Yes.
I'M FINE, BUT BE CARE-FUL.
Next time.
I'm so sorry.
REALLY...
...
KAHOKO?
WHAT THE HECK ARE YOU DOING HERE?
AND DRESSED LIKE THAT?
LEN!

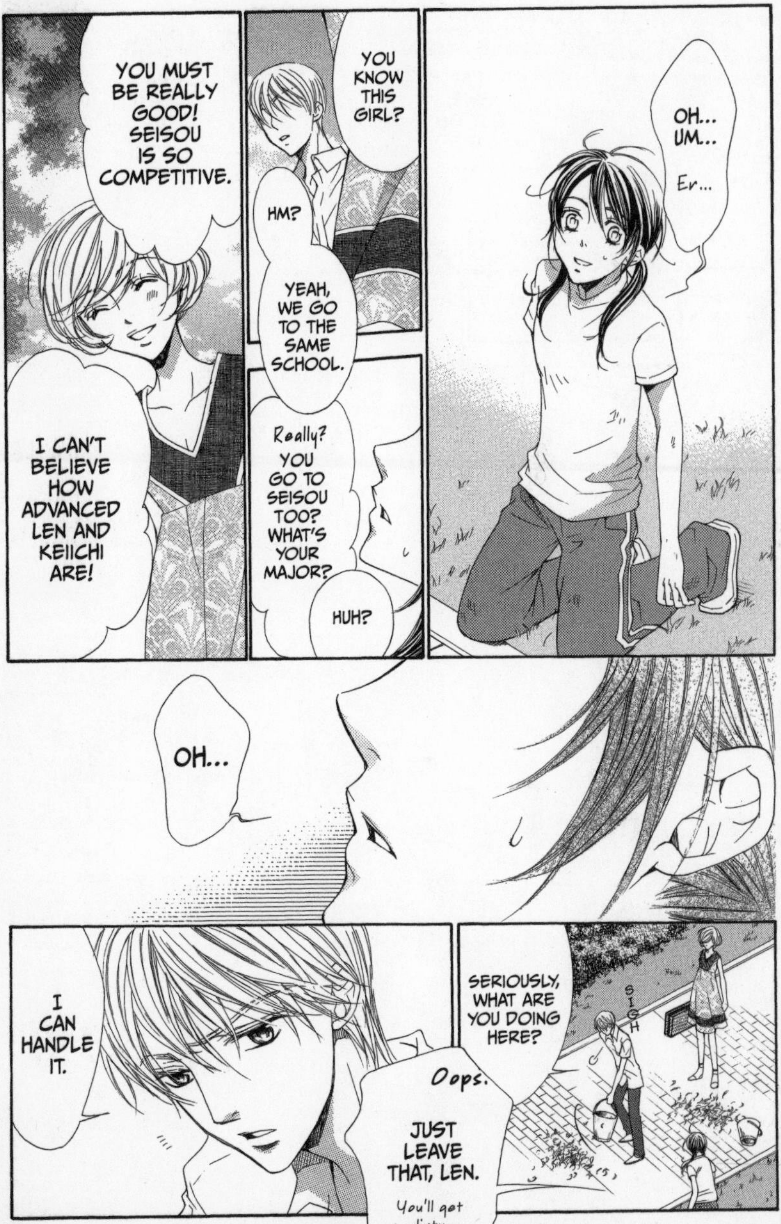
OH... UM...
Er...
YOU KNOW THIS GIRL?
HM?
YEAH, WE GO TO THE SAME SCHOOL.
Really? YOU GO TO SEISOU TOO? WHAT'S YOUR MAJOR?
HUH?
YOU MUST BE REALLY GOOD! SEISOU IS SO COMPETITIVE.
I CAN'T BELIEVE HOW ADVANCED LEN AND KEIICHI ARE!
OH...
SERIOUSLY, WHAT ARE YOU DOING HERE?
SIGH
Oops.
JUST LEAVE THAT, LEN.
You'll get dirty.
I CAN HANDLE IT.

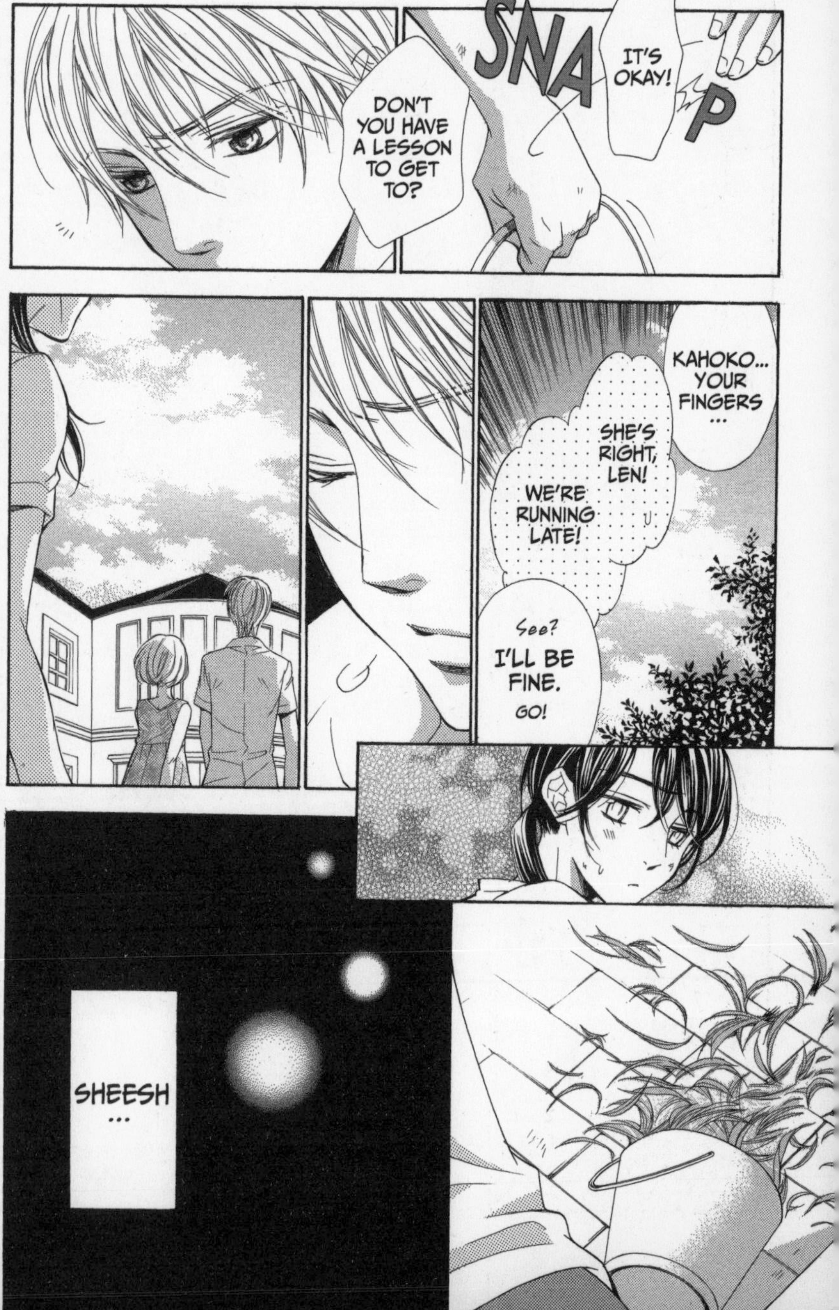
SNAP
IT'S OKAY!
DON'T YOU HAVE A LESSON TO GET TO?
KAHOKO... YOUR FINGERS...
SHE'S RIGHT, LEN!
WE'RE RUNNING LATE!
See? I'LL BE FINE.
GO!
SHEESH...

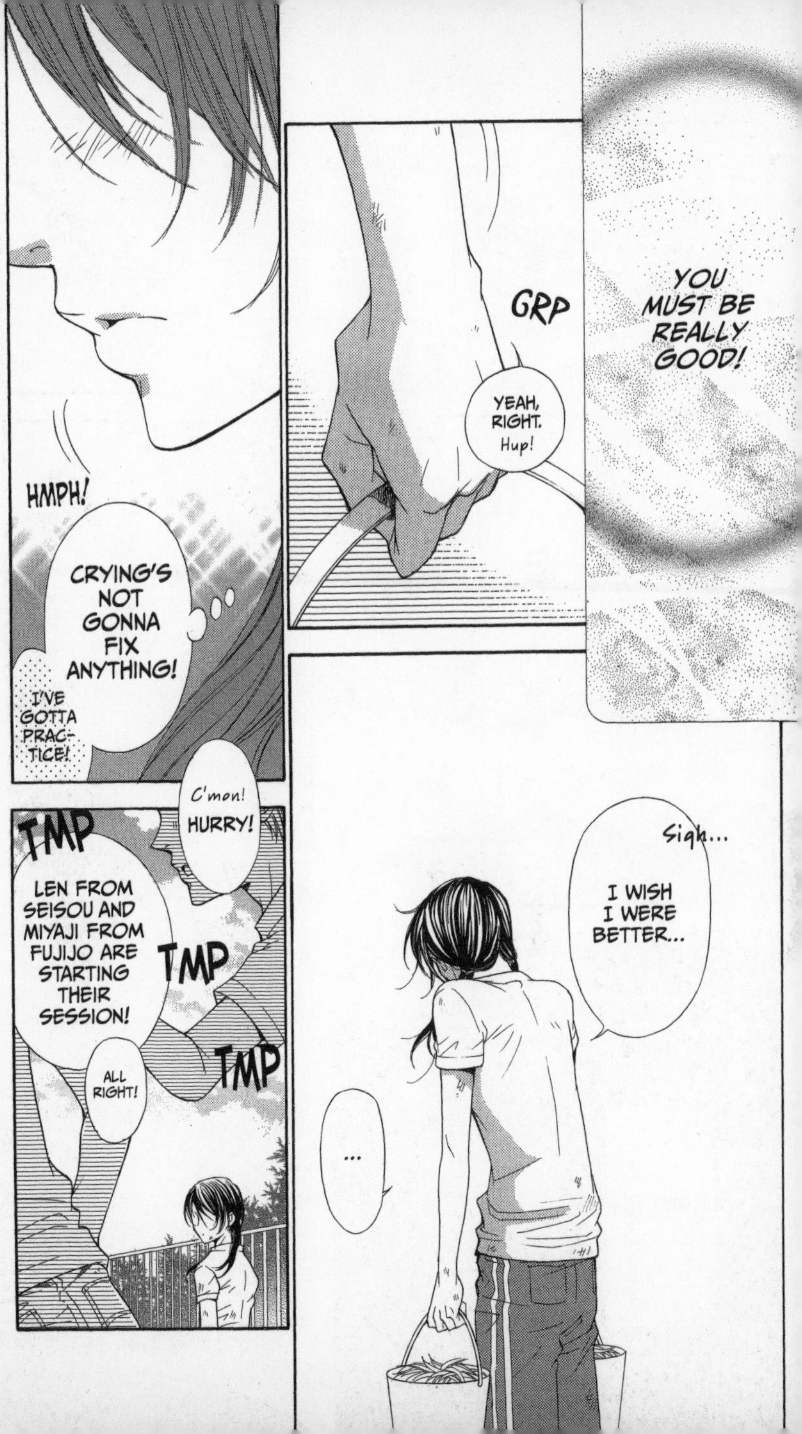
YOU MUST BE REALLY GOOD!
GRP
YEAH, RIGHT. Hup!
HMPH!
CRYING'S NOT GONNA FIX ANYTHING!
I'VE GOTTA PRAC-TICE!
Sigh...
I WISH I WERE BETTER...
...
C'mon! HURRY!
TMP
LEN FROM SEISOU AND MIYAJI FROM FUJIJO ARE STARTING THEIR SESSION!
TMP
ALL RIGHT!
TMP

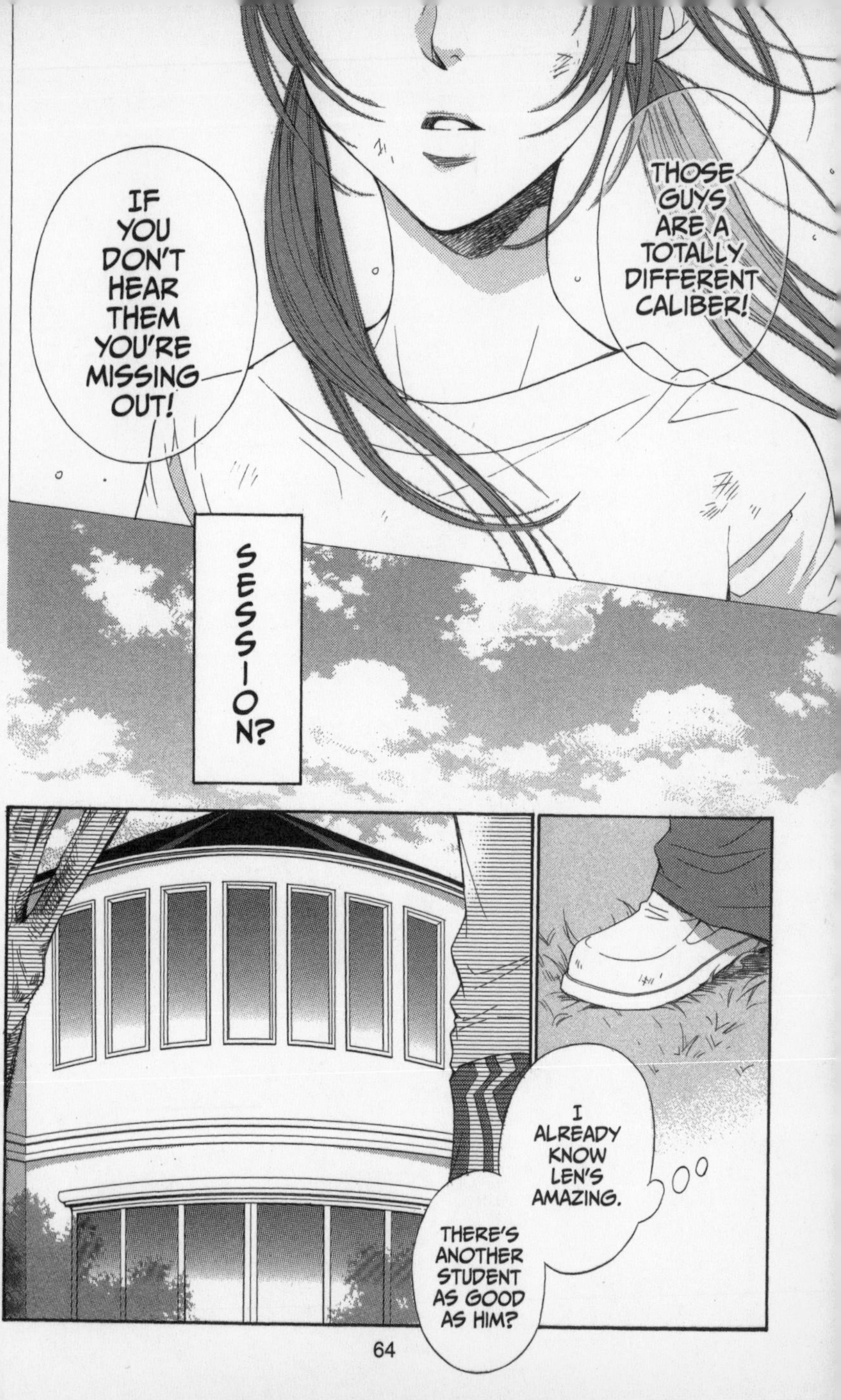
THOSE GUYS ARE A TOTALLY DIFFERENT CALIBER!
IF YOU DON'T HEAR THEM YOU'RE MISSING OUT!
SESSION?
I ALREADY KNOW LEN'S AMAZING.
THERE'S ANOTHER STUDENT AS GOOD AS HIM?

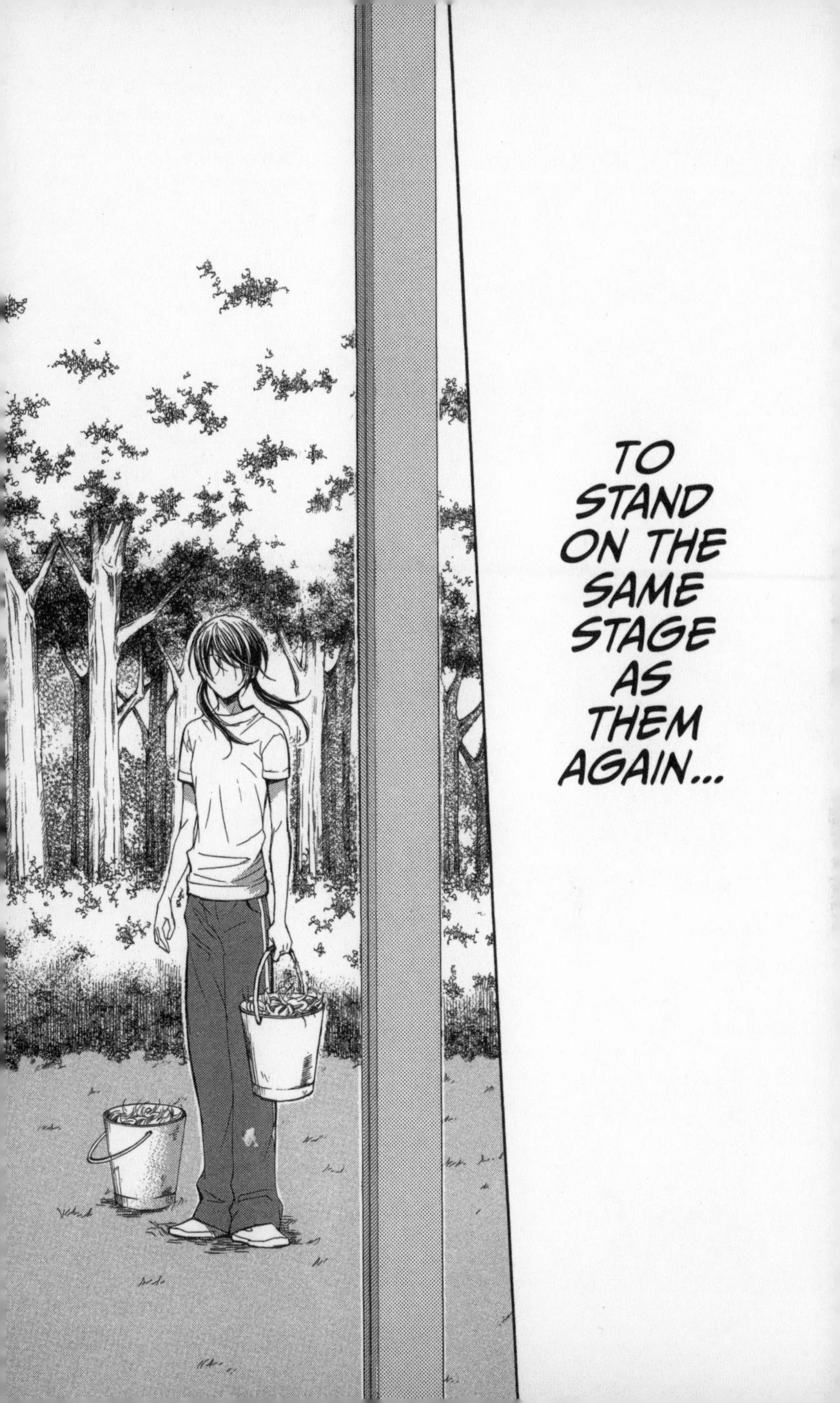
TO STAND ON THE SAME STAGE AS THEM AGAIN...

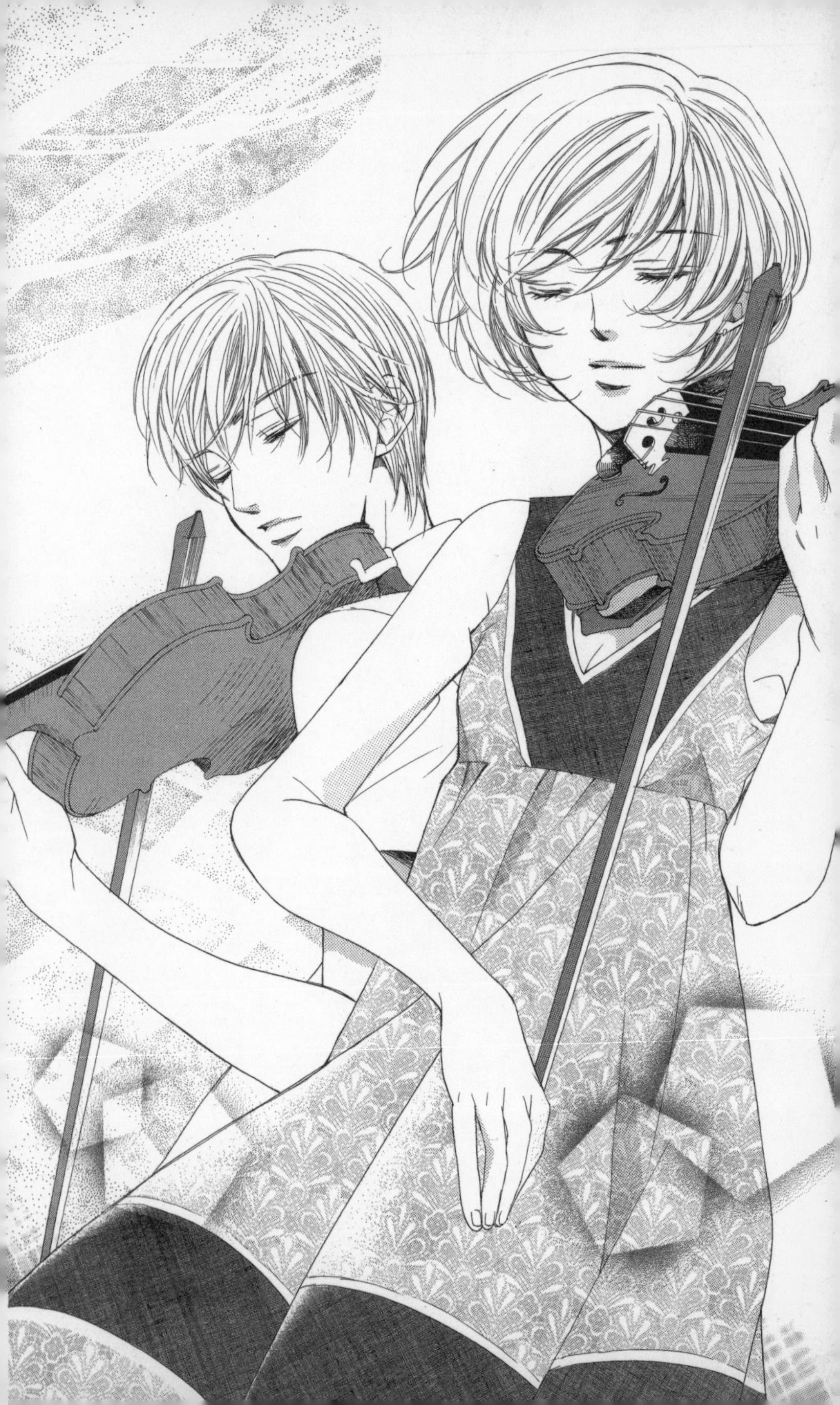

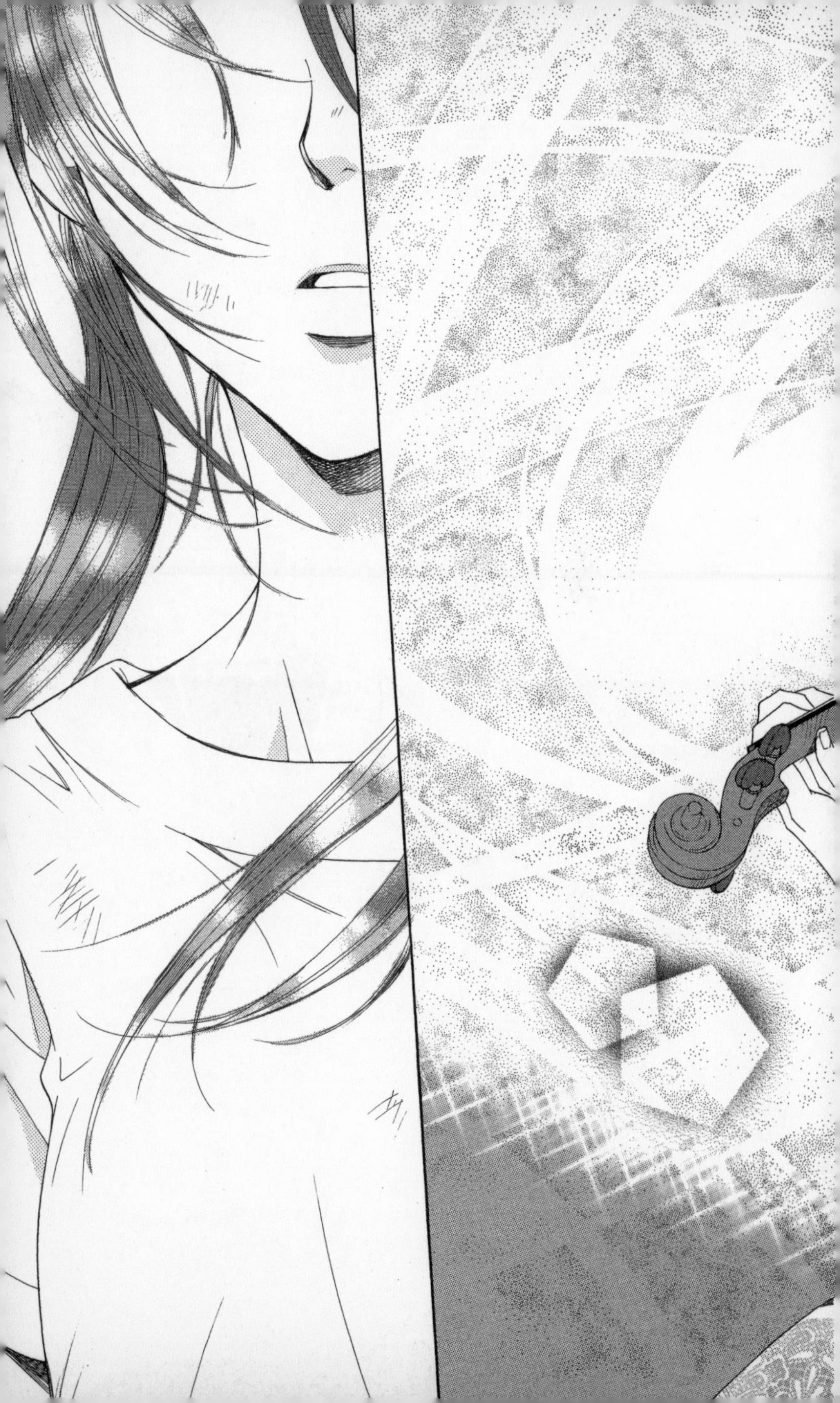

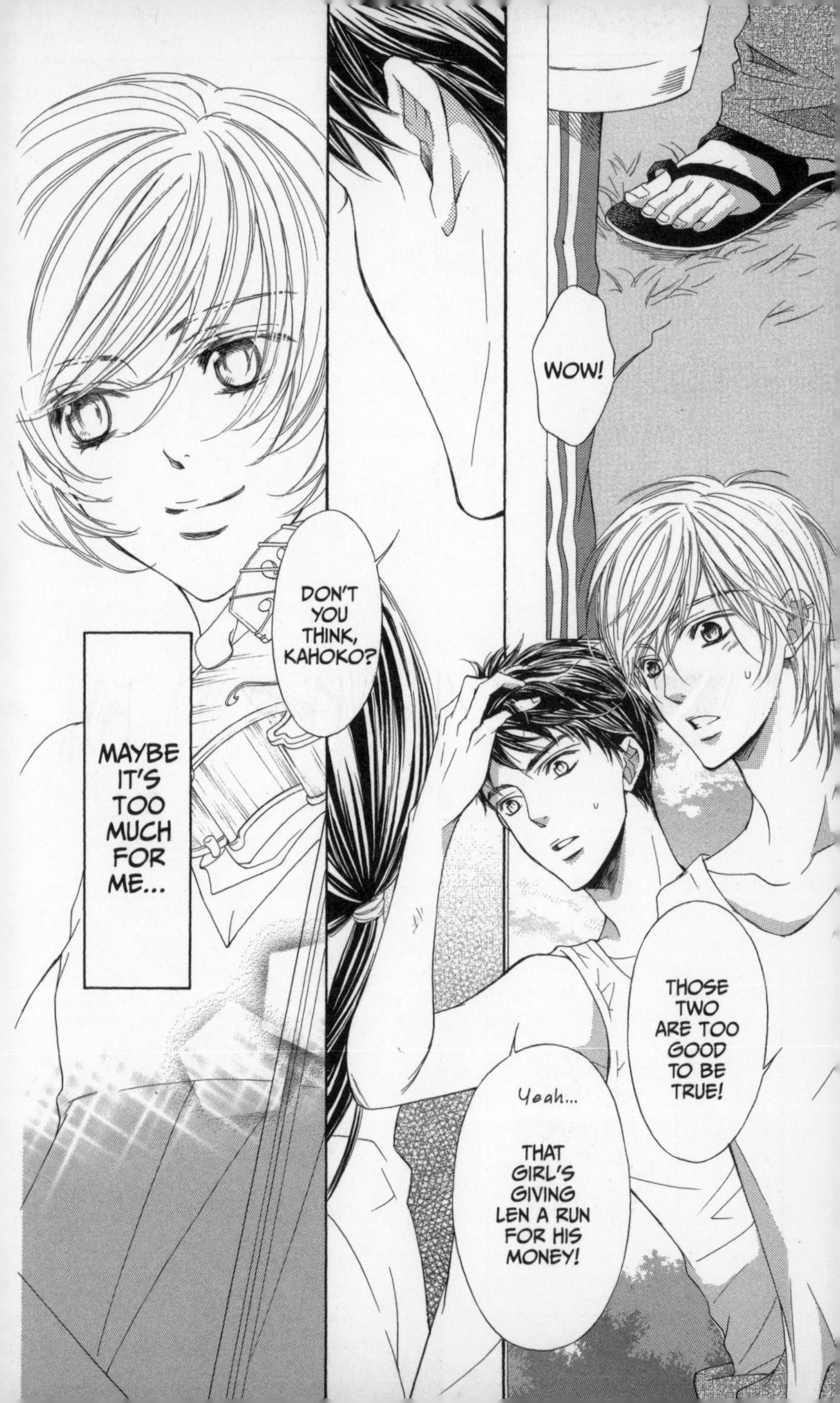
WOW!
THOSE TWO ARE TOO GOOD TO BE TRUE!
Yeah...
THAT GIRL'S GIVING LEN A RUN FOR HIS MONEY!
DON'T YOU THINK, KAHOKO?
MAYBE IT'S TOO MUCH FOR ME...

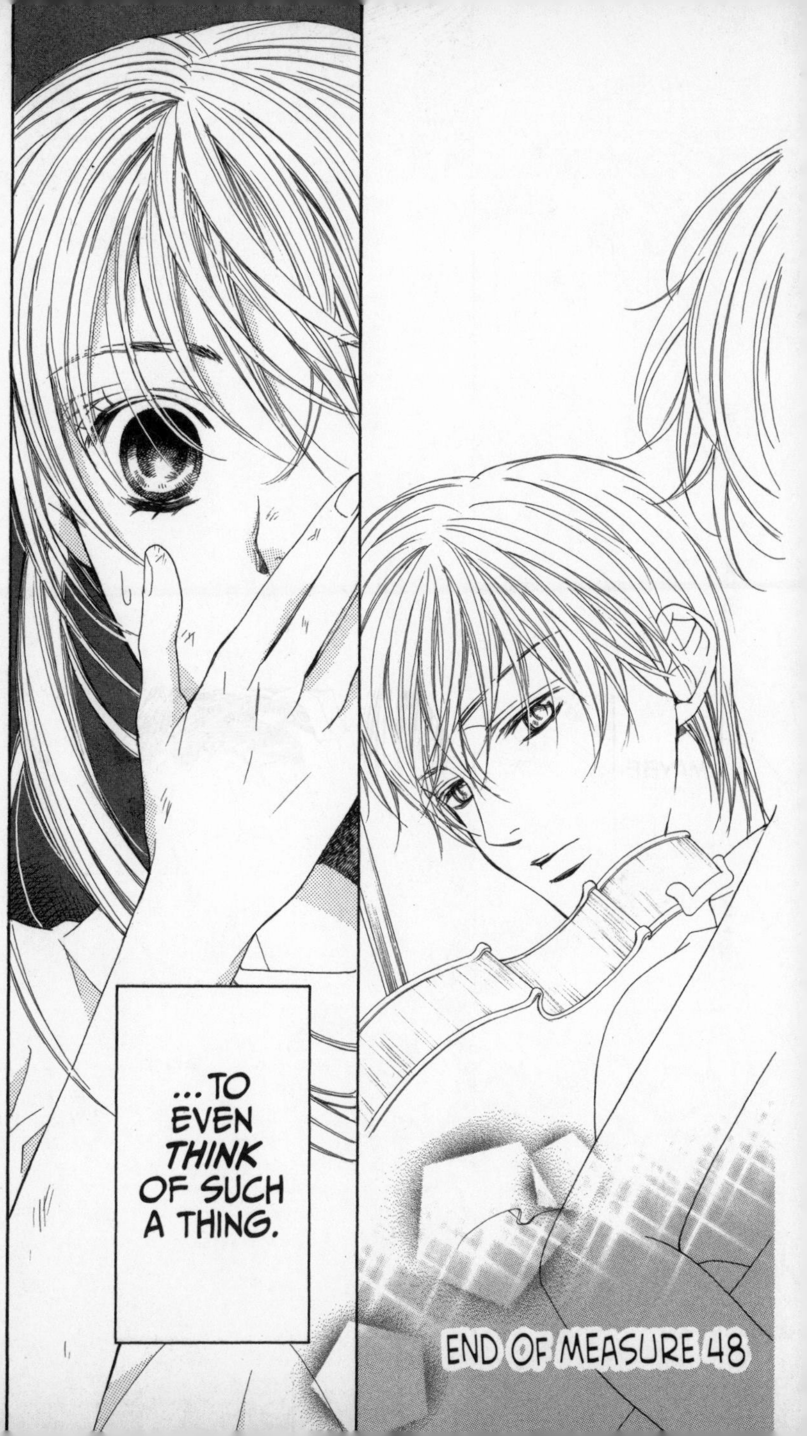
END OF MEASURE 48
...TO EVEN *THINK* OF SUCH A THING.

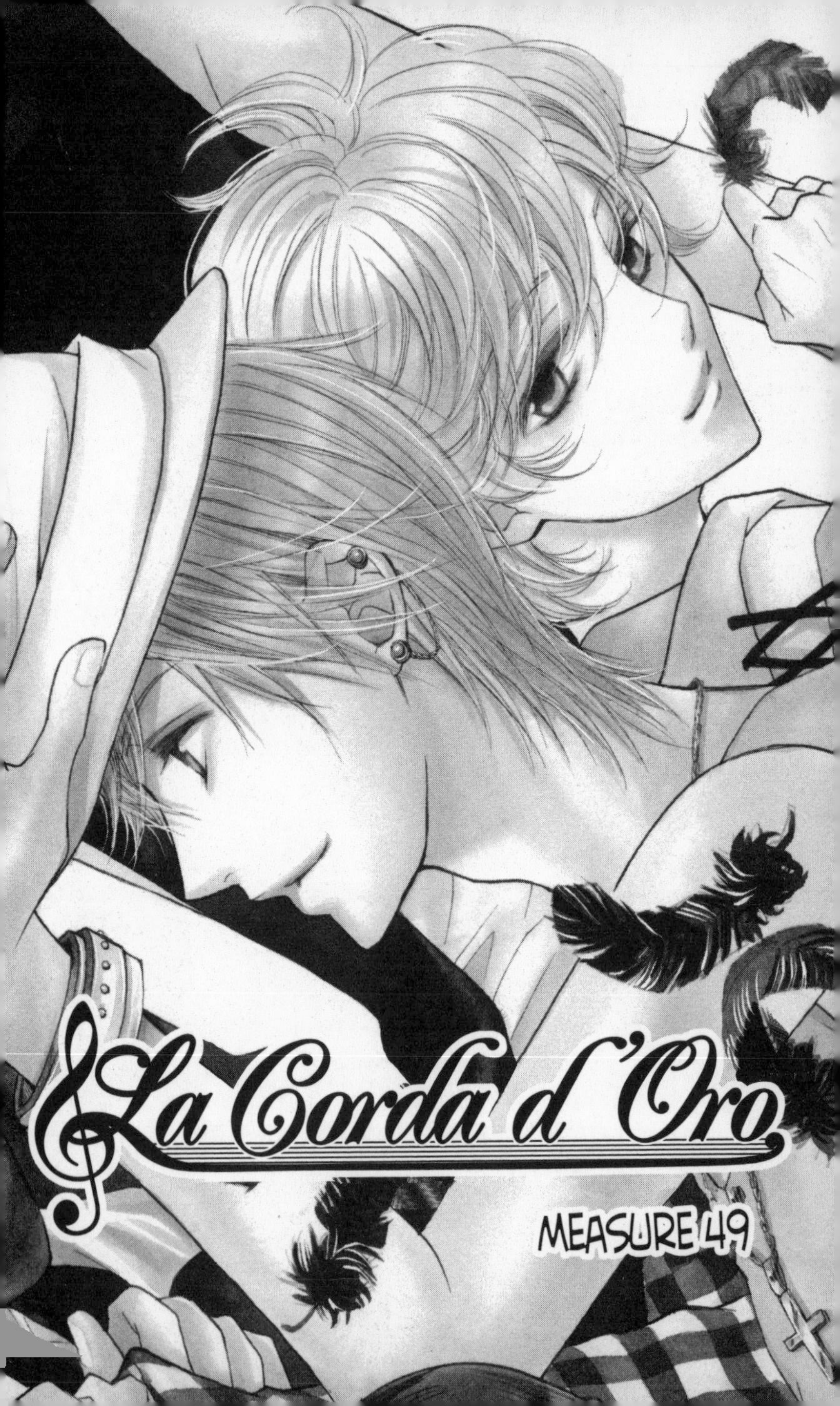
La Corda d'Oro
MEASURE 49

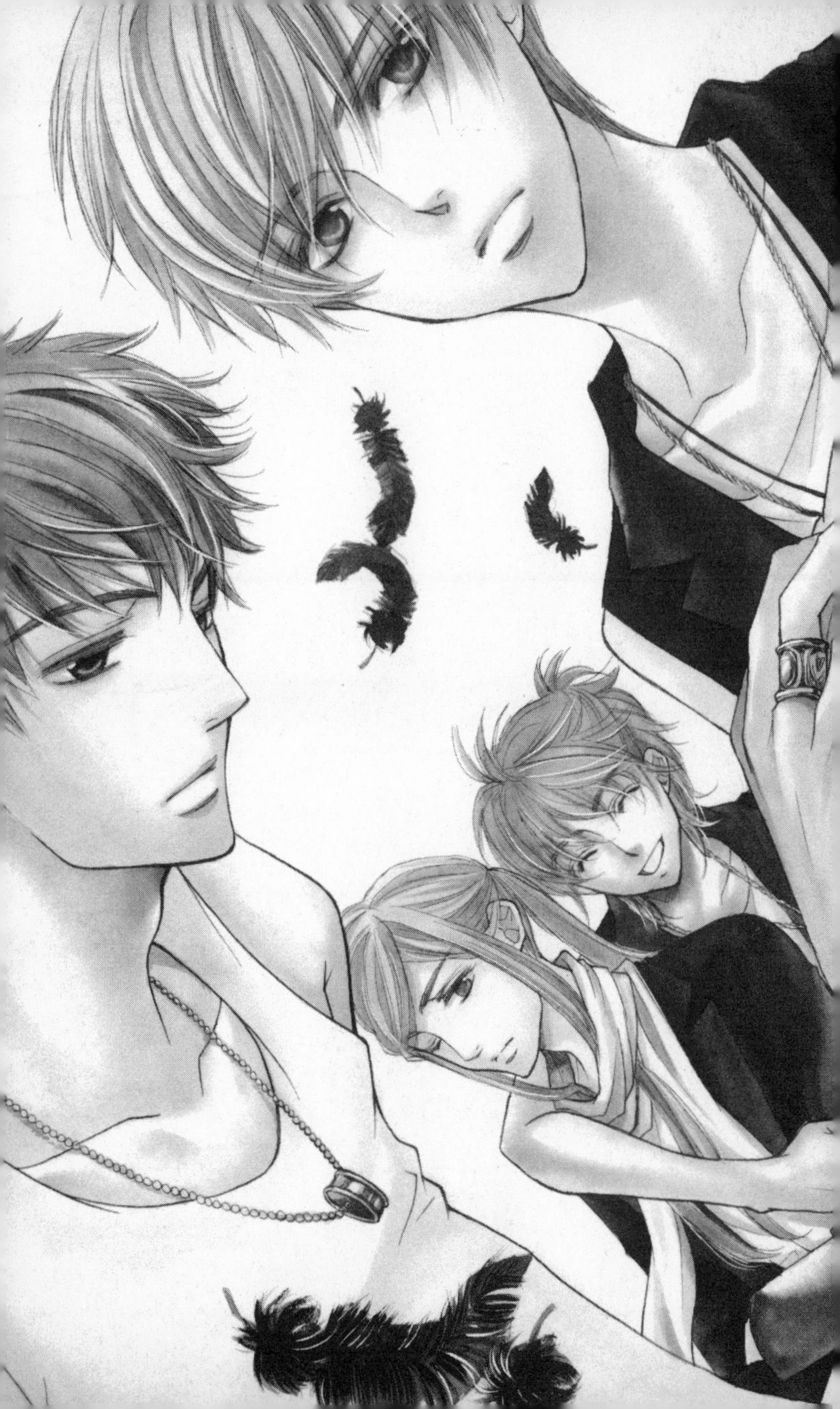

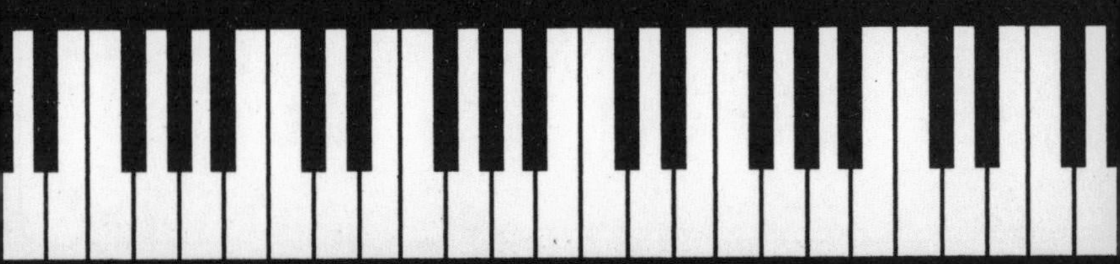

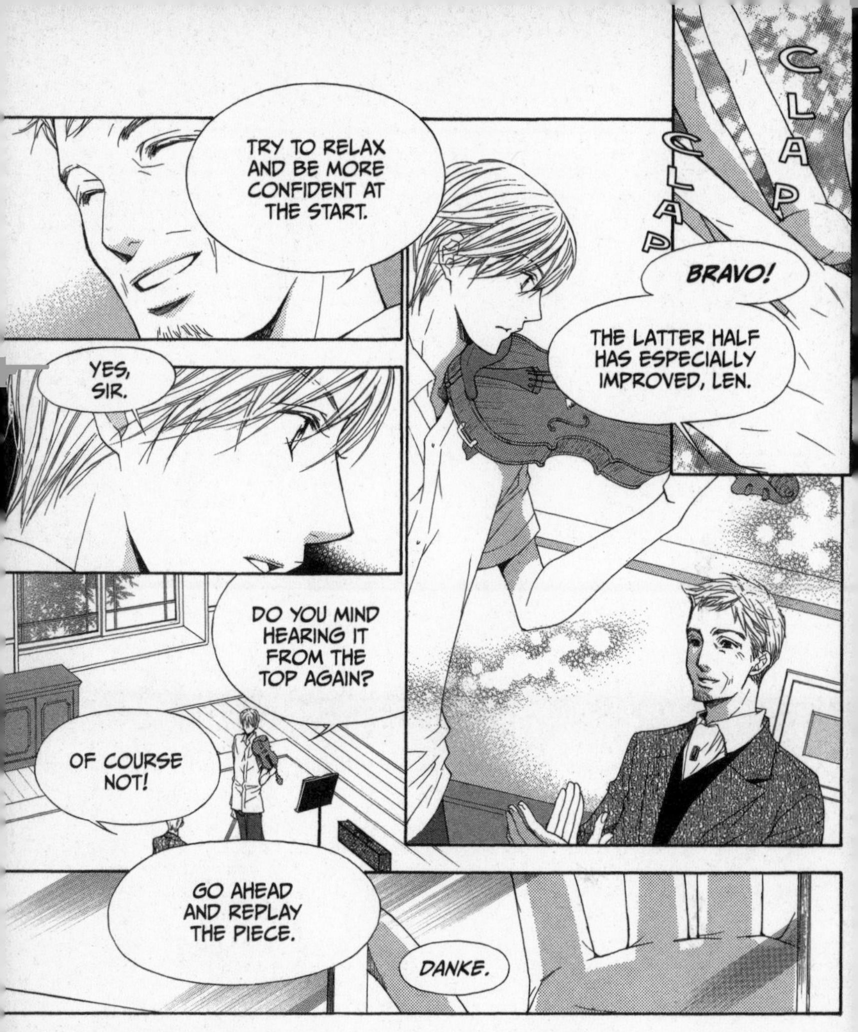
CLAP CLAP
BRAVO!
THE LATTER HALF HAS ESPECIALLY IMPROVED, LEN.
TRY TO RELAX AND BE MORE CONFIDENT AT THE START.
YES, SIR.
DO YOU MIND HEARING IT FROM THE TOP AGAIN?
OF COURSE NOT!
GO AHEAD AND REPLAY THE PIECE.
DANKE.

Daily Happenings ④①

Alcohol...

I've always liked drinking, but my drinks of choice are usually beer, shochu, sake, whiskey...all drinks associated with middle-aged men. I've never been into wine, but I tried a Moscato d'Asti my friend got me the other day, and it was so smooth. ♡ I recommend it for anyone who likes sweet drinks. Even the bottle's fancy.♪

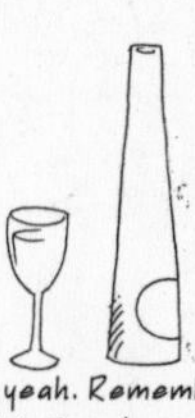

Oh, yeah. Remember, don't drink if you're underage!

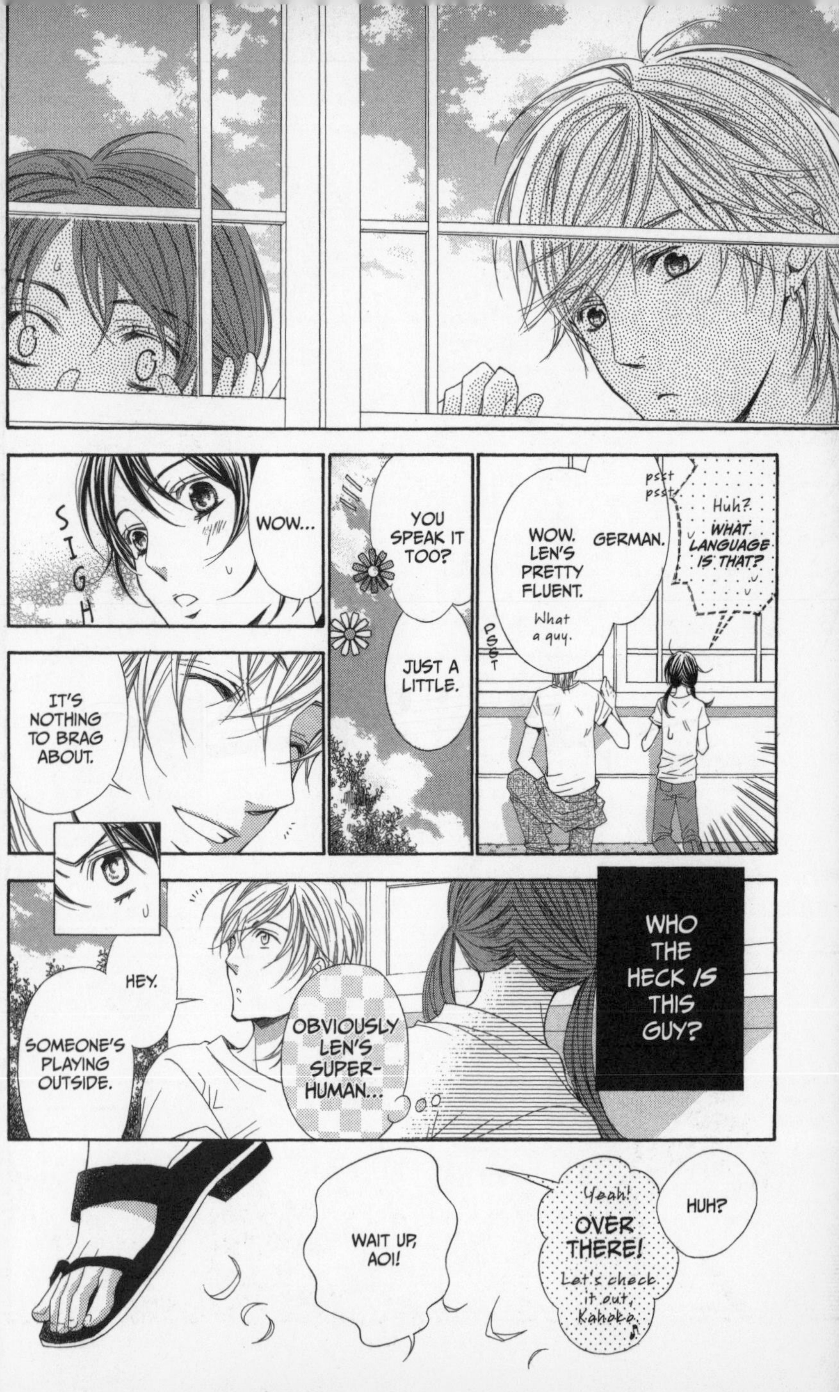
psst psst
Huh? WHAT LANGUAGE IS THAT?
GERMAN.
WOW. LEN'S PRETTY FLUENT.
What a guy.
PSST
YOU SPEAK IT TOO?
JUST A LITTLE.
WOW...
SIGH
IT'S NOTHING TO BRAG ABOUT.
WHO THE HECK IS THIS GUY?
OBVIOUSLY LEN'S SUPER-HUMAN...
HEY.
SOMEONE'S PLAYING OUTSIDE.
HUH?
Yeah! OVER THERE! Let's check it out, Kahoko.
WAIT UP, AOI!

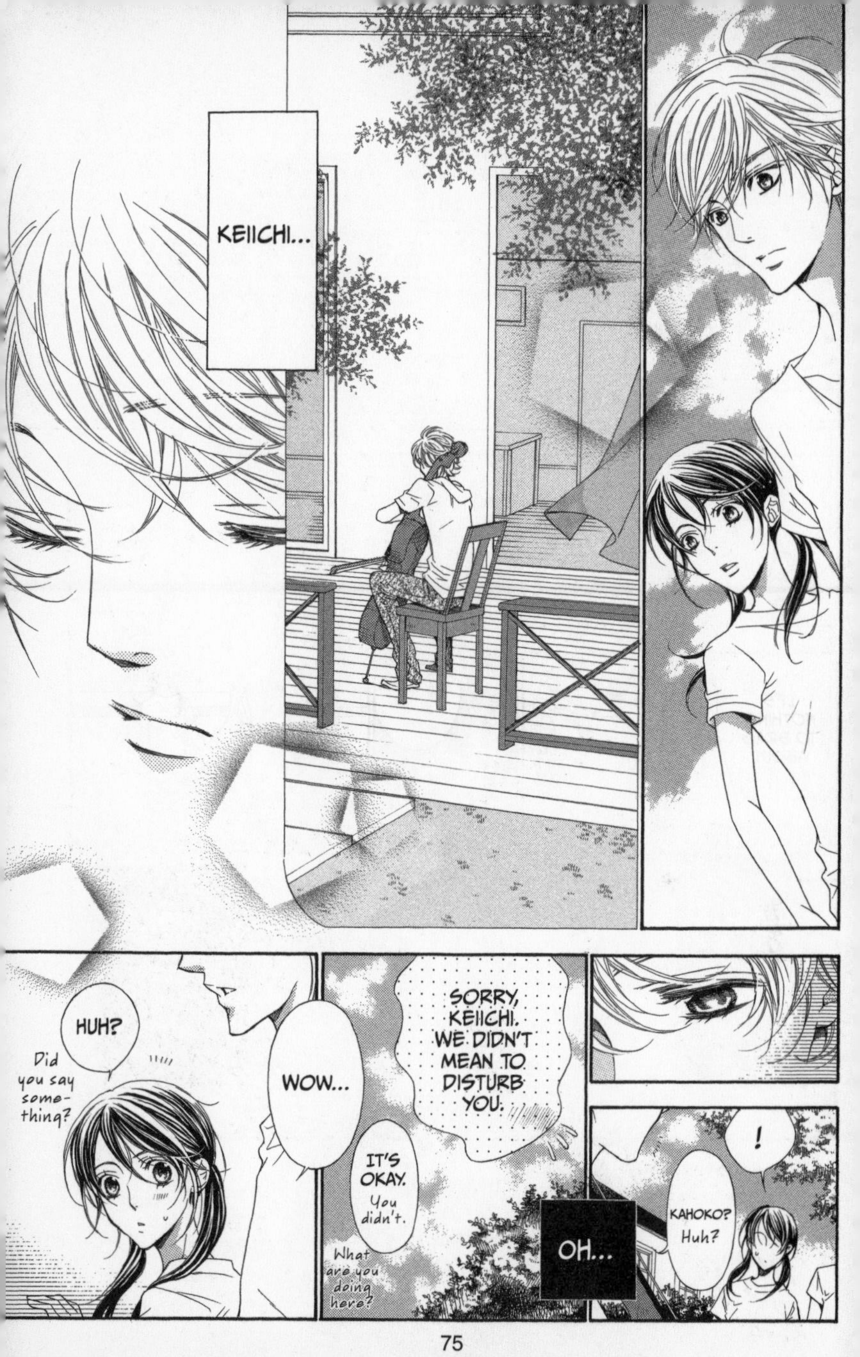
KEIICHI...
!
KAHOKO? Huh?
OH...
SORRY, KEIICHI. WE DIDN'T MEAN TO DISTURB YOU.
IT'S OKAY. You didn't.
What are you doing here?
WOW...
HUH?
Did you say some-thing?

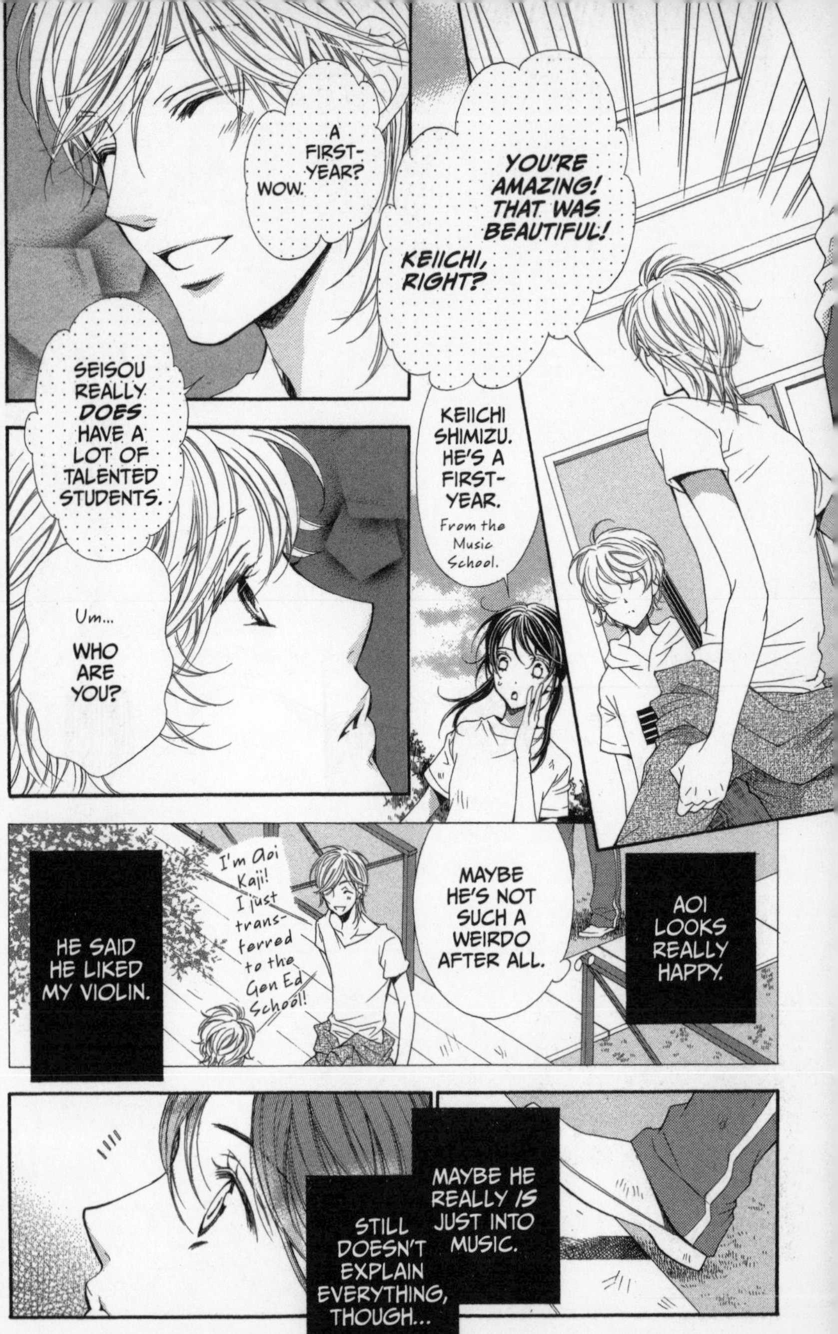
YOU'RE AMAZING! THAT WAS BEAUTIFUL!
KEIICHI, RIGHT?
KEIICHI SHIMIZU. HE'S A FIRST-YEAR.
From the Music School.
A FIRST-YEAR? WOW.
SEISOU REALLY *DOES* HAVE A LOT OF TALENTED STUDENTS.
Um...
WHO ARE YOU?
AOI LOOKS REALLY HAPPY.
MAYBE HE'S NOT SUCH A WEIRDO AFTER ALL.
I'm Aoi Kaji! I just transferred to the Gen Ed School!
HE SAID HE LIKED MY VIOLIN.
MAYBE HE REALLY *IS* JUST INTO MUSIC.
STILL DOESN'T EXPLAIN EVERYTHING, THOUGH...

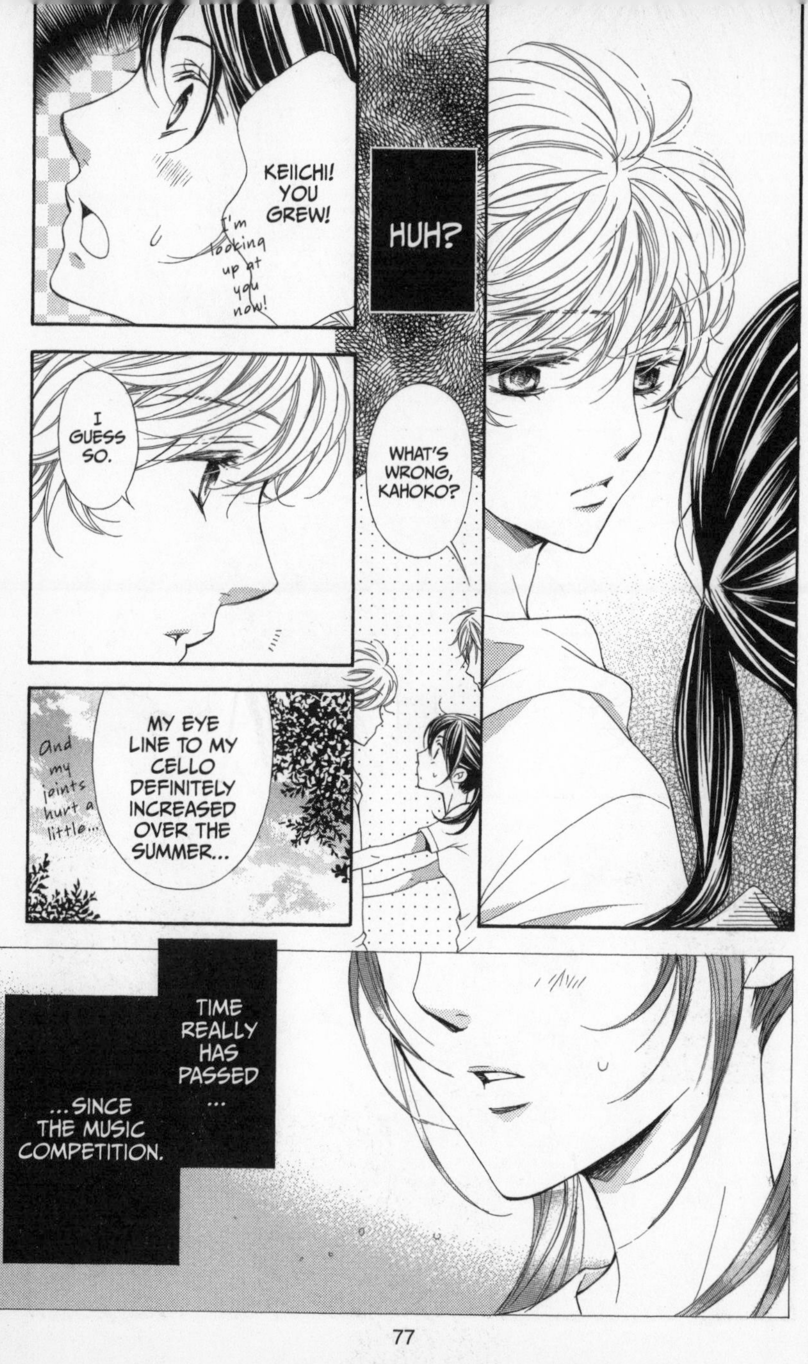
HUH?
WHAT'S WRONG, KAHOKO?
KEIICHI! YOU GREW!
I'm looking up at you now!
I GUESS SO.
MY EYE LINE TO MY CELLO DEFINITELY INCREASED OVER THE SUMMER...
And my joints hurt a little...
TIME REALLY HAS PASSED ...
...SINCE THE MUSIC COMPETITION.

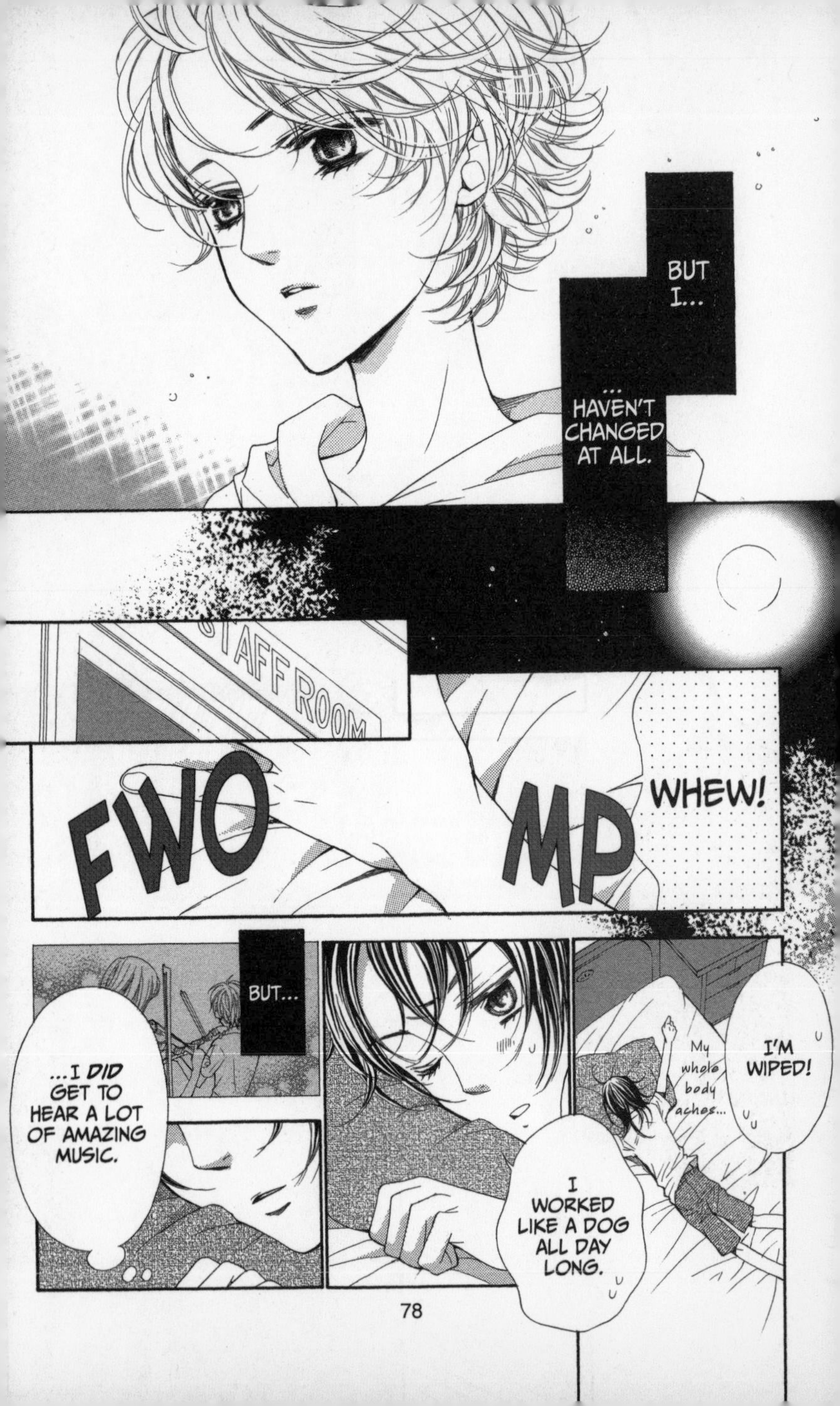
BUT I...
...HAVEN'T CHANGED AT ALL.
STAFF ROOM
WHEW!
FWOMP
I'M WIPED!
My whole body aches...
I WORKED LIKE A DOG ALL DAY LONG.
BUT...
...I *DID* GET TO HEAR A LOT OF AMAZING MUSIC.

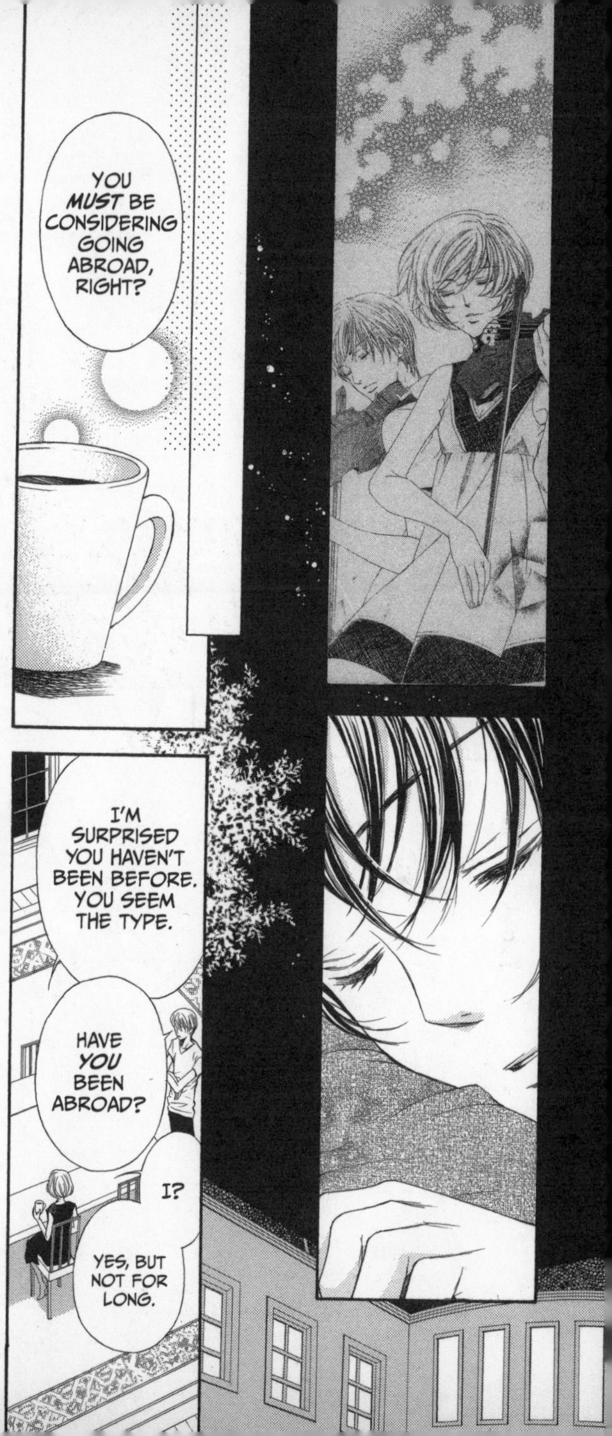
YOU *MUST* BE CONSIDERING GOING ABROAD, RIGHT?
I'M SURPRISED YOU HAVEN'T BEEN BEFORE. YOU SEEM THE TYPE.
HAVE *YOU* BEEN ABROAD?
I?
YES, BUT NOT FOR LONG.

Let's talk about the story a little. Aoi is from the *La Corda 2* game. (So is Kira, the board director.) I know he's pretty hard to read, but I hope he finds his place in the gang. Visually, I enjoy drawing him. It feels fresh. By the way, he's 180 cm and his blood type is AB.

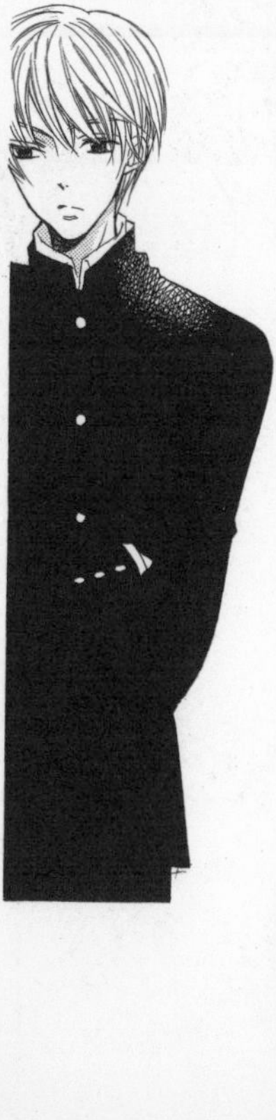

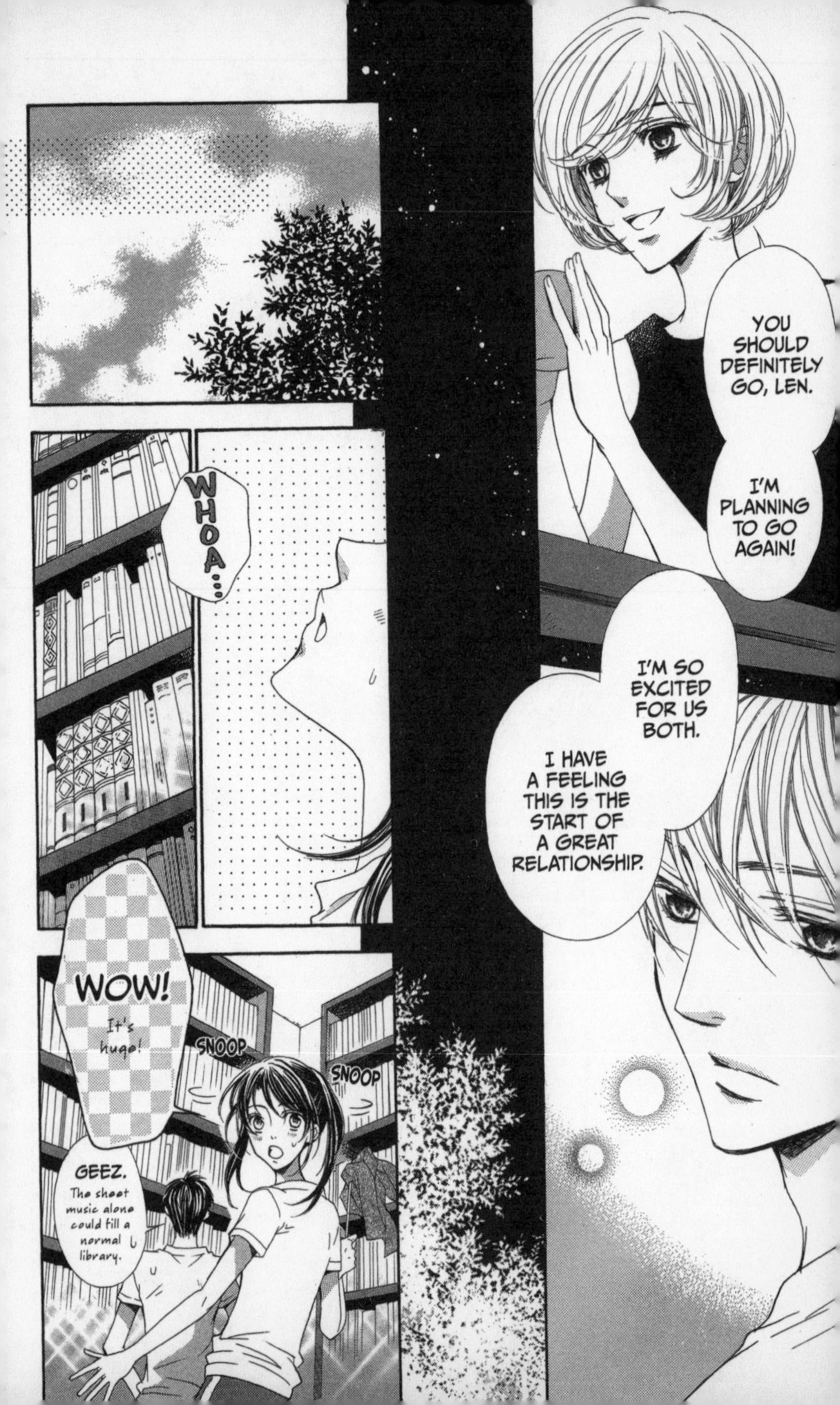
YOU SHOULD DEFINITELY GO, LEN.
I'M PLANNING TO GO AGAIN!
I'M SO EXCITED FOR US BOTH.
I HAVE A FEELING THIS IS THE START OF A GREAT RELATIONSHIP.
WHOA...
WOW! It's huge!
SNOOP
SNOOP
GEEZ. The sheet music alone could fill a normal library.

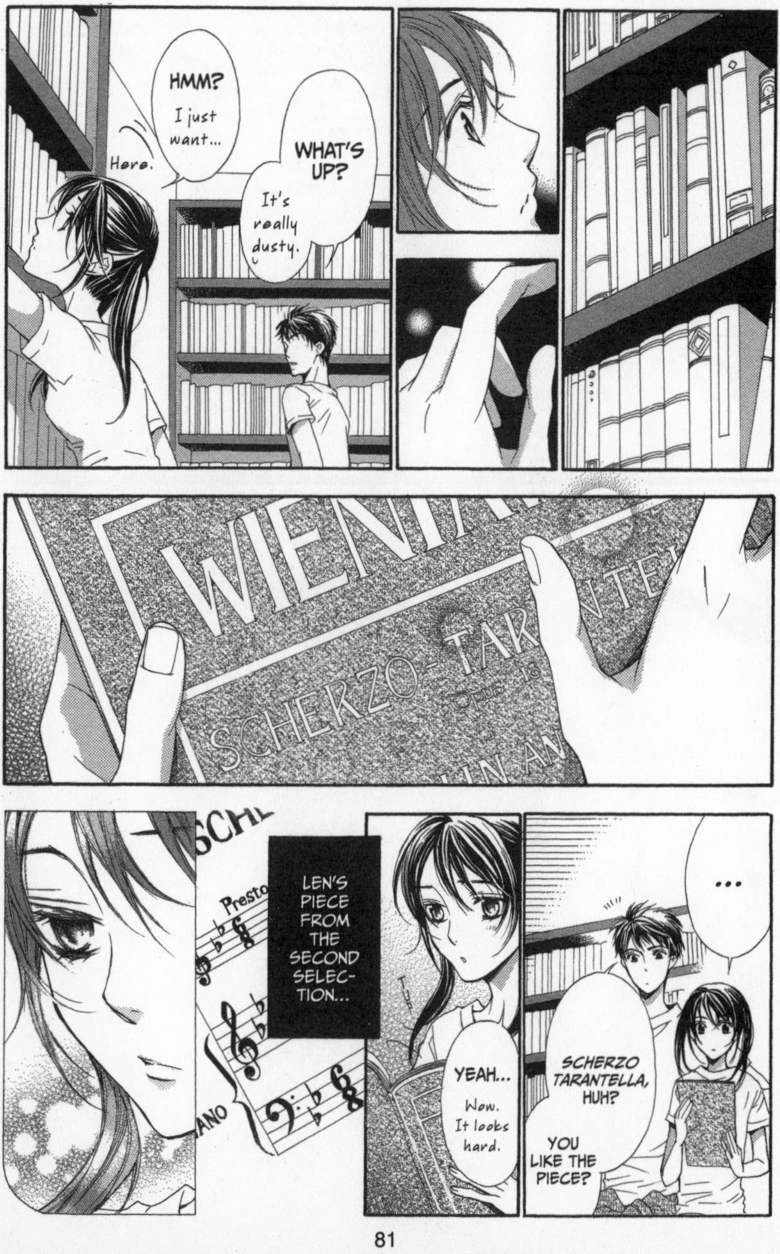
WHAT'S UP?
It's really dusty.
HMM?
I just want...
Here.
WIENIA
SCHERZO-TARANTEL
OPUS 16
...
SCHERZO TARANTELLA, HUH?
YOU LIKE THE PIECE?
YEAH...
Wow. It looks hard.
LEN'S PIECE FROM THE SECOND SELECTION...
Presto

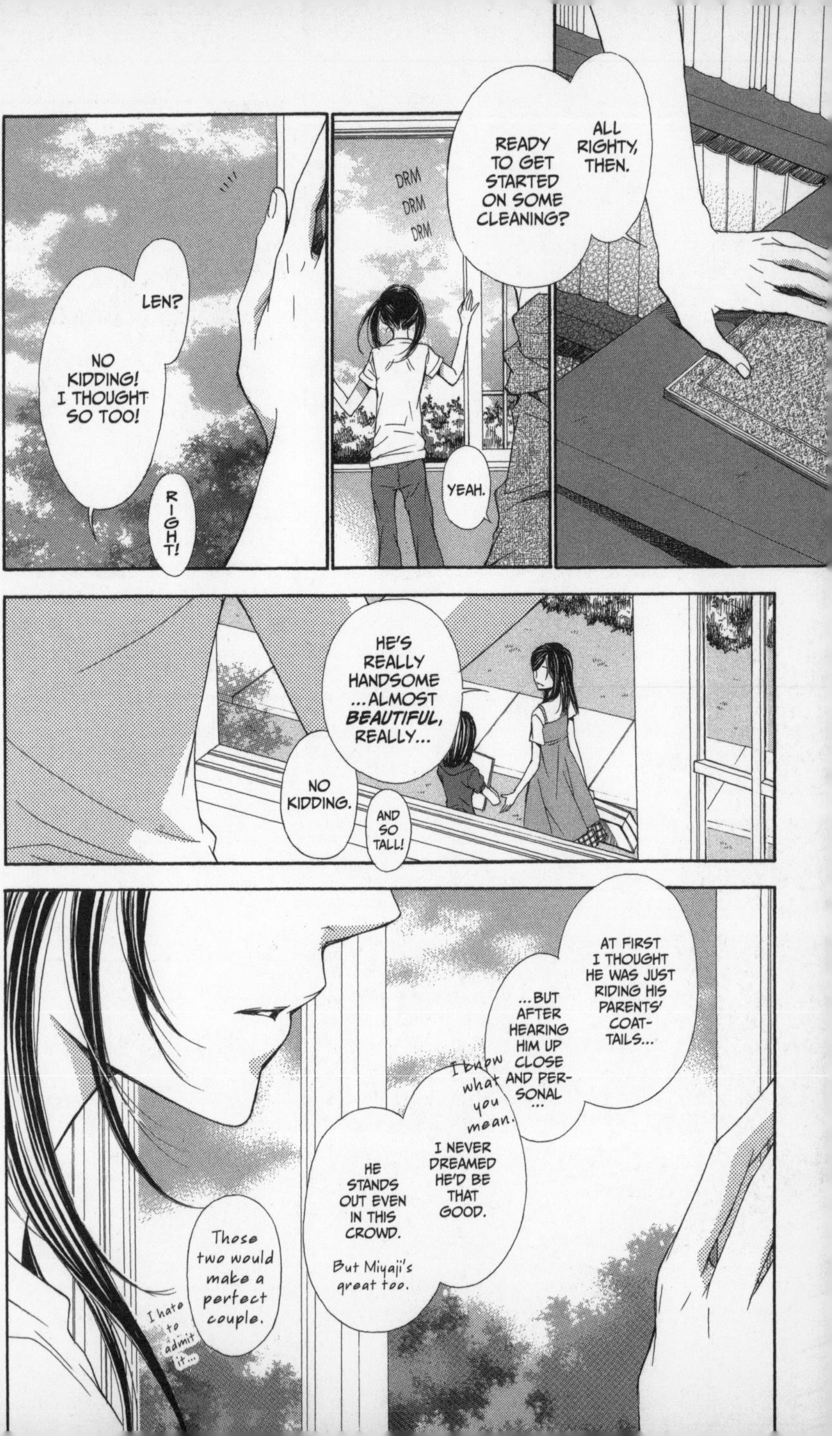
ALL RIGHTY, THEN.
READY TO GET STARTED ON SOME CLEANING?
DRM DRM DRM
YEAH.
LEN?
NO KIDDING! I THOUGHT SO TOO!
RIGHT!
HE'S REALLY HANDSOME ...ALMOST *BEAUTIFUL*, REALLY...
AND SO TALL!
NO KIDDING.
AT FIRST I THOUGHT HE WAS JUST RIDING HIS PARENTS' COAT-TAILS...
...BUT AFTER HEARING HIM UP CLOSE AND PER-SONAL...
I know what you mean.
I NEVER DREAMED HE'D BE THAT GOOD.
HE STANDS OUT EVEN IN THIS CROWD.
But Miyaji's great too.
Those two would make a perfect couple.
I hate to admit it...

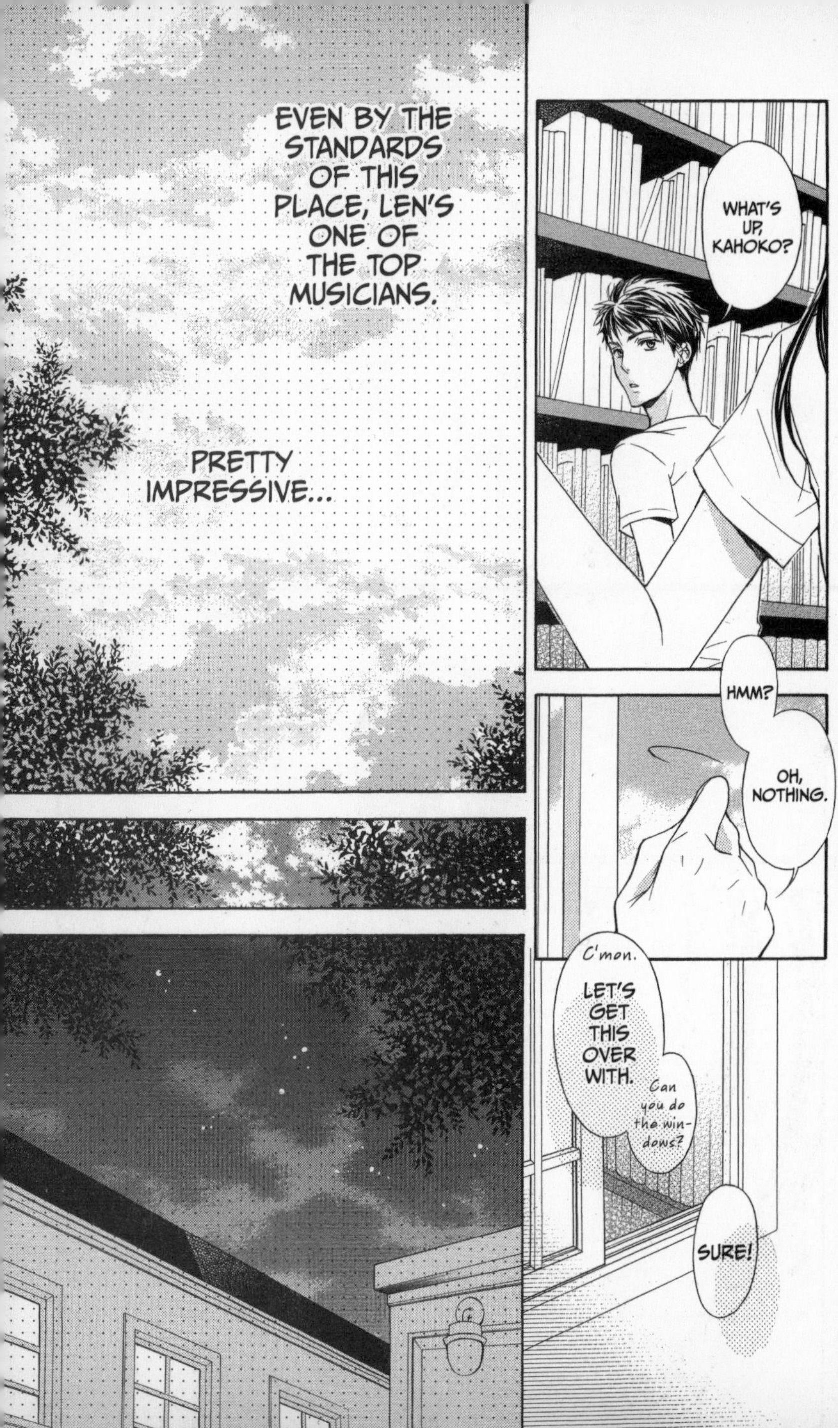
WHAT'S UP, KAHOKO?
HMM?
OH, NOTHING.
C'mon.
LET'S GET THIS OVER WITH.
Can you do the win-dows?
SURE!
EVEN BY THE STANDARDS OF THIS PLACE, LEN'S ONE OF THE TOP MUSICIANS.
PRETTY IMPRESSIVE...

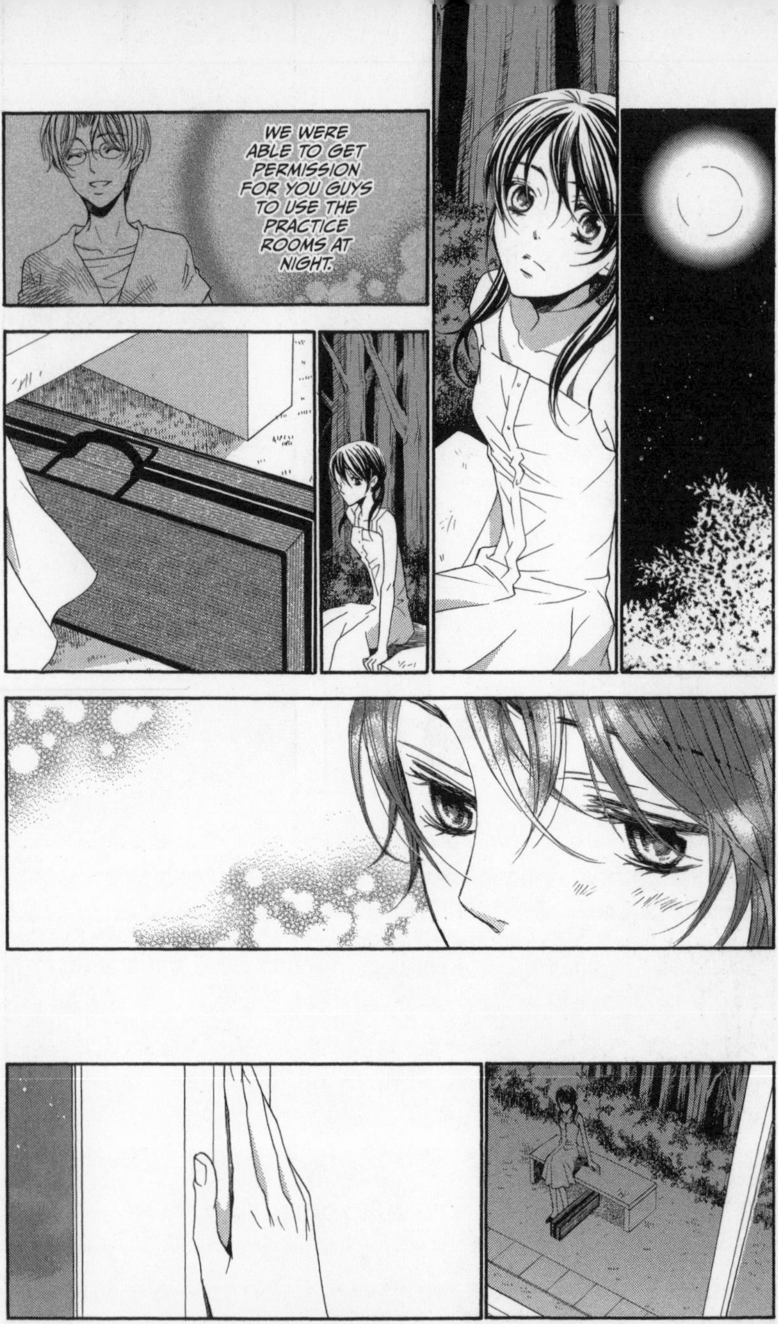
WE WERE ABLE TO GET PERMISSION FOR YOU GUYS TO USE THE PRACTICE ROOMS AT NIGHT.

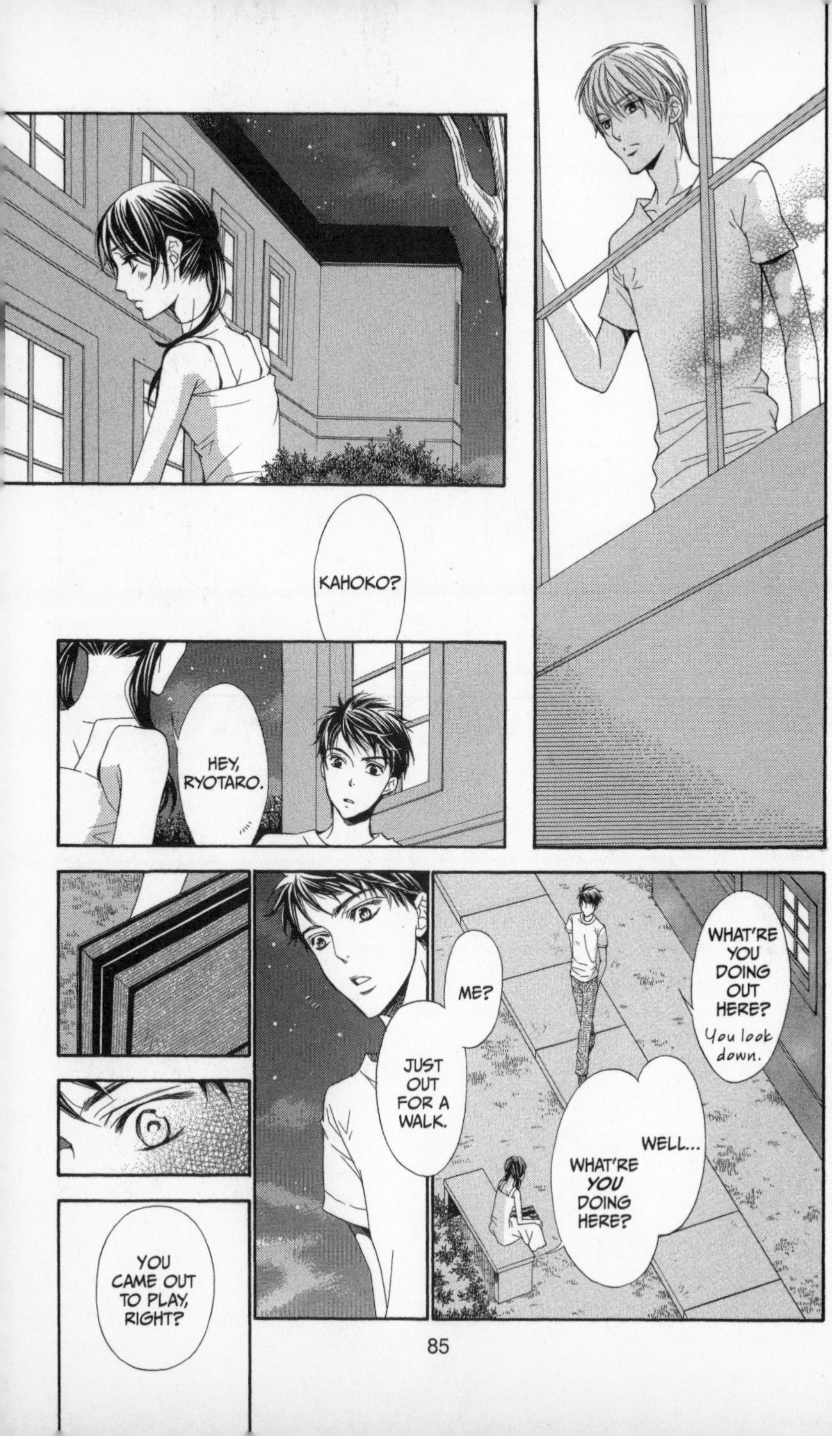
KAHOKO?
HEY, RYOTARO.
WHAT'RE YOU DOING OUT HERE? You look down.
WELL... WHAT'RE *YOU* DOING HERE?
ME?
JUST OUT FOR A WALK.
YOU CAME OUT TO PLAY, RIGHT?

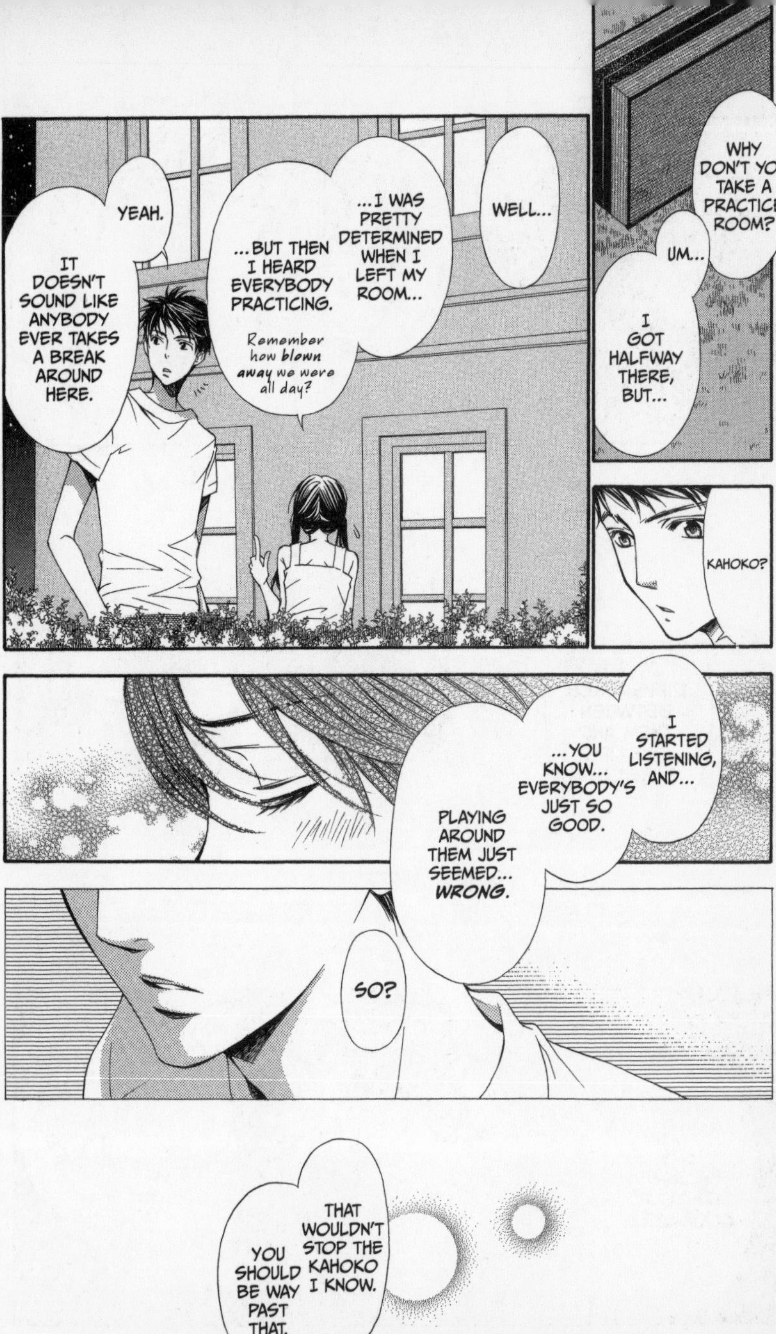
WHY DON'T YOU TAKE A PRACTICE ROOM?
UM...
I GOT HALFWAY THERE, BUT...
WELL...
...I WAS PRETTY DETERMINED WHEN I LEFT MY ROOM...
...BUT THEN I HEARD EVERYBODY PRACTICING.
Remember how *blown away* we were all day?
YEAH.
IT DOESN'T SOUND LIKE ANYBODY EVER TAKES A BREAK AROUND HERE.
KAHOKO?
I STARTED LISTENING, AND...
...YOU KNOW... EVERYBODY'S JUST SO GOOD.
PLAYING AROUND THEM JUST SEEMED... *WRONG*.
SO?
THAT WOULDN'T STOP THE KAHOKO I KNOW.
YOU SHOULD BE WAY PAST THAT.

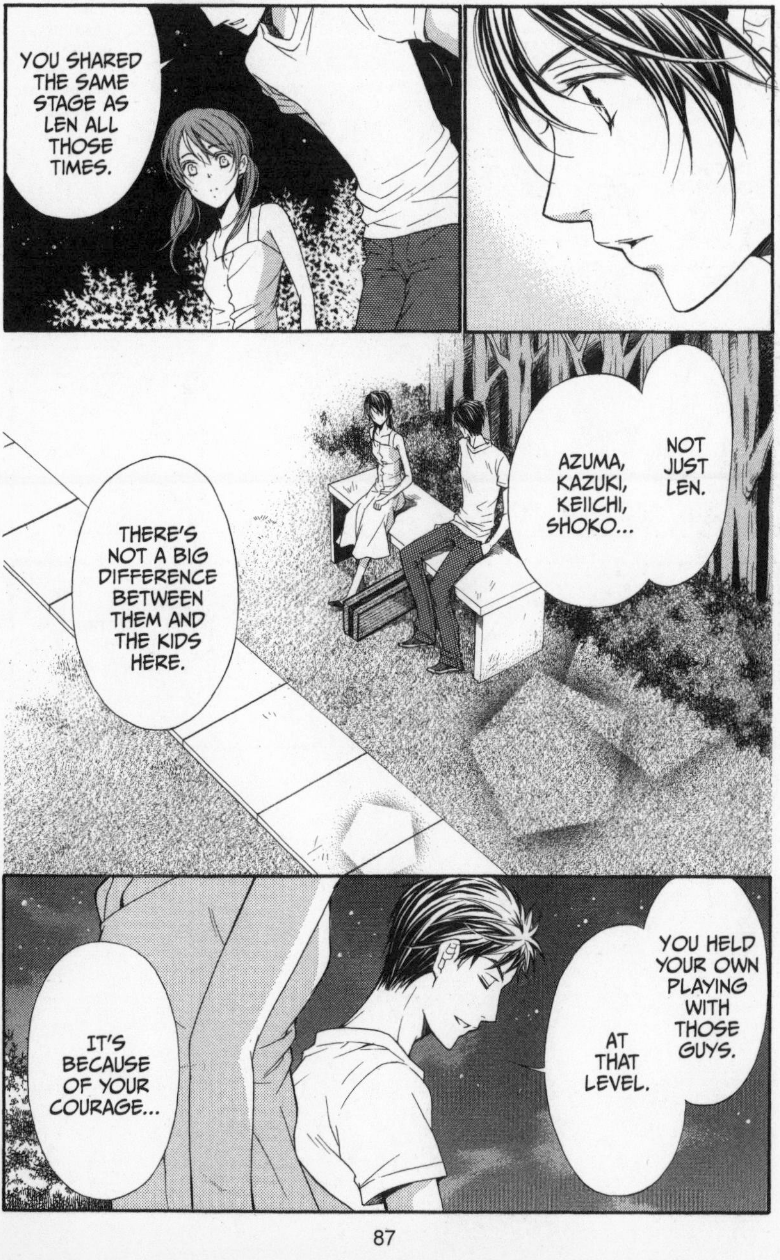
YOU SHARED THE SAME STAGE AS LEN ALL THOSE TIMES.
NOT JUST LEN.
AZUMA, KAZUKI, KEIICHI, SHOKO...
THERE'S NOT A BIG DIFFERENCE BETWEEN THEM AND THE KIDS HERE.
YOU HELD YOUR OWN PLAYING WITH THOSE GUYS.
AT THAT LEVEL.
IT'S BECAUSE OF YOUR COURAGE...

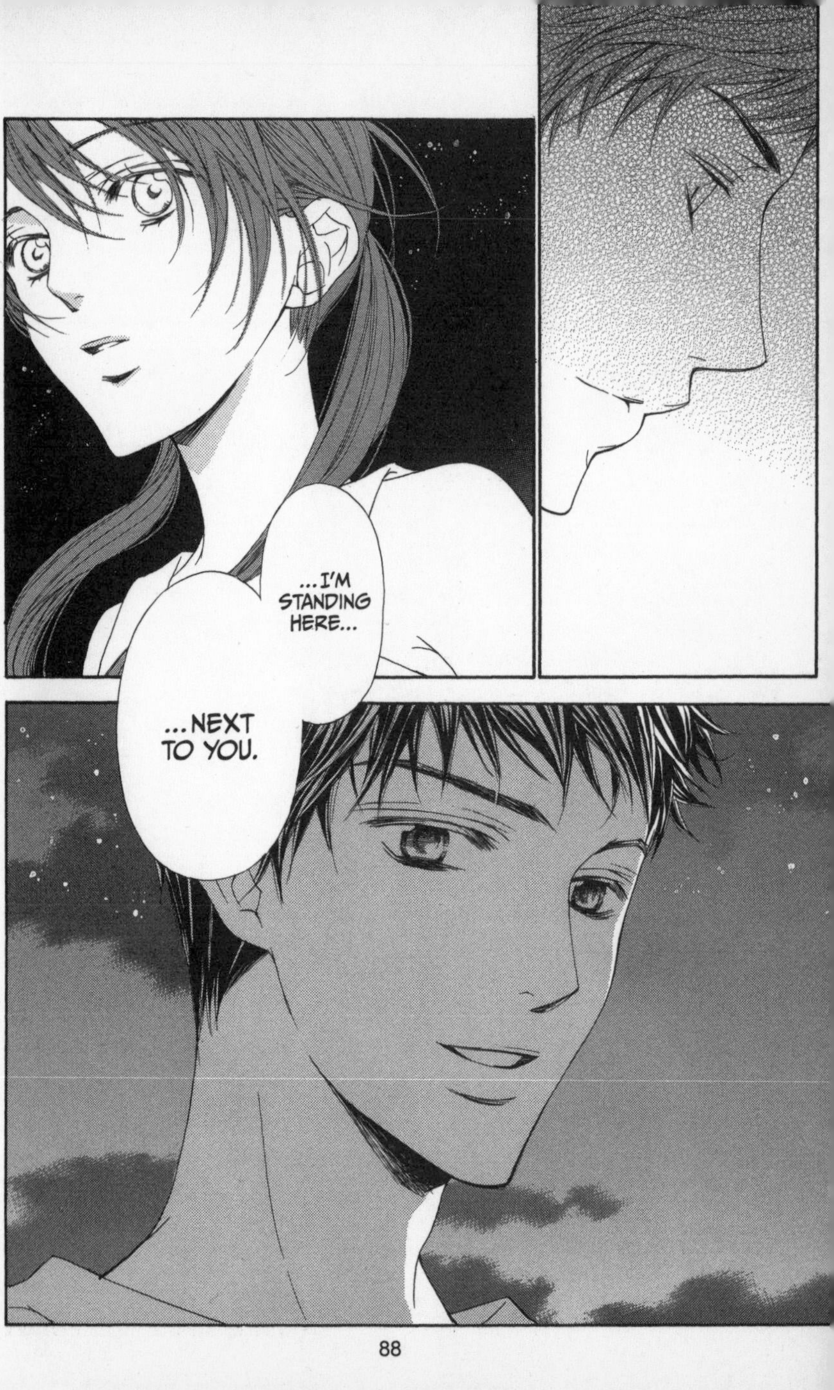
...I'M STANDING HERE...
...NEXT TO YOU.

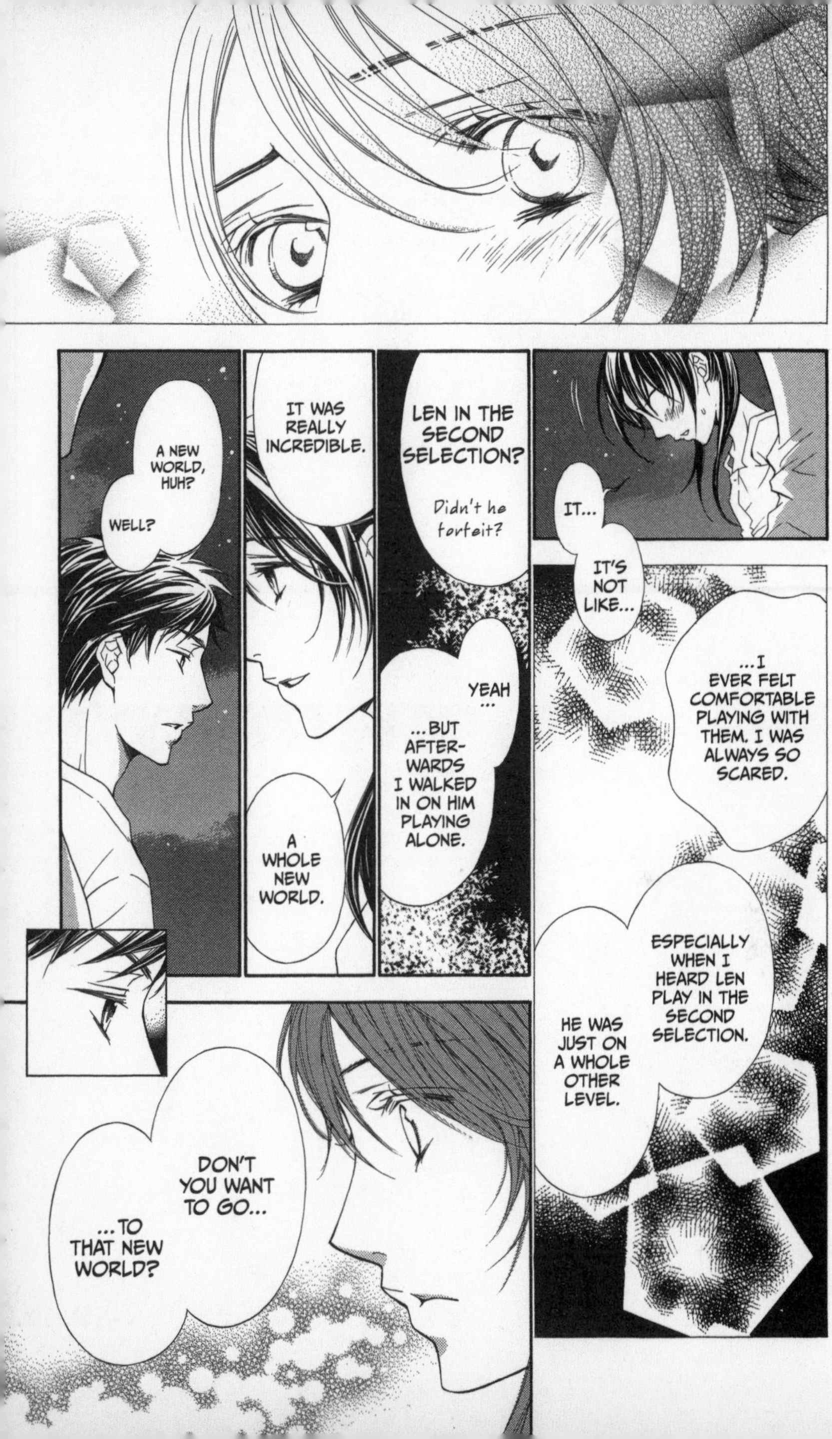
IT...
IT'S NOT LIKE...
...I EVER FELT COMFORTABLE PLAYING WITH THEM. I WAS ALWAYS SO SCARED.
ESPECIALLY WHEN I HEARD LEN PLAY IN THE SECOND SELECTION.
HE WAS JUST ON A WHOLE OTHER LEVEL.
LEN IN THE SECOND SELECTION?
Didn't he forfeit?
YEAH...
...BUT AFTERWARDS I WALKED IN ON HIM PLAYING ALONE.
IT WAS REALLY INCREDIBLE.
A WHOLE NEW WORLD.
A NEW WORLD, HUH?
WELL?
DON'T YOU WANT TO GO...
...TO THAT NEW WORLD?

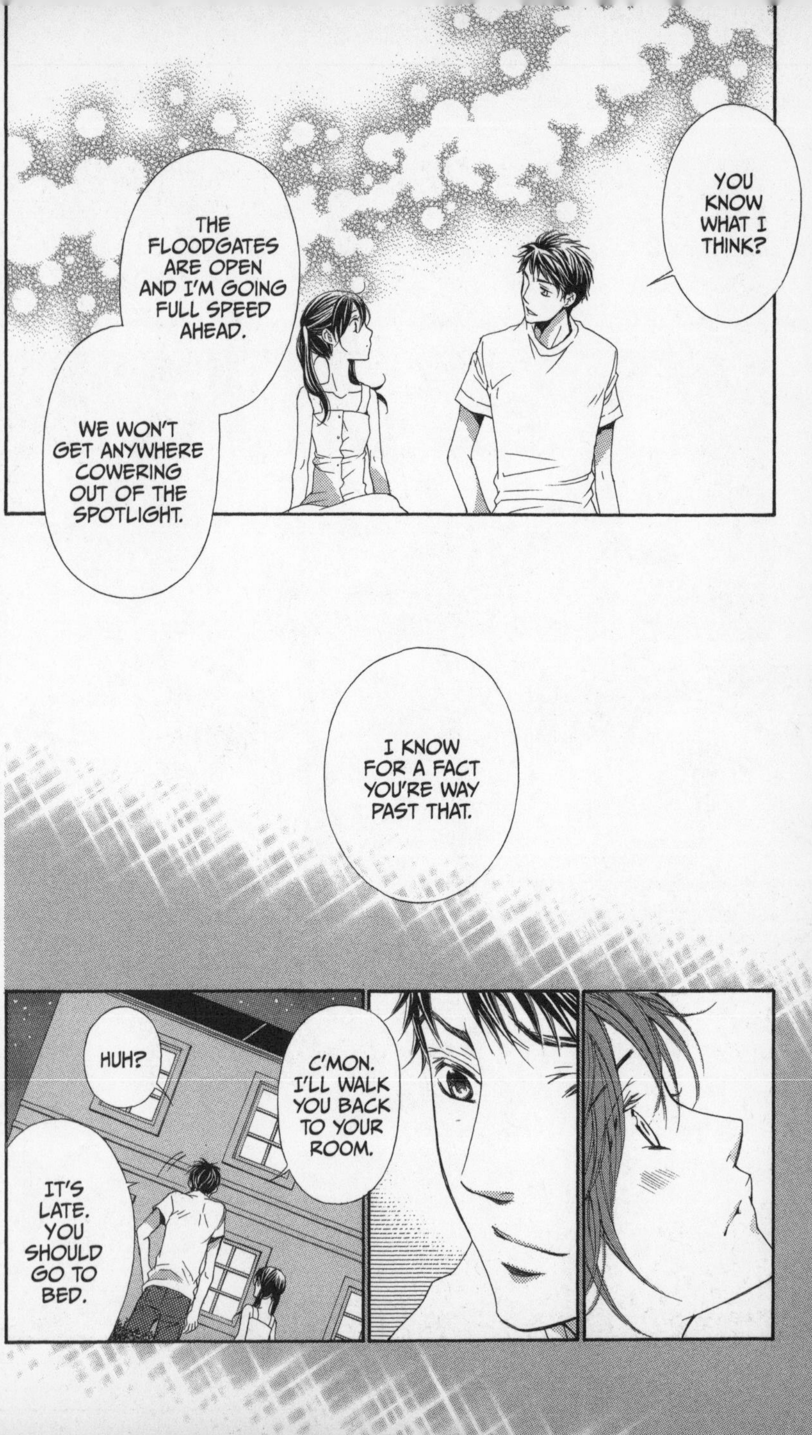
YOU KNOW WHAT I THINK?
THE FLOODGATES ARE OPEN AND I'M GOING FULL SPEED AHEAD.
WE WON'T GET ANYWHERE COWERING OUT OF THE SPOTLIGHT.
I KNOW FOR A FACT YOU'RE WAY PAST THAT.
C'MON. I'LL WALK YOU BACK TO YOUR ROOM.
HUH?
IT'S LATE. YOU SHOULD GO TO BED.

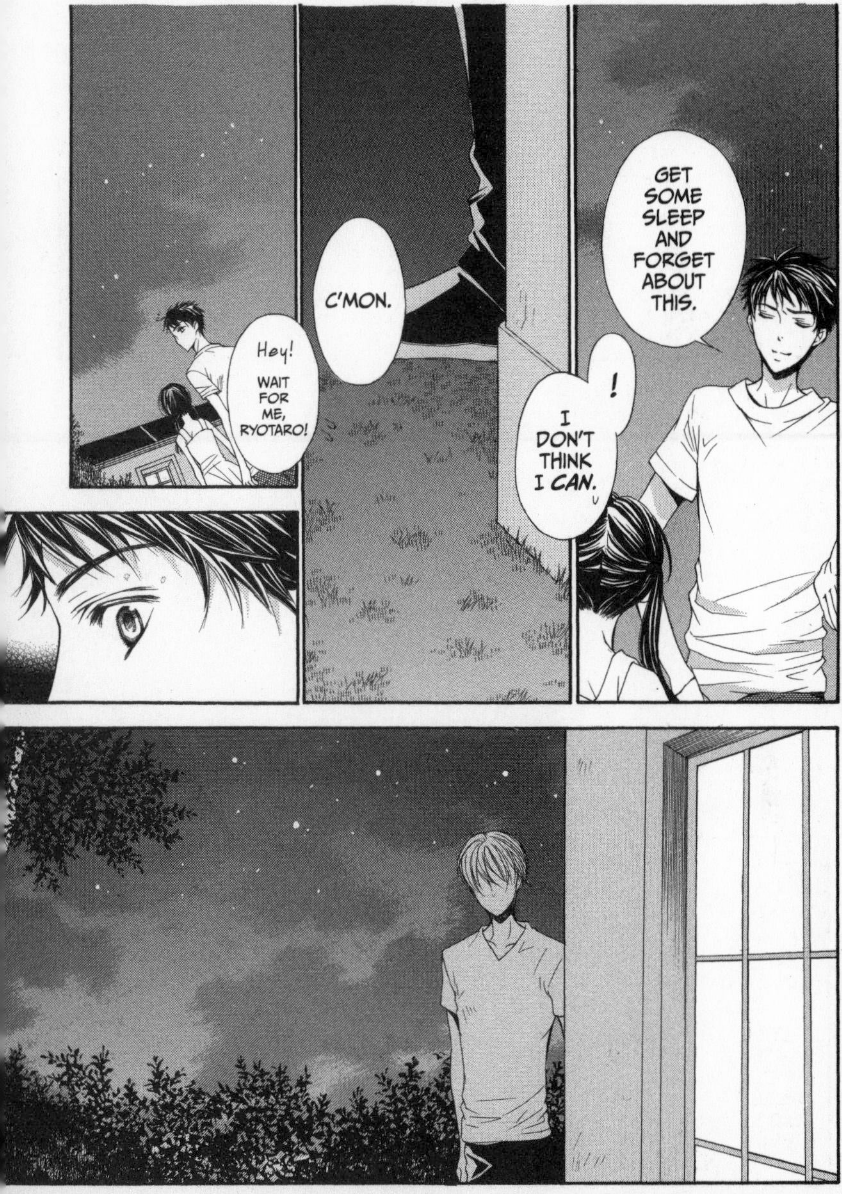
GET SOME SLEEP AND FORGET ABOUT THIS.
!
I DON'T THINK I CAN.
C'MON.
Hey!
WAIT FOR ME, RYOTARO!

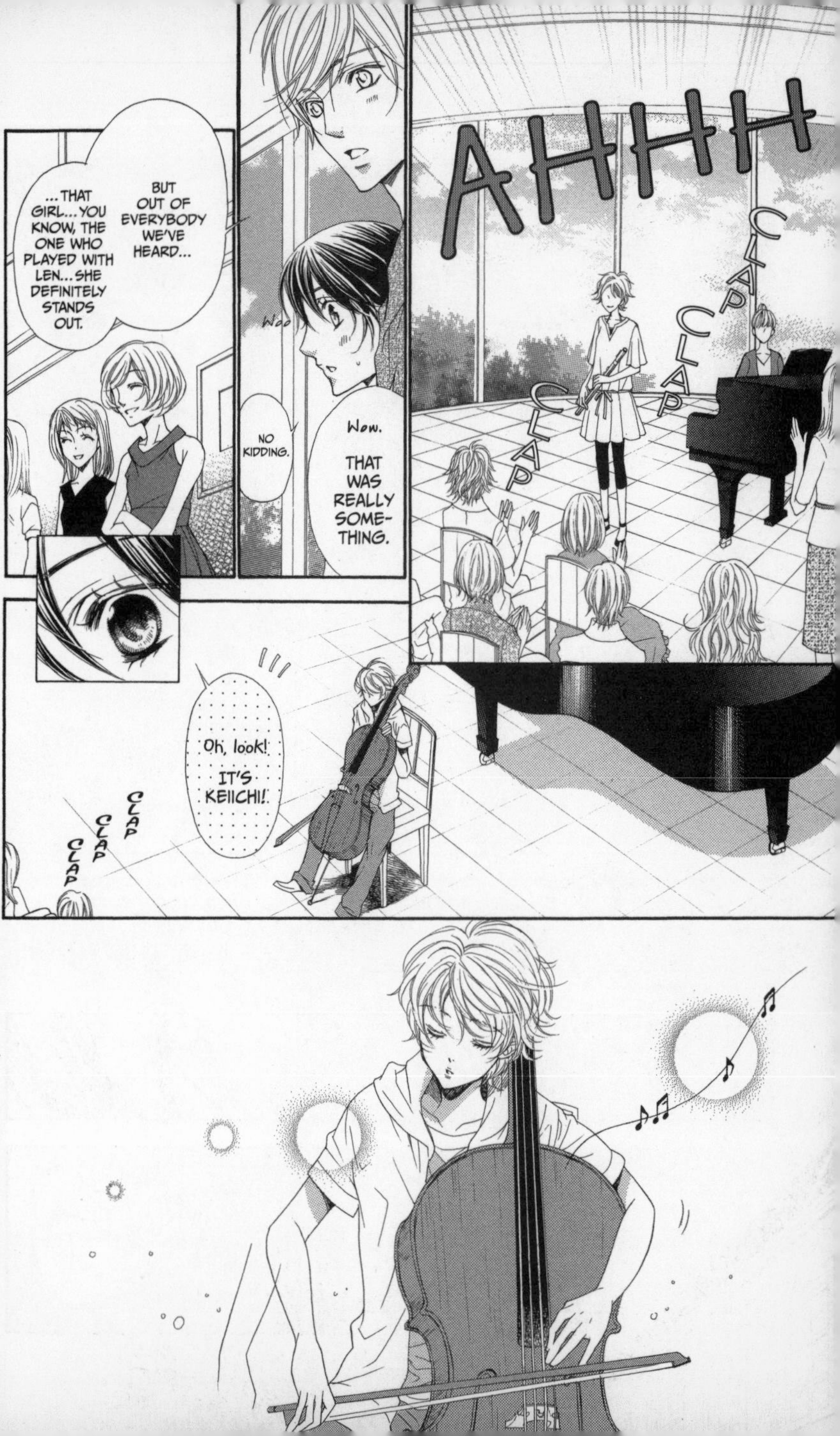
AHHHH
CLAP CLAP
CLAP
CLAP
Woo
Wow. THAT WAS REALLY SOME- THING.
NO KIDDING.
BUT OUT OF EVERYBODY WE'VE HEARD...
...THAT GIRL...YOU KNOW, THE ONE WHO PLAYED WITH LEN...SHE DEFINITELY STANDS OUT.
Oh, look! IT'S KEIICHI!
CLAP
CLAP
CLAP

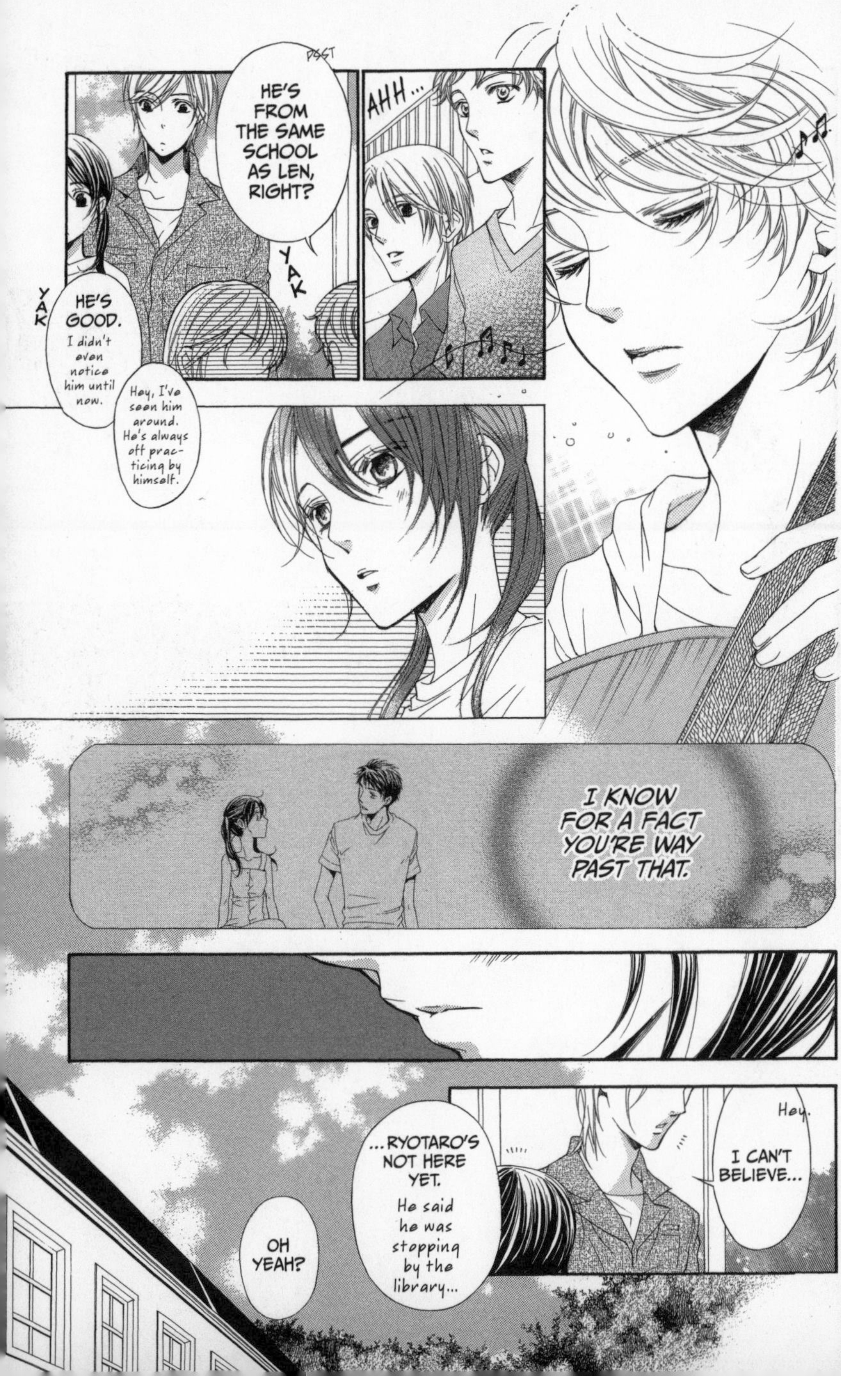
AHH...
PSST
HE'S FROM THE SAME SCHOOL AS LEN, RIGHT?
YAK
YAK
HE'S GOOD.
I didn't even notice him until now.
Hey, I've seen him around. He's always off prac-ticing by himself.
I KNOW FOR A FACT YOU'RE WAY PAST THAT.
Hey.
I CAN'T BELIEVE...
...RYOTARO'S NOT HERE YET.
He said he was stopping by the library...
OH YEAH?

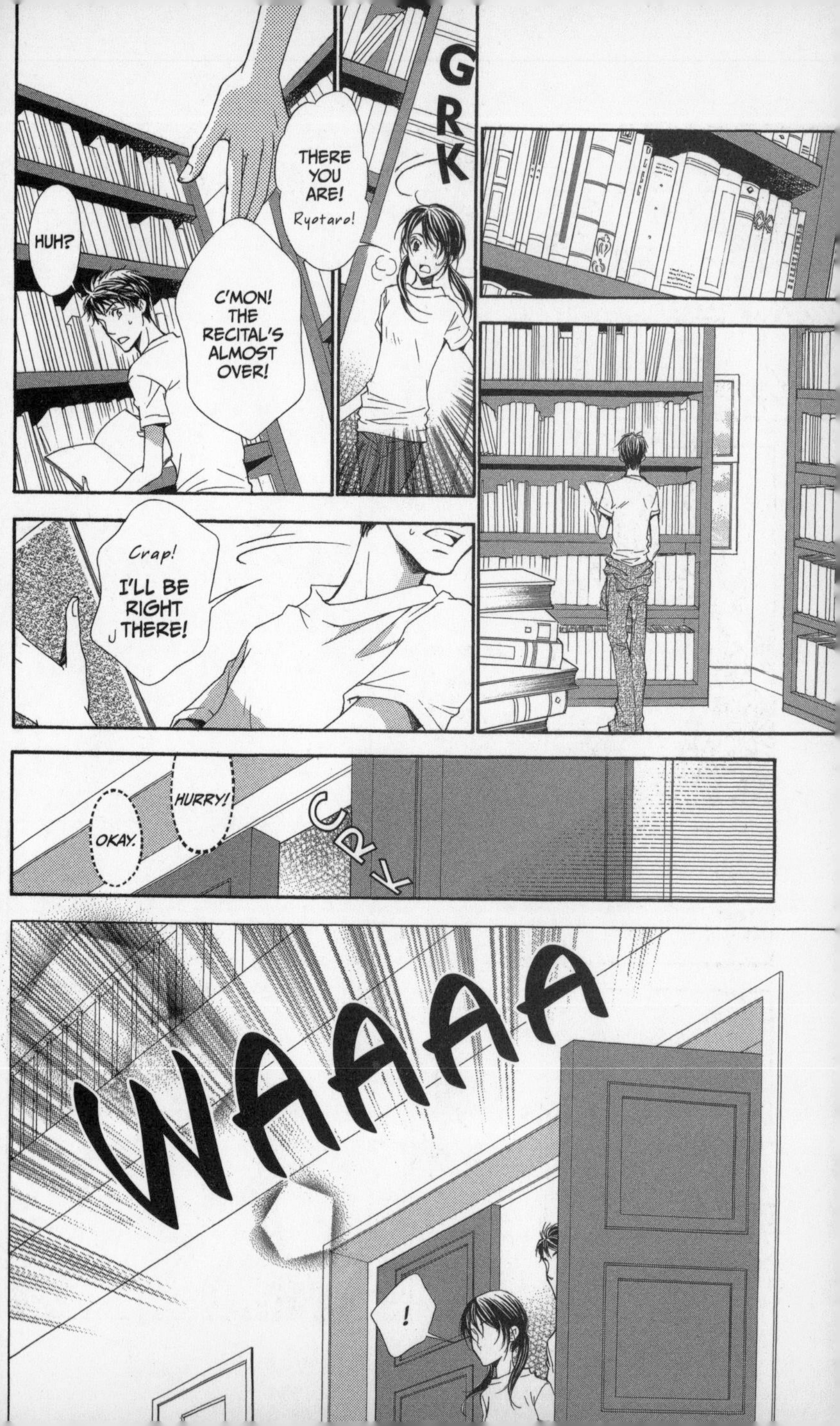
GRK
THERE YOU ARE! Ryotaro!
HUH?
C'MON! THE RECITAL'S ALMOST OVER!
Crap! I'LL BE RIGHT THERE!
HURRY!
OKAY.
CRK
WAAAA
!

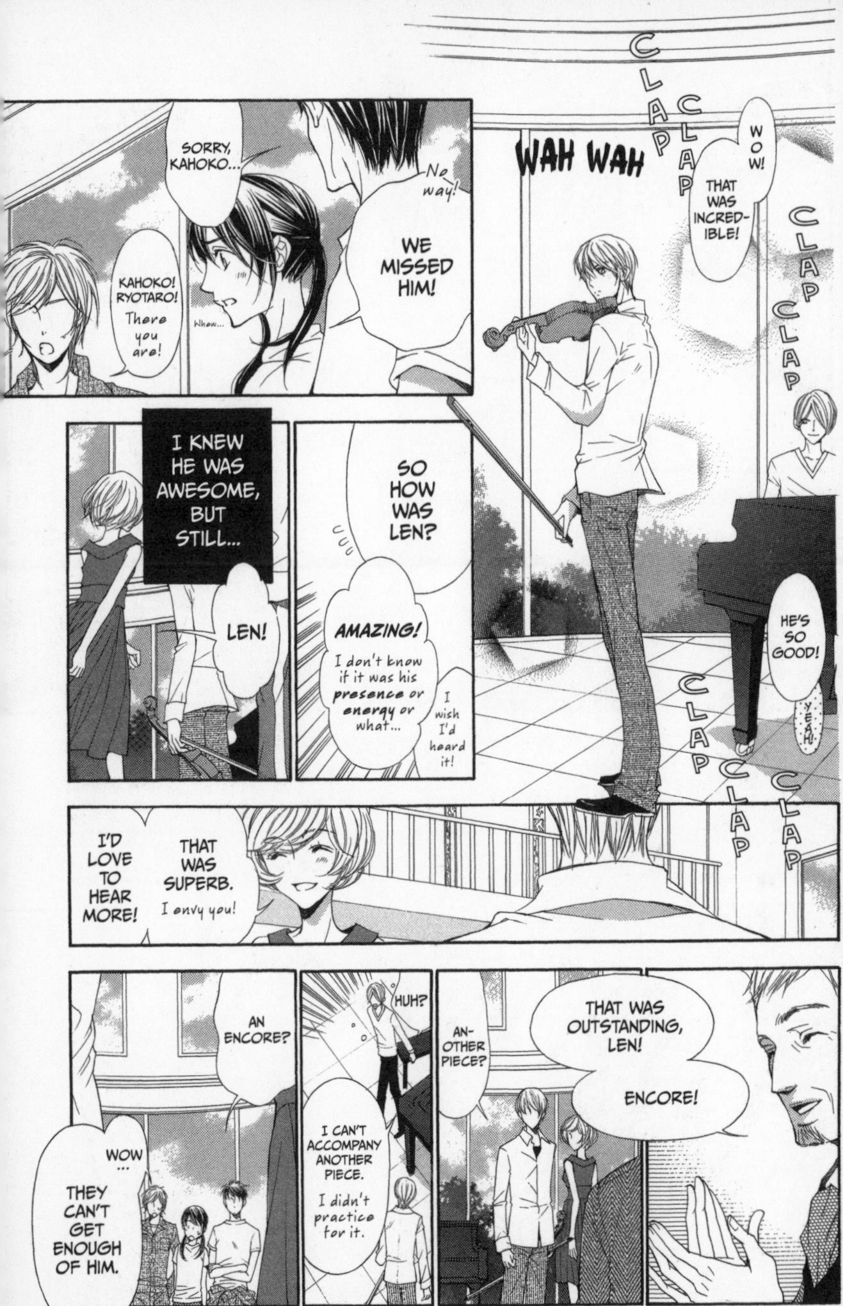
CLAP CLAP
WOW! THAT WAS INCREDIBLE!
WAH WAH
CLAP CLAP
HE'S SO GOOD!
YEAH!
CLAP CLAP CLAP
No way!
WE MISSED HIM!
SORRY, KAHOKO...
Whew...
KAHOKO! RYOTARO! There you are!
SO HOW WAS LEN?
AMAZING! I don't know if it was his presence or energy or what...
I wish I'd heard it!
I KNEW HE WAS AWESOME, BUT STILL...
LEN!
THAT WAS SUPERB. I envy you!
I'D LOVE TO HEAR MORE!
THAT WAS OUTSTANDING, LEN!
ENCORE!
AN-OTHER PIECE?
HUH?
I CAN'T ACCOMPANY ANOTHER PIECE. I didn't practice for it.
AN ENCORE?
WOW...
THEY CAN'T GET ENOUGH OF HIM.

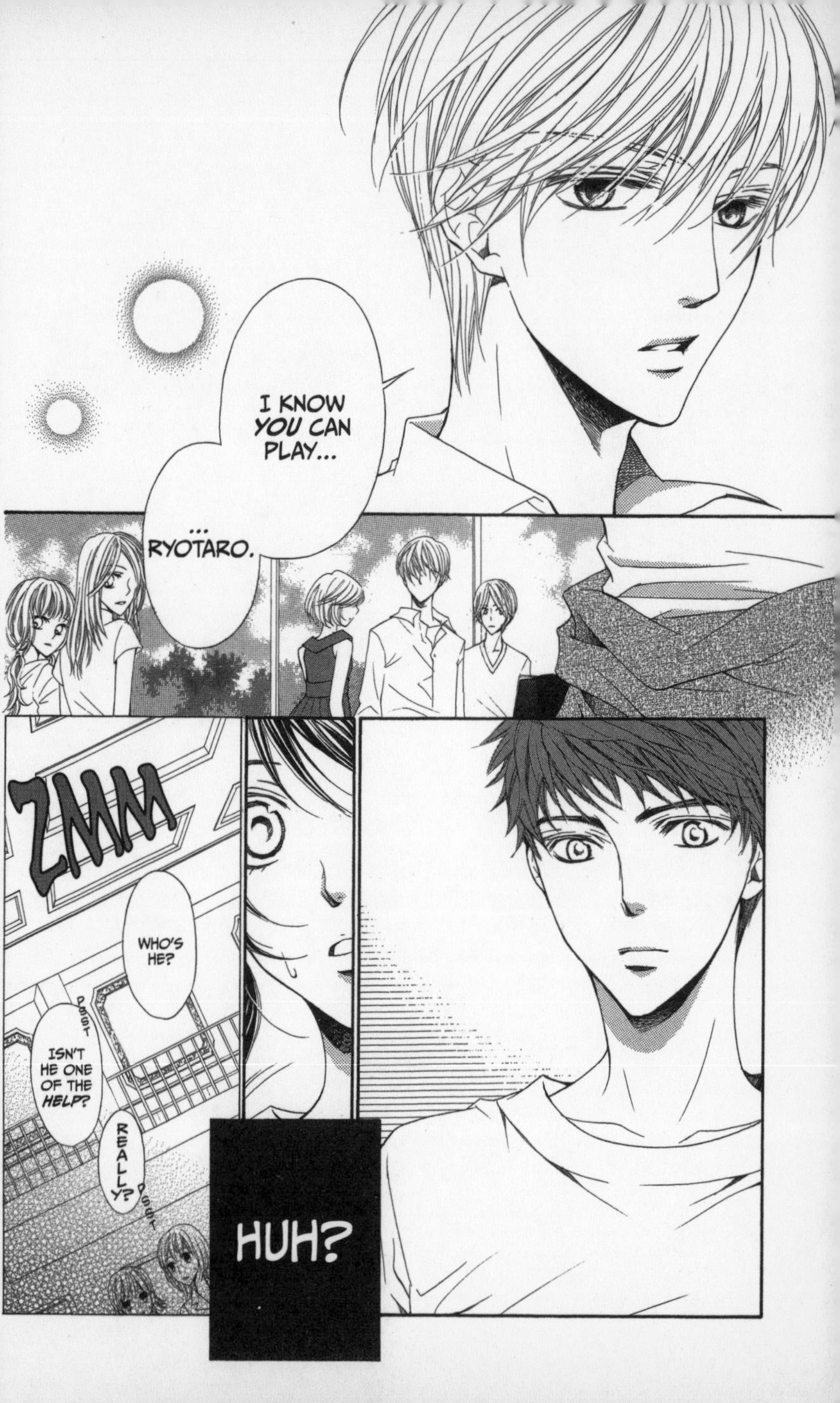
I KNOW YOU CAN PLAY...
... RYOTARO.
ZMM
HUH?
WHO'S HE?
PSST
ISN'T HE ONE OF THE HELP?
REALLY?
PSST

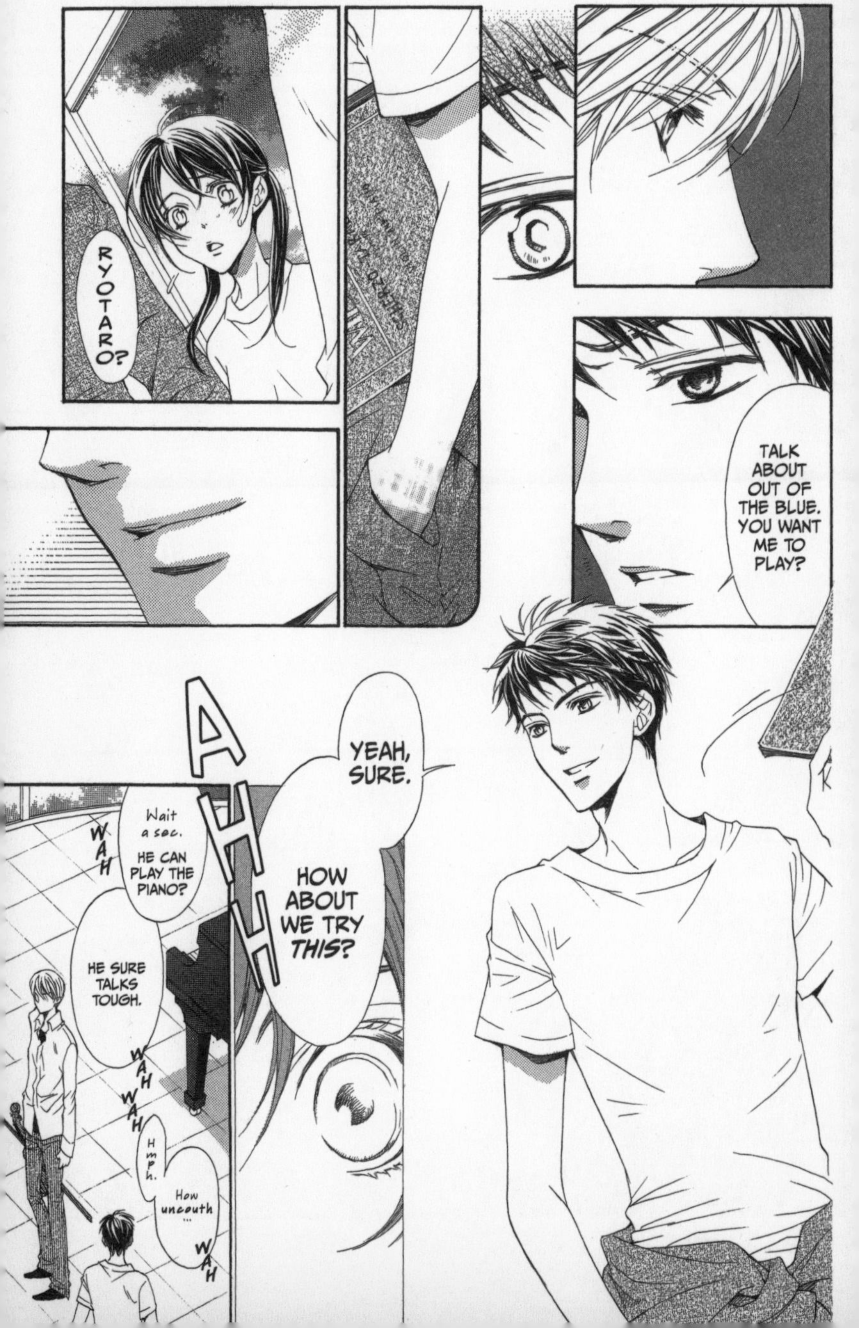

TALK ABOUT OUT OF THE BLUE. YOU WANT ME TO PLAY?
RYOTARO?
YEAH, SURE.
HOW ABOUT WE TRY THIS?
AHHH
Wait a sec.
HE CAN PLAY THE PIANO?
WAH
WAH
HE SURE TALKS TOUGH.
WAH
WAH
Hmph.
How uncouth...
WAH

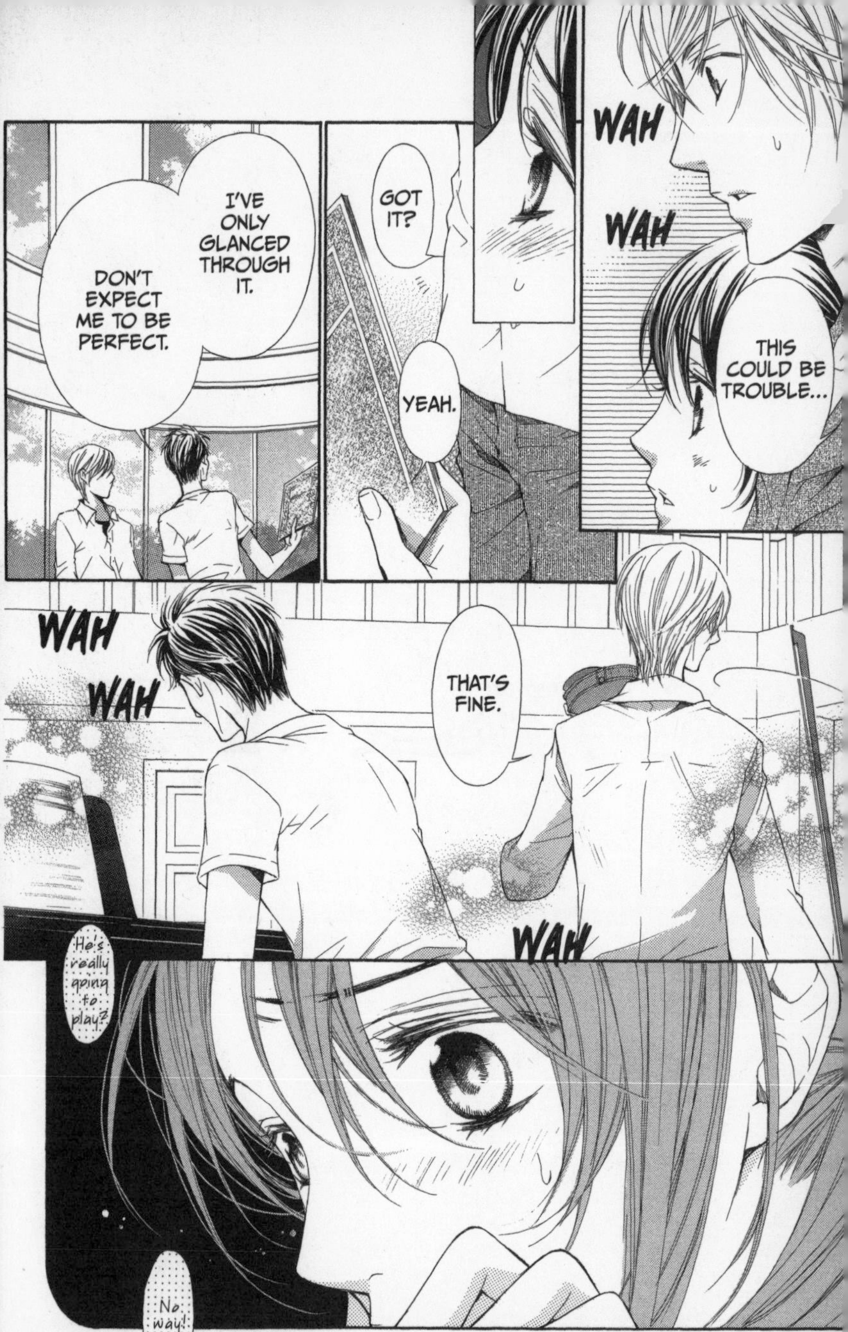
WAH
WAH
THIS COULD BE TROUBLE...
GOT IT?
YEAH.
I'VE ONLY GLANCED THROUGH IT.
DON'T EXPECT ME TO BE PERFECT.
THAT'S FINE.
WAH
WAH
WAH
He's really going to play?
No way!

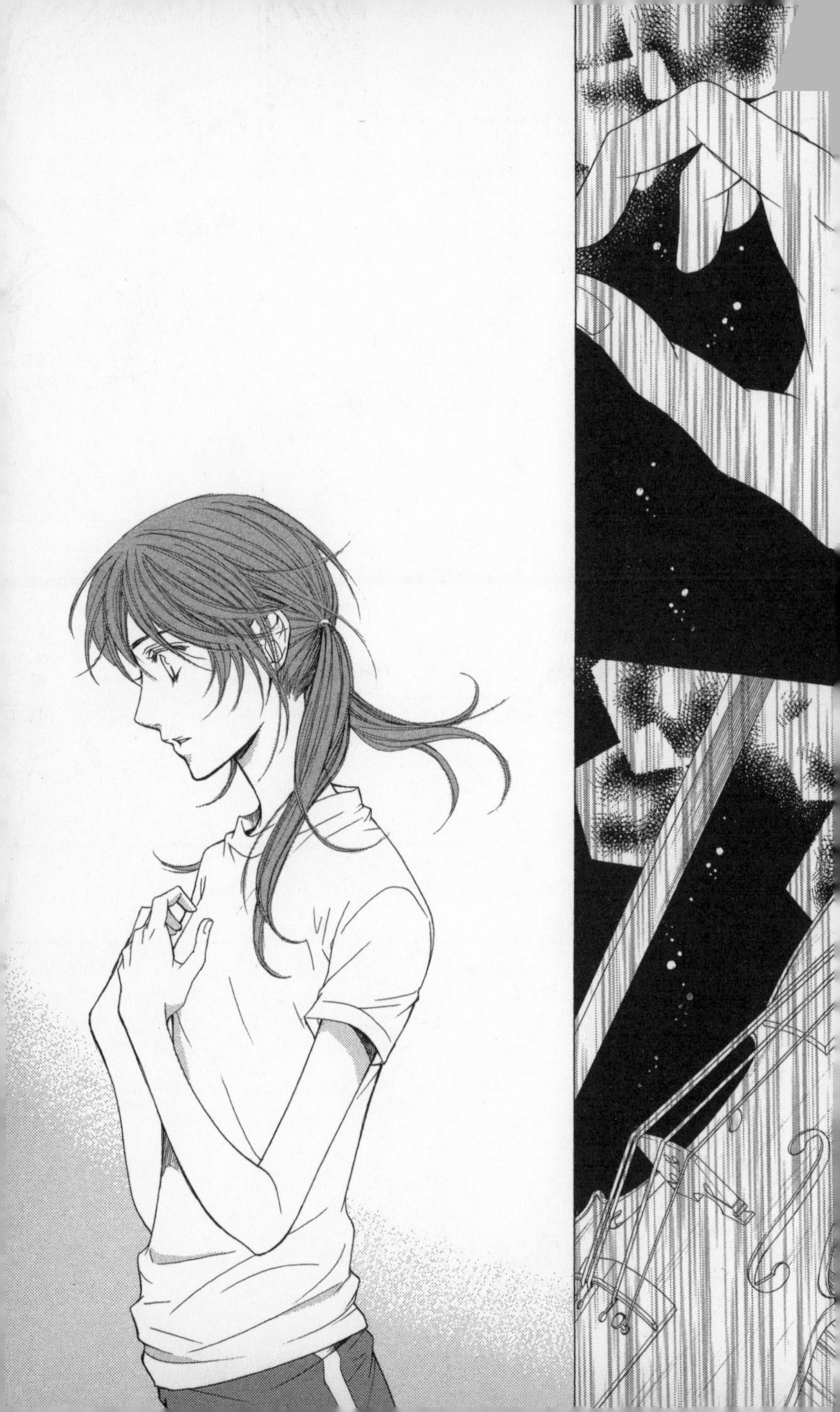

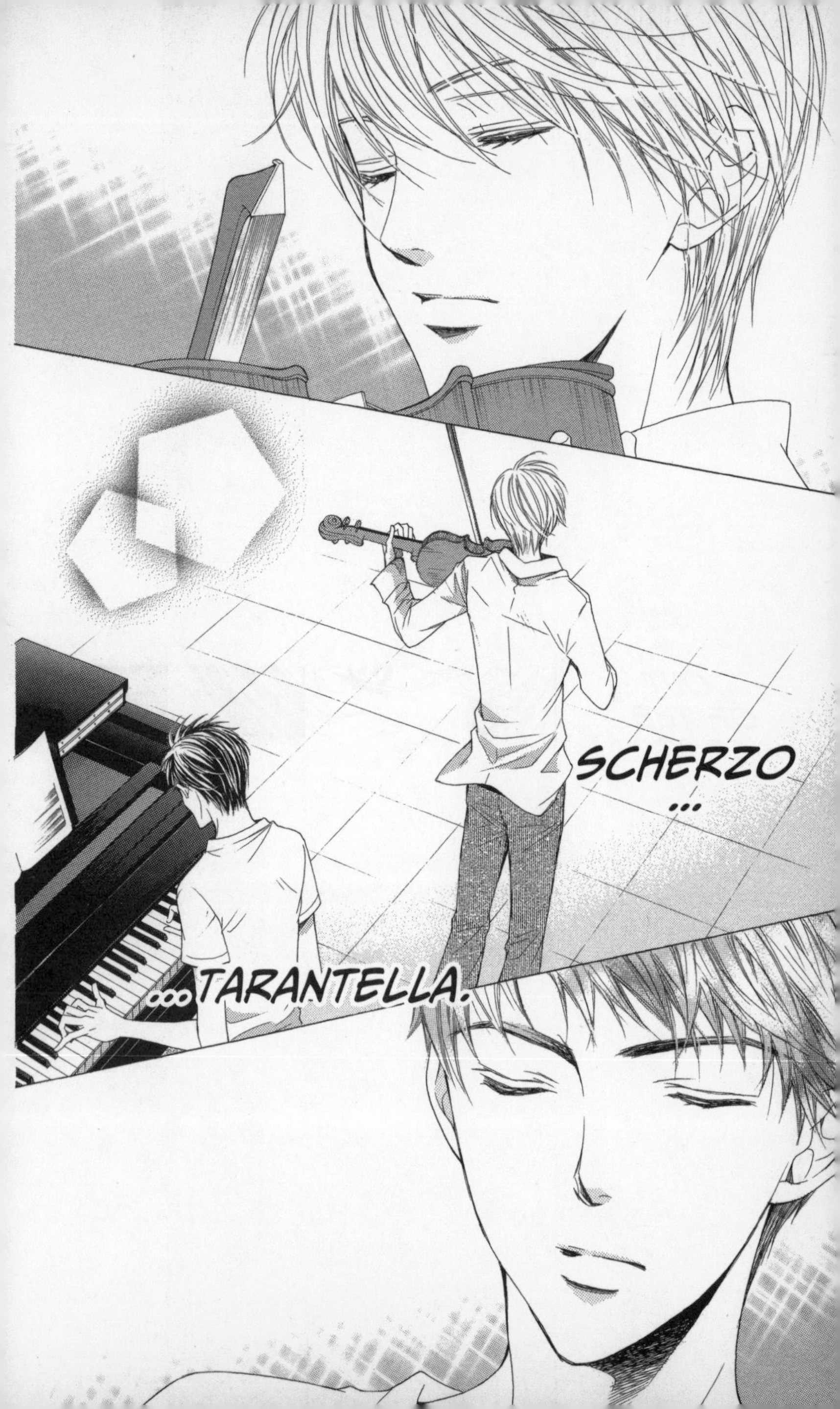
SCHERZO
...
...TARANTELLA.

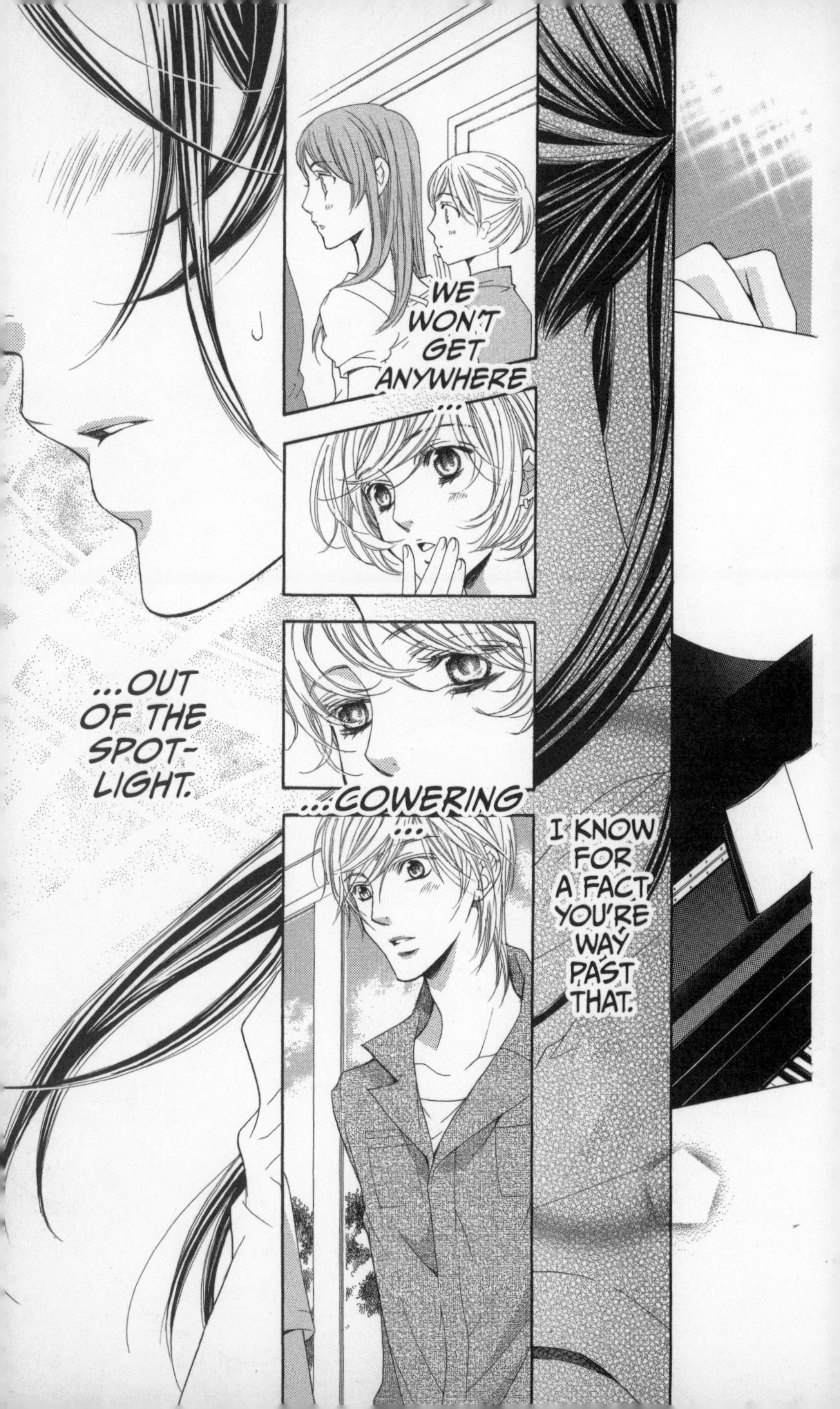
WE WON'T GET ANYWHERE...
...COWERING...
...OUT OF THE SPOT-LIGHT.
I KNOW FOR A FACT YOU'RE WAY PAST THAT.

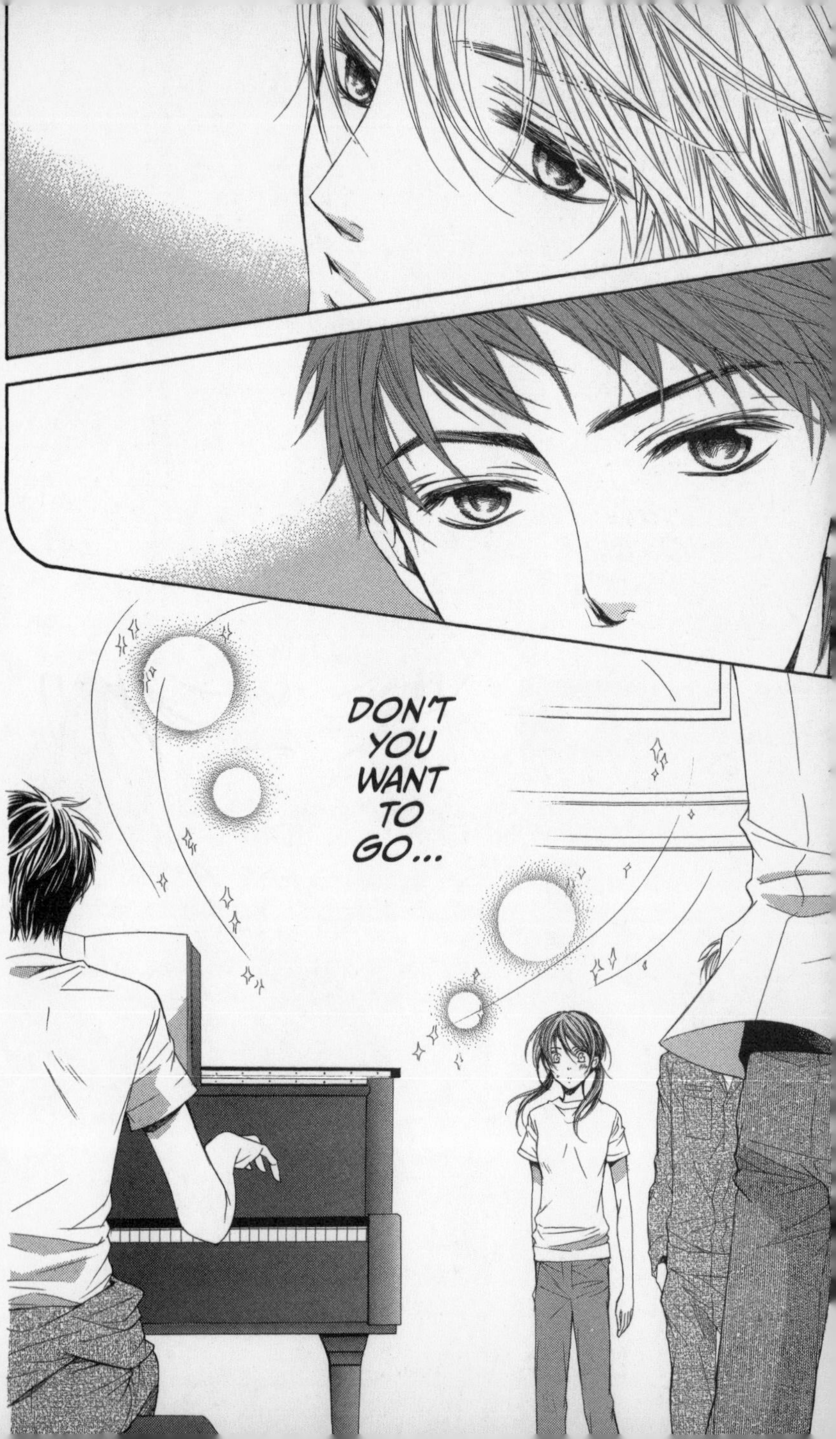
DON'T YOU WANT TO GO...

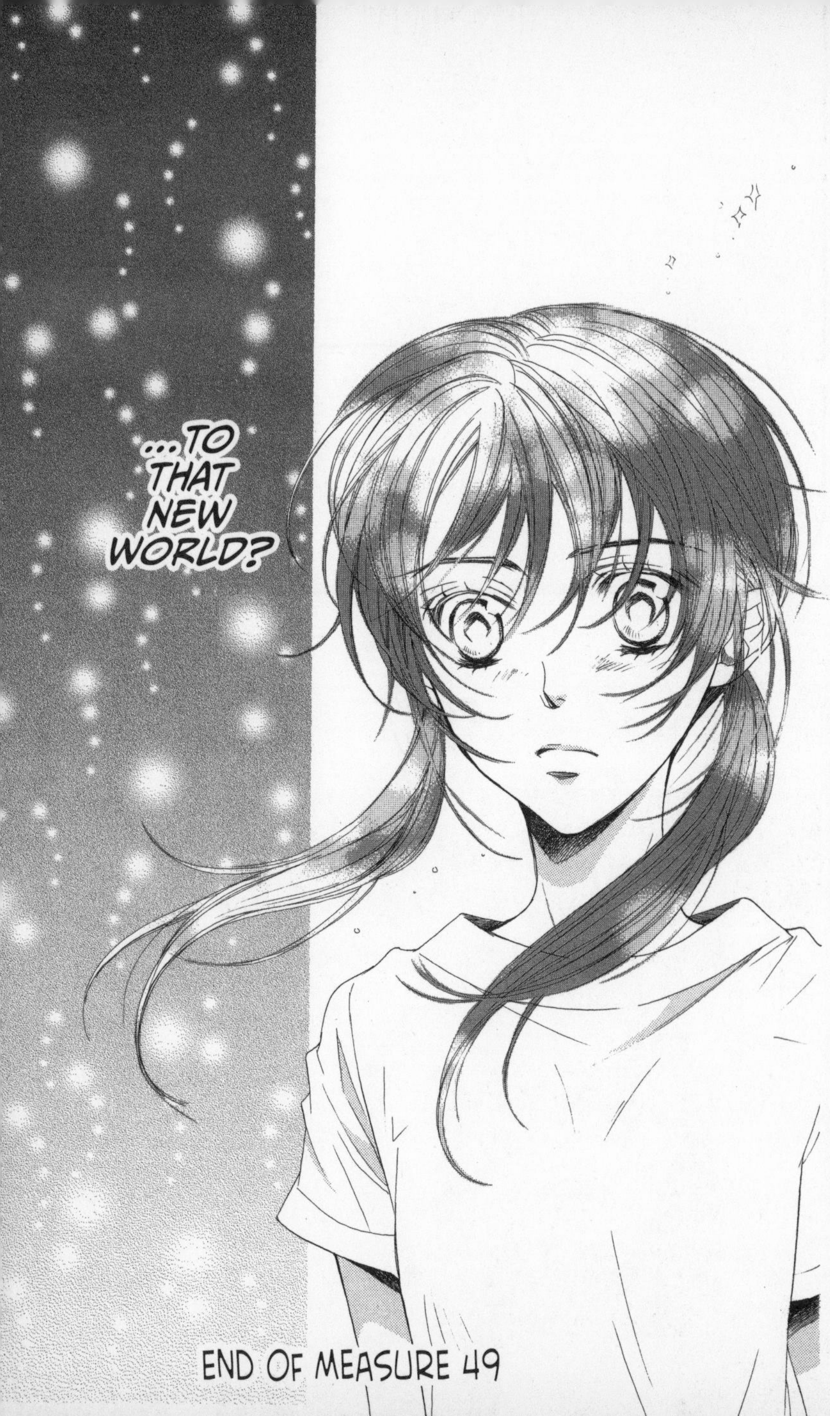
...TO THAT NEW WORLD?
END OF MEASURE 49

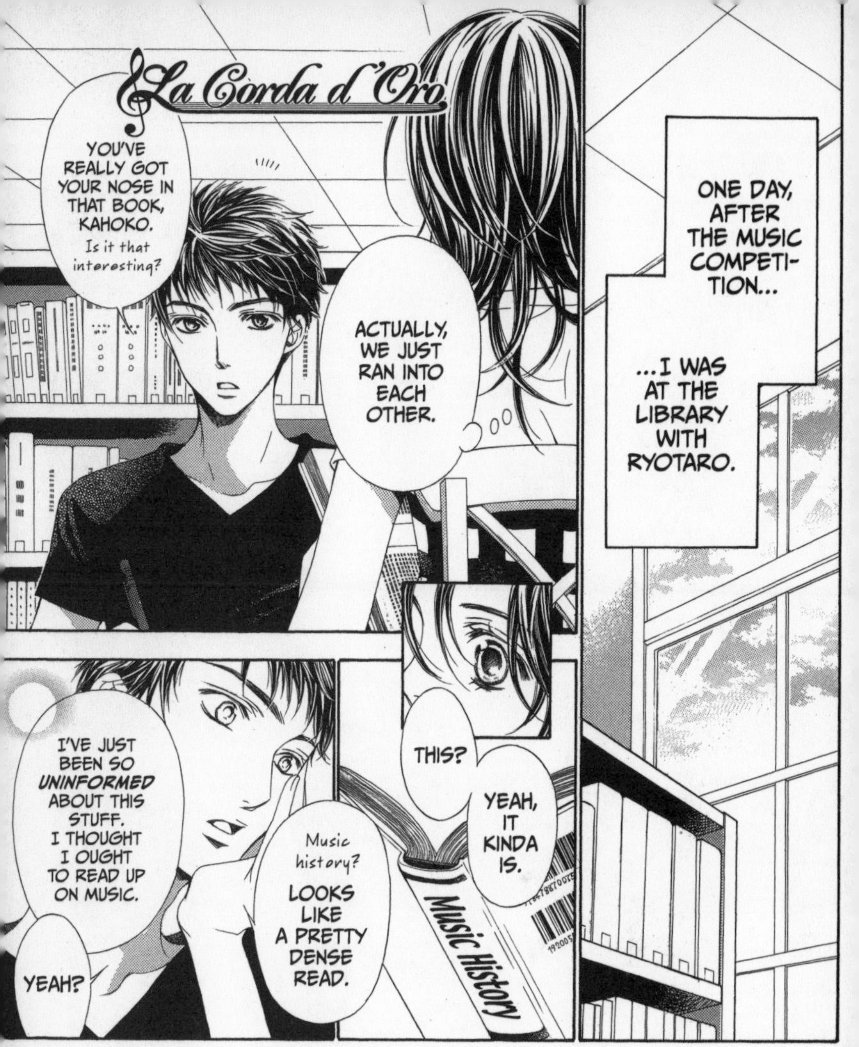
La Corda d'Oro
ONE DAY, AFTER THE MUSIC COMPETITION...
...I WAS AT THE LIBRARY WITH RYOTARO.
ACTUALLY, WE JUST RAN INTO EACH OTHER.
YOU'VE REALLY GOT YOUR NOSE IN THAT BOOK, KAHOKO. Is it that interesting?
THIS?
YEAH, IT KINDA IS.
Music history? LOOKS LIKE A PRETTY DENSE READ.
I'VE JUST BEEN SO *UNINFORMED* ABOUT THIS STUFF. I THOUGHT I OUGHT TO READ UP ON MUSIC.
YEAH?
Music History

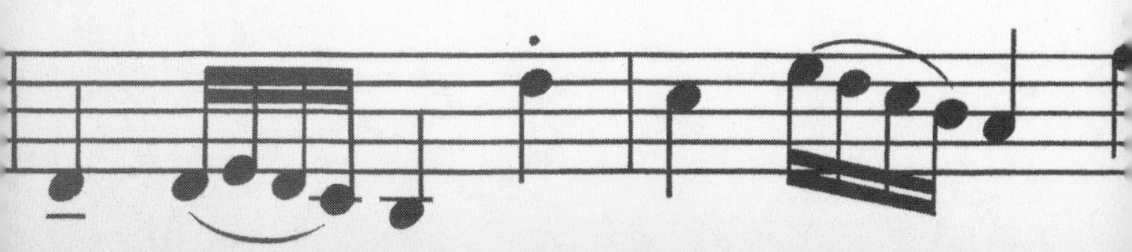

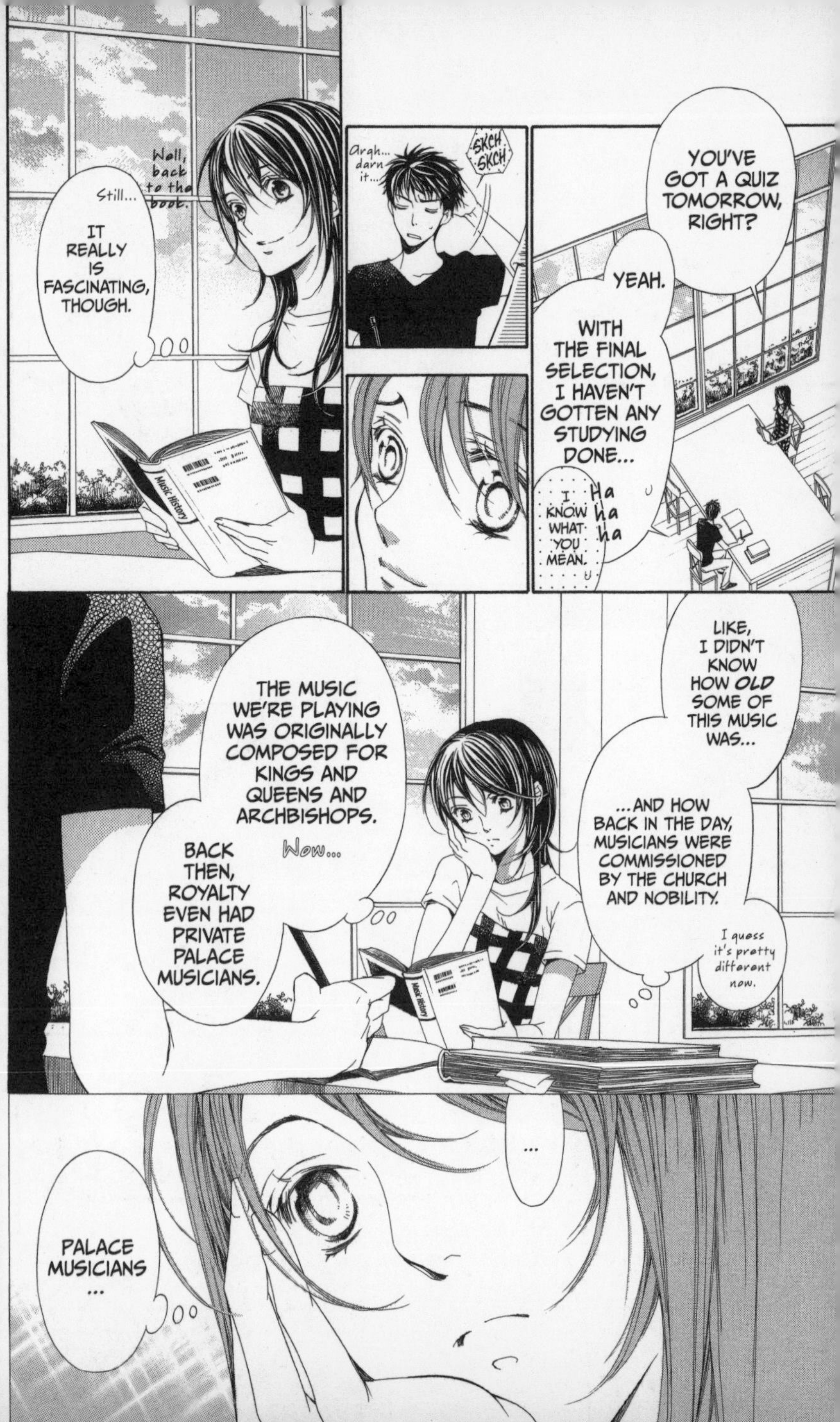
YOU'VE GOT A QUIZ TOMORROW, RIGHT?
YEAH.
WITH THE FINAL SELECTION, I HAVEN'T GOTTEN ANY STUDYING DONE...
Ha ha ha
I KNOW WHAT YOU MEAN.
SKCH SKCH
Argh... darn it...
Well, back to the book.
Still...
IT REALLY IS FASCINATING, THOUGH.
LIKE, I DIDN'T KNOW HOW *OLD* SOME OF THIS MUSIC WAS...
...AND HOW BACK IN THE DAY, MUSICIANS WERE COMMISSIONED BY THE CHURCH AND NOBILITY.
I guess it's pretty different now.
THE MUSIC WE'RE PLAYING WAS ORIGINALLY COMPOSED FOR KINGS AND QUEENS AND ARCHBISHOPS.
Wow...
BACK THEN, ROYALTY EVEN HAD PRIVATE PALACE MUSICIANS.
Music History
...
PALACE MUSICIANS ...

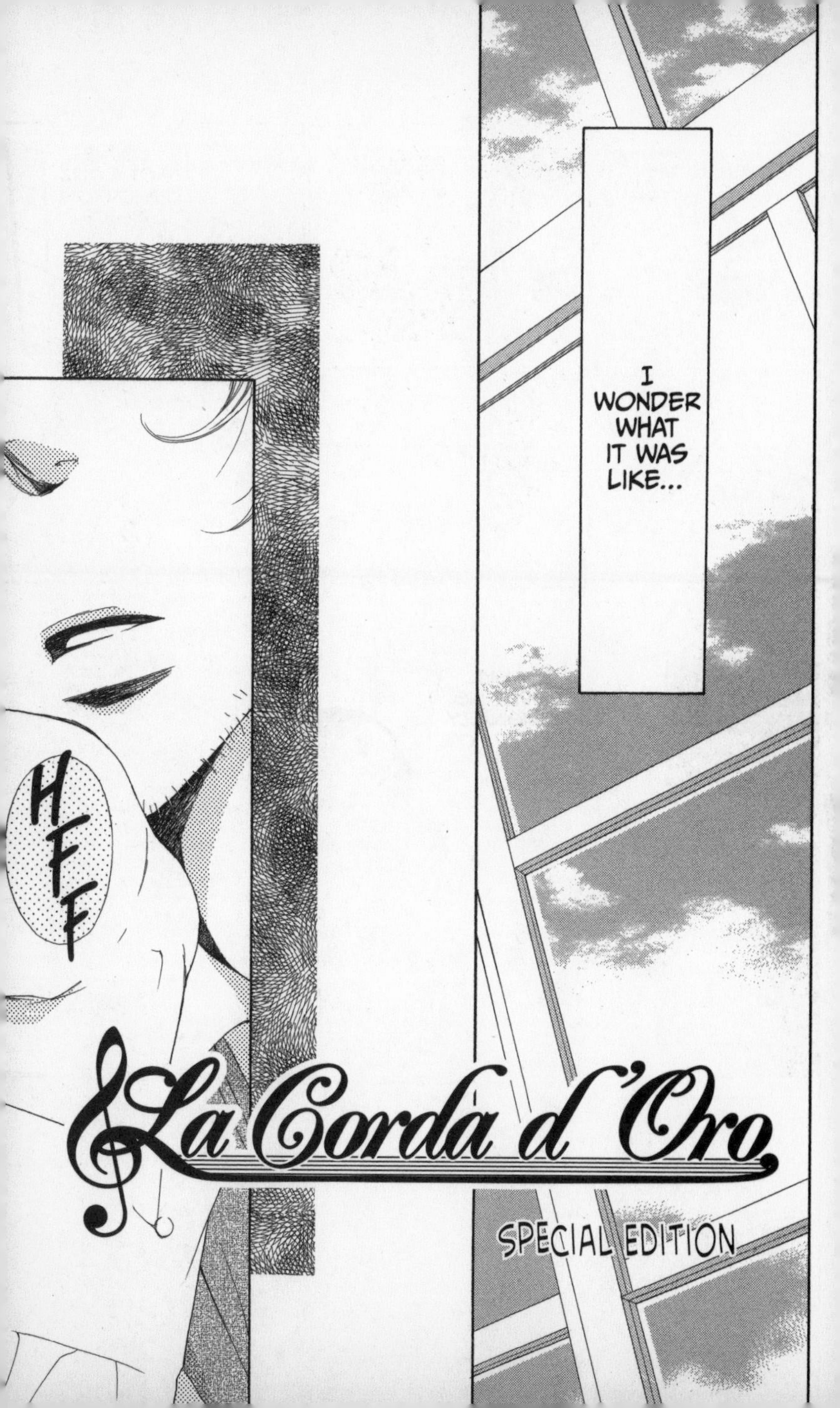
I WONDER WHAT IT WAS LIKE...
HFF
La Corda d'Oro
SPECIAL EDITION

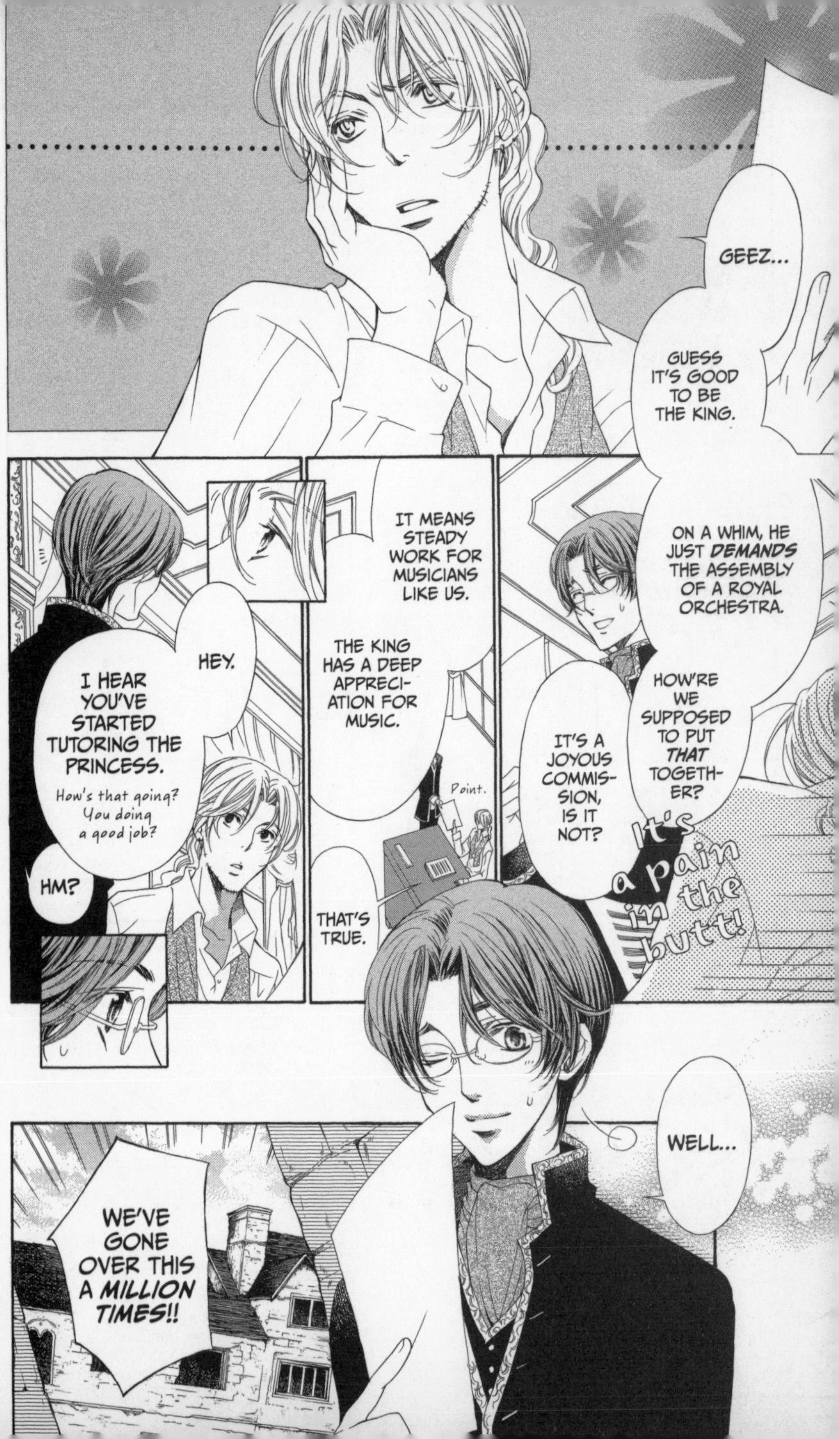
GEEZ...
GUESS IT'S GOOD TO BE THE KING.
ON A WHIM, HE JUST DEMANDS THE ASSEMBLY OF A ROYAL ORCHESTRA.
HOW'RE WE SUPPOSED TO PUT THAT TOGETHER?
It's a pain in the butt!
IT'S A JOYOUS COMMISSION, IS IT NOT?
IT MEANS STEADY WORK FOR MUSICIANS LIKE US.
THE KING HAS A DEEP APPRECIATION FOR MUSIC.
Point.
THAT'S TRUE.
HEY.
I HEAR YOU'VE STARTED TUTORING THE PRINCESS.
How's that going? You doing a good job?
HM?
WELL...
WE'VE GONE OVER THIS A MILLION TIMES!!

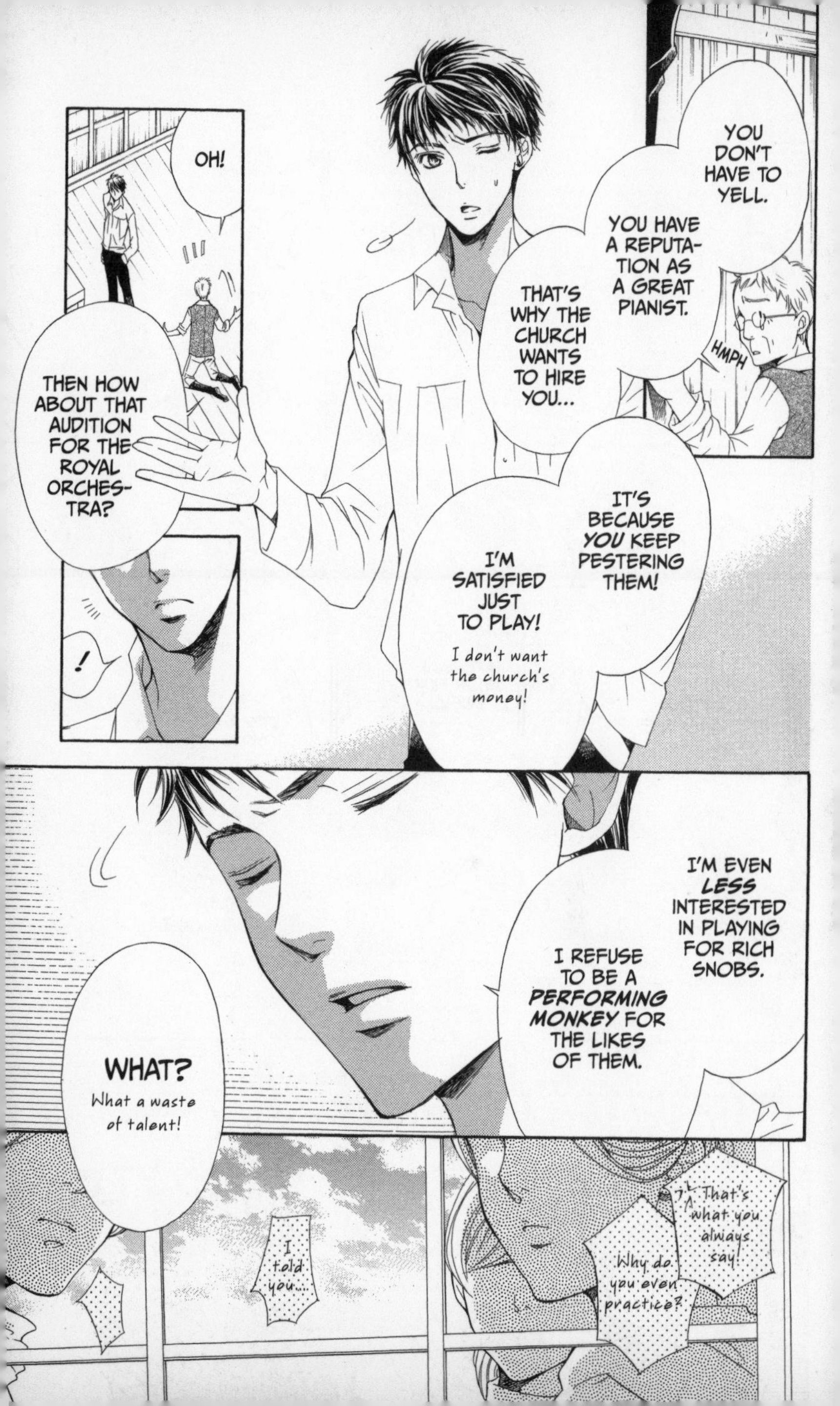
YOU DON'T HAVE TO YELL.
YOU HAVE A REPUTATION AS A GREAT PIANIST.
HMPH
THAT'S WHY THE CHURCH WANTS TO HIRE YOU...
IT'S BECAUSE YOU KEEP PESTERING THEM!
I'M SATISFIED JUST TO PLAY!
I don't want the church's money!
OH!
THEN HOW ABOUT THAT AUDITION FOR THE ROYAL ORCHESTRA?
!
I'M EVEN LESS INTERESTED IN PLAYING FOR RICH SNOBS.
I REFUSE TO BE A PERFORMING MONKEY FOR THE LIKES OF THEM.
WHAT?
What a waste of talent!
That's what you always say!
Why do you even practice?
I told you...

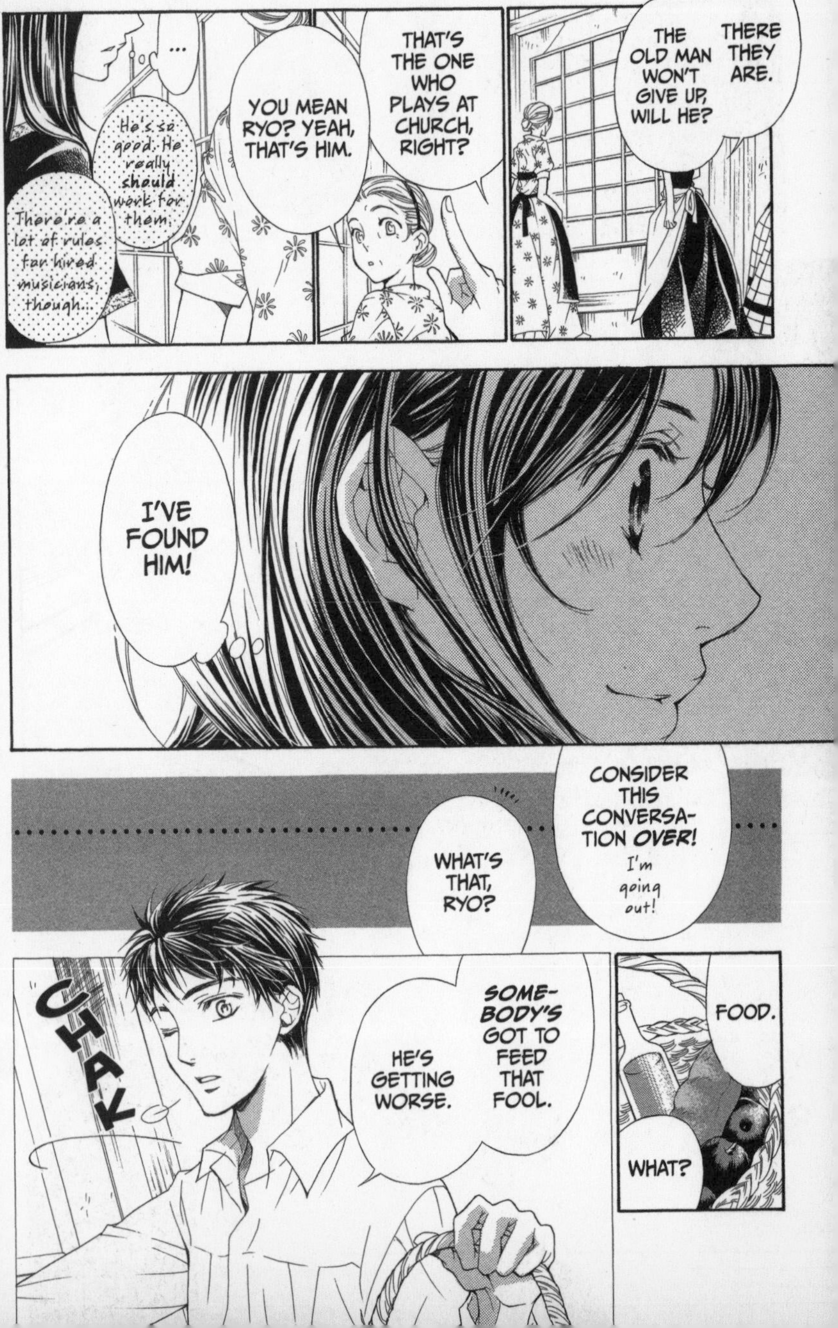
THERE THEY ARE.
THE OLD MAN WON'T GIVE UP, WILL HE?
THAT'S THE ONE WHO PLAYS AT CHURCH, RIGHT?
YOU MEAN RYO? YEAH, THAT'S HIM.
...
He's so good. He really *should* work for them.
There're a lot of rules for hired musicians, though...
I'VE FOUND HIM!
CONSIDER THIS CONVERSATION *OVER!* I'm going out!
WHAT'S THAT, RYO?
FOOD.
WHAT?
SOMEBODY'S GOT TO FEED THAT FOOL.
HE'S GETTING WORSE.
CHAK

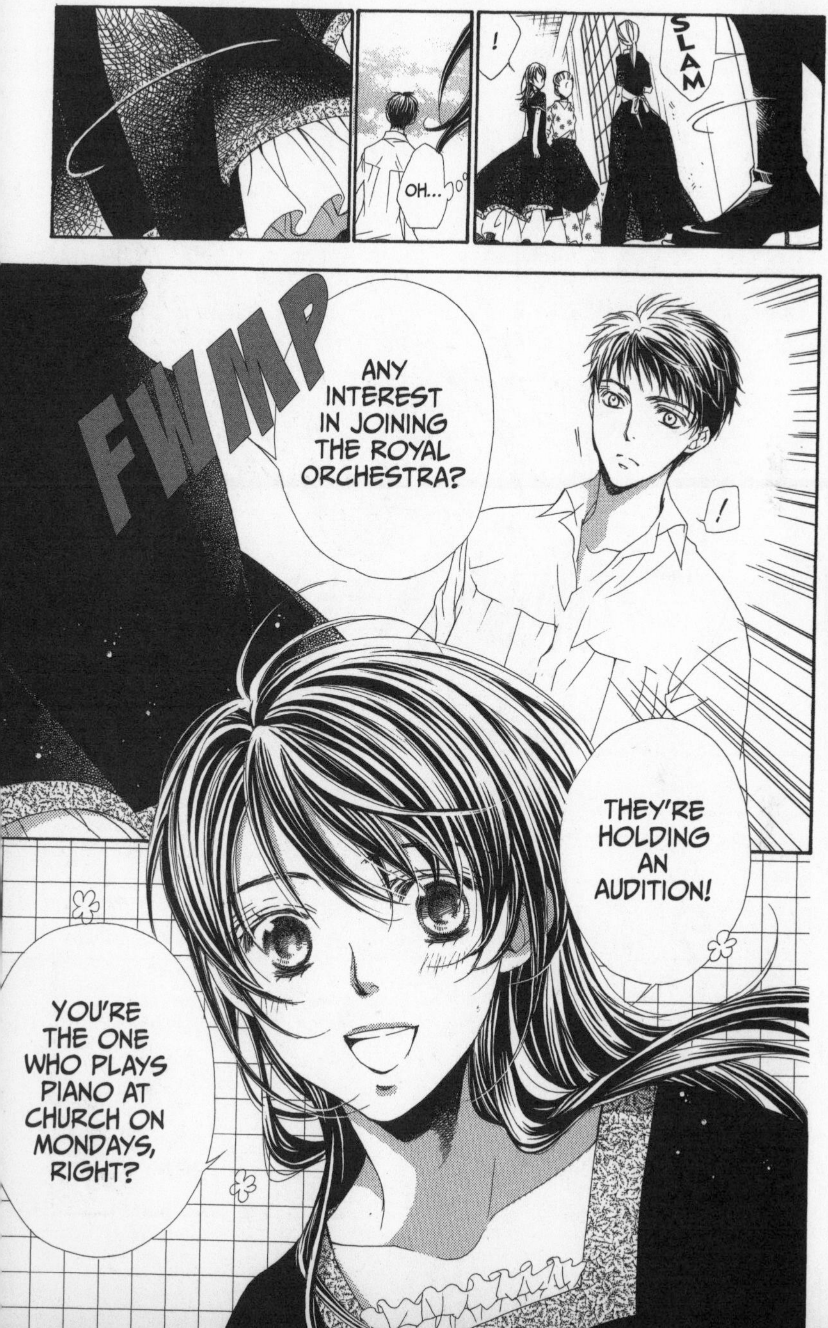
!
SLAM
OH...
!
ANY INTEREST IN JOINING THE ROYAL ORCHESTRA?
FWMP
THEY'RE HOLDING AN AUDITION!
YOU'RE THE ONE WHO PLAYS PIANO AT CHURCH ON MONDAYS, RIGHT?

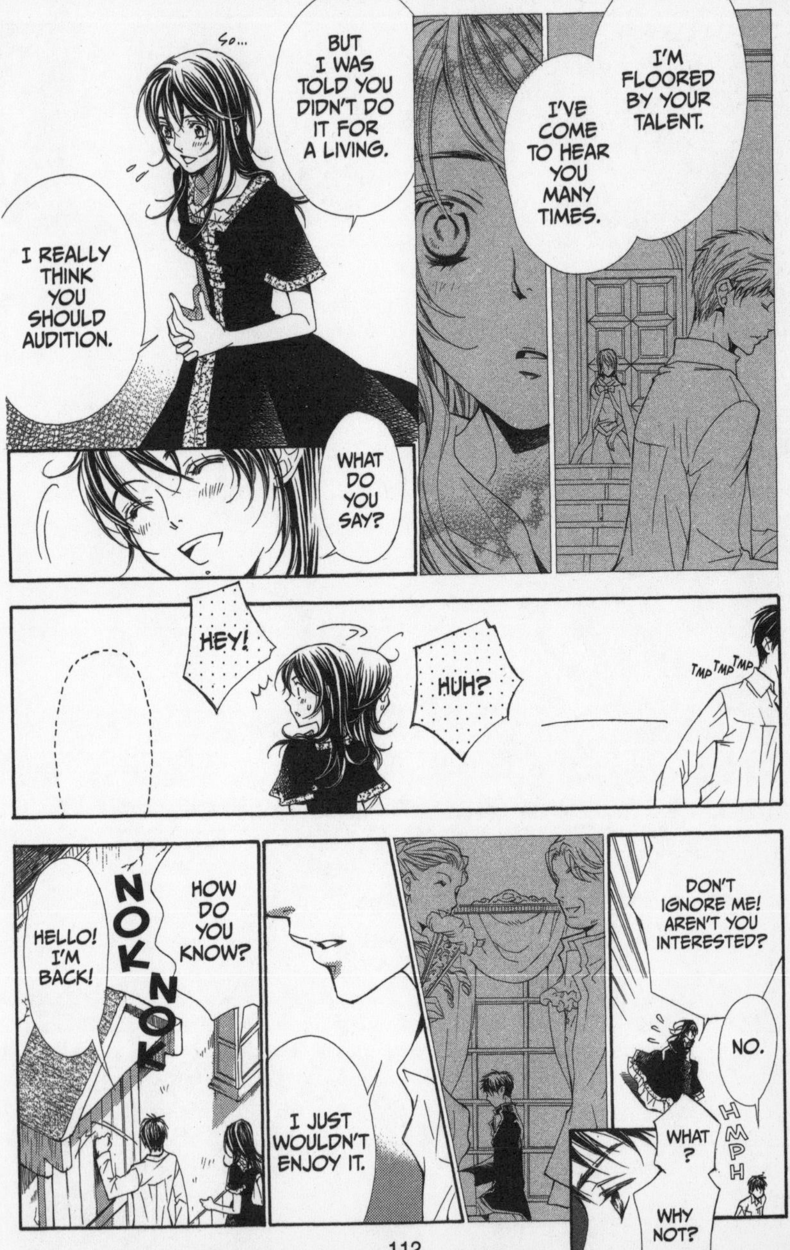
I'M FLOORED BY YOUR TALENT.
I'VE COME TO HEAR YOU MANY TIMES.
So...
BUT I WAS TOLD YOU DIDN'T DO IT FOR A LIVING.
I REALLY THINK YOU SHOULD AUDITION.
WHAT DO YOU SAY?
TMP TMP TMP
HUH?
HEY!
DON'T IGNORE ME! AREN'T YOU INTERESTED?
NO.
HMPH
WHAT?
WHY NOT?
I JUST WOULDN'T ENJOY IT.
HOW DO YOU KNOW?
NOK NOK
HELLO! I'M BACK!

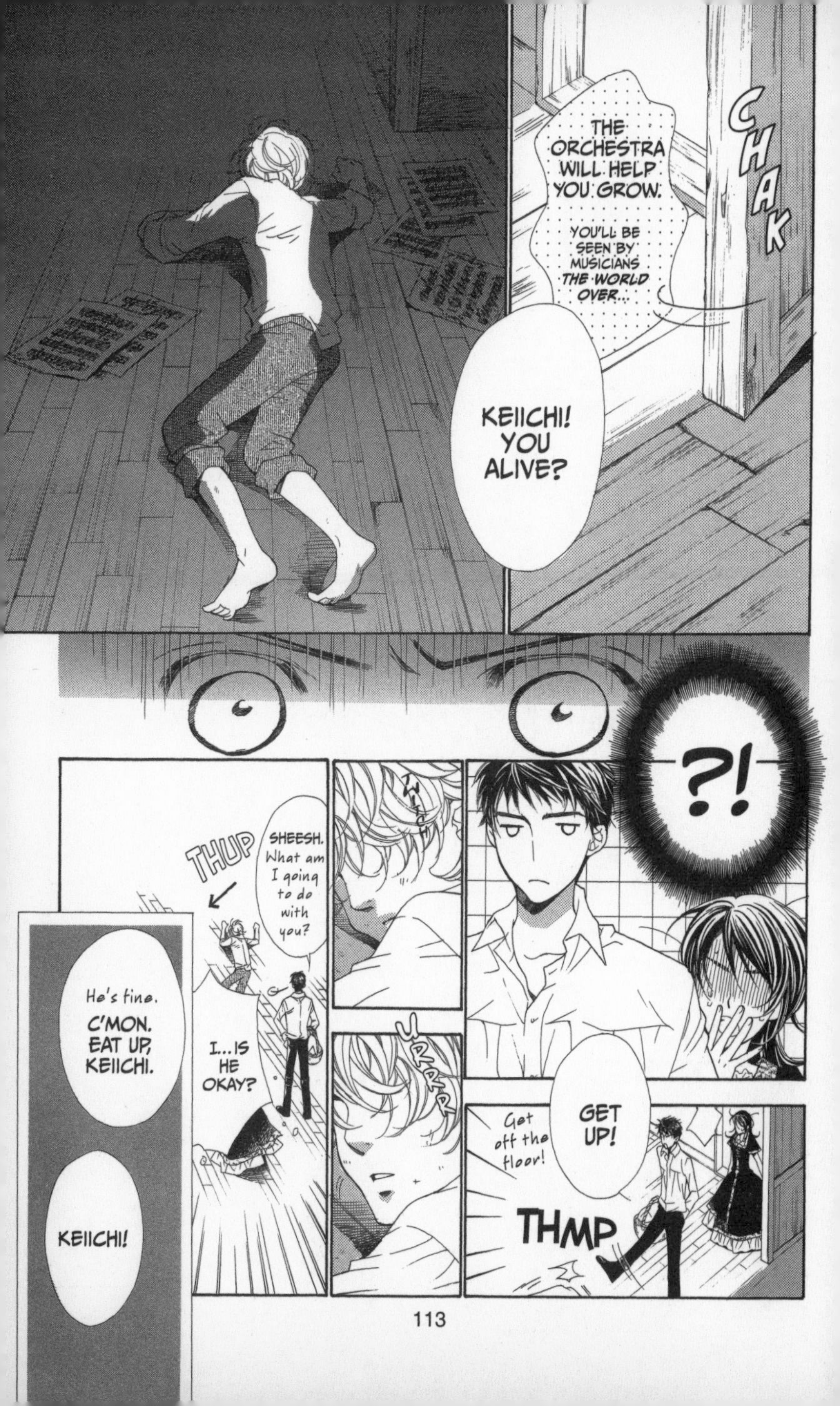
CHAK
THE ORCHESTRA WILL HELP YOU GROW.
YOU'LL BE SEEN BY MUSICIANS THE WORLD OVER...
KEIICHI! YOU ALIVE?
?!
TWITCH
GET UP!
Get off the floor!
THMP
URARR
THUP
SHEESH. What am I going to do with you?
I...IS HE OKAY?
He's fine.
C'MON. EAT UP, KEIICHI.
KEIICHI!

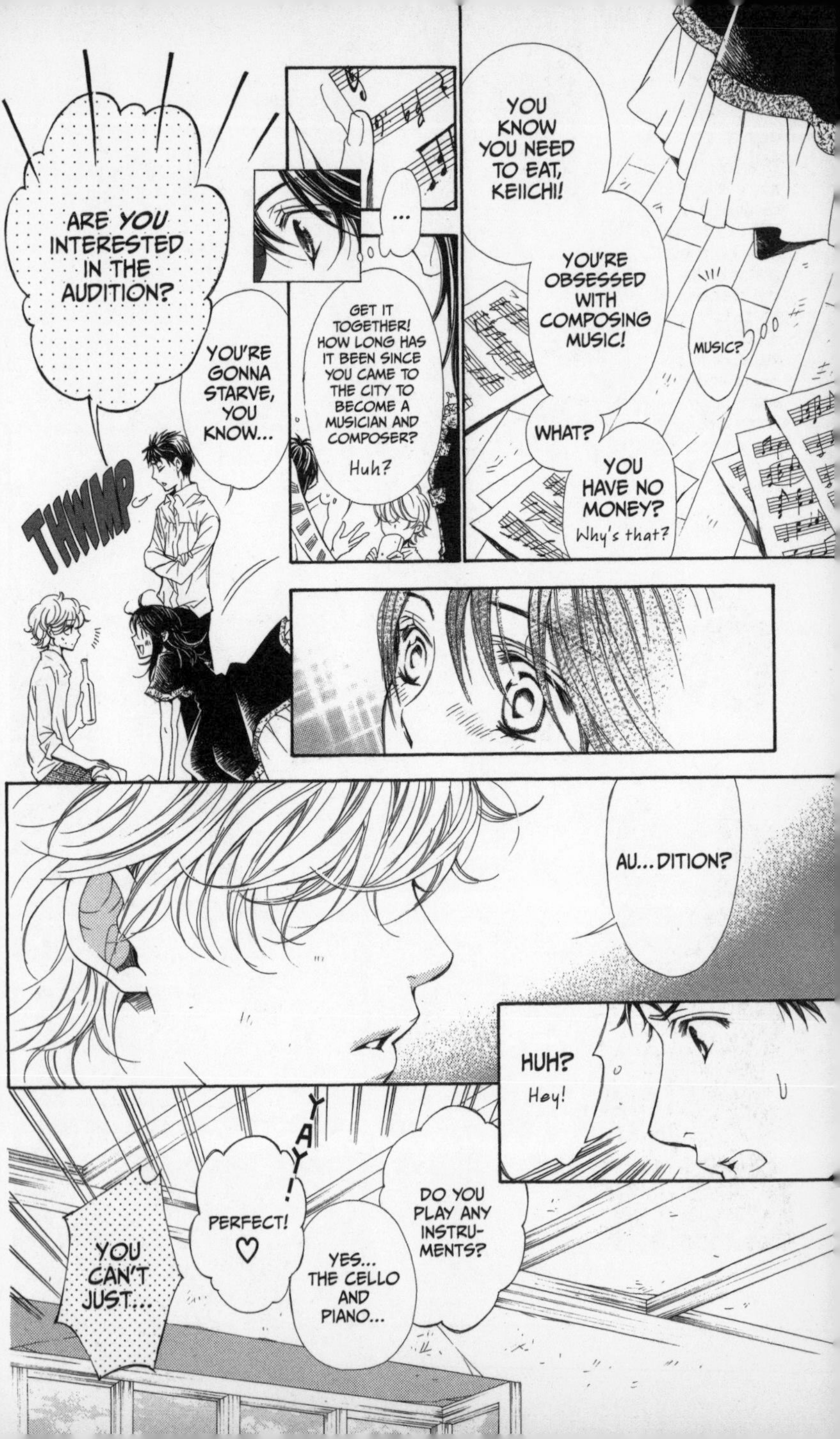
YOU KNOW YOU NEED TO EAT, KEIICHI!
YOU'RE OBSESSED WITH COMPOSING MUSIC!
MUSIC?
WHAT?
YOU HAVE NO MONEY?
Why's that?
...
GET IT TOGETHER! HOW LONG HAS IT BEEN SINCE YOU CAME TO THE CITY TO BECOME A MUSICIAN AND COMPOSER?
Huh?
YOU'RE GONNA STARVE, YOU KNOW...
ARE YOU INTERESTED IN THE AUDITION?
THWMP
AU...DITION?
HUH?
Hey!
DO YOU PLAY ANY INSTRU-MENTS?
YES... THE CELLO AND PIANO...
PERFECT! ♡
YAY!
YOU CAN'T JUST...

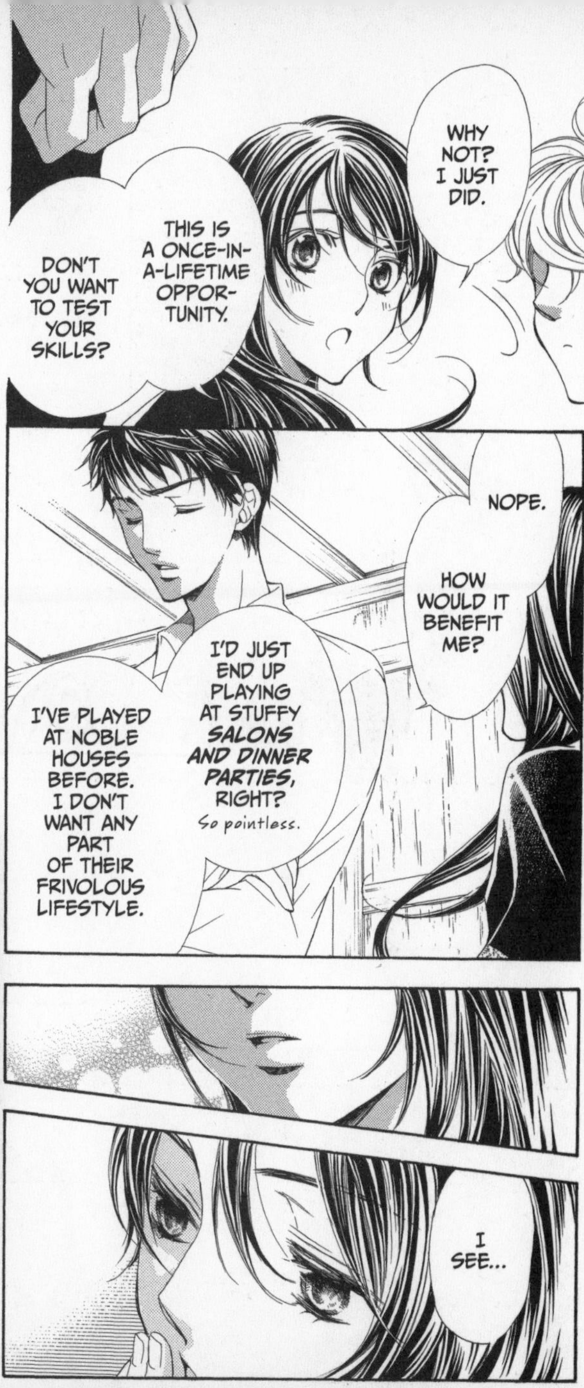
WHY NOT? I JUST DID.
THIS IS A ONCE-IN-A-LIFETIME OPPOR-TUNITY.
DON'T YOU WANT TO TEST YOUR SKILLS?
NOPE.
HOW WOULD IT BENEFIT ME?
I'D JUST END UP PLAYING AT STUFFY *SALONS AND DINNER PARTIES,* RIGHT?
So pointless.
I'VE PLAYED AT NOBLE HOUSES BEFORE. I DON'T WANT ANY PART OF THEIR FRIVOLOUS LIFESTYLE.
I SEE...

I realize this side story is kind of random. Azuma fits right in, though, huh? He almost seems more at home in a costume drama. This story appeared in *LaLa* before Measure 47, where Aoi is introduced, which is why he doesn't make an appearance. I guess he'd be nobility of some kind. He might be good as a commoner, though.

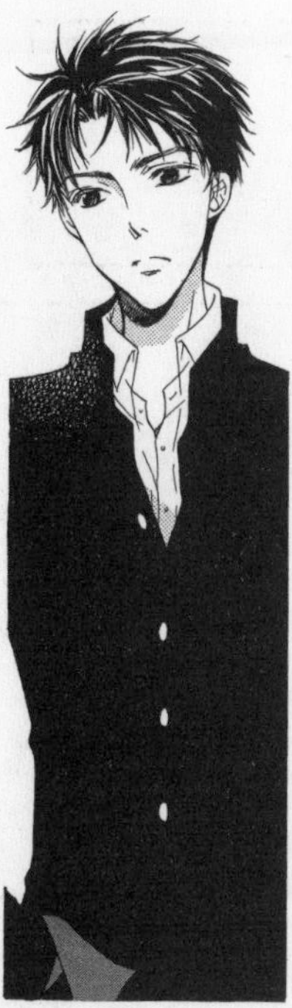

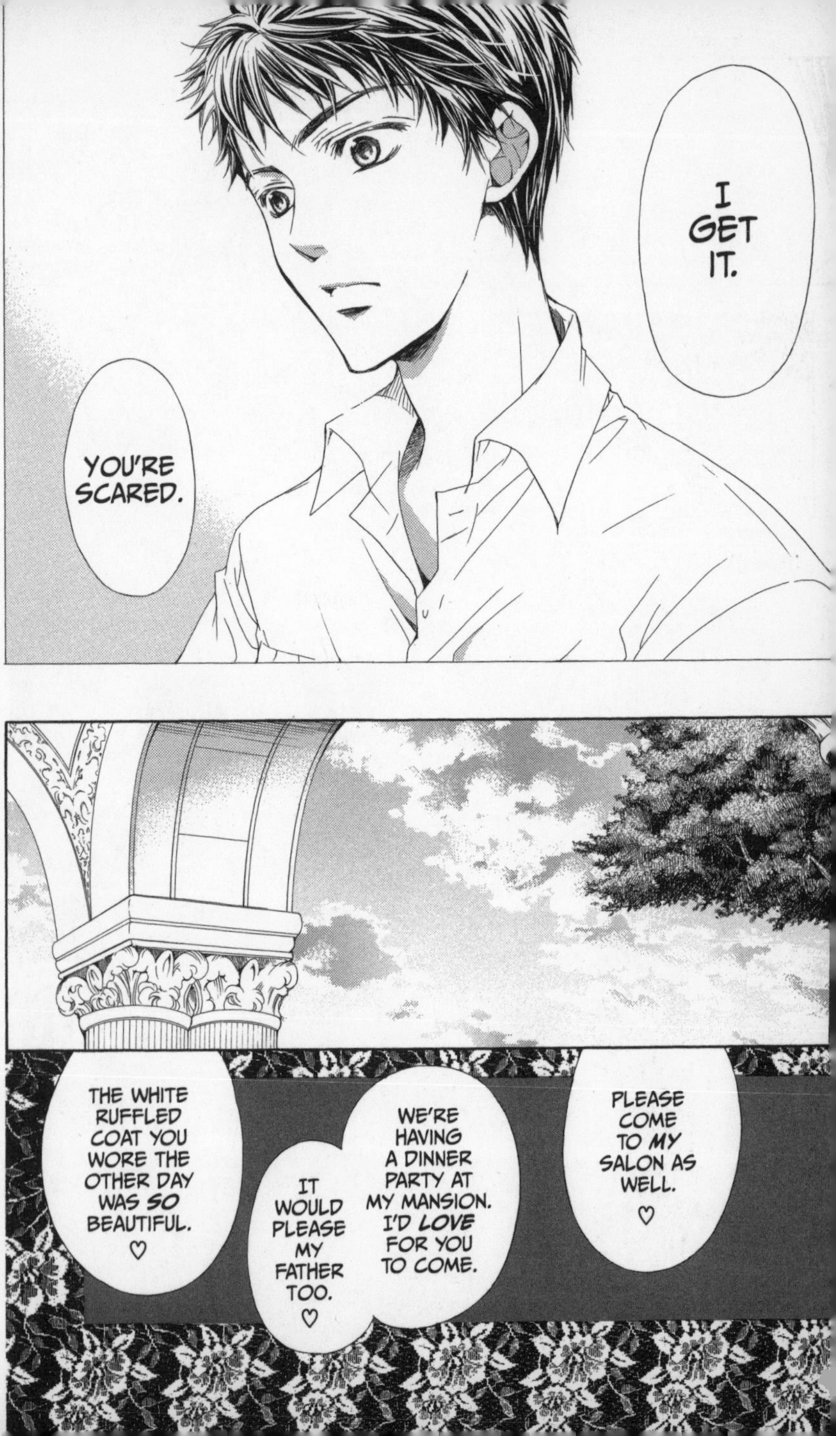
I GET IT.
YOU'RE SCARED.
PLEASE COME TO *MY* SALON AS WELL. ♡
WE'RE HAVING A DINNER PARTY AT MY MANSION. I'D *LOVE* FOR YOU TO COME.
IT WOULD PLEASE MY FATHER TOO. ♡
THE WHITE RUFFLED COAT YOU WORE THE OTHER DAY WAS *SO* BEAUTIFUL. ♡

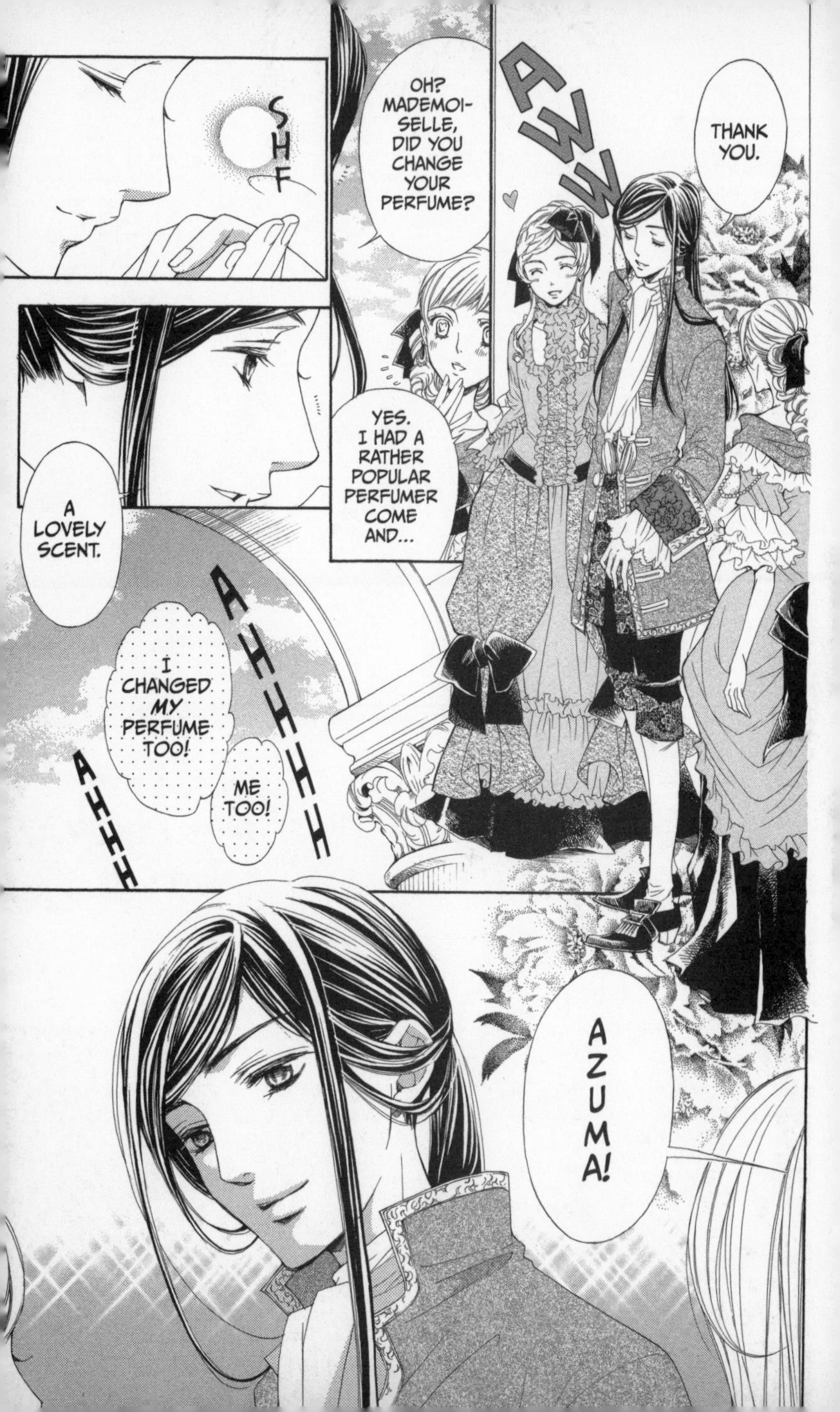
AWW
THANK YOU.
OH? MADEMOI-SELLE, DID YOU CHANGE YOUR PERFUME?
YES. I HAD A RATHER POPULAR PERFUMER COME AND...
SHF
A LOVELY SCENT.
AHHHHHH
I CHANGED MY PERFUME TOO!
ME TOO!
AHHHH
AZUMA!

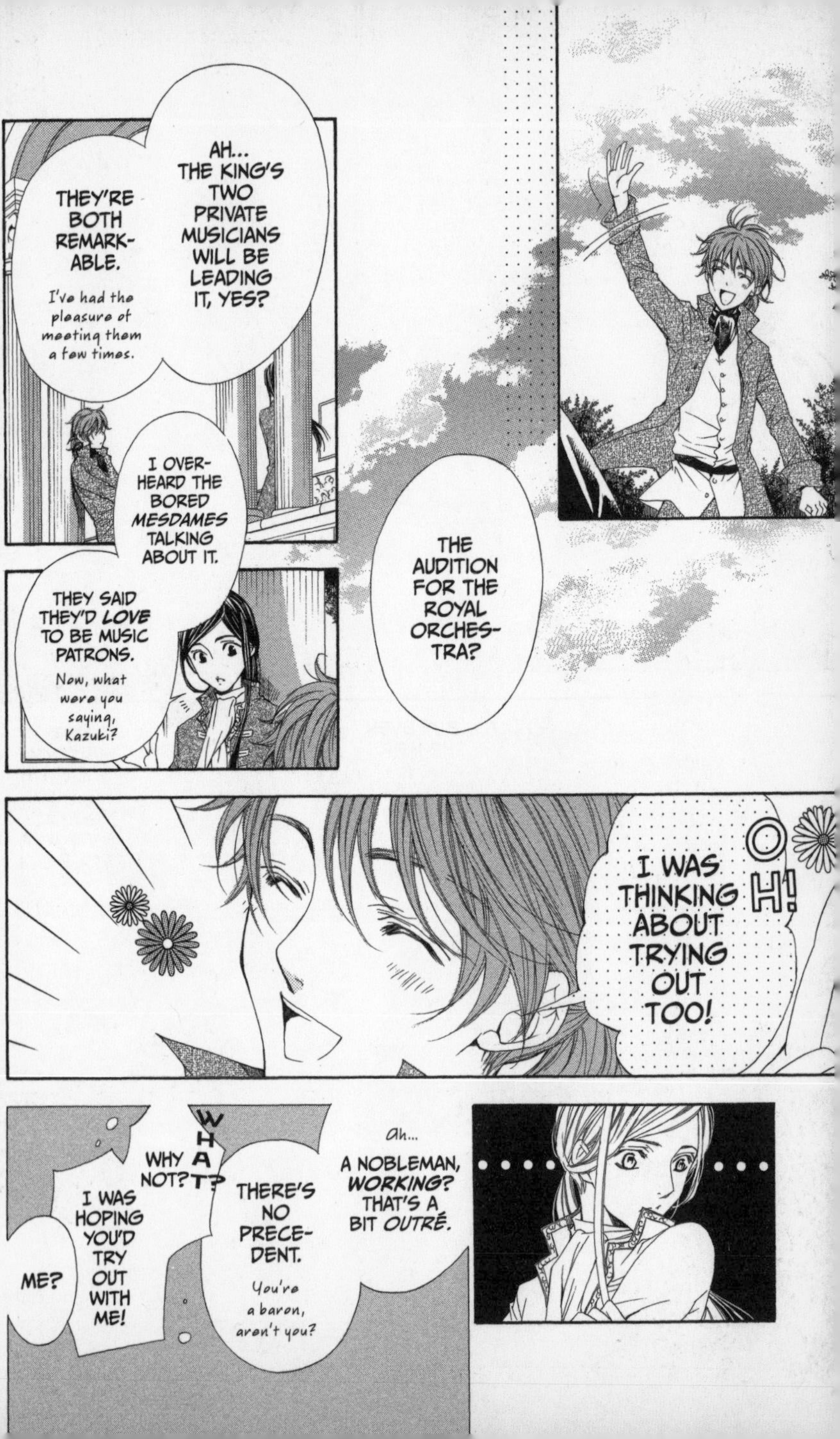
THE AUDITION FOR THE ROYAL ORCHESTRA?
AH... THE KING'S TWO PRIVATE MUSICIANS WILL BE LEADING IT, YES?
THEY'RE BOTH REMARKABLE.
I've had the pleasure of meeting them a few times.
I OVERHEARD THE BORED *MESDAMES* TALKING ABOUT IT.
THEY SAID THEY'D ***LOVE*** TO BE MUSIC PATRONS.
Now, what were you saying, Kazuki?
OH!
I WAS THINKING ABOUT TRYING OUT TOO!
. . . .
. . .
Ah...
A NOBLEMAN, ***WORKING?*** THAT'S A BIT *OUTRÉ.*
THERE'S NO PRECEDENT.
You're a baron, aren't you?
WHAT?
WHY NOT?
I WAS HOPING YOU'D TRY OUT WITH ME!
ME?

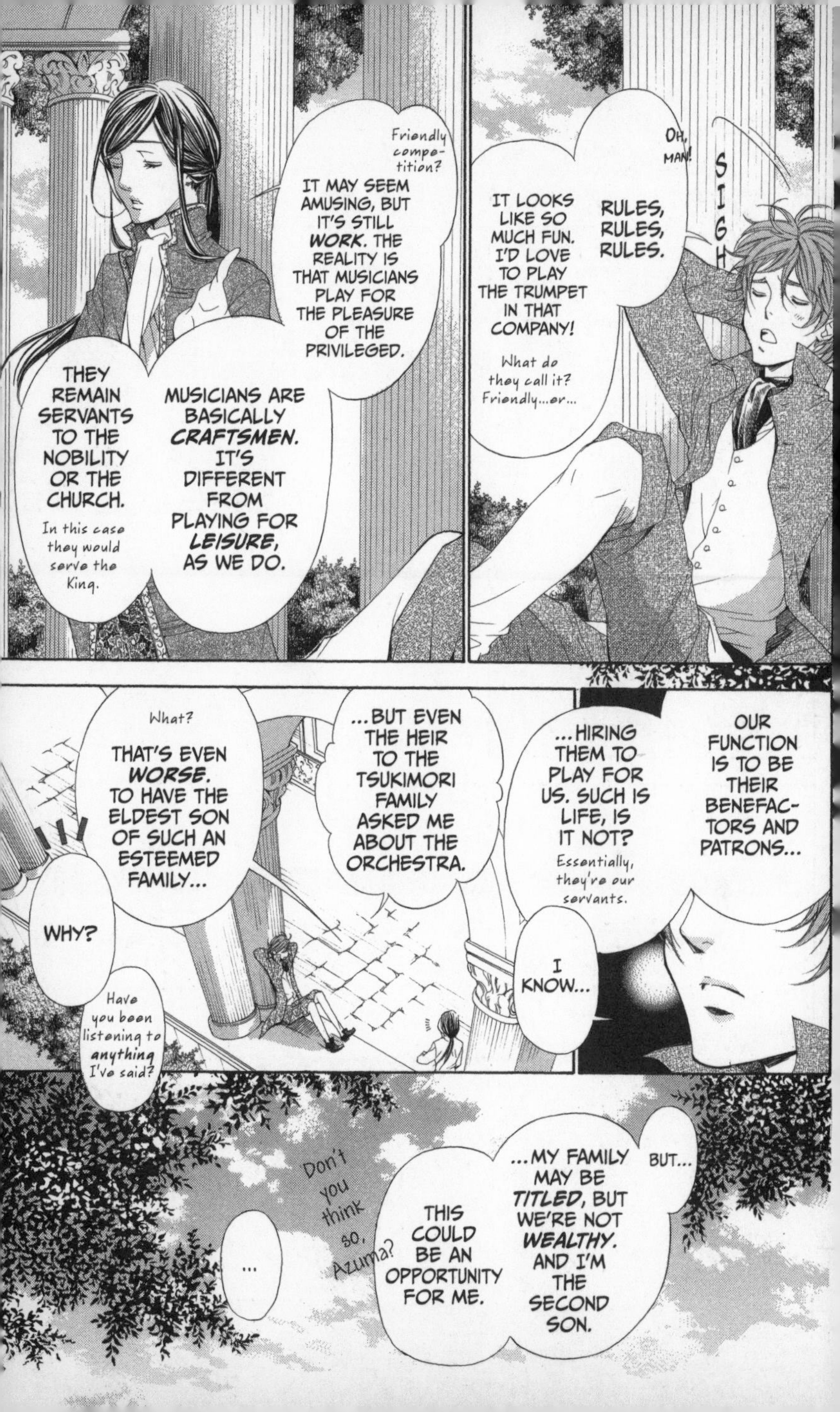

OH, MAN!
SIGH
RULES, RULES, RULES.
IT LOOKS LIKE SO MUCH FUN. I'D LOVE TO PLAY THE TRUMPET IN THAT COMPANY!
What do they call it? Friendly...er...
Friendly competition?
IT MAY SEEM AMUSING, BUT IT'S STILL WORK. THE REALITY IS THAT MUSICIANS PLAY FOR THE PLEASURE OF THE PRIVILEGED.
MUSICIANS ARE BASICALLY CRAFTSMEN. IT'S DIFFERENT FROM PLAYING FOR LEISURE, AS WE DO.
THEY REMAIN SERVANTS TO THE NOBILITY OR THE CHURCH.
In this case they would serve the King.
OUR FUNCTION IS TO BE THEIR BENEFACTORS AND PATRONS...
...HIRING THEM TO PLAY FOR US. SUCH IS LIFE, IS IT NOT?
Essentially, they're our servants.
I KNOW...
...BUT EVEN THE HEIR TO THE TSUKIMORI FAMILY ASKED ME ABOUT THE ORCHESTRA.
What?
THAT'S EVEN WORSE. TO HAVE THE ELDEST SON OF SUCH AN ESTEEMED FAMILY...
WHY?
Have you been listening to anything I've said?
BUT...
...MY FAMILY MAY BE TITLED, BUT WE'RE NOT WEALTHY. AND I'M THE SECOND SON.
THIS COULD BE AN OPPORTUNITY FOR ME.
Don't you think so, Azuma?
...

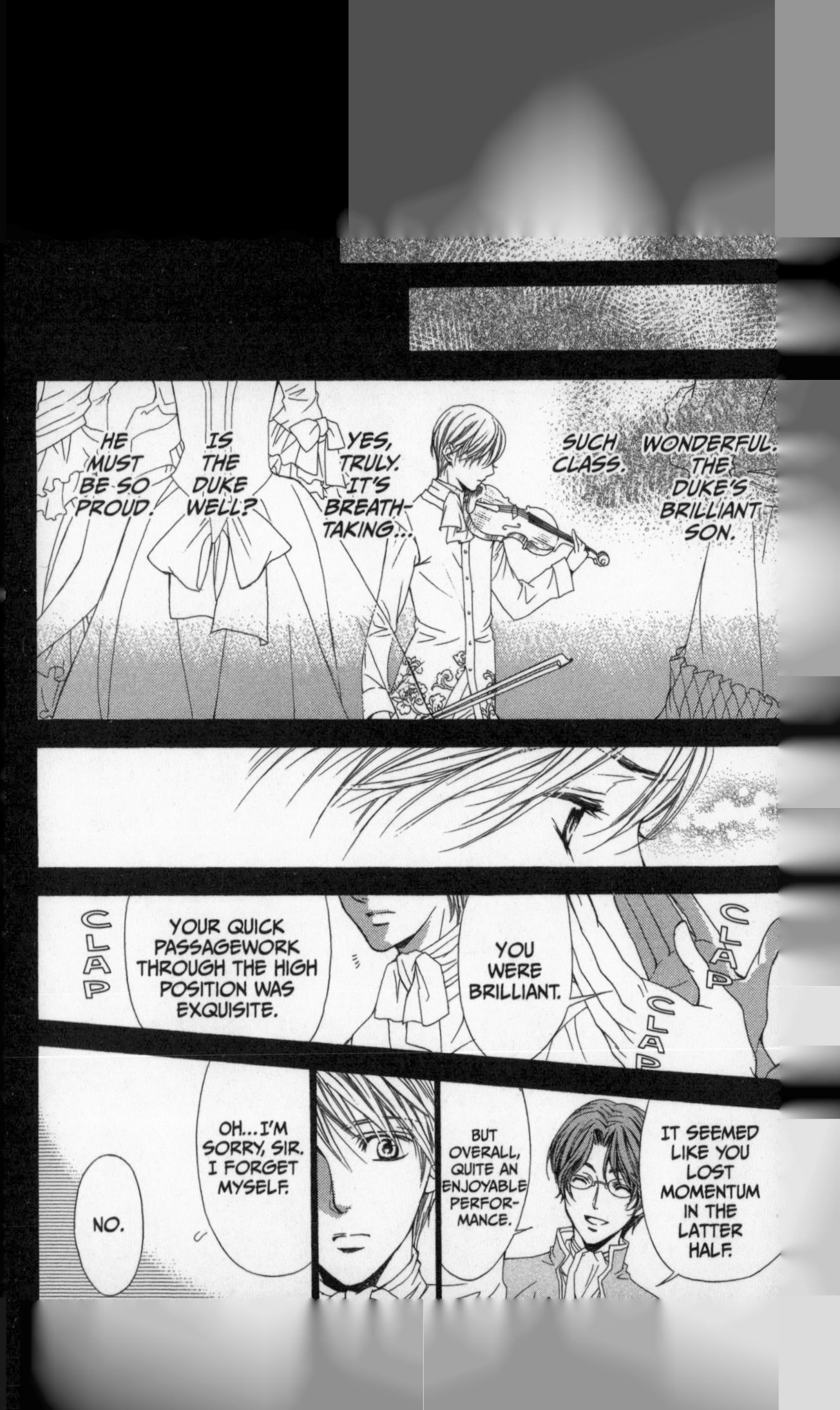
WONDERFUL. THE DUKE'S BRILLIANT SON.
SUCH CLASS.
YES, TRULY. IT'S BREATHTAKING...
IS THE DUKE WELL?
HE MUST BE SO PROUD.
CLAP
CLAP
YOU WERE BRILLIANT.
YOUR QUICK PASSAGEWORK THROUGH THE HIGH POSITION WAS EXQUISITE.
CLAP
IT SEEMED LIKE YOU LOST MOMENTUM IN THE LATTER HALF.
BUT OVERALL, QUITE AN ENJOYABLE PERFORMANCE.
OH...I'M SORRY, SIR. I FORGET MYSELF.
NO.

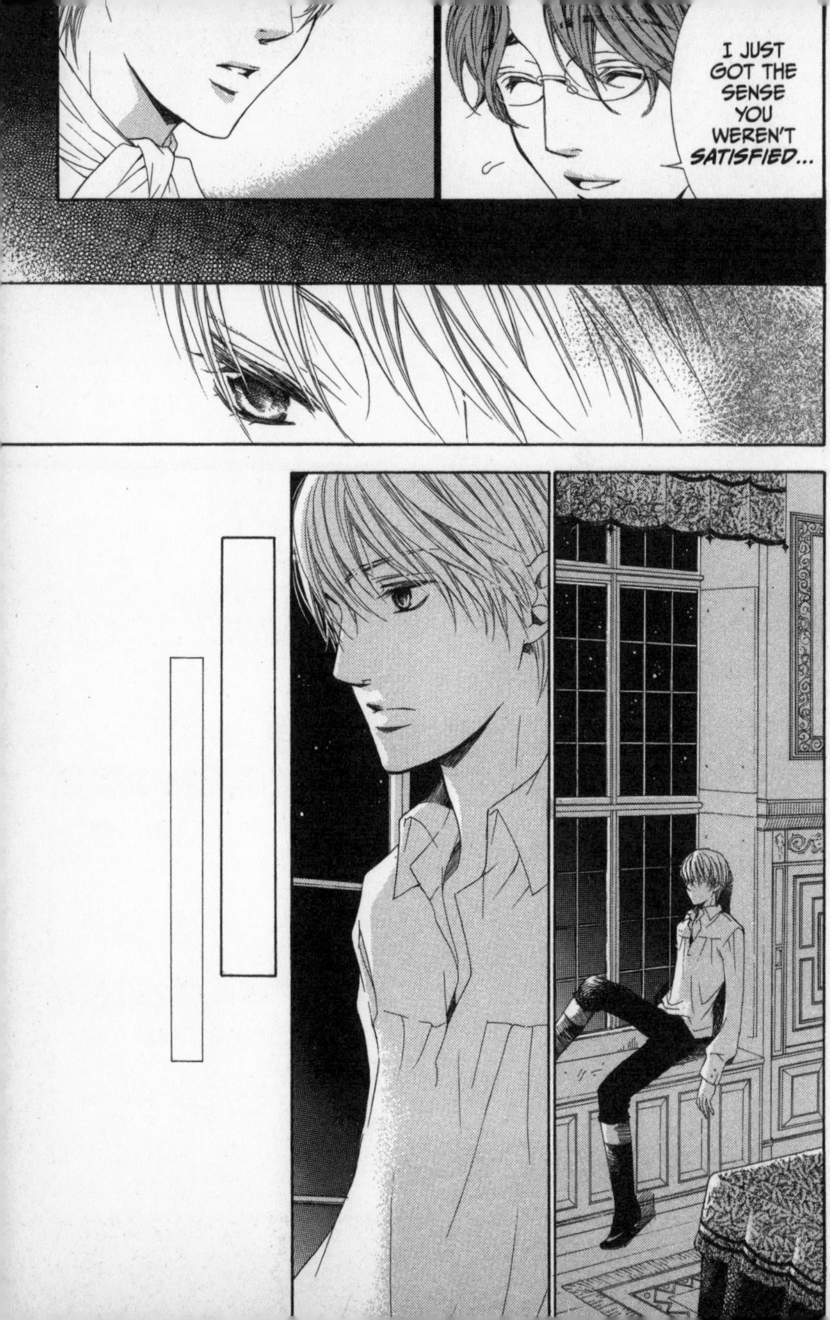
I JUST GOT THE SENSE YOU WEREN'T SATISFIED...

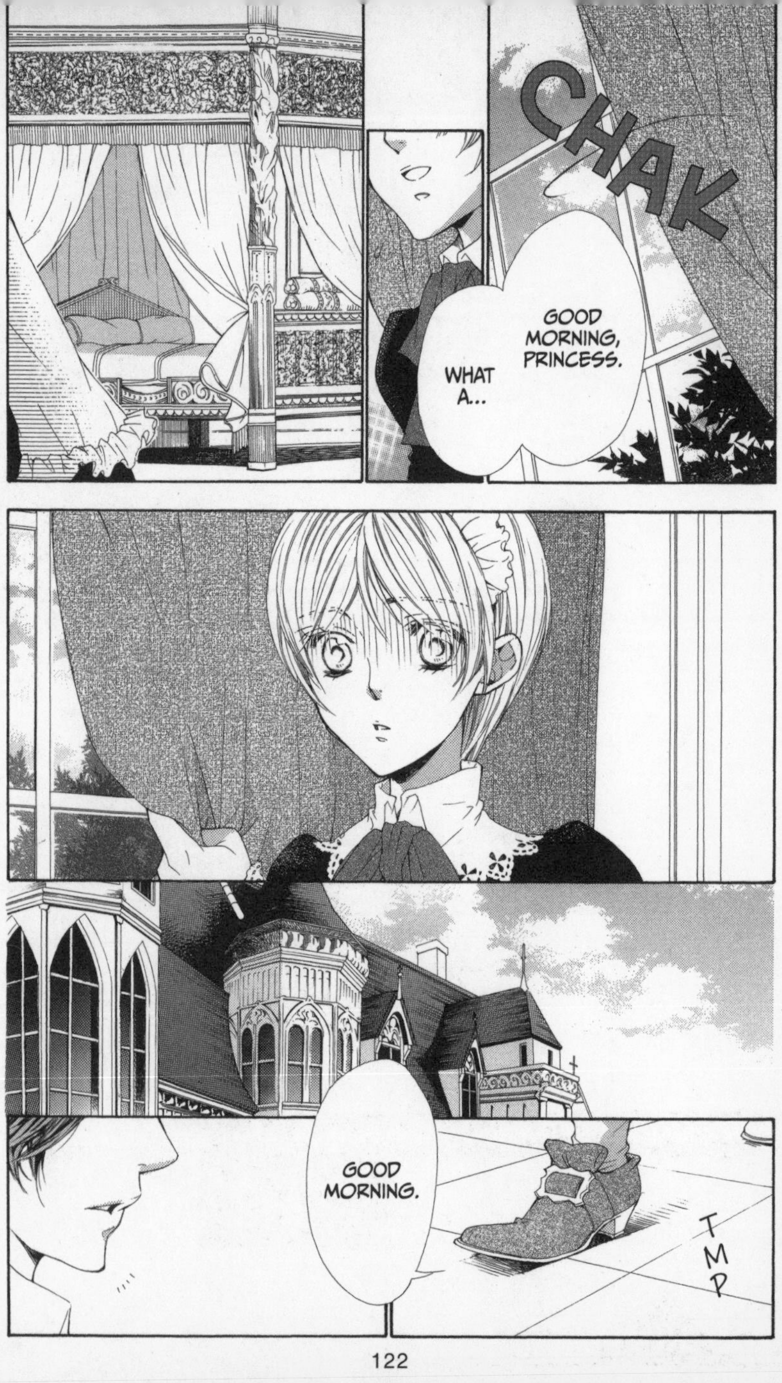
CHAK
GOOD MORNING, PRINCESS.
WHAT A...
TMP
GOOD MORNING.

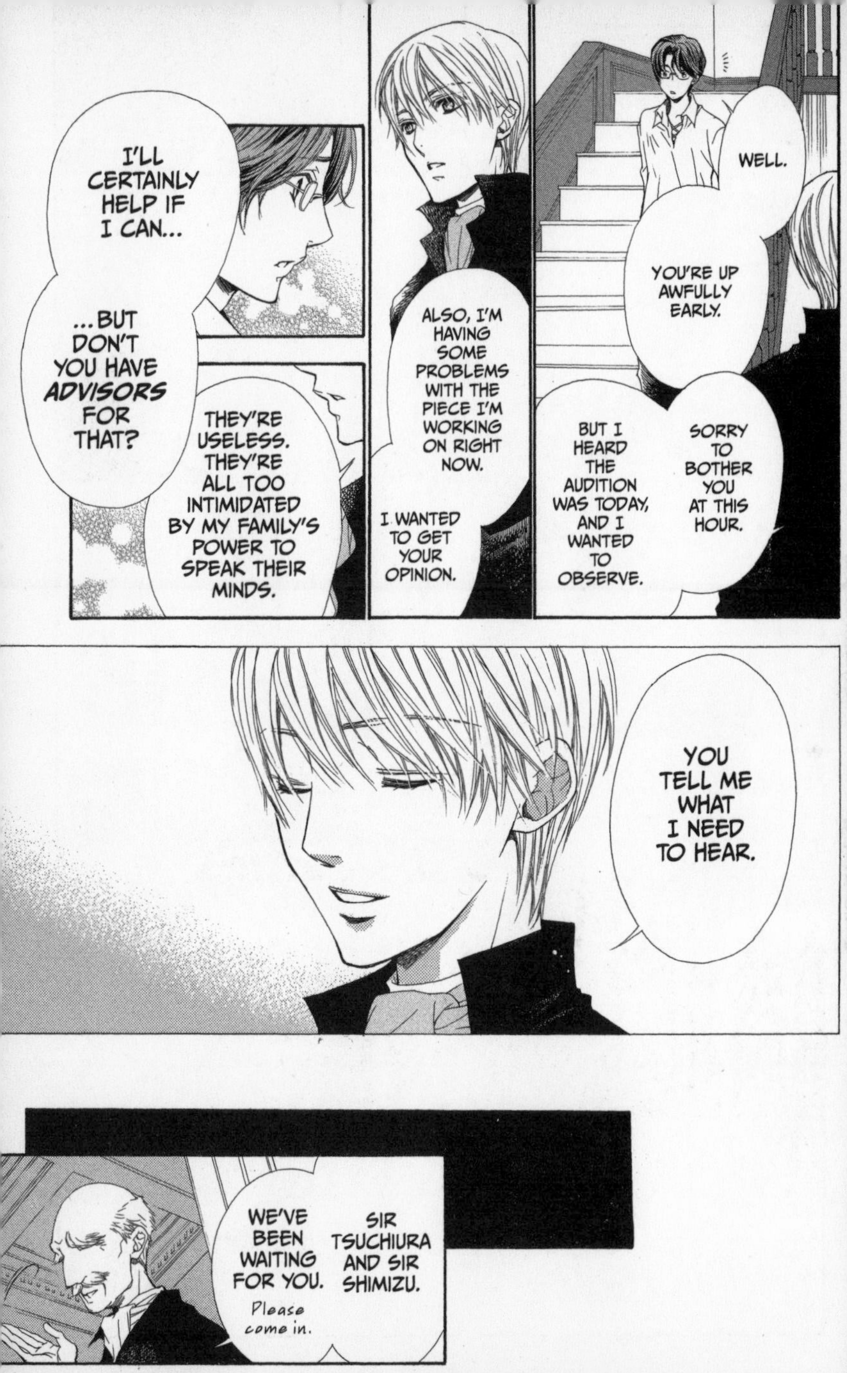
WELL.
YOU'RE UP AWFULLY EARLY.
SORRY TO BOTHER YOU AT THIS HOUR.
BUT I HEARD THE AUDITION WAS TODAY, AND I WANTED TO OBSERVE.
ALSO, I'M HAVING SOME PROBLEMS WITH THE PIECE I'M WORKING ON RIGHT NOW.
I WANTED TO GET YOUR OPINION.
I'LL CERTAINLY HELP IF I CAN...
...BUT DON'T YOU HAVE ADVISORS FOR THAT?
THEY'RE USELESS. THEY'RE ALL TOO INTIMIDATED BY MY FAMILY'S POWER TO SPEAK THEIR MINDS.
YOU TELL ME WHAT I NEED TO HEAR.
SIR TSUCHIURA AND SIR SHIMIZU.
WE'VE BEEN WAITING FOR YOU.
Please come in.

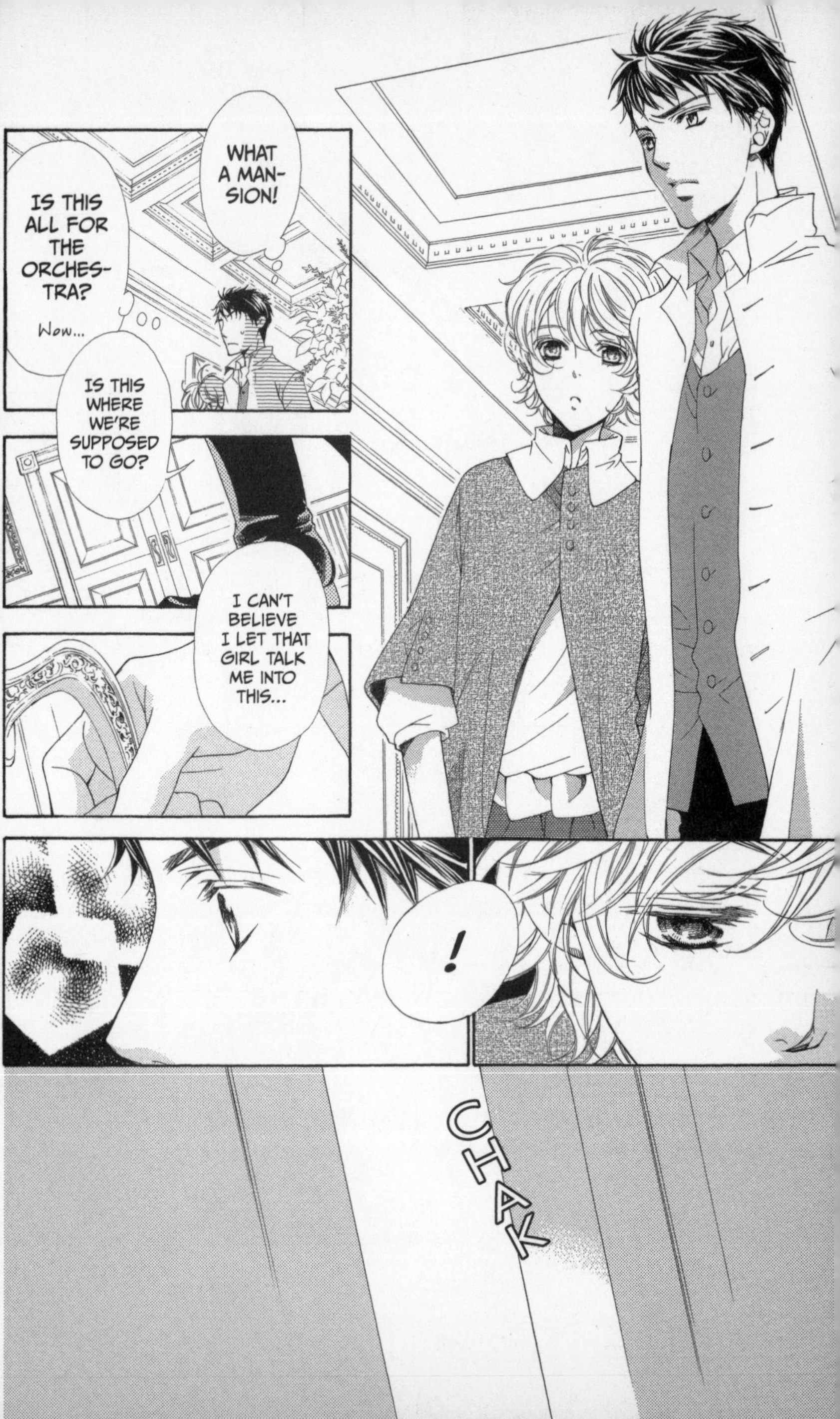

WHAT A MAN-SION!
IS THIS ALL FOR THE ORCHES-TRA?
Wow...
IS THIS WHERE WE'RE SUPPOSED TO GO?
I CAN'T BELIEVE I LET THAT GIRL TALK ME INTO THIS...
!
CHAK

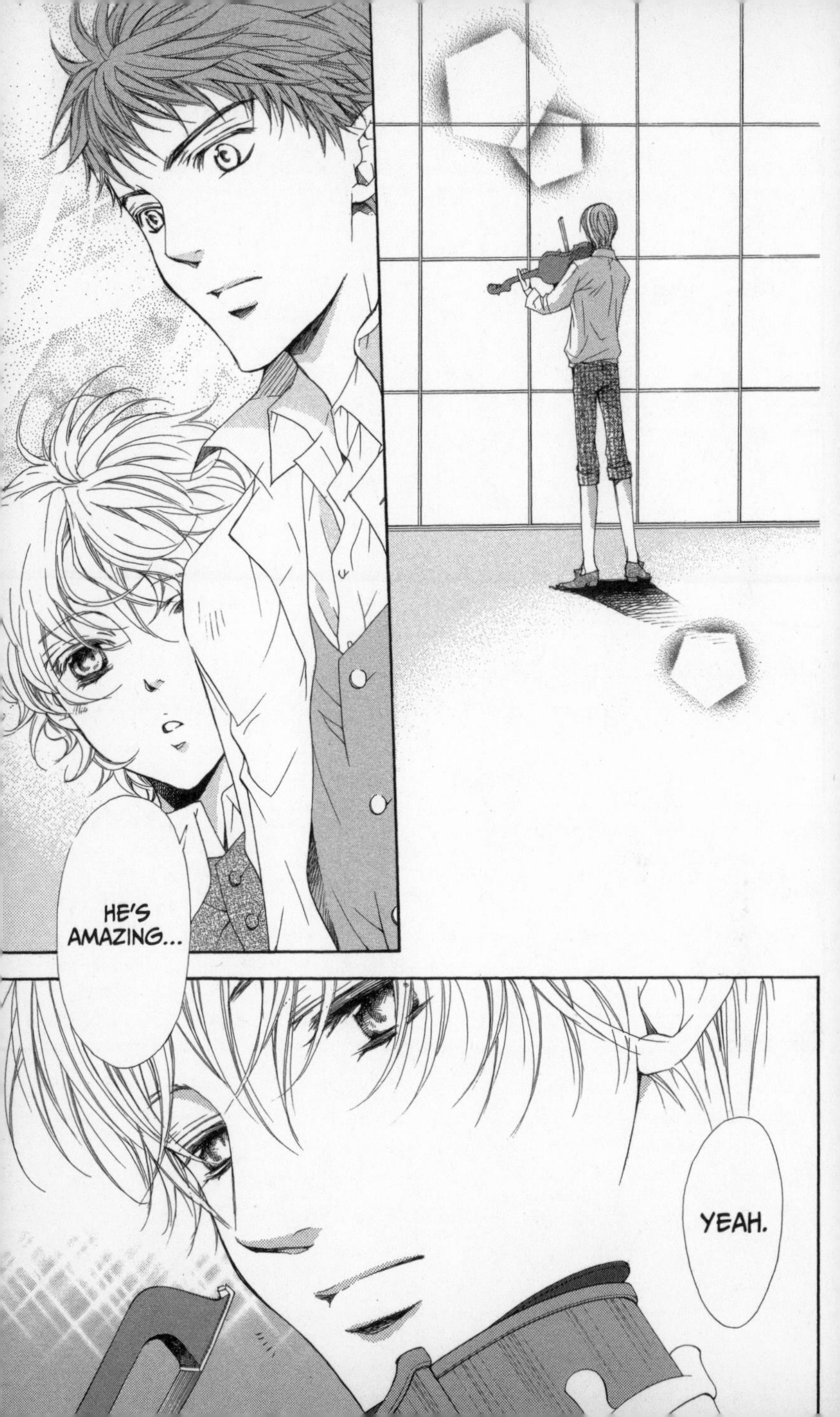
HE'S AMAZING...
YEAH.

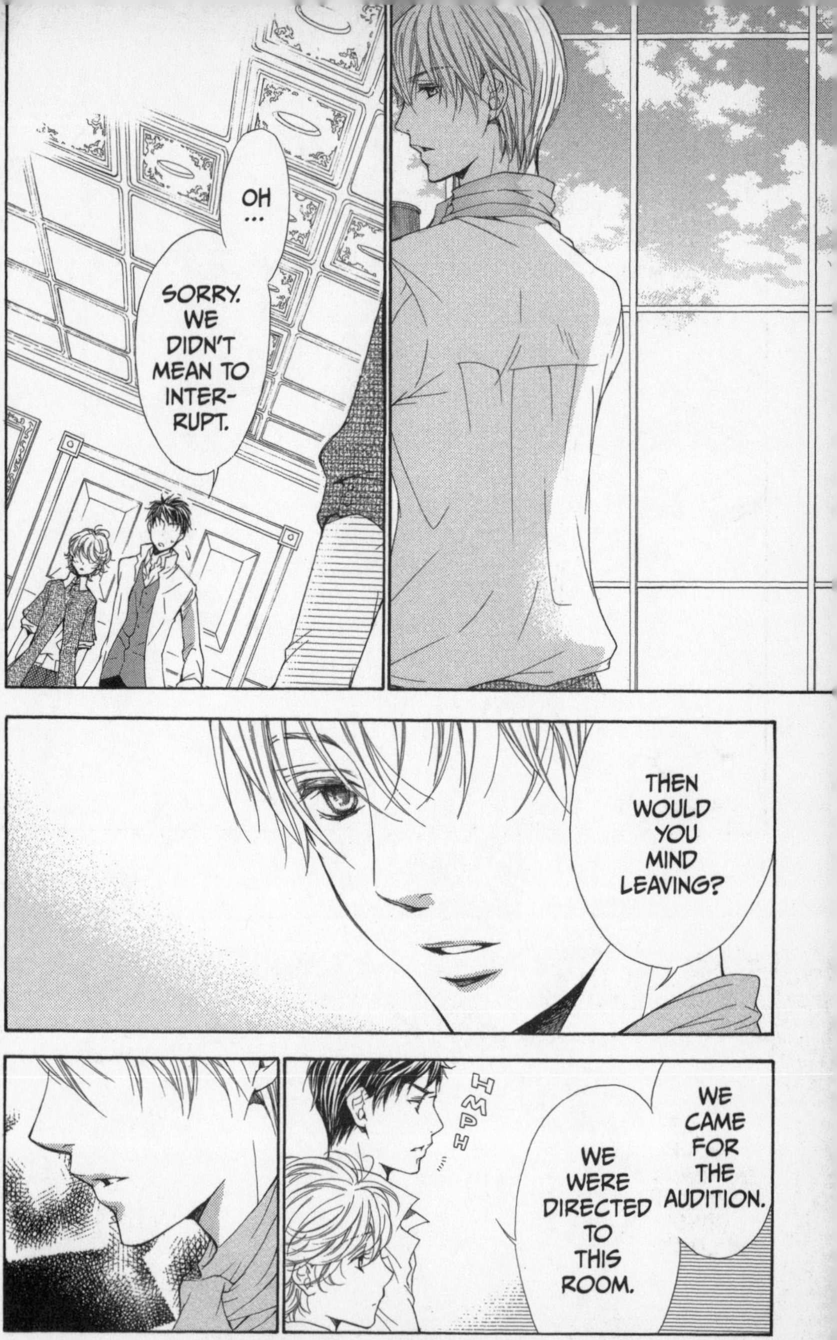
OH ...
SORRY. WE DIDN'T MEAN TO INTER-RUPT.
THEN WOULD YOU MIND LEAVING?
HMPH
WE CAME FOR THE AUDITION.
WE WERE DIRECTED TO THIS ROOM.

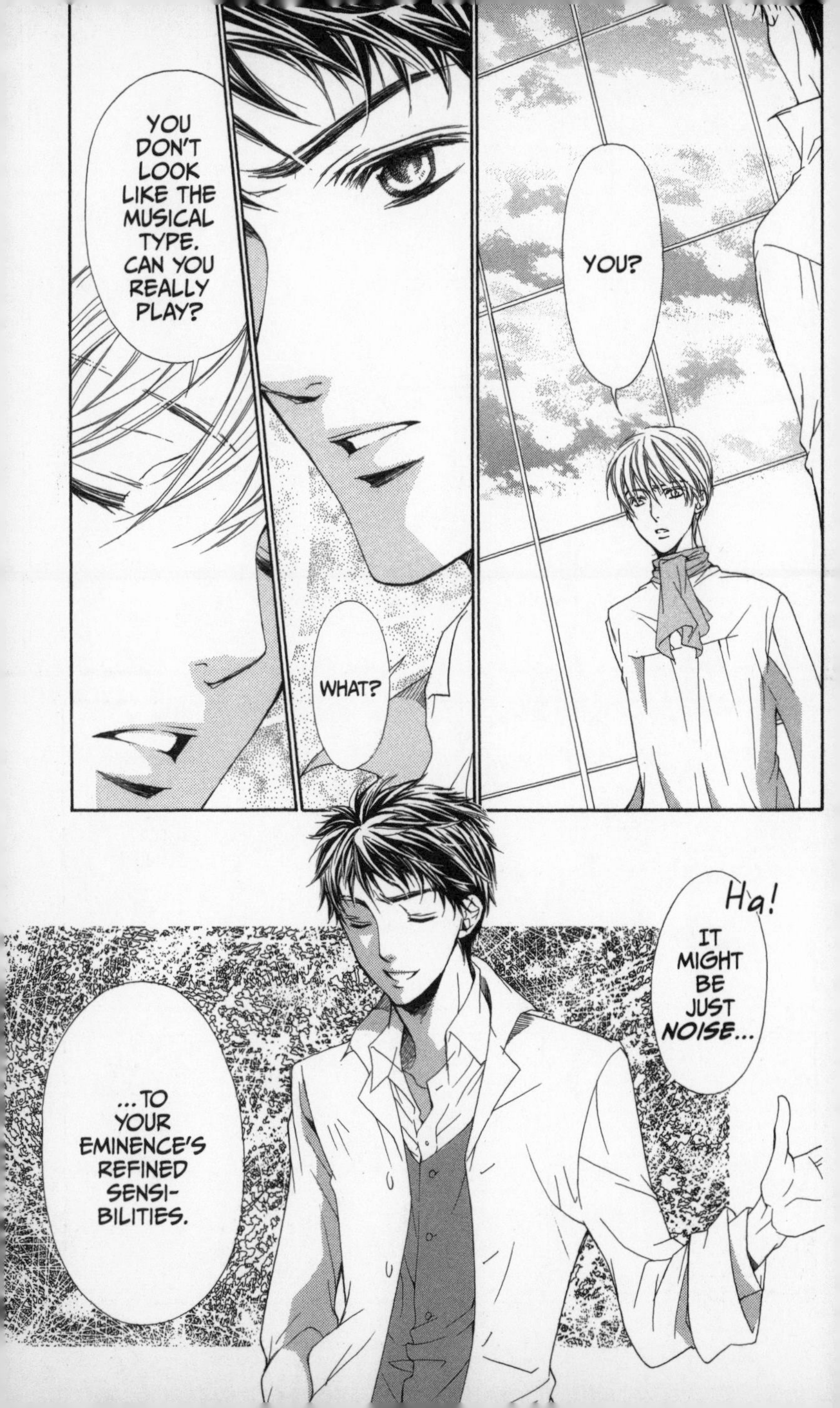
YOU?
WHAT?
YOU DON'T LOOK LIKE THE MUSICAL TYPE. CAN YOU REALLY PLAY?
Ha!
IT MIGHT BE JUST *NOISE*...
...TO YOUR EMINENCE'S REFINED SENSI-BILITIES.

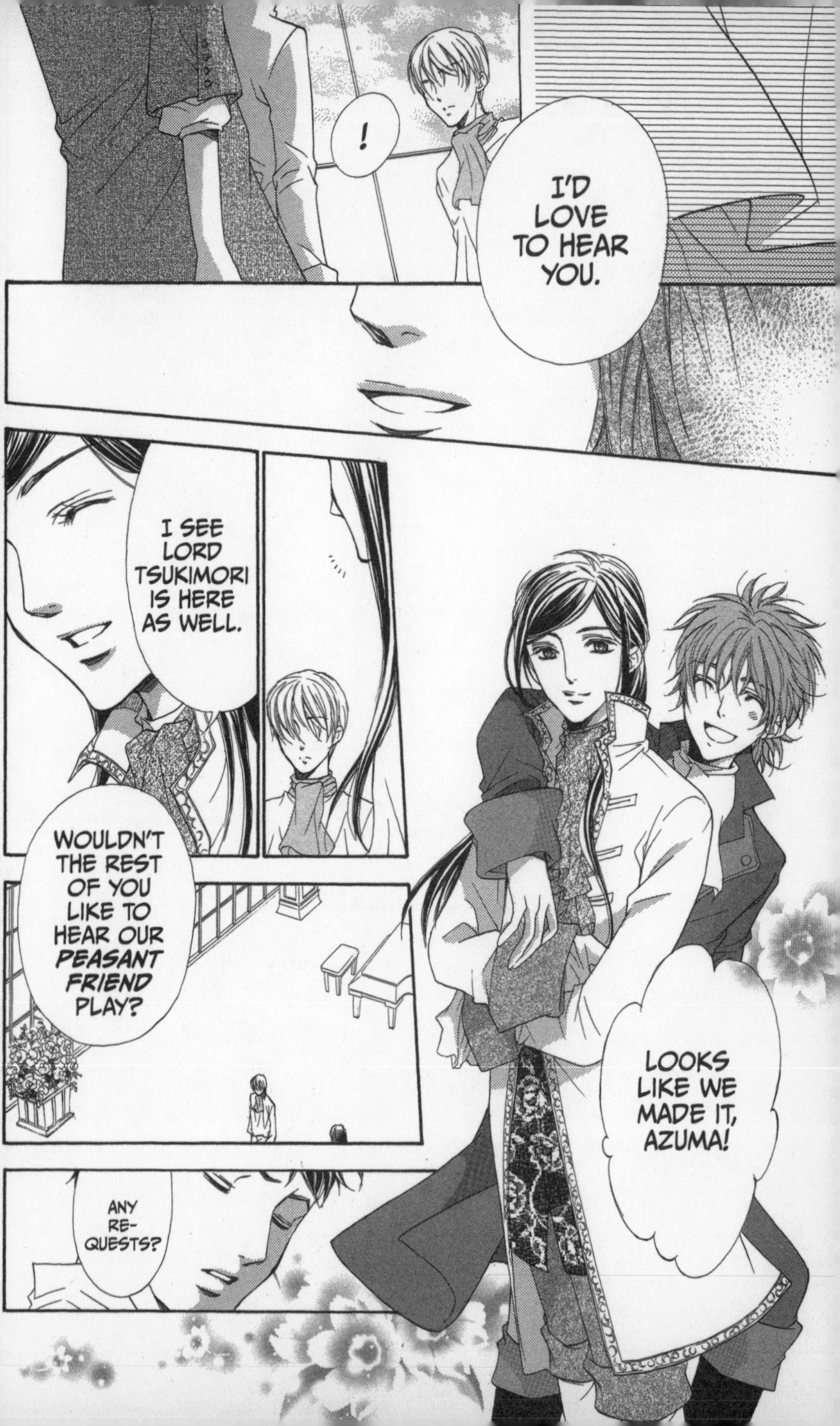
I'D LOVE TO HEAR YOU.
!
LOOKS LIKE WE MADE IT, AZUMA!
I SEE LORD TSUKIMORI IS HERE AS WELL.
WOULDN'T THE REST OF YOU LIKE TO HEAR OUR *PEASANT FRIEND* PLAY?
ANY RE-QUESTS?

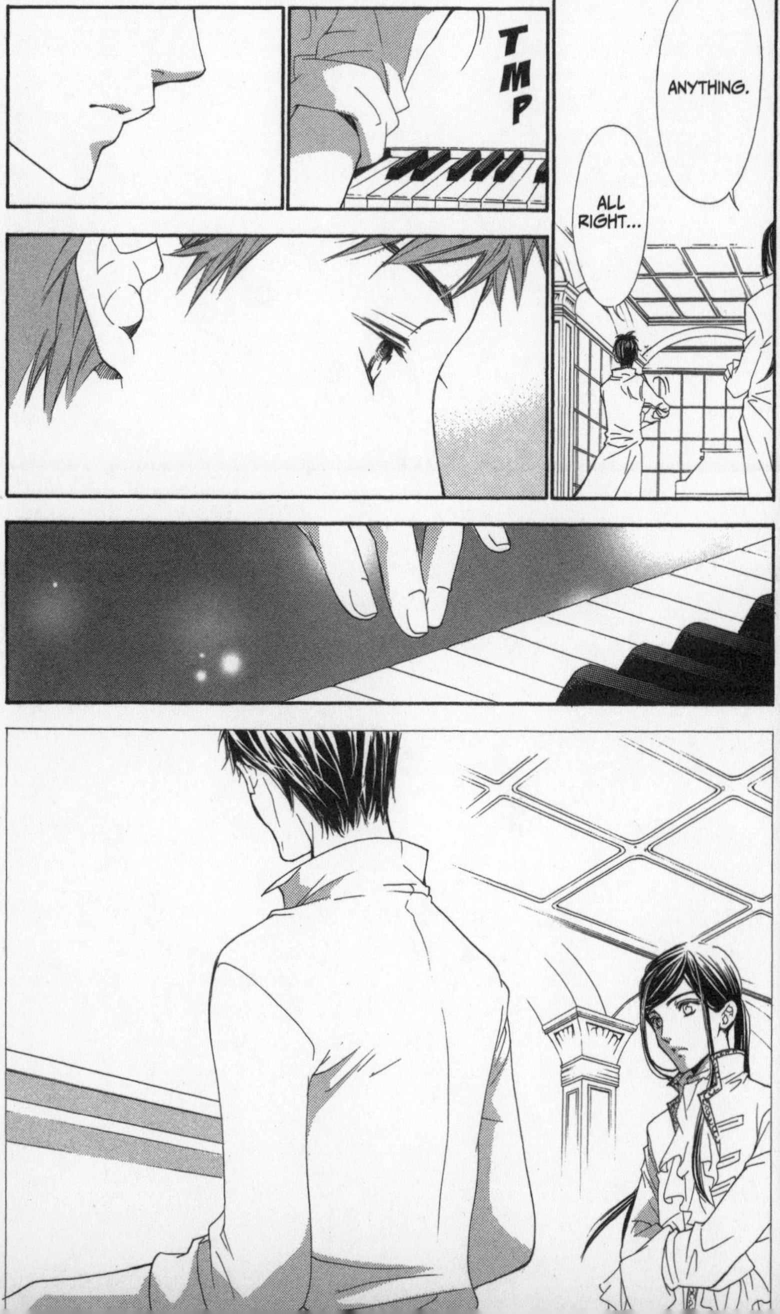
ANYTHING.
ALL RIGHT...
TMP

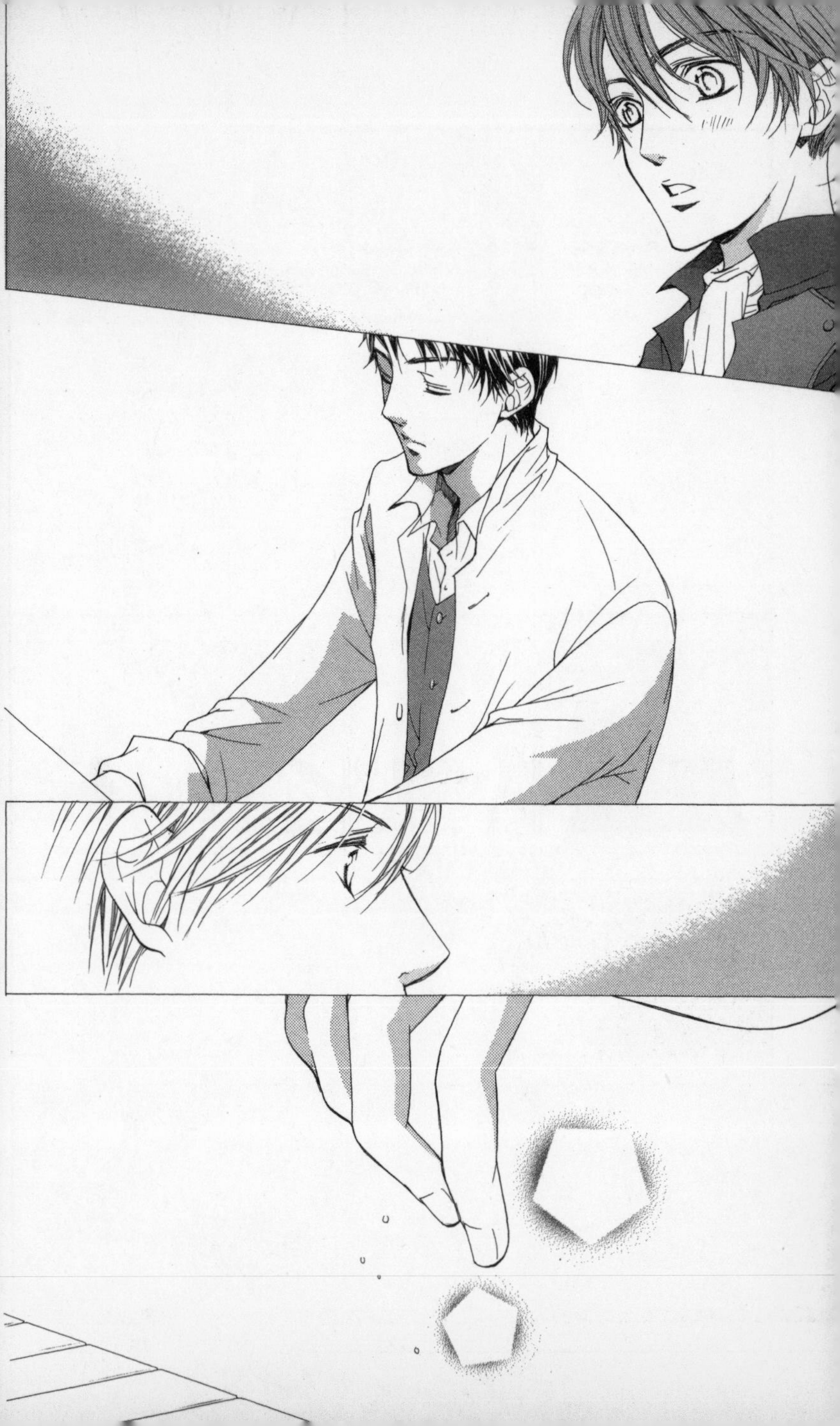

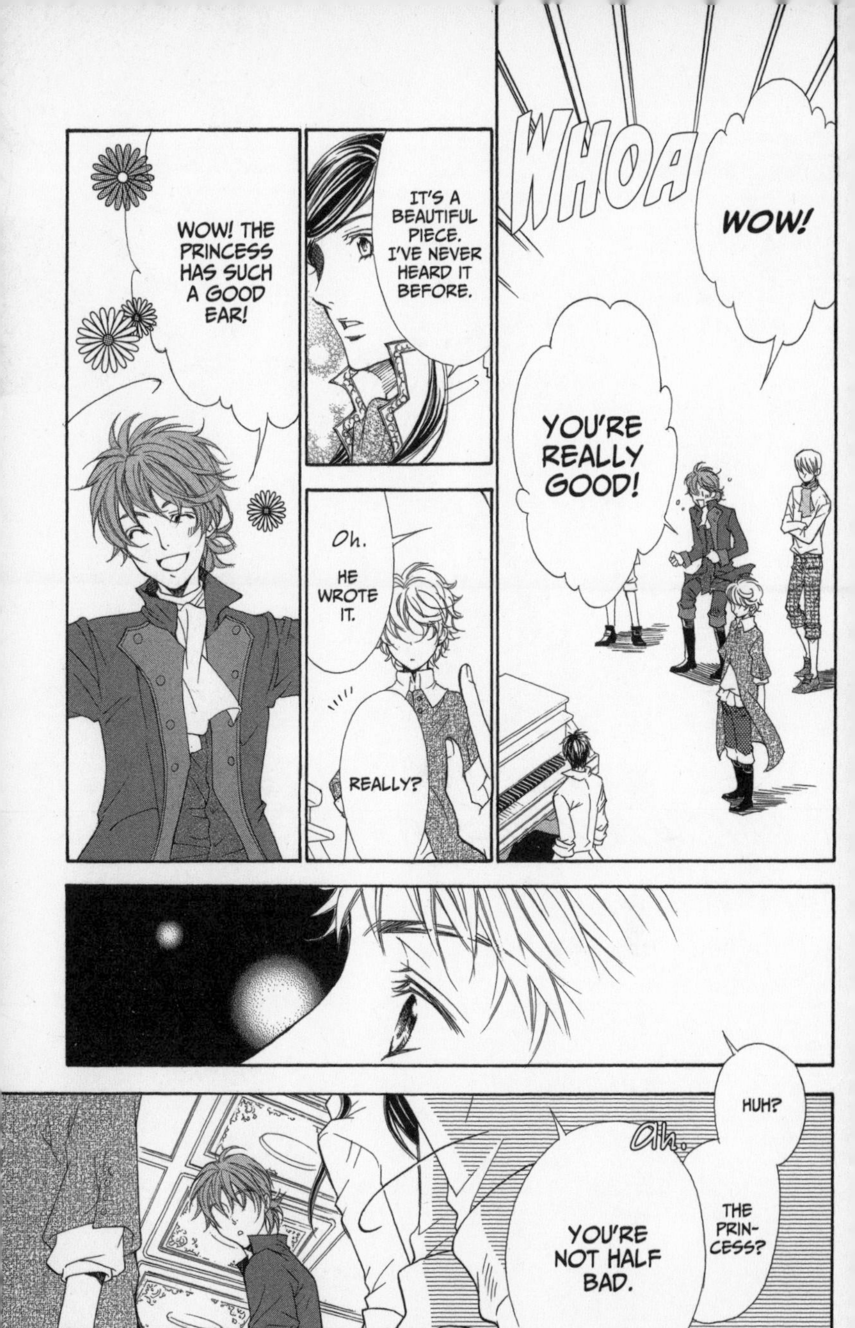
WHOA
WOW!
YOU'RE REALLY GOOD!
IT'S A BEAUTIFUL PIECE. I'VE NEVER HEARD IT BEFORE.
Oh.
HE WROTE IT.
REALLY?
WOW! THE PRINCESS HAS SUCH A GOOD EAR!
HUH?
THE PRIN-CESS?
Ah.
YOU'RE NOT HALF BAD.

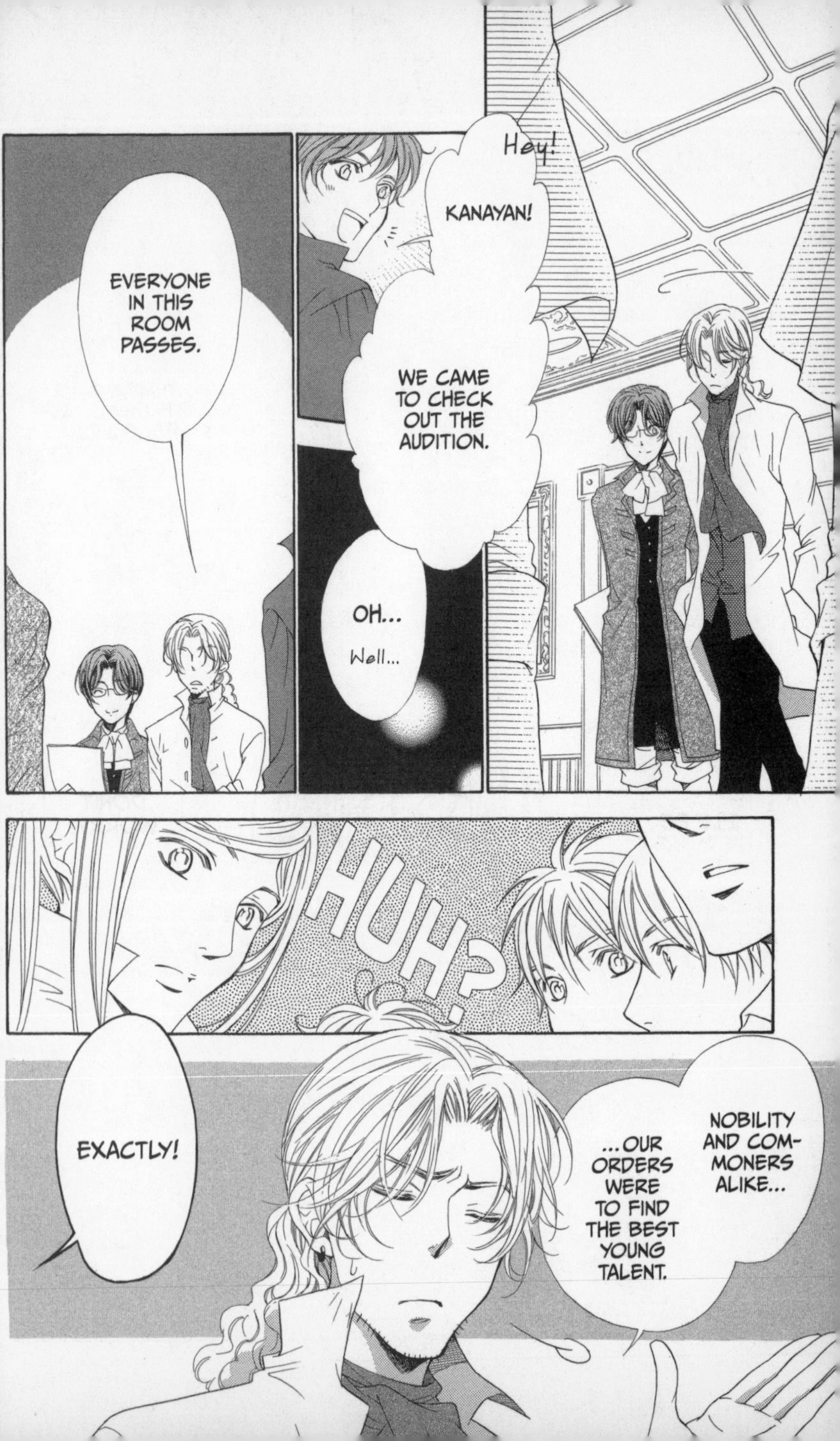
Hey!
KANAYAN!
WE CAME TO CHECK OUT THE AUDITION.
OH...
Well...
EVERYONE IN THIS ROOM PASSES.
HUH?
NOBILITY AND COMMONERS ALIKE...
...OUR ORDERS WERE TO FIND THE BEST YOUNG TALENT.
EXACTLY!

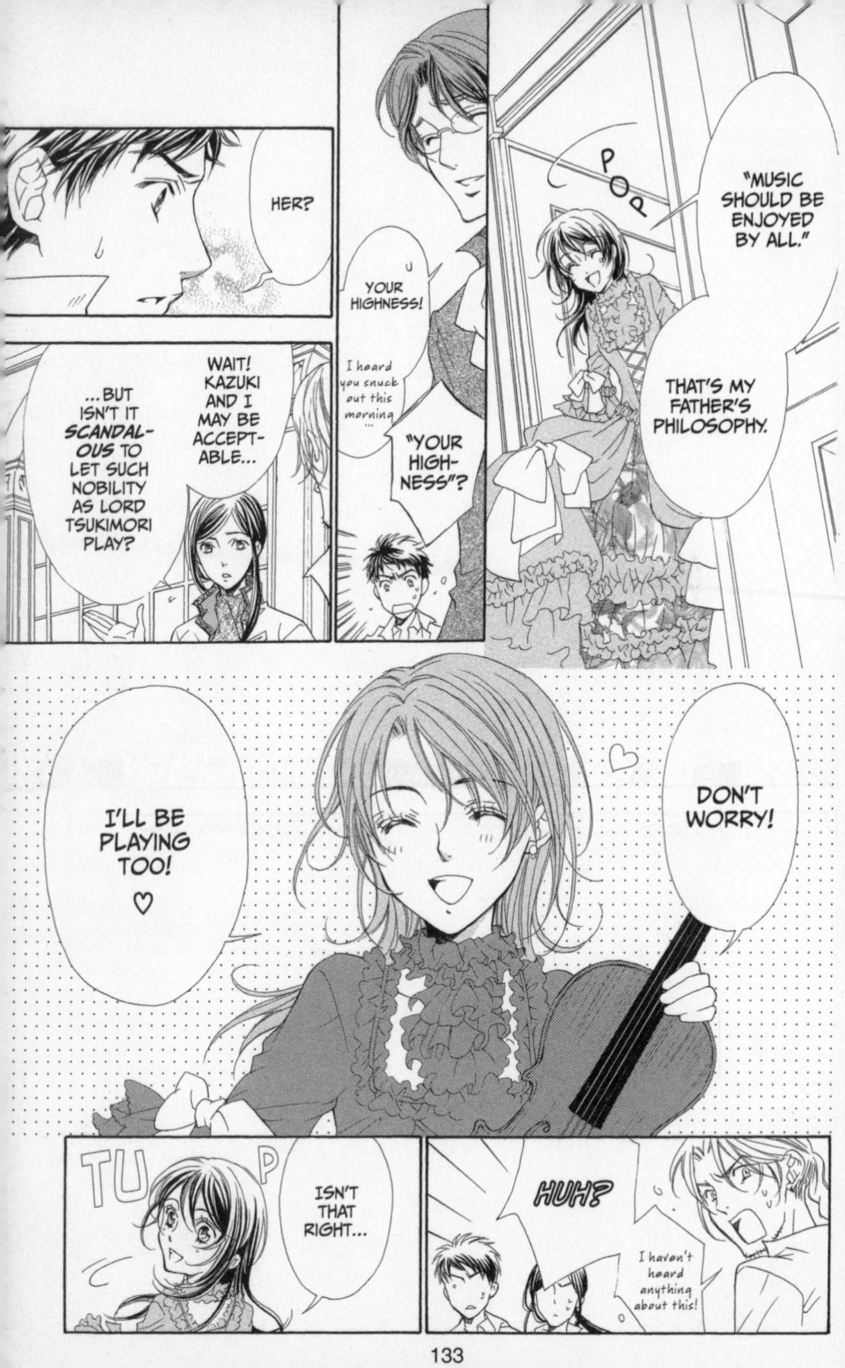
POP
"MUSIC SHOULD BE ENJOYED BY ALL."
THAT'S MY FATHER'S PHILOSOPHY.
YOUR HIGHNESS!
I heard you snuck out this morning...
"YOUR HIGHNESS"?
HER?
WAIT! KAZUKI AND I MAY BE ACCEPTABLE...
...BUT ISN'T IT *SCANDALOUS* TO LET SUCH NOBILITY AS LORD TSUKIMORI PLAY?
DON'T WORRY!
I'LL BE PLAYING TOO! ♡
HUH?
I haven't heard anything about this!
TUP
ISN'T THAT RIGHT...

...FATHER?
♡

OF COURSE!
♡

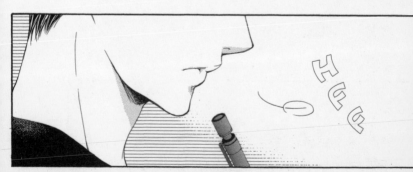

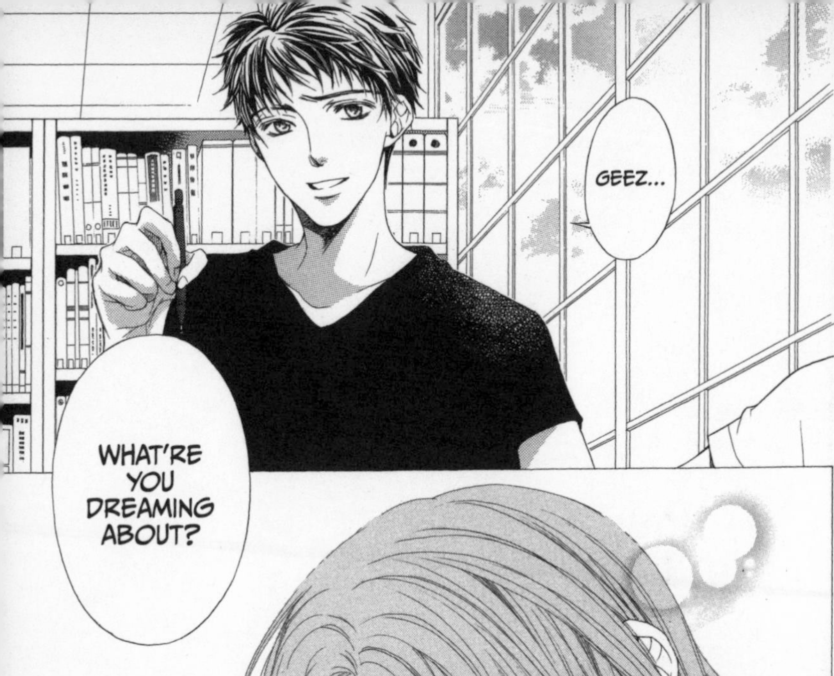
GEEZ...
WHAT'RE YOU DREAMING ABOUT?

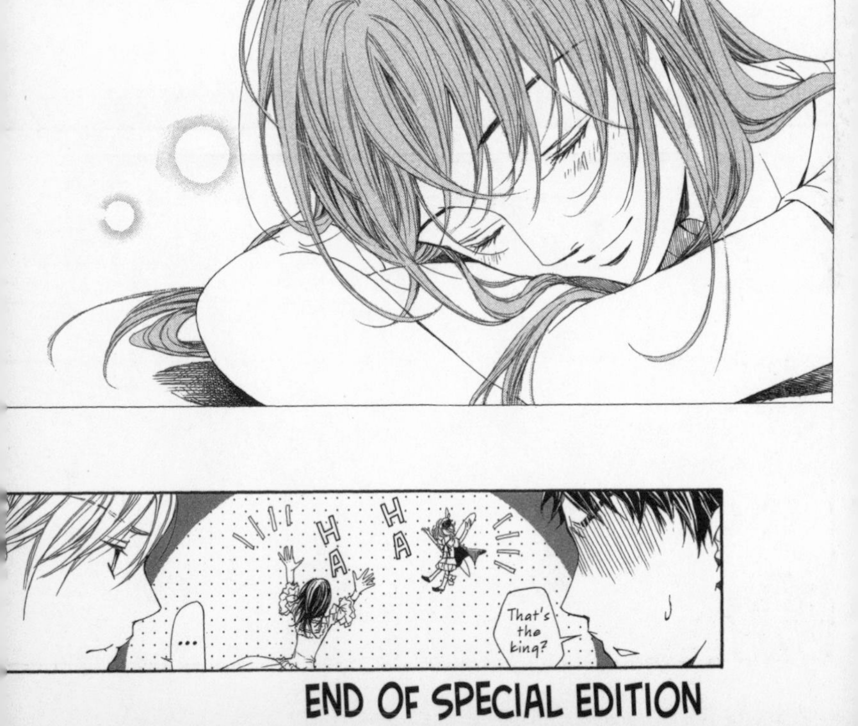
HA HA
That's the king?
...

END OF SPECIAL EDITION

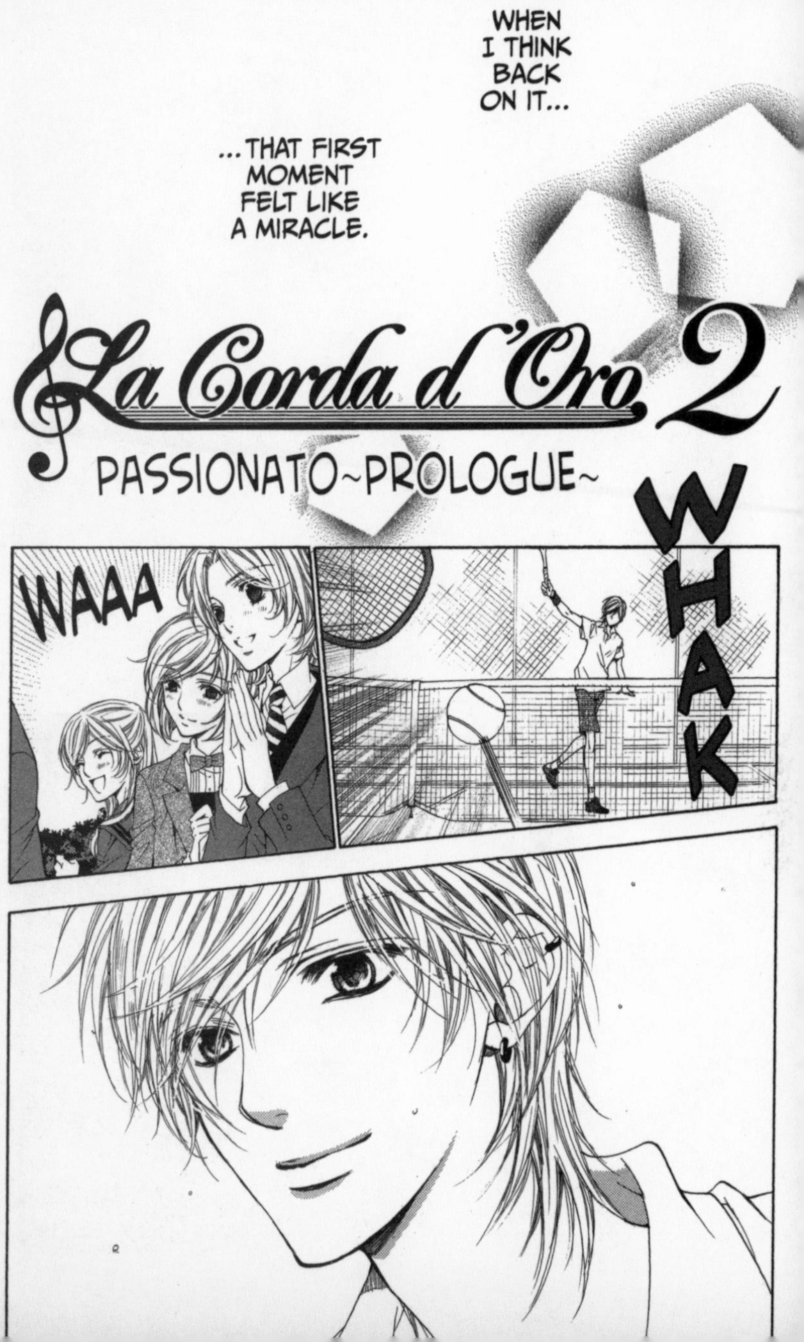
WHEN I THINK BACK ON IT...
...THAT FIRST MOMENT FELT LIKE A MIRACLE.
La Corda d'Oro 2
PASSIONATO~PROLOGUE~
WHAK
WAAA

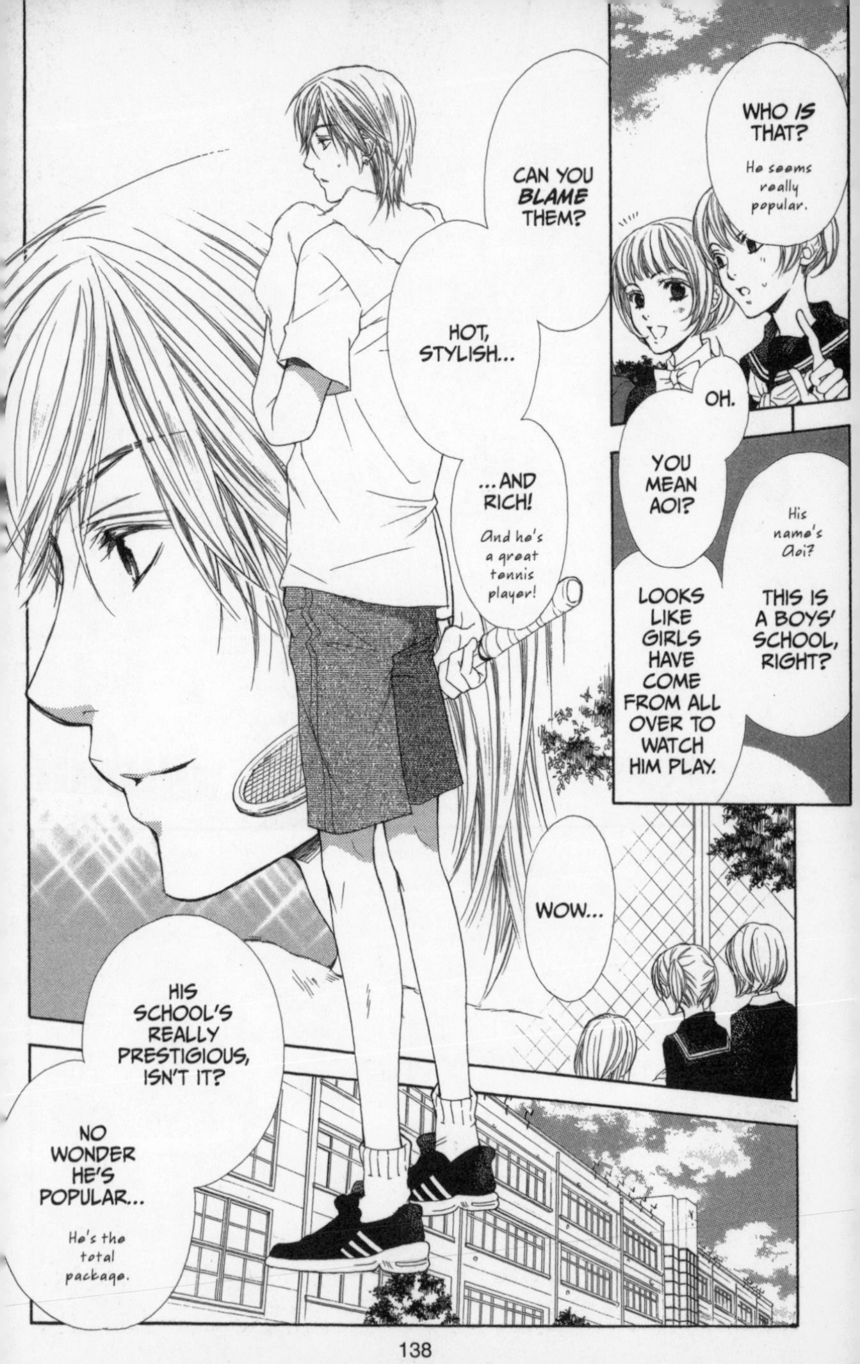

WHO *IS* THAT?
He seems really popular.
OH.
YOU MEAN AOI?
His name's Aoi?
THIS IS A BOYS' SCHOOL, RIGHT?
LOOKS LIKE GIRLS HAVE COME FROM ALL OVER TO WATCH HIM PLAY.
CAN YOU *BLAME* THEM?
HOT, STYLISH...
...AND RICH!
And he's a great tennis player!
WOW...
HIS SCHOOL'S REALLY PRESTIGIOUS, ISN'T IT?
NO WONDER HE'S POPULAR...
He's the total package.

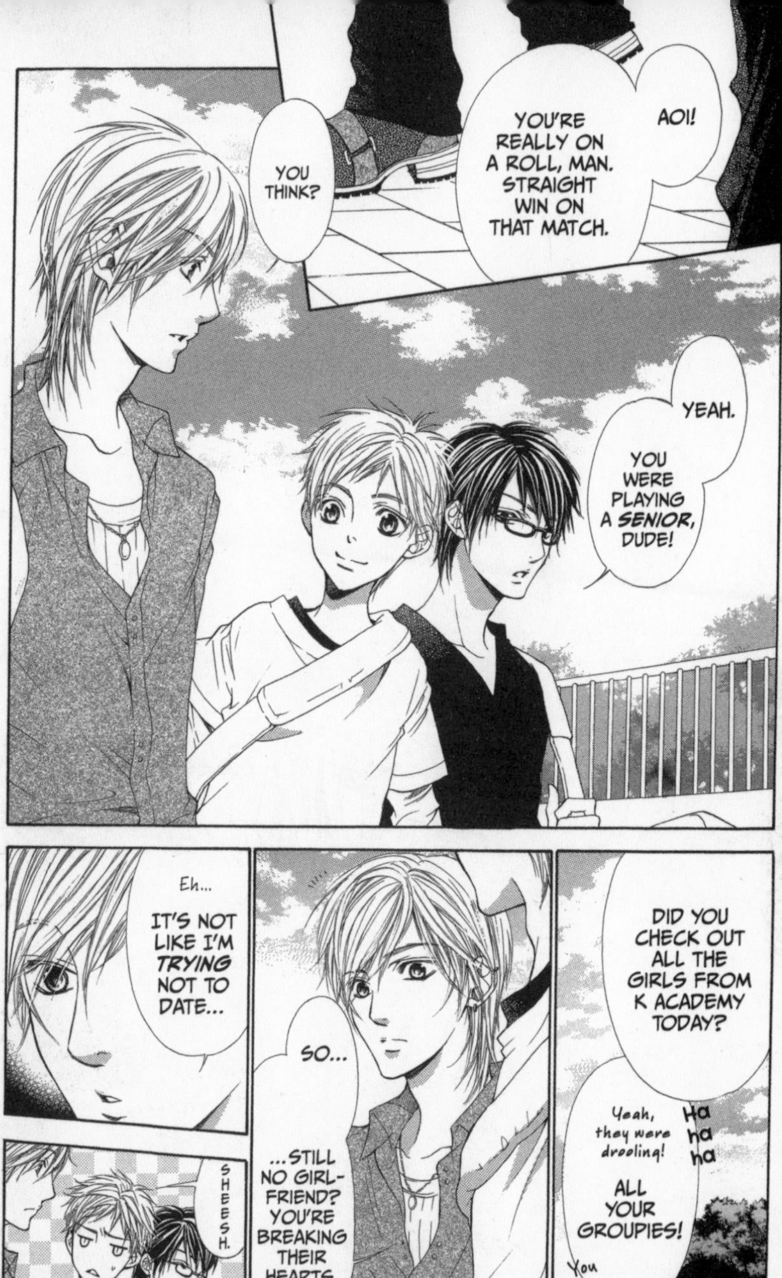
AOI!
YOU'RE REALLY ON A ROLL, MAN. STRAIGHT WIN ON THAT MATCH.
YOU THINK?
YEAH.
YOU WERE PLAYING A *SENIOR*, DUDE!
DID YOU CHECK OUT ALL THE GIRLS FROM K ACADEMY TODAY?
Yeah, they were drooling!
Ha ha ha
ALL YOUR GROUPIES!
You stud.
SO...
...STILL NO GIRL-FRIEND? YOU'RE BREAKING THEIR HEARTS.
Eh...
IT'S NOT LIKE I'M *TRYING* NOT TO DATE...
SHEESH.
HA HA

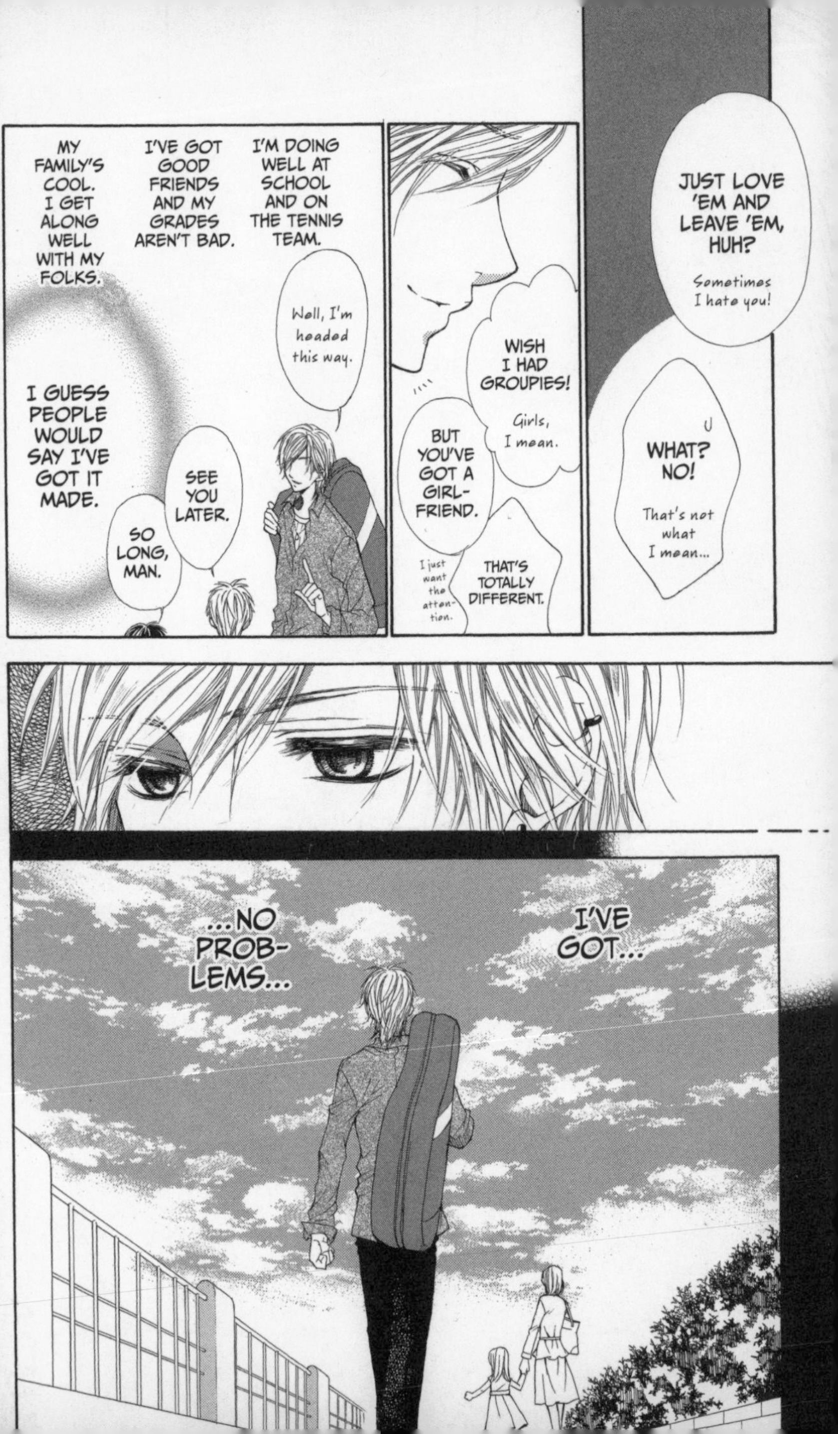
JUST LOVE 'EM AND LEAVE 'EM, HUH?
Sometimes I hate you!
WHAT? NO!
That's not what I mean...
WISH I HAD GROUPIES!
Girls, I mean.
BUT YOU'VE GOT A GIRLFRIEND.
THAT'S TOTALLY DIFFERENT.
I just want the attention.
I'M DOING WELL AT SCHOOL AND ON THE TENNIS TEAM.
I'VE GOT GOOD FRIENDS AND MY GRADES AREN'T BAD.
MY FAMILY'S COOL. I GET ALONG WELL WITH MY FOLKS.
Well, I'm headed this way.
SEE YOU LATER.
I GUESS PEOPLE WOULD SAY I'VE GOT IT MADE.
SO LONG, MAN.
I'VE GOT...
...NO PROBLEMS...

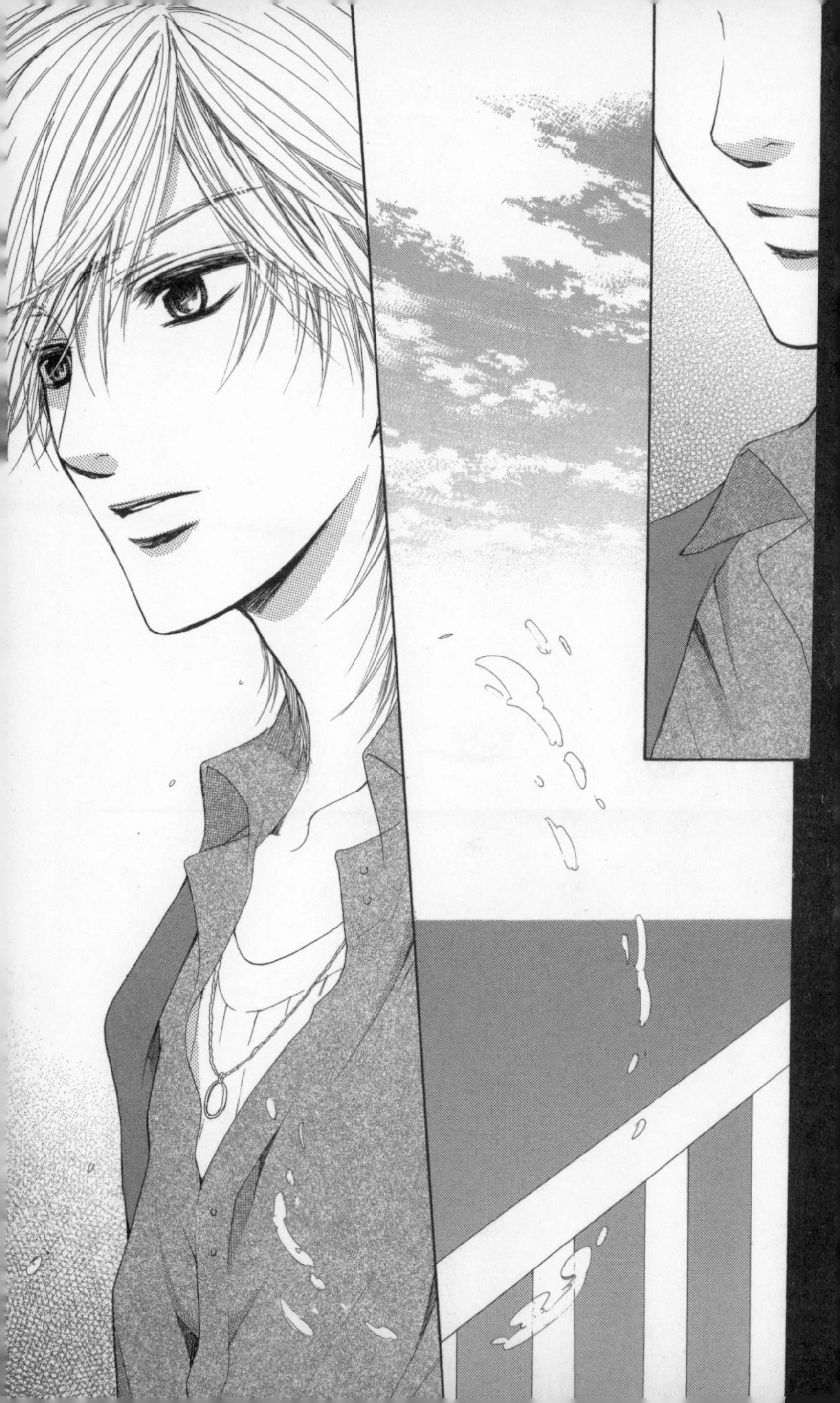

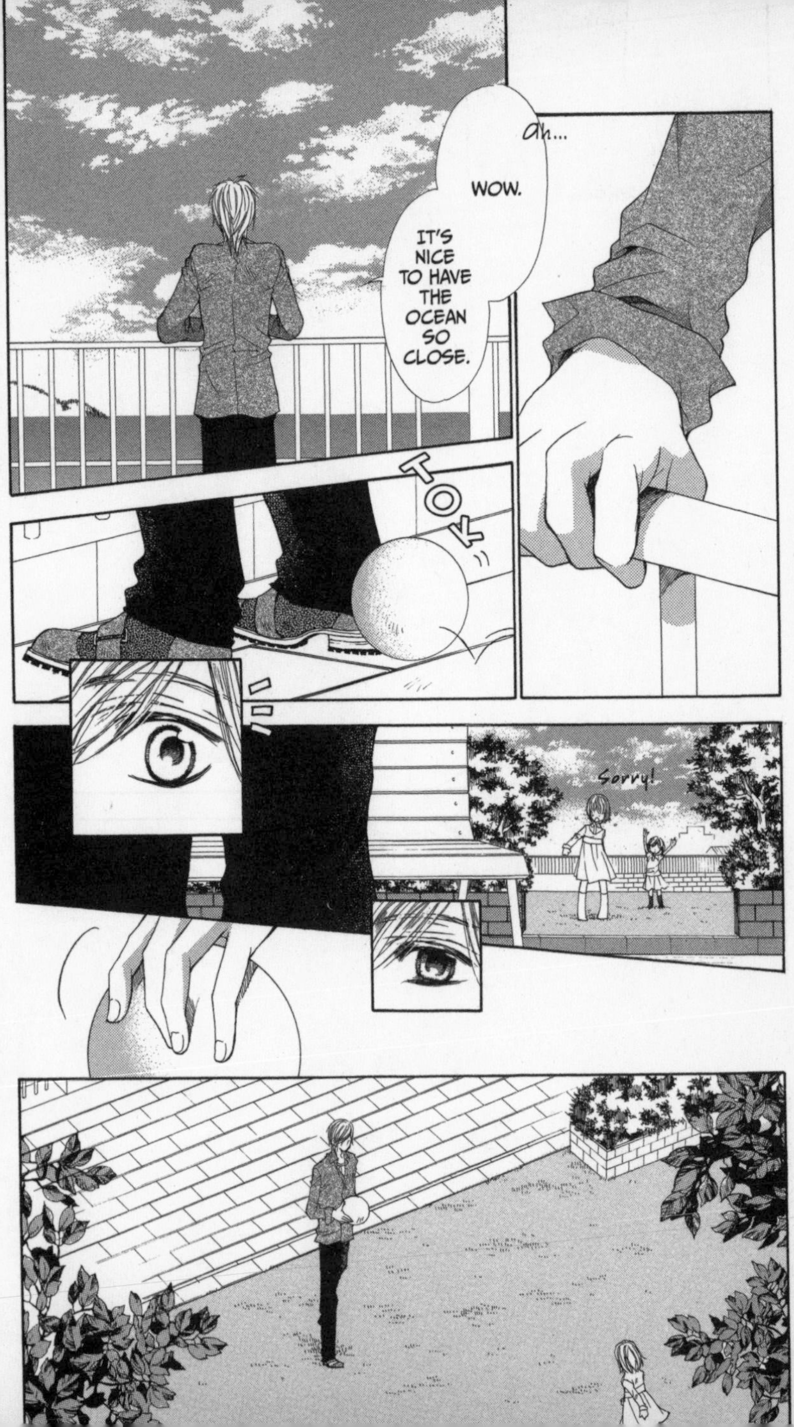
ah...
WOW.
IT'S NICE TO HAVE THE OCEAN SO CLOSE.
TOK
Sorry!

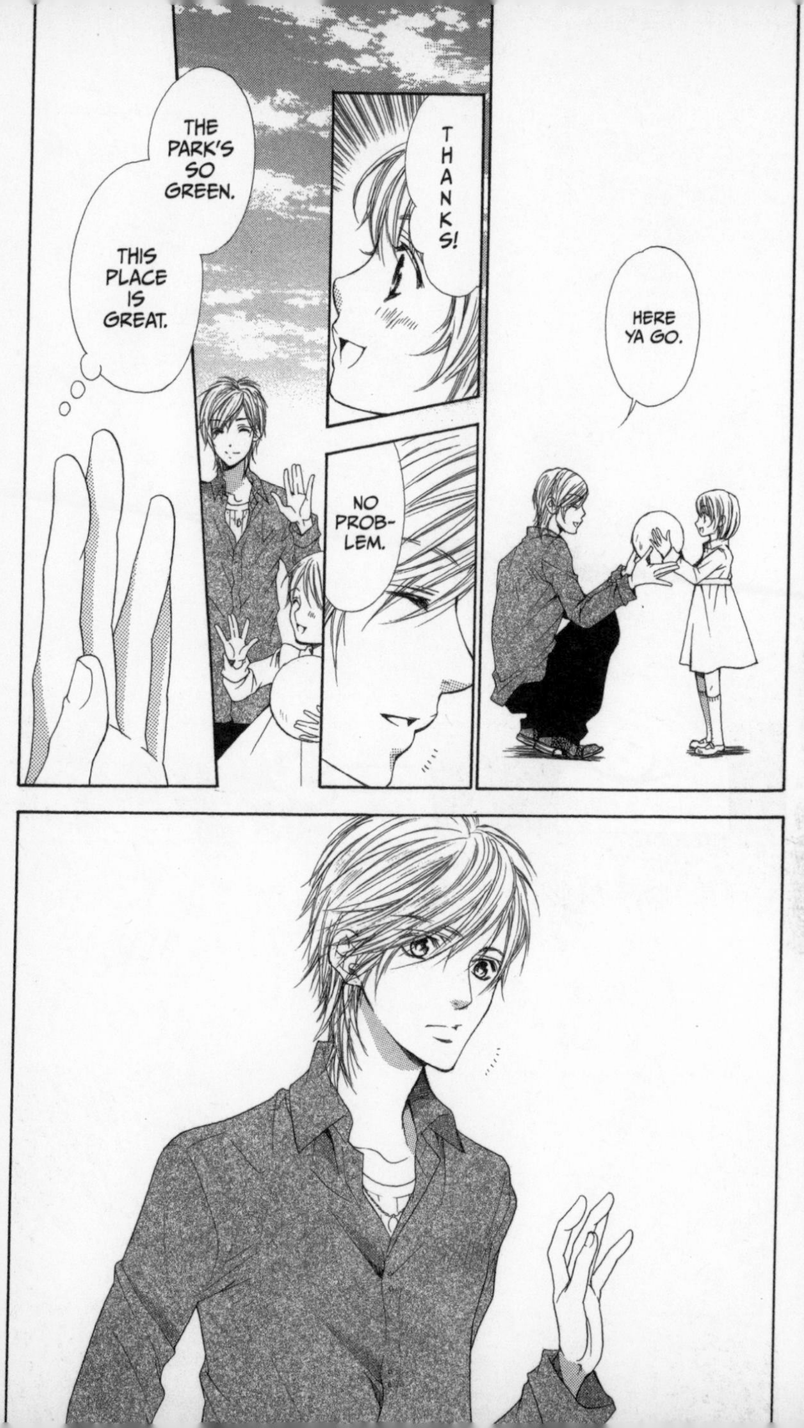
HERE YA GO.
THANKS!
NO PROB-LEM.
THE PARK'S SO GREEN.
THIS PLACE IS GREAT.

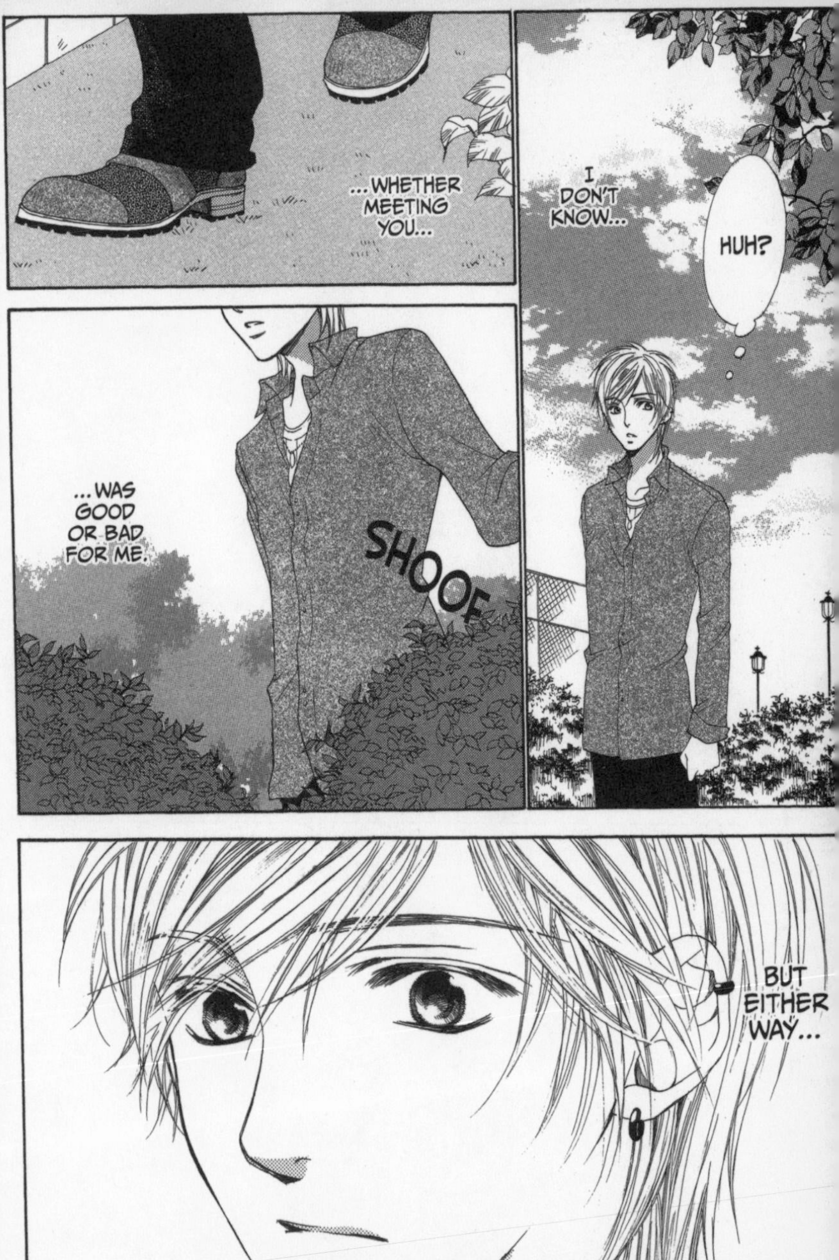
I DON'T KNOW...
HUH?
...WHETHER MEETING YOU...
...WAS GOOD OR BAD FOR ME.
SHOOF
BUT EITHER WAY...

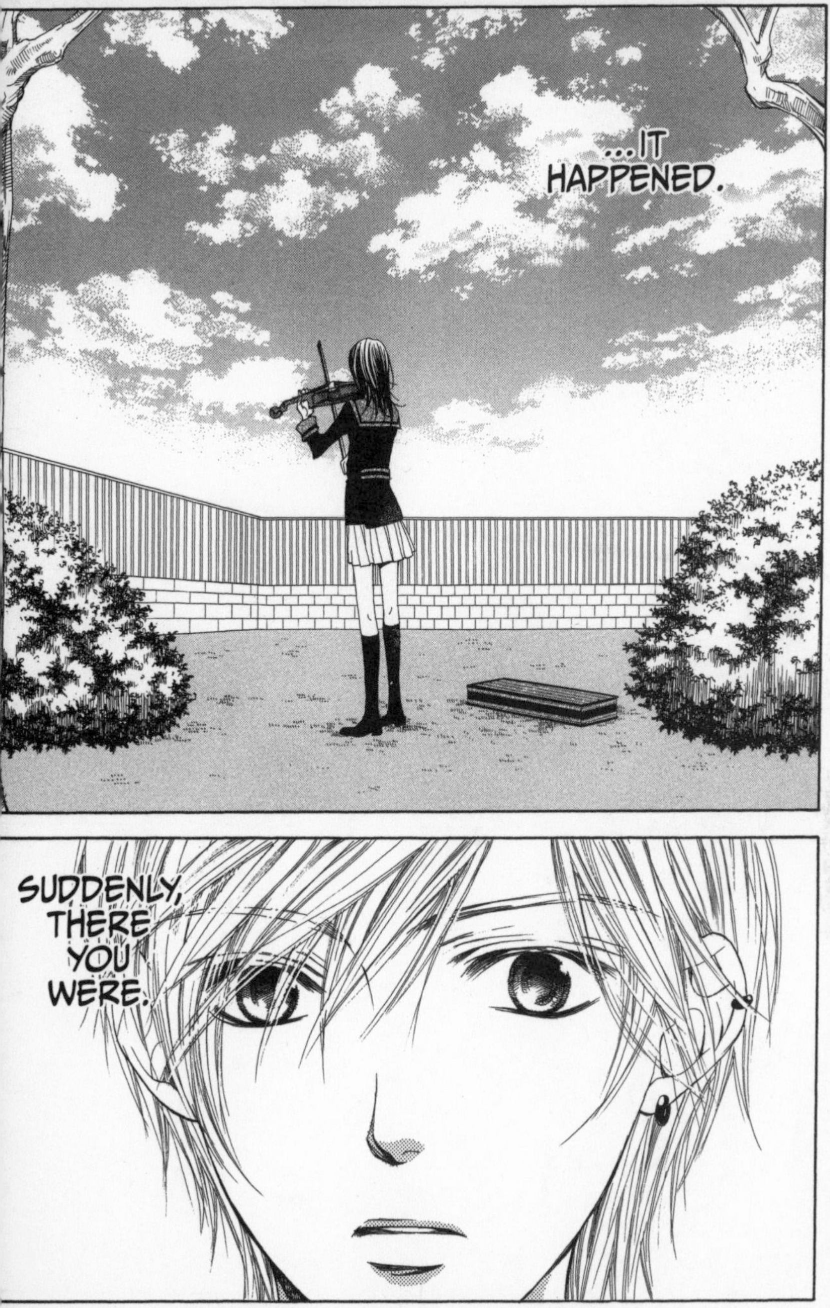
...IT HAPPENED.
SUDDENLY, THERE YOU WERE.

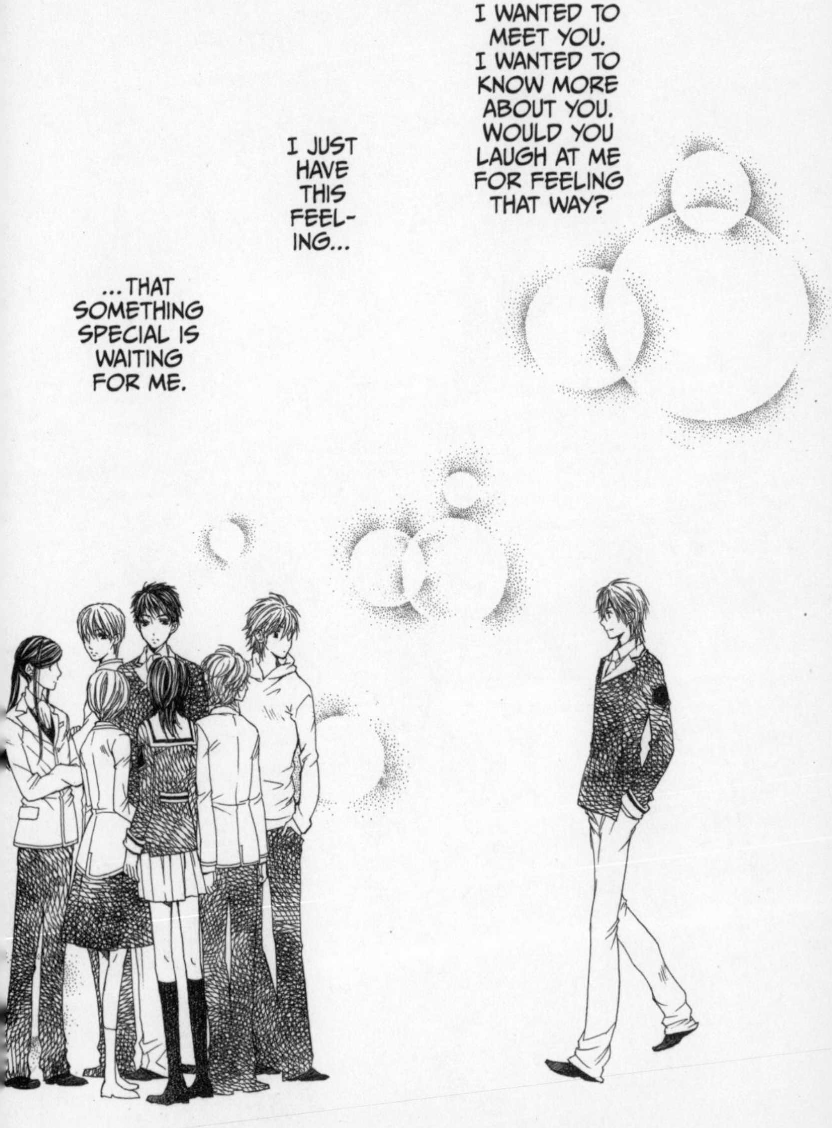
I WANTED TO MEET YOU. I WANTED TO KNOW MORE ABOUT YOU. WOULD YOU LAUGH AT ME FOR FEELING THAT WAY?
I JUST HAVE THIS FEEL- ING...
...THAT SOMETHING SPECIAL IS WAITING FOR ME.

END OF PASSIONATO~PROLOGUE~

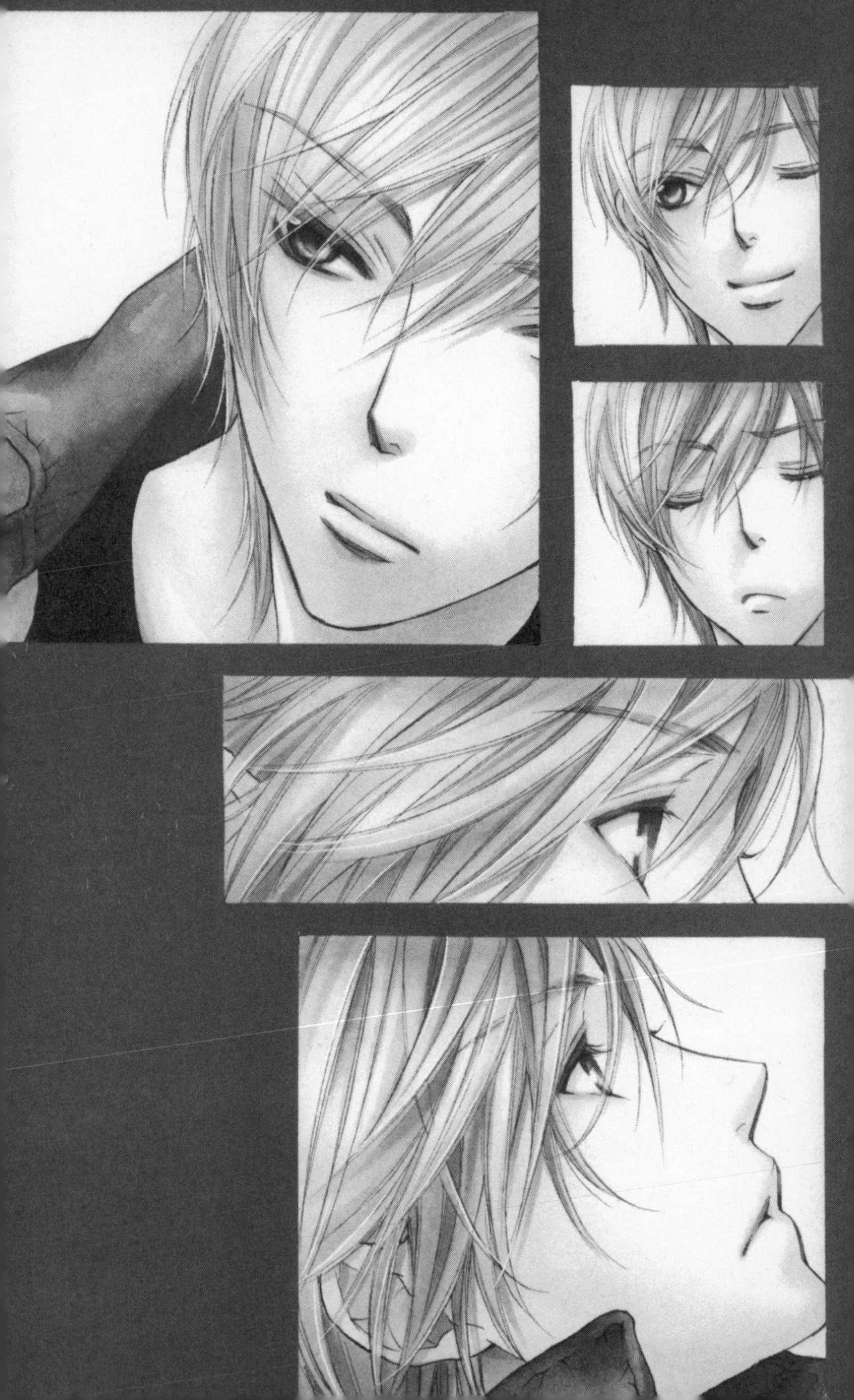

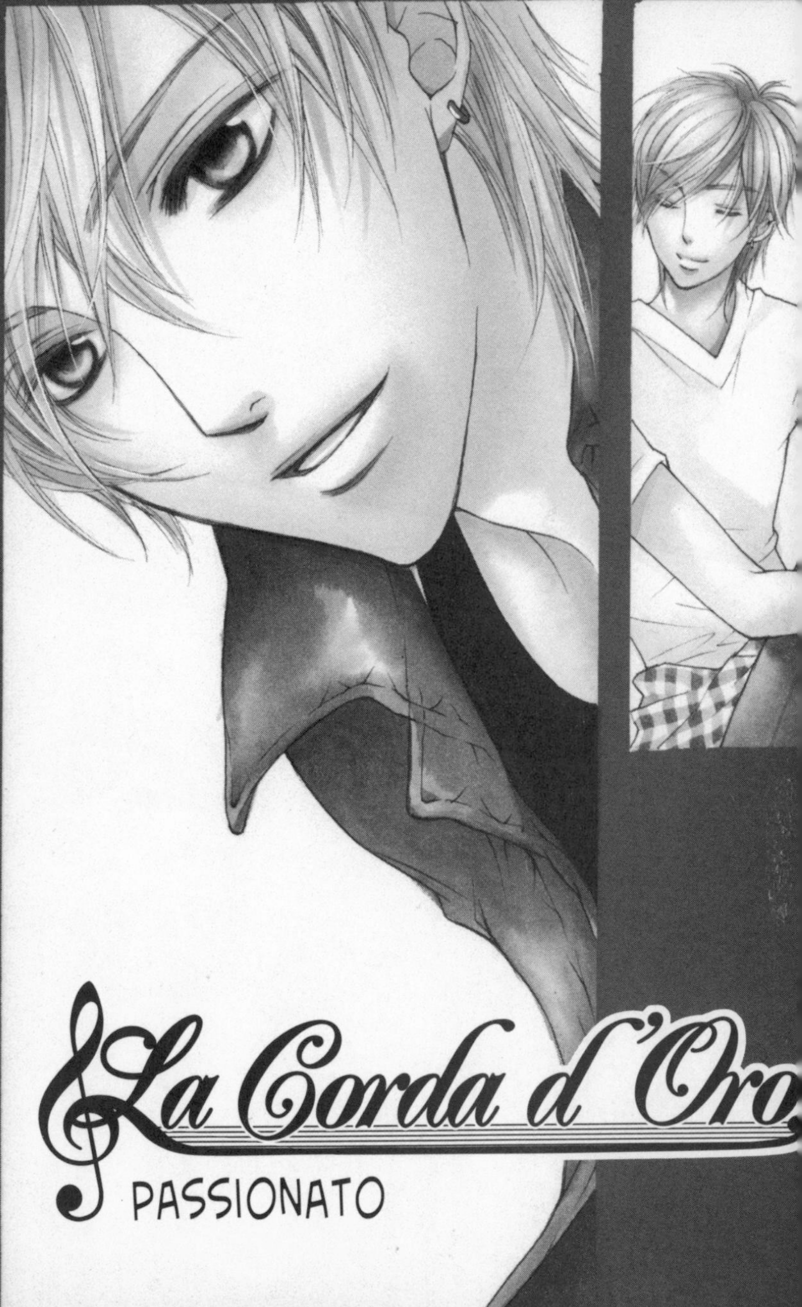
La Corda d'Oro
PASSIONATO

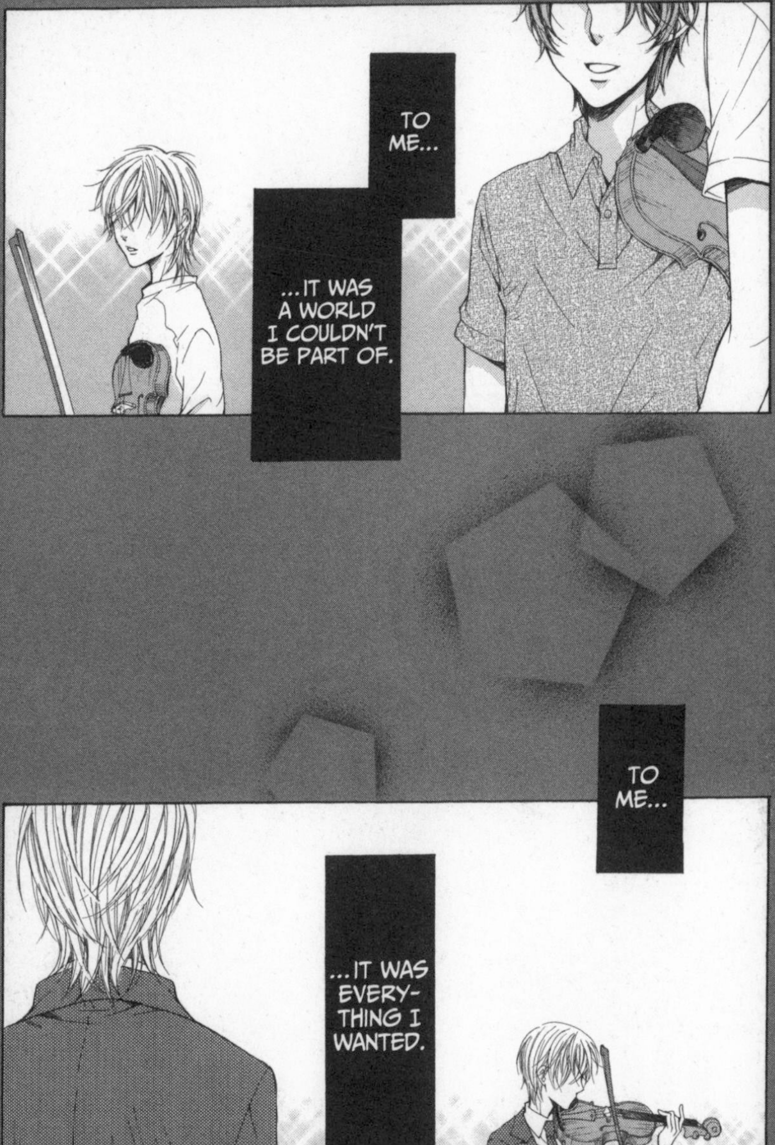
TO ME...
...IT WAS A WORLD I COULDN'T BE PART OF.
TO ME...
...IT WAS EVERY-THING I WANTED.

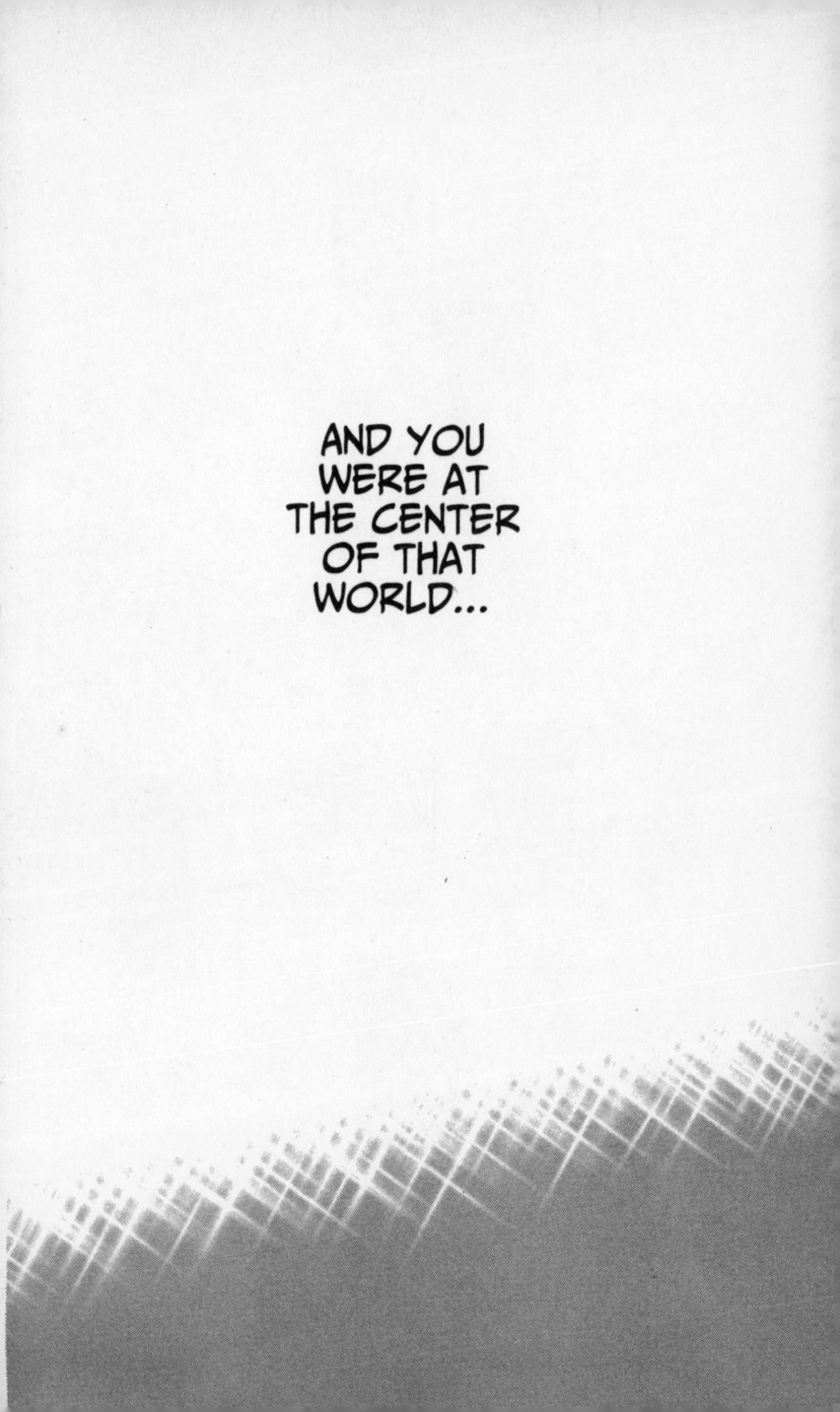
AND YOU WERE AT THE CENTER OF THAT WORLD...

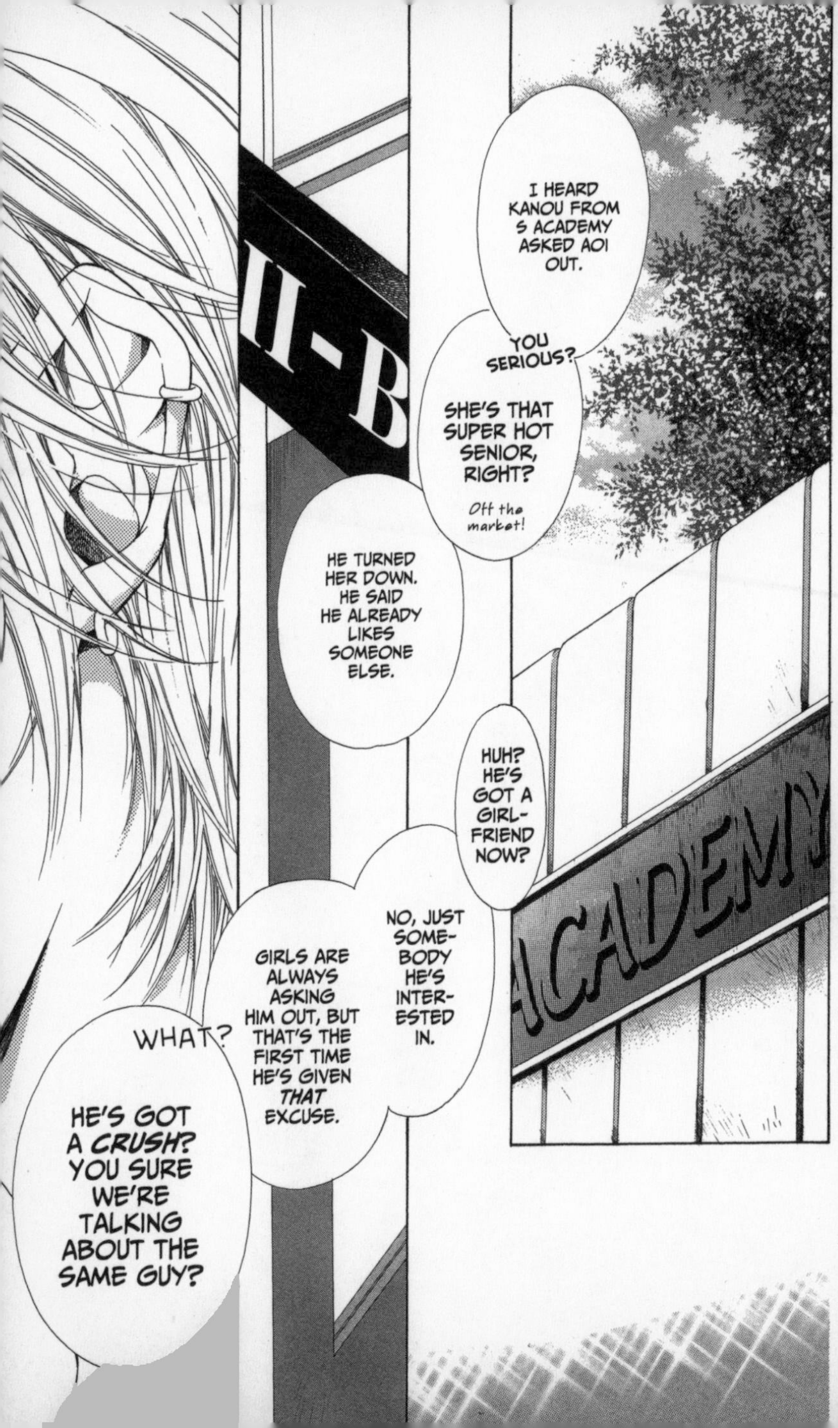

I HEARD KANOU FROM S ACADEMY ASKED AOI OUT.
YOU SERIOUS?
SHE'S THAT SUPER HOT SENIOR, RIGHT?
Off the market!
HE TURNED HER DOWN. HE SAID HE ALREADY LIKES SOMEONE ELSE.
HUH? HE'S GOT A GIRLFRIEND NOW?
ACADEMY
NO, JUST SOMEBODY HE'S INTERESTED IN.
GIRLS ARE ALWAYS ASKING HIM OUT, BUT THAT'S THE FIRST TIME HE'S GIVEN *THAT* EXCUSE.
II-B
WHAT?
HE'S GOT A *CRUSH*? YOU SURE WE'RE TALKING ABOUT THE SAME GUY?

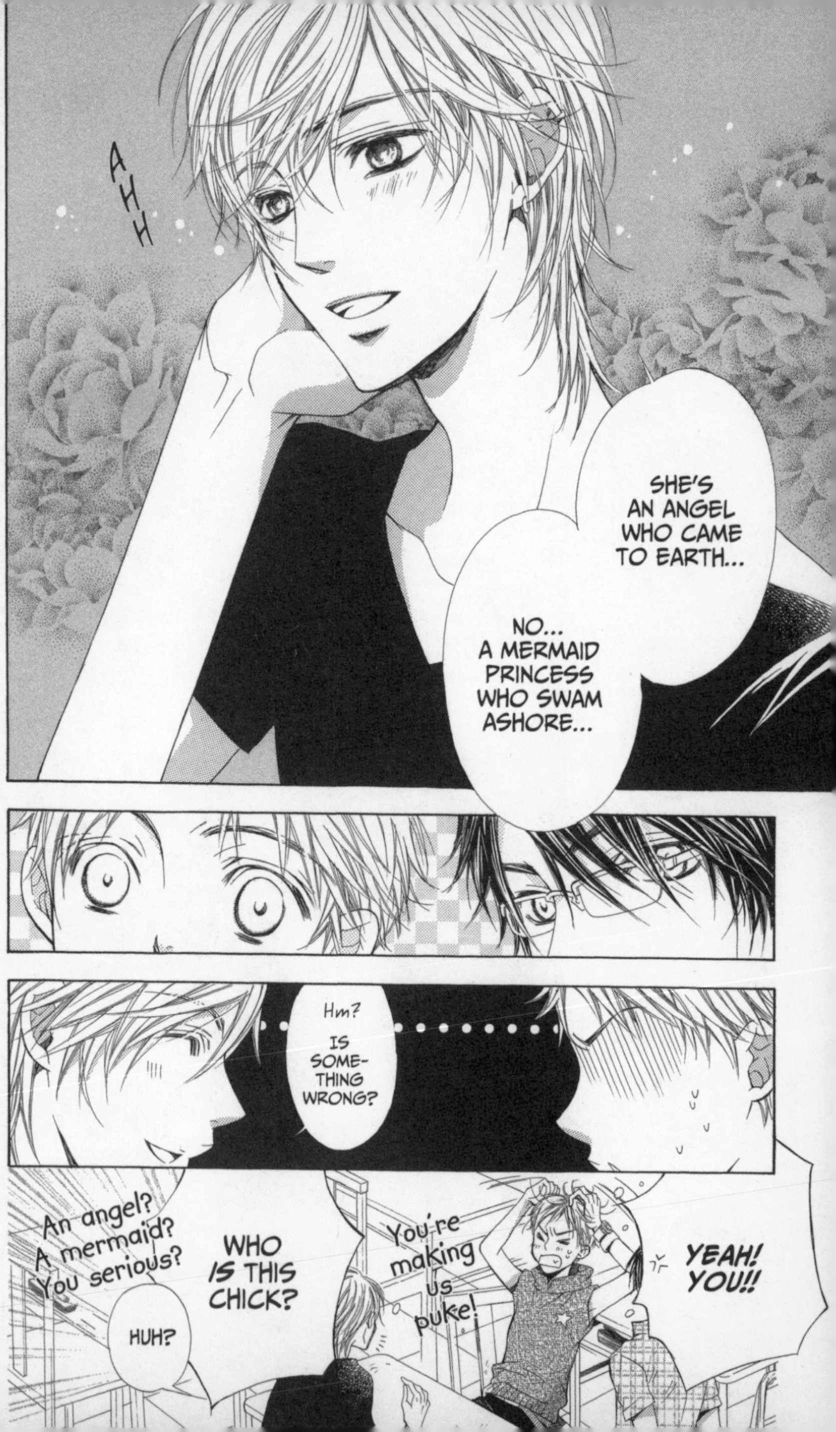
AHHH
SHE'S AN ANGEL WHO CAME TO EARTH...
NO... A MERMAID PRINCESS WHO SWAM ASHORE...
Hm? IS SOME-THING WRONG?
YEAH! YOU!!
You're making us puke!
WHO *IS* THIS CHICK?
An angel? A mermaid? You serious?
HUH?

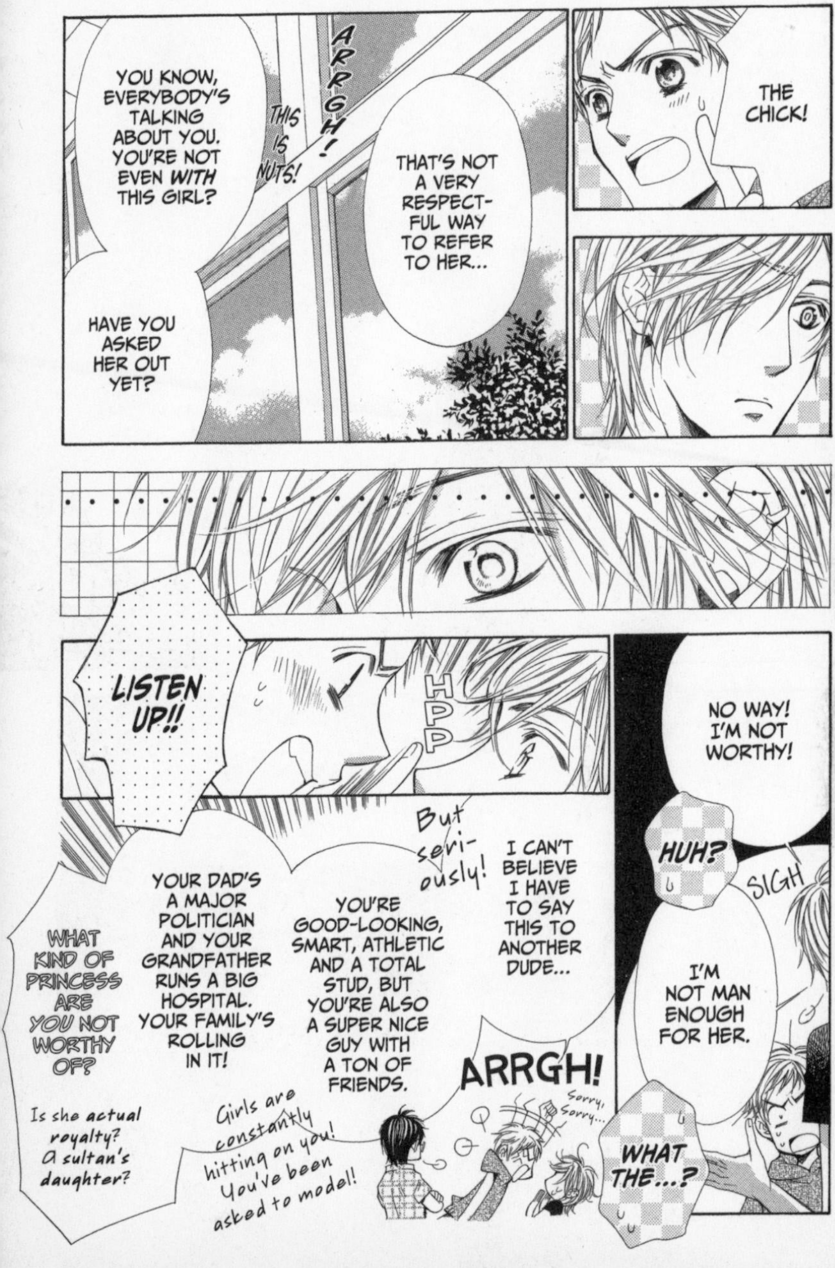
THE CHICK!
ARRGH!
THAT'S NOT A VERY RESPECT-FUL WAY TO REFER TO HER...
THIS IS NUTS!
YOU KNOW, EVERYBODY'S TALKING ABOUT YOU. YOU'RE NOT EVEN WITH THIS GIRL?
HAVE YOU ASKED HER OUT YET?
NO WAY! I'M NOT WORTHY!
HUH?
SIGH
I'M NOT MAN ENOUGH FOR HER.
Sorry, Sorry...
WHAT THE...?
HPP
LISTEN UP!!
But seri-ously!
I CAN'T BELIEVE I HAVE TO SAY THIS TO ANOTHER DUDE...
YOU'RE GOOD-LOOKING, SMART, ATHLETIC AND A TOTAL STUD, BUT YOU'RE ALSO A SUPER NICE GUY WITH A TON OF FRIENDS.
YOUR DAD'S A MAJOR POLITICIAN AND YOUR GRANDFATHER RUNS A BIG HOSPITAL. YOUR FAMILY'S ROLLING IN IT!
WHAT KIND OF PRINCESS ARE YOU NOT WORTHY OF?
ARRGH!
Girls are constantly hitting on you! You've been asked to model!
Is she actual royalty? A sultan's daughter?

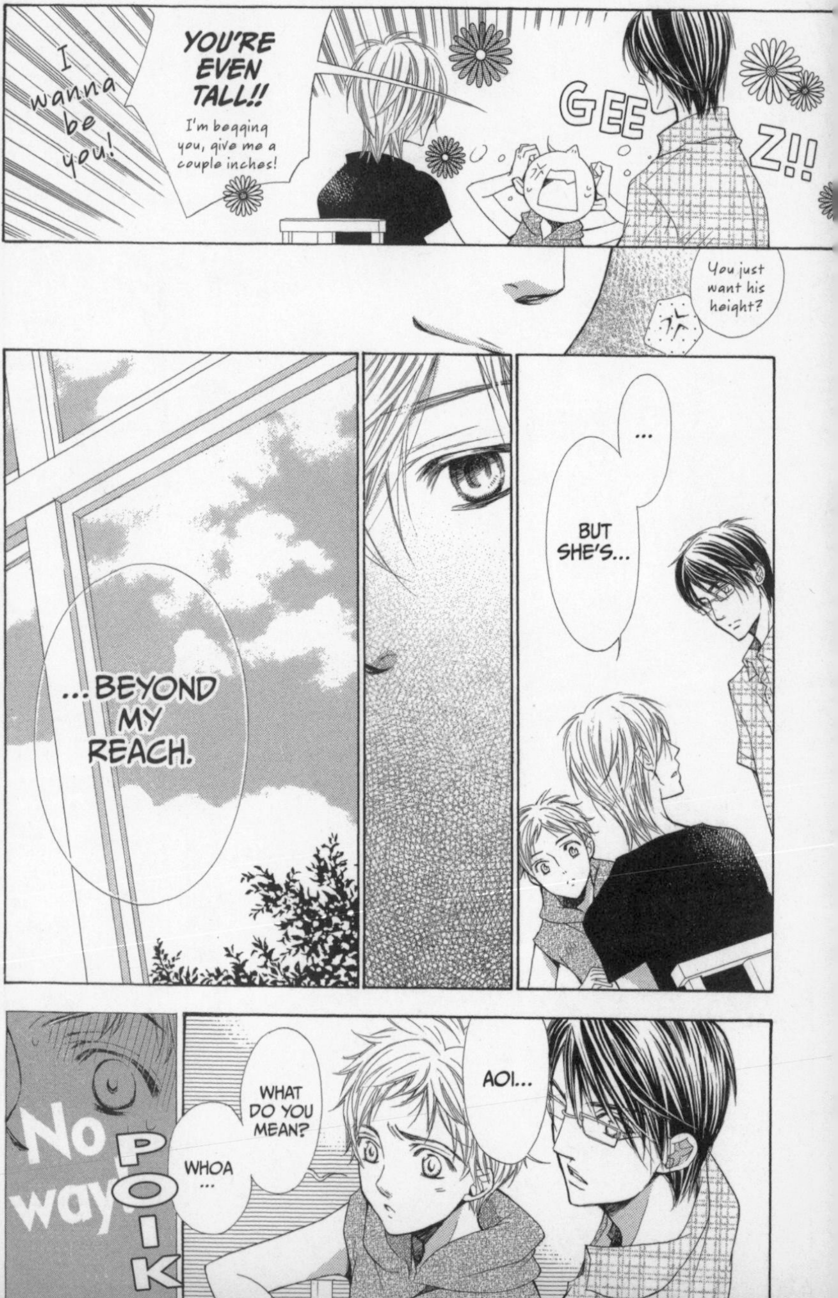
GEEZ!!
YOU'RE EVEN TALL!!
I'm begging you, give me a couple inches!
I wanna be you!
You just want his height?
...
BUT SHE'S...
...BEYOND MY REACH.
AOI...
WHAT DO YOU MEAN?
WHOA ...
POIK
No way!

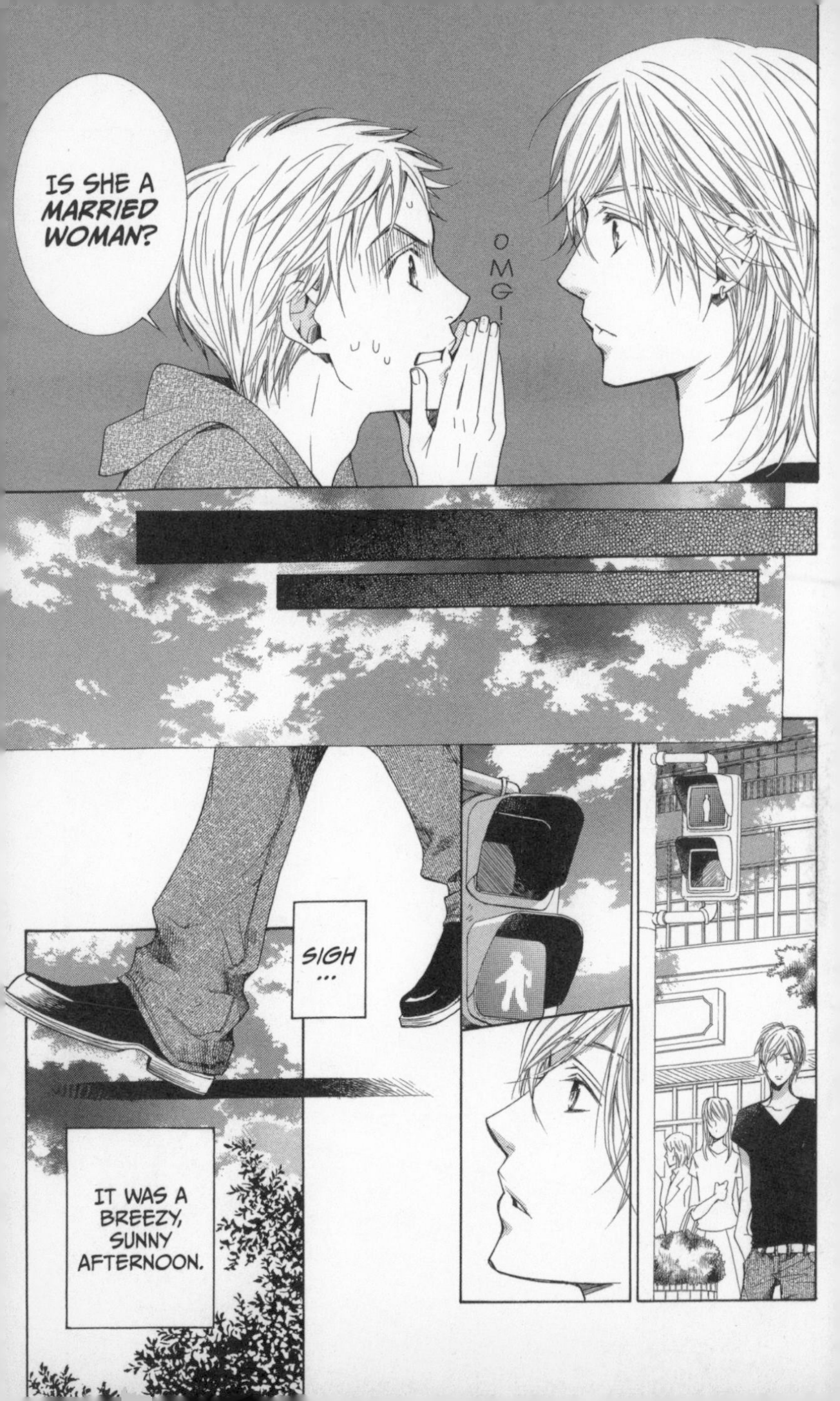
IS SHE A MARRIED WOMAN?
OMG!
SIGH...
IT WAS A BREEZY, SUNNY AFTERNOON.

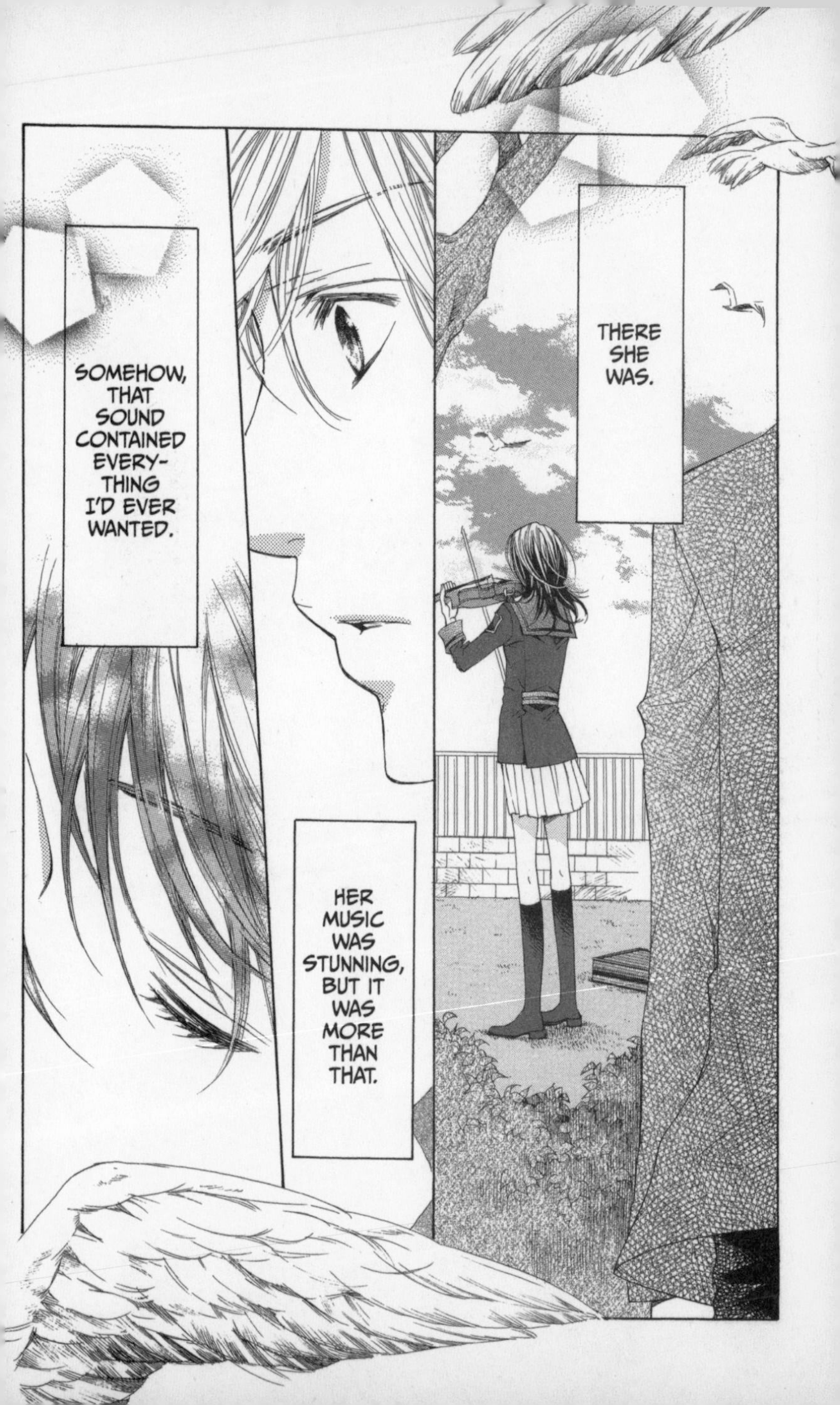

THERE SHE WAS.
HER MUSIC WAS STUNNING, BUT IT WAS MORE THAN THAT.
SOMEHOW, THAT SOUND CONTAINED EVERY-THING I'D EVER WANTED.

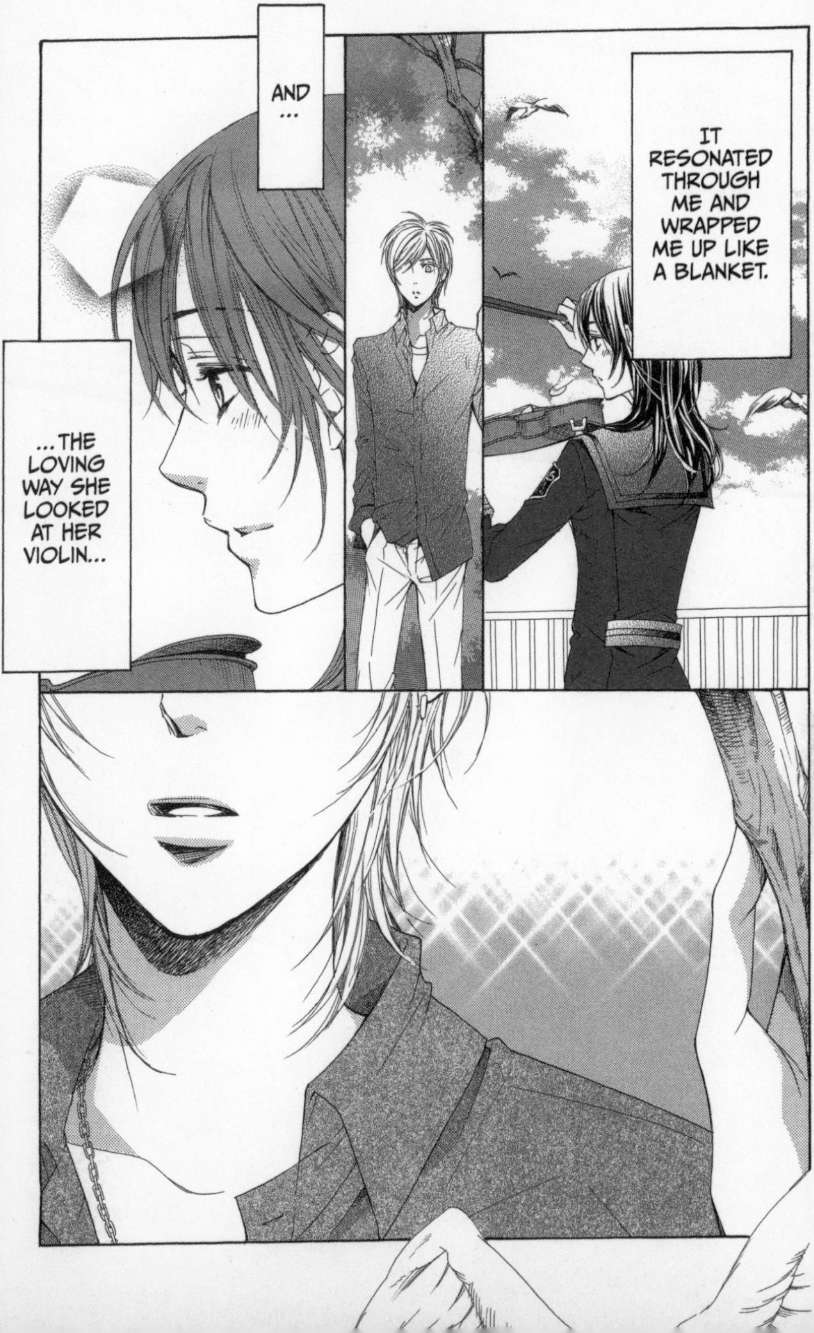

IT RESONATED THROUGH ME AND WRAPPED ME UP LIKE A BLANKET.
AND ...
...THE LOVING WAY SHE LOOKED AT HER VIOLIN...

THE IMAGE IS SEARED INTO MY HEART.

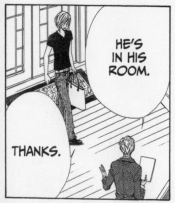

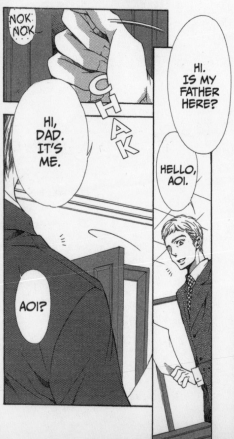

HE'S IN HIS ROOM.
THANKS.
HI. IS MY FATHER HERE?
HELLO, AOI.
NOK NOK
CHAK
HI, DAD. IT'S ME.
AOI?

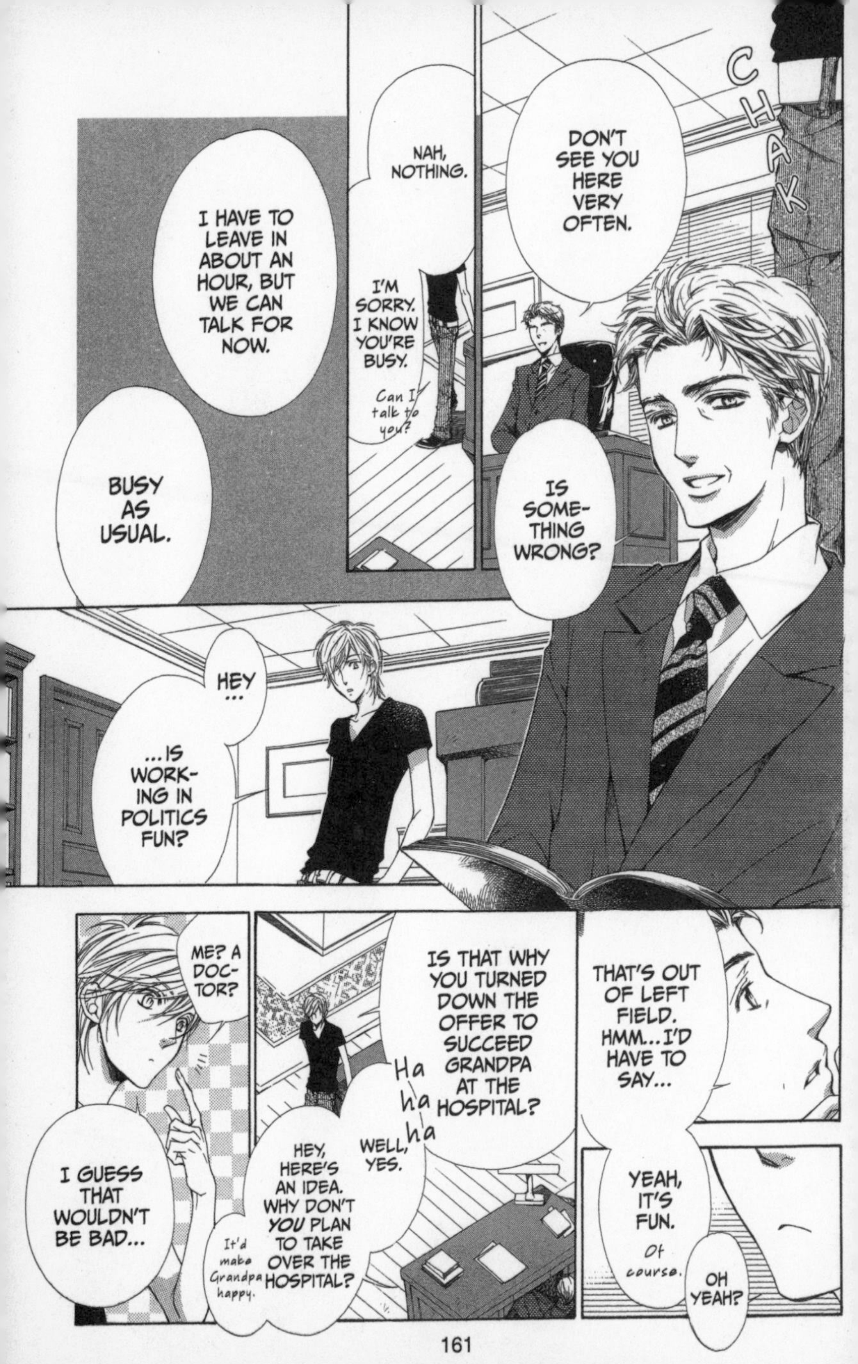
CHAK
DON'T SEE YOU HERE VERY OFTEN.
IS SOMETHING WRONG?
NAH, NOTHING.
I'M SORRY. I KNOW YOU'RE BUSY.
Can I talk to you?
I HAVE TO LEAVE IN ABOUT AN HOUR, BUT WE CAN TALK FOR NOW.
BUSY AS USUAL.
HEY...
...IS WORKING IN POLITICS FUN?
THAT'S OUT OF LEFT FIELD. HMM...I'D HAVE TO SAY...
YEAH, IT'S FUN.
Of course.
OH YEAH?
IS THAT WHY YOU TURNED DOWN THE OFFER TO SUCCEED GRANDPA AT THE HOSPITAL?
Ha ha ha
WELL, YES.
HEY, HERE'S AN IDEA. WHY DON'T *YOU* PLAN TO TAKE OVER THE HOSPITAL?
It'd make Grandpa happy.
ME? A DOCTOR?
I GUESS THAT WOULDN'T BE BAD...

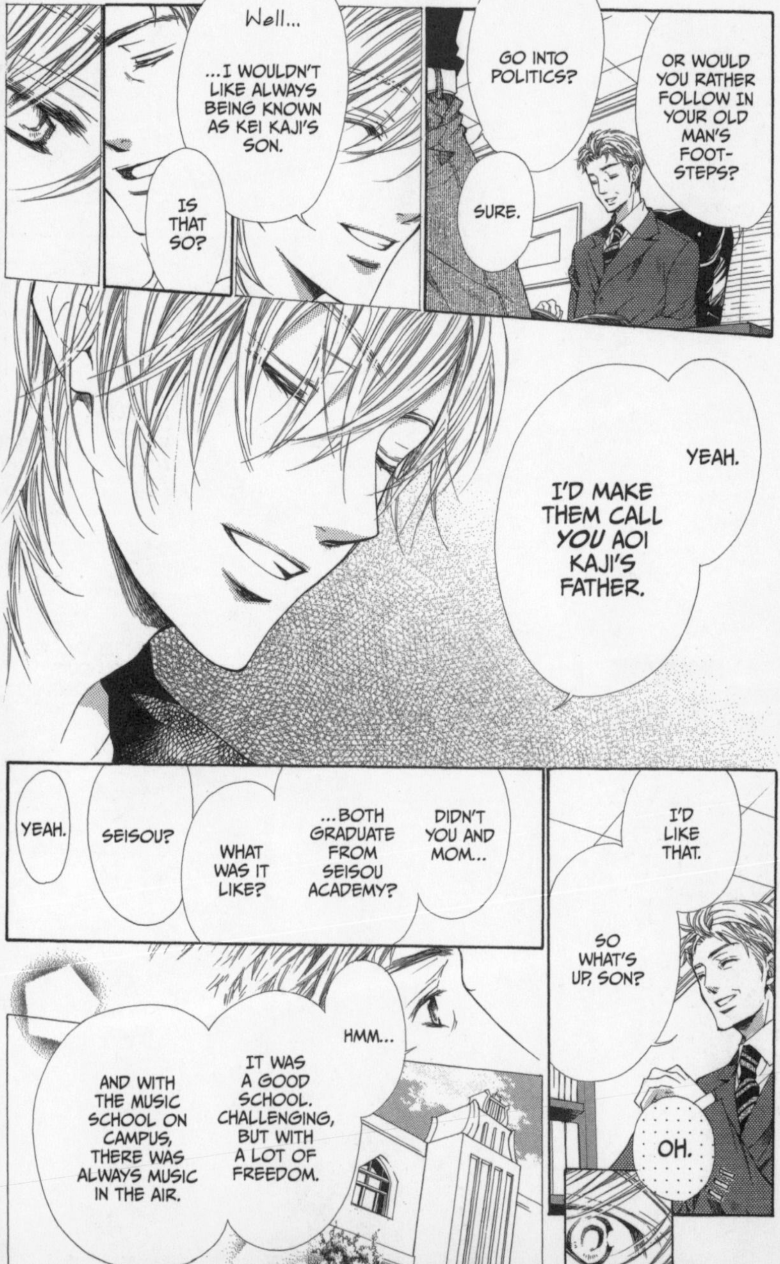
OR WOULD YOU RATHER FOLLOW IN YOUR OLD MAN'S FOOT-STEPS?
GO INTO POLITICS?
SURE.
Well...
...I WOULDN'T LIKE ALWAYS BEING KNOWN AS KEI KAJI'S SON.
IS THAT SO?
YEAH.
I'D MAKE THEM CALL *YOU* AOI KAJI'S FATHER.
I'D LIKE THAT.
SO WHAT'S UP, SON?
OH.
DIDN'T YOU AND MOM...
...BOTH GRADUATE FROM SEISOU ACADEMY?
WHAT WAS IT LIKE?
SEISOU?
YEAH.
HMM...
IT WAS A GOOD SCHOOL. CHALLENGING, BUT WITH A LOT OF FREEDOM.
AND WITH THE MUSIC SCHOOL ON CAMPUS, THERE WAS ALWAYS MUSIC IN THE AIR.

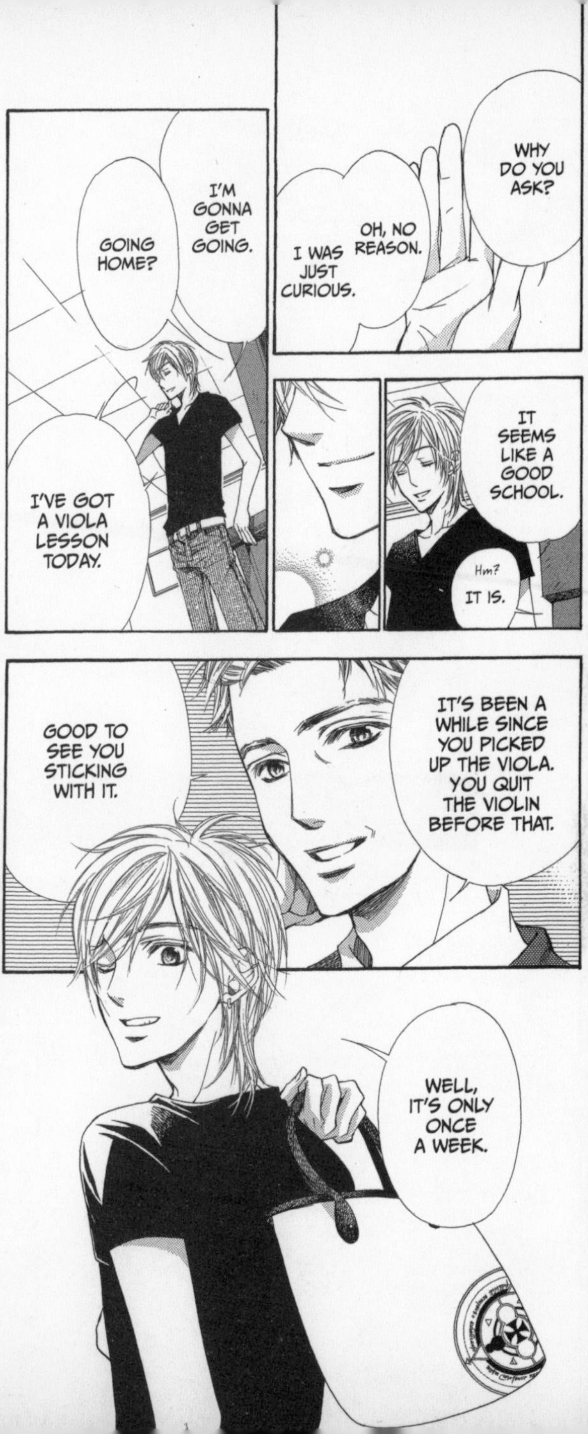
WHY DO YOU ASK?
OH, NO REASON.
I WAS JUST CURIOUS.
IT SEEMS LIKE A GOOD SCHOOL.
Hm?
IT IS.
I'M GONNA GET GOING.
GOING HOME?
I'VE GOT A VIOLA LESSON TODAY.
IT'S BEEN A WHILE SINCE YOU PICKED UP THE VIOLA. YOU QUIT THE VIOLIN BEFORE THAT.
GOOD TO SEE YOU STICKING WITH IT.
WELL, IT'S ONLY ONCE A WEEK.

This volume has a lot of side stories, so I feel sorry for the readers waiting to get back to the main story. I really like drawing Aoi's two friends, though. My assistants love them too. I'll make sure to give the other characters a bigger part in the next volume! Please be patient!

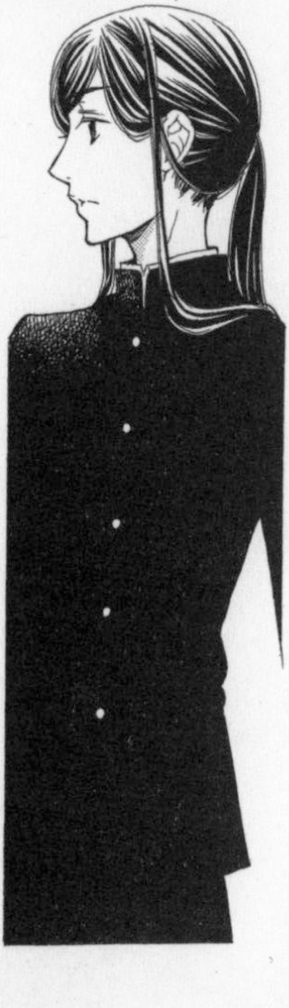

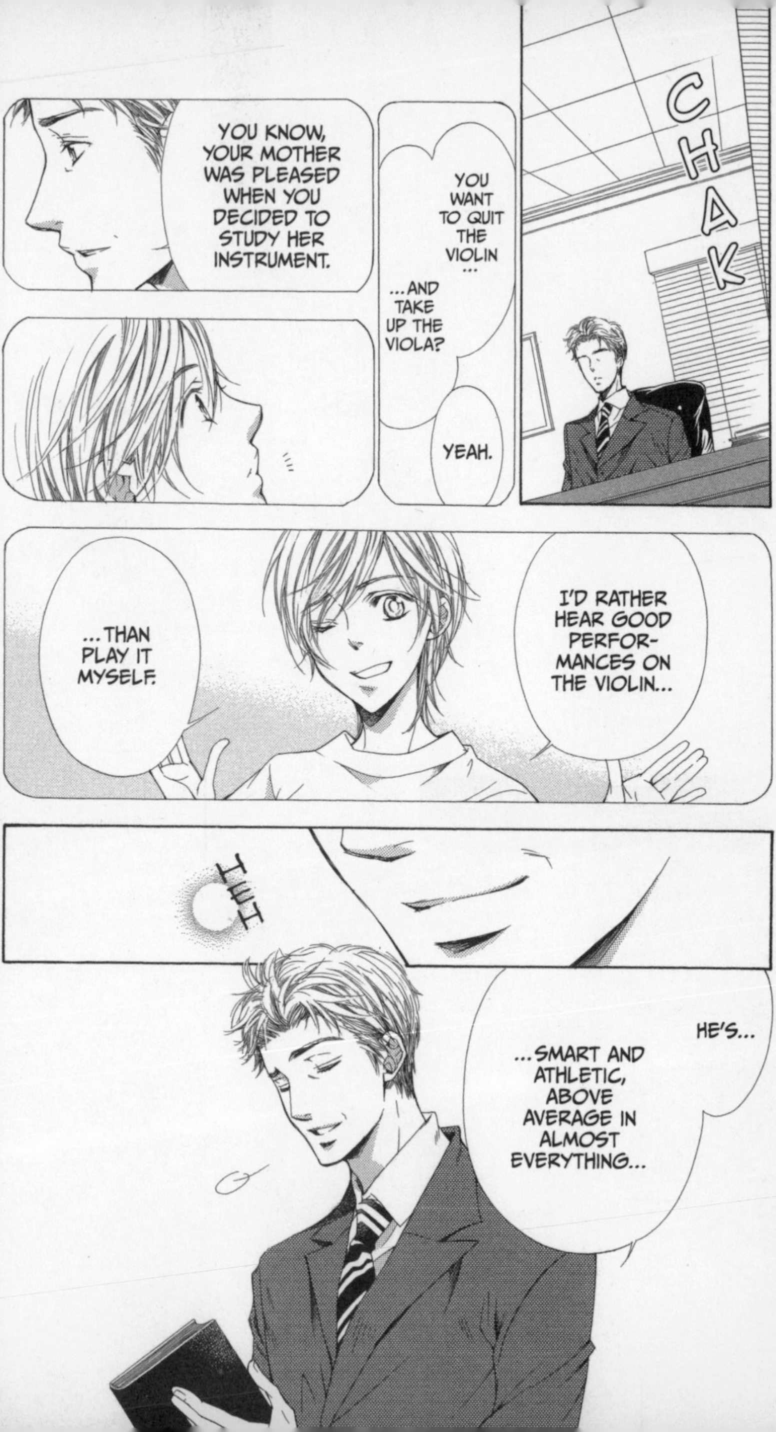
CHAK
YOU WANT TO QUIT THE VIOLIN ...
...AND TAKE UP THE VIOLA?
YEAH.
YOU KNOW, YOUR MOTHER WAS PLEASED WHEN YOU DECIDED TO STUDY HER INSTRUMENT.
I'D RATHER HEAR GOOD PERFOR-MANCES ON THE VIOLIN...
...THAN PLAY IT MYSELF.
HEH
HE'S...
...SMART AND ATHLETIC, ABOVE AVERAGE IN ALMOST EVERYTHING...

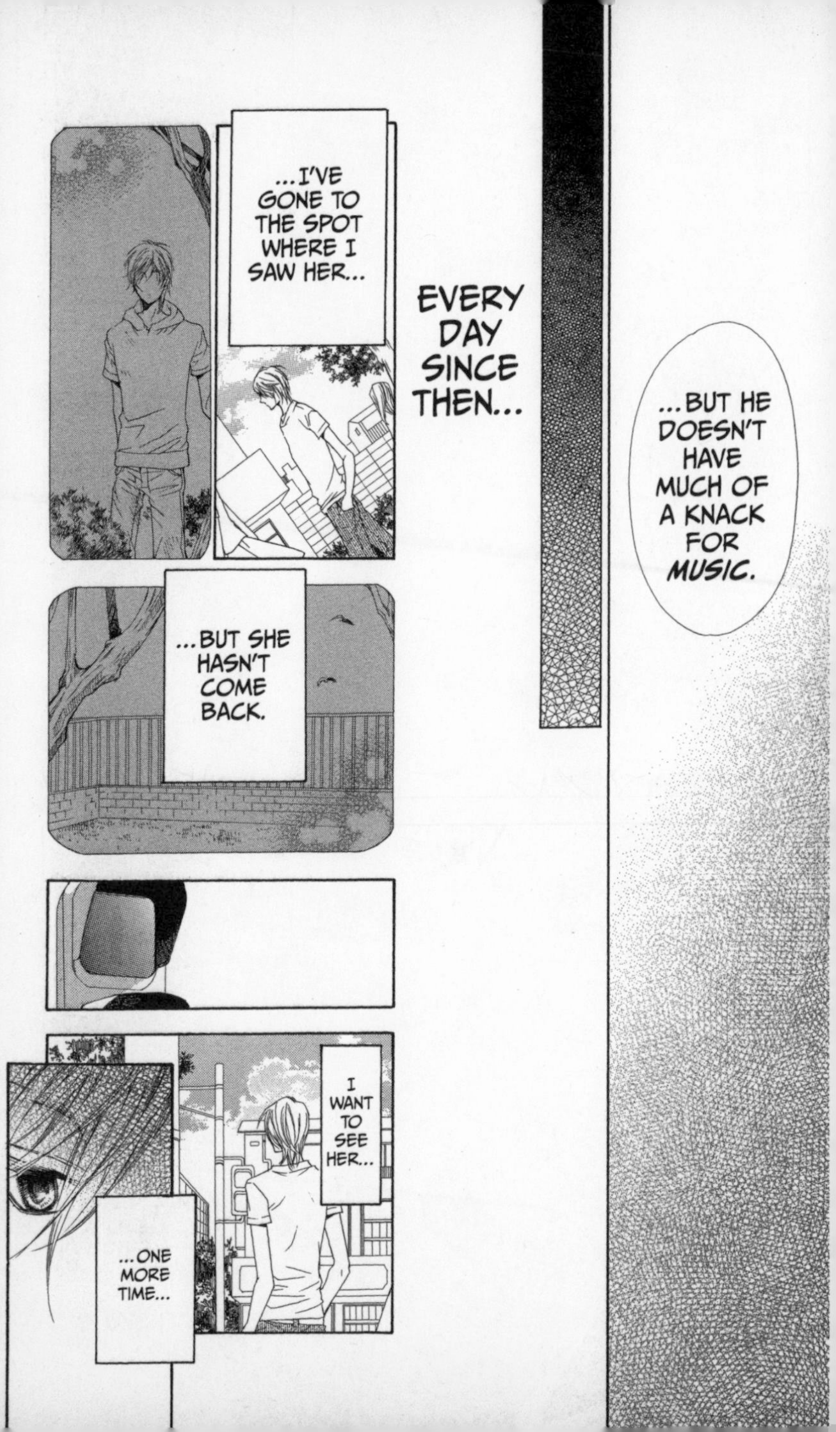
...BUT HE DOESN'T HAVE MUCH OF A KNACK FOR MUSIC.
EVERY DAY SINCE THEN...
...I'VE GONE TO THE SPOT WHERE I SAW HER...
...BUT SHE HASN'T COME BACK.
I WANT TO SEE HER...
...ONE MORE TIME...

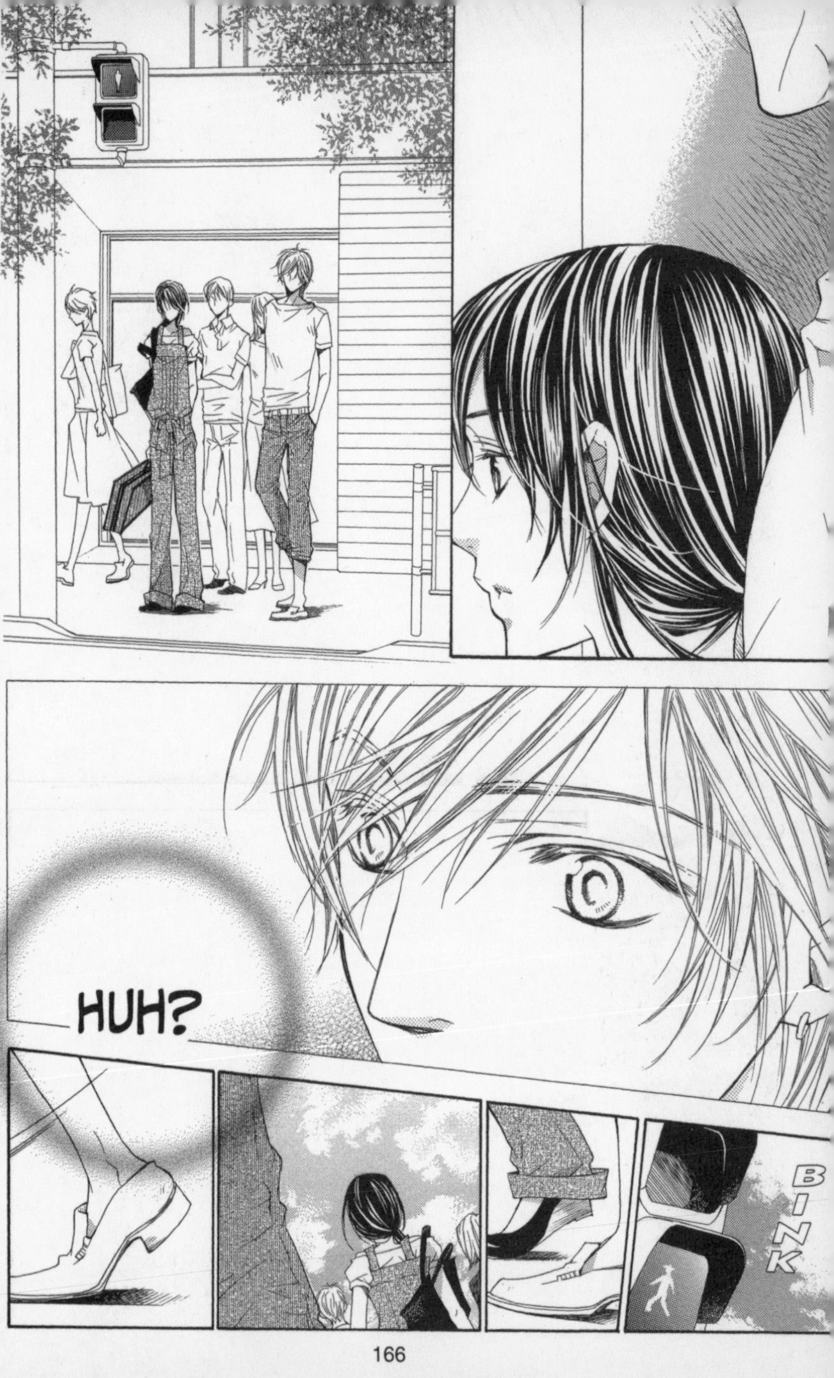
HUH?
BLINK

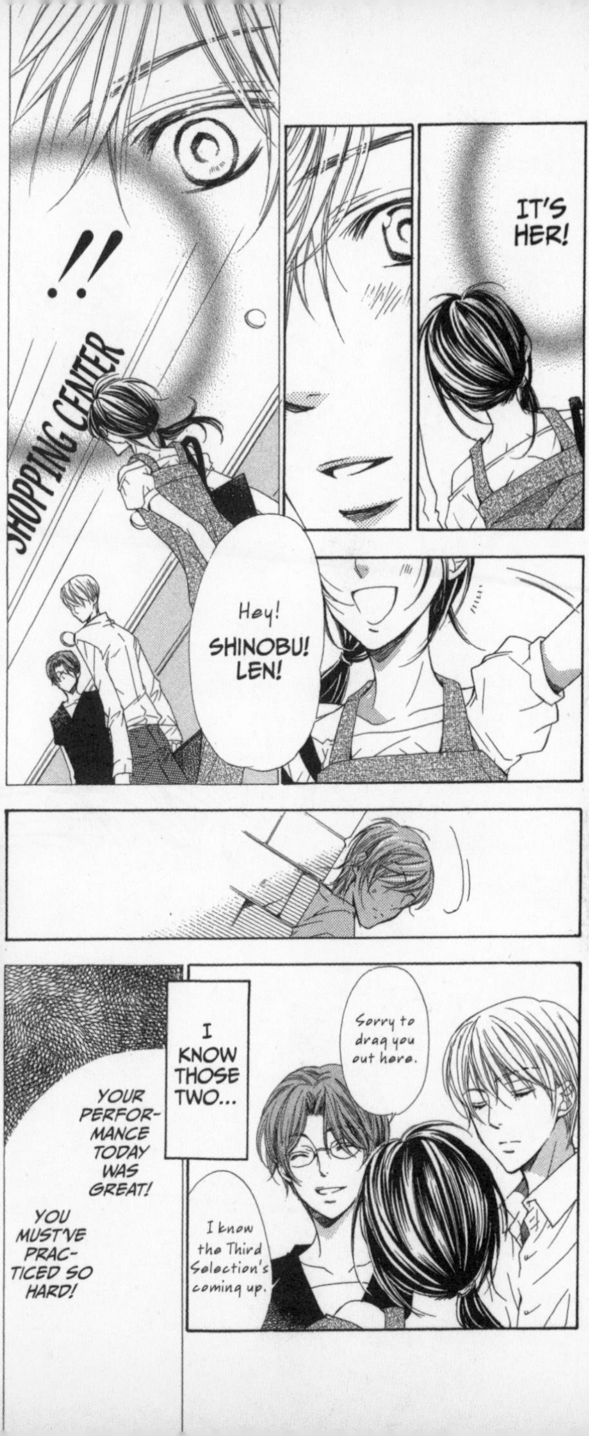
IT'S HER!
!!
SHOPPING CENTER
Hey! SHINOBU! LEN!
I KNOW THOSE TWO...
Sorry to drag you out here.
I know the Third Selection's coming up.
YOUR PERFORMANCE TODAY WAS GREAT!
YOU MUST'VE PRACTICED SO HARD!

Here's the last of the school uniform sketches. Keiichi seems like the type to stick to the rules when it comes to uniforms, but I made him wear a sweatshirt underneath.

Thanks so much for reading! Until next time...

Yuki Kure 2008

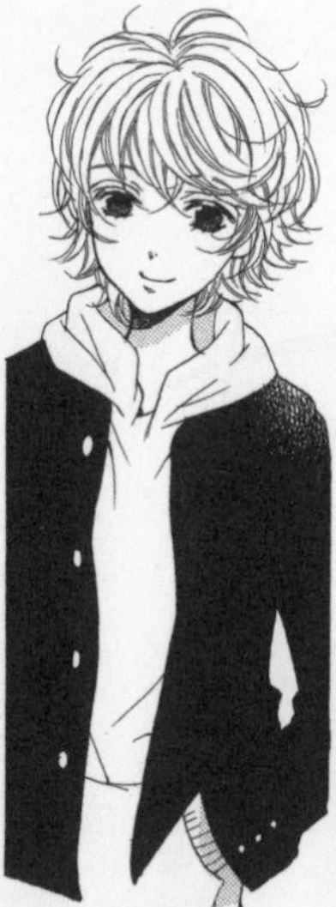

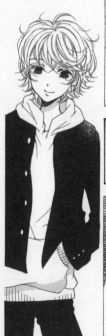

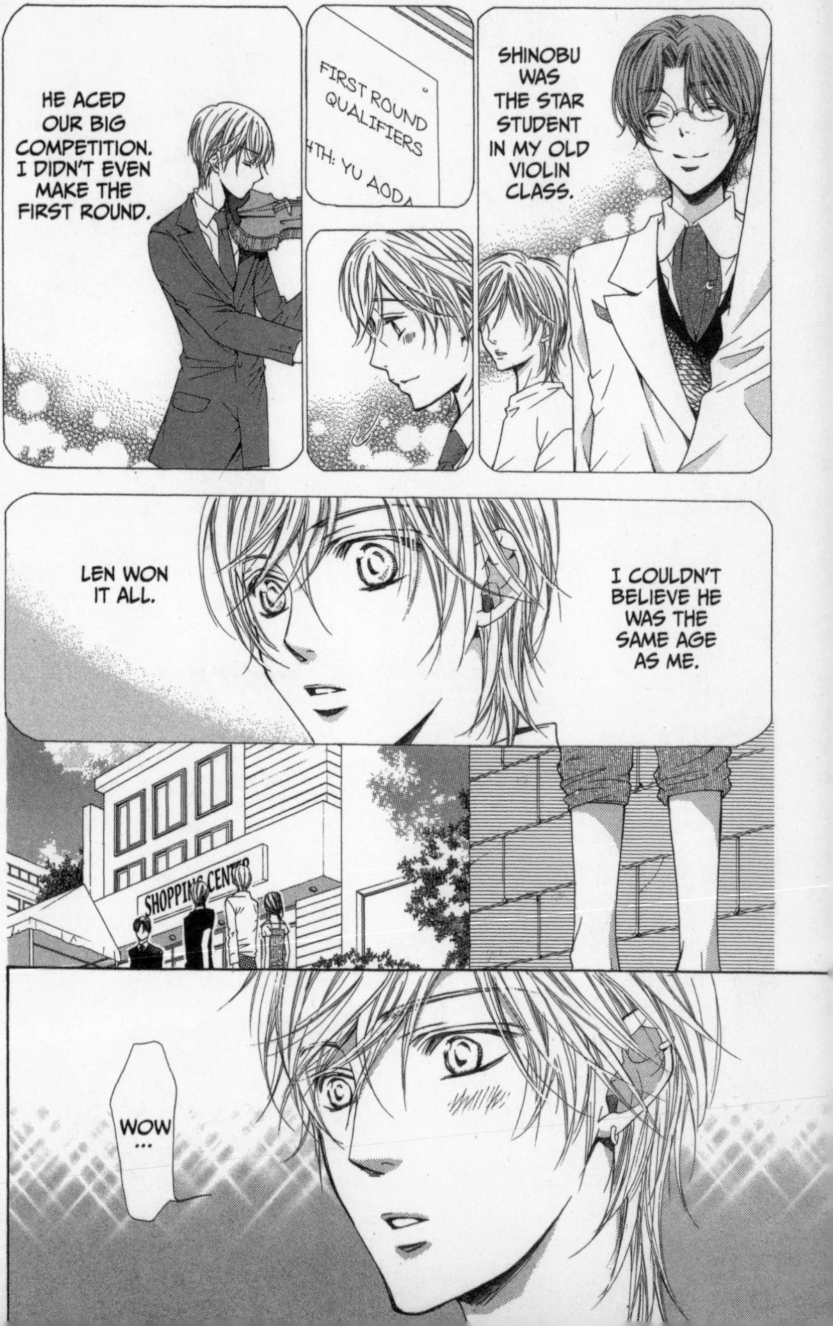
SHINOBU WAS THE STAR STUDENT IN MY OLD VIOLIN CLASS.
FIRST ROUND QUALIFIERS
4TH: YU AODA
HE ACED OUR BIG COMPETITION. I DIDN'T EVEN MAKE THE FIRST ROUND.
I COULDN'T BELIEVE HE WAS THE SAME AGE AS ME.
LEN WON IT ALL.
WOW ...

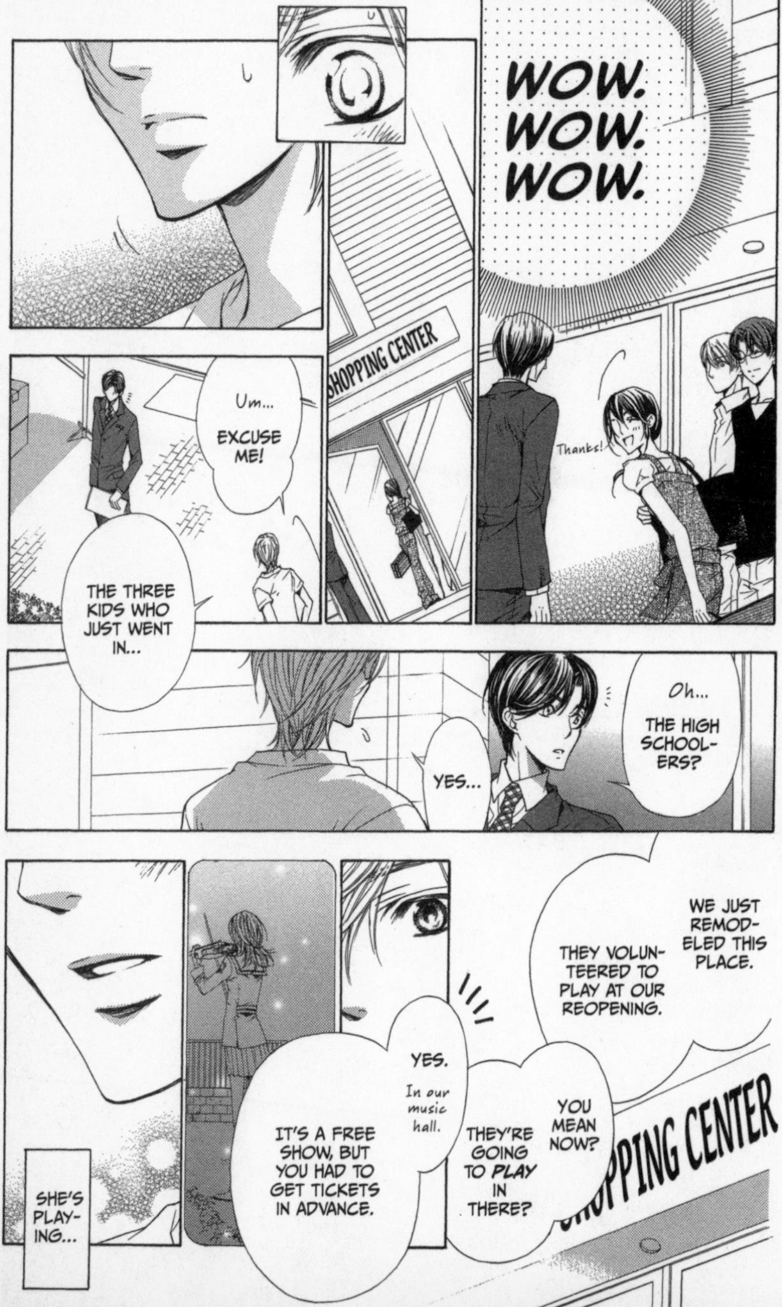
WOW. WOW. WOW.
Thanks!
SHOPPING CENTER
Um... EXCUSE ME!
THE THREE KIDS WHO JUST WENT IN...
Oh... THE HIGH SCHOOL-ERS?
YES...
WE JUST REMOD-ELED THIS PLACE.
THEY VOLUN-TEERED TO PLAY AT OUR REOPENING.
OPPING CENTER
YOU MEAN NOW?
THEY'RE GOING TO *PLAY* IN THERE?
YES.
In our music hall.
IT'S A FREE SHOW, BUT YOU HAD TO GET TICKETS IN ADVANCE.
SHE'S PLAY-ING...

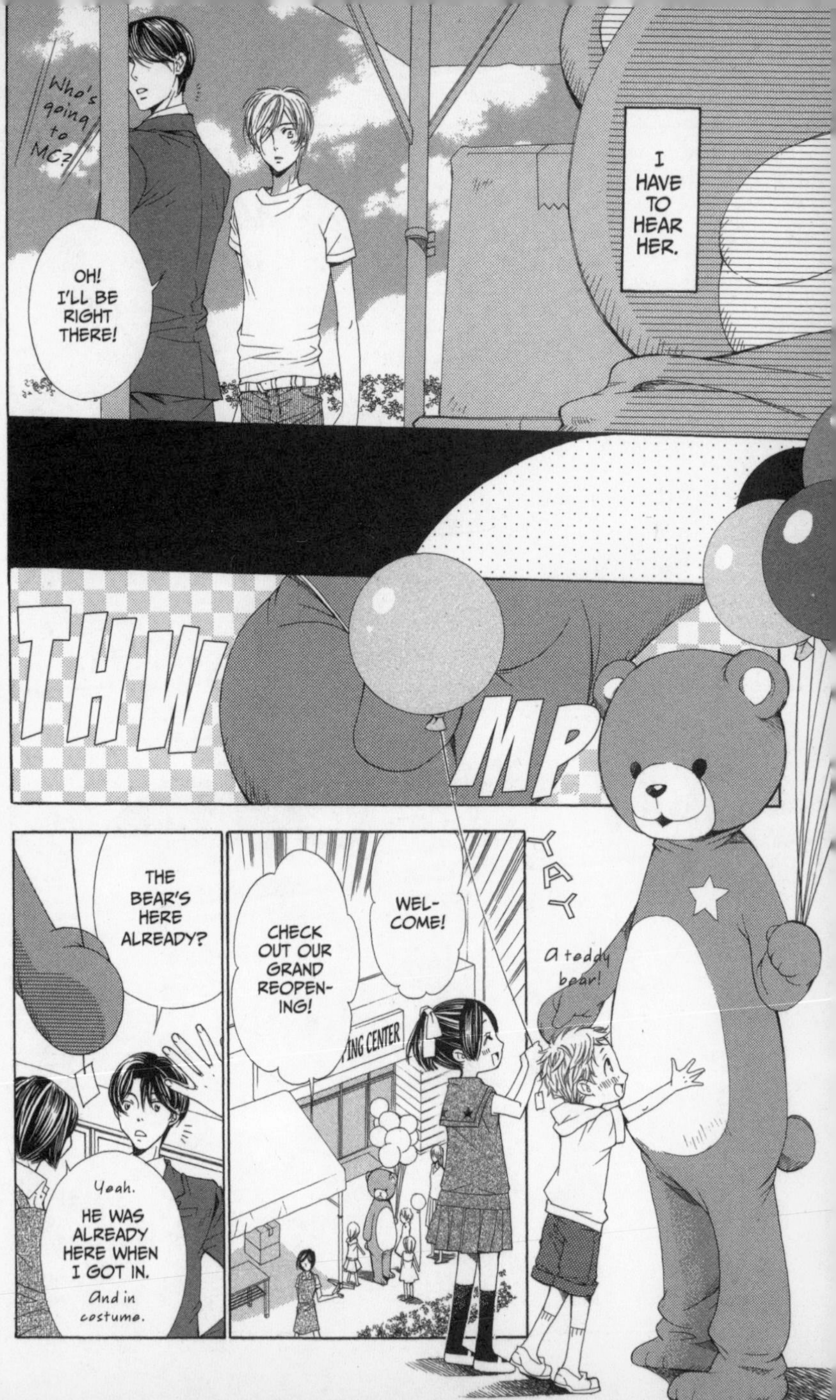
I HAVE TO HEAR HER.
Who's going to MC?
OH! I'LL BE RIGHT THERE!
THWMP
YAY
A teddy bear!
WEL-COME!
CHECK OUT OUR GRAND REOPEN-ING!
THE BEAR'S HERE ALREADY?
Yeah.
HE WAS ALREADY HERE WHEN I GOT IN.
And in costume.

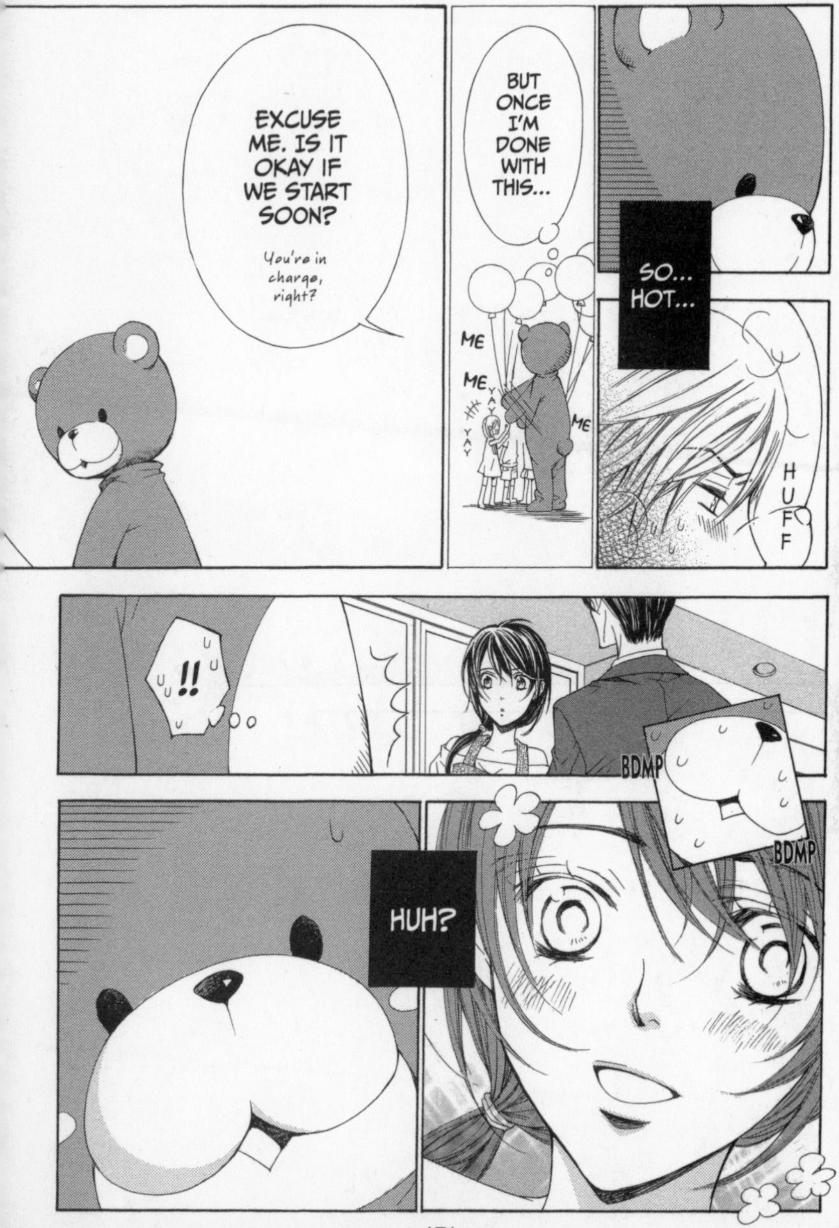
SO... HOT...
HUFF
HUFF
BUT ONCE I'M DONE WITH THIS...
ME
ME
YAY YAY
YAY YAY
ME
EXCUSE ME. IS IT OKAY IF WE START SOON?
You're in charge, right?
!!
BDMP
BDMP
HUH?

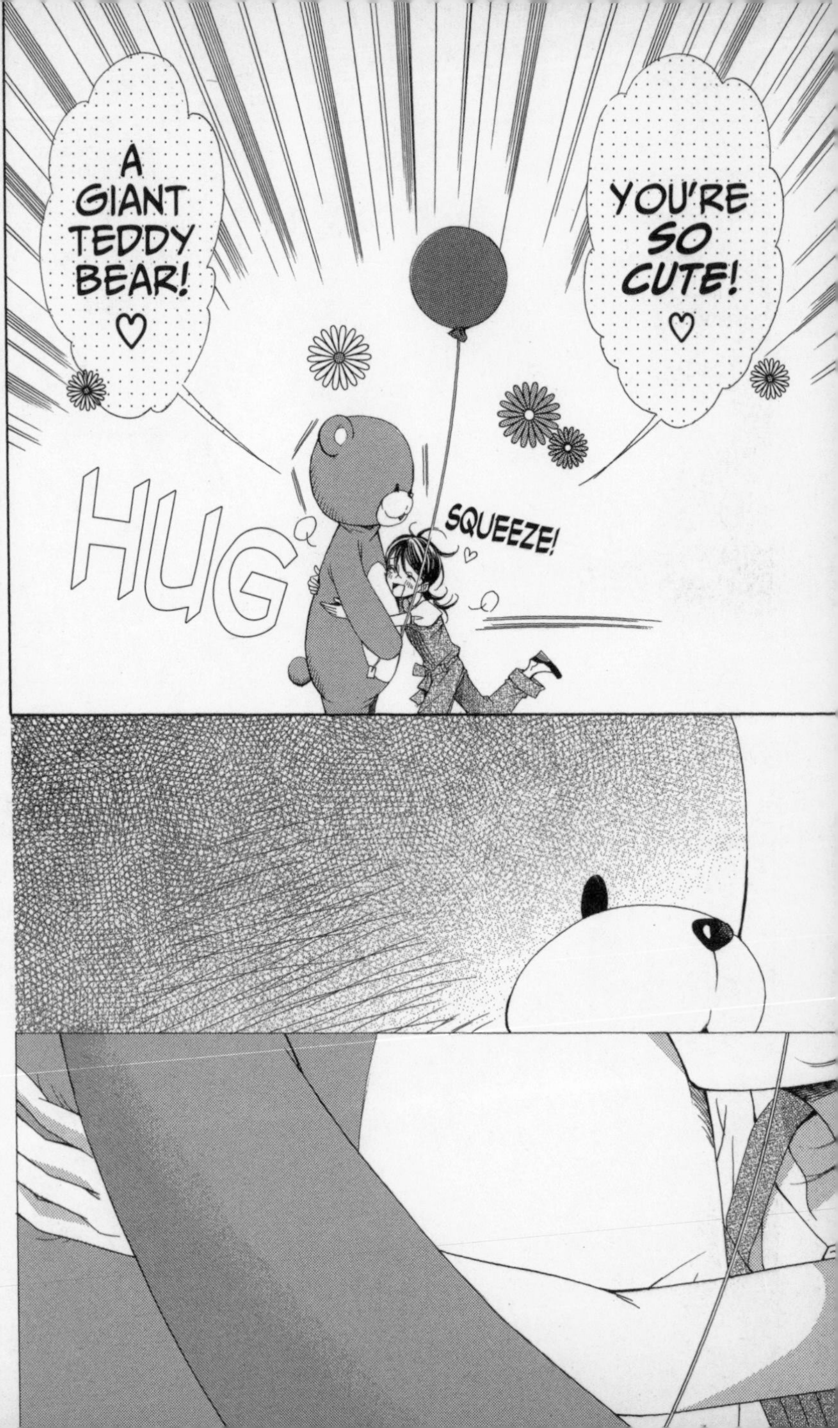
YOU'RE SO CUTE! ♡
A GIANT TEDDY BEAR! ♡
SQUEEZE! ♡
HUG

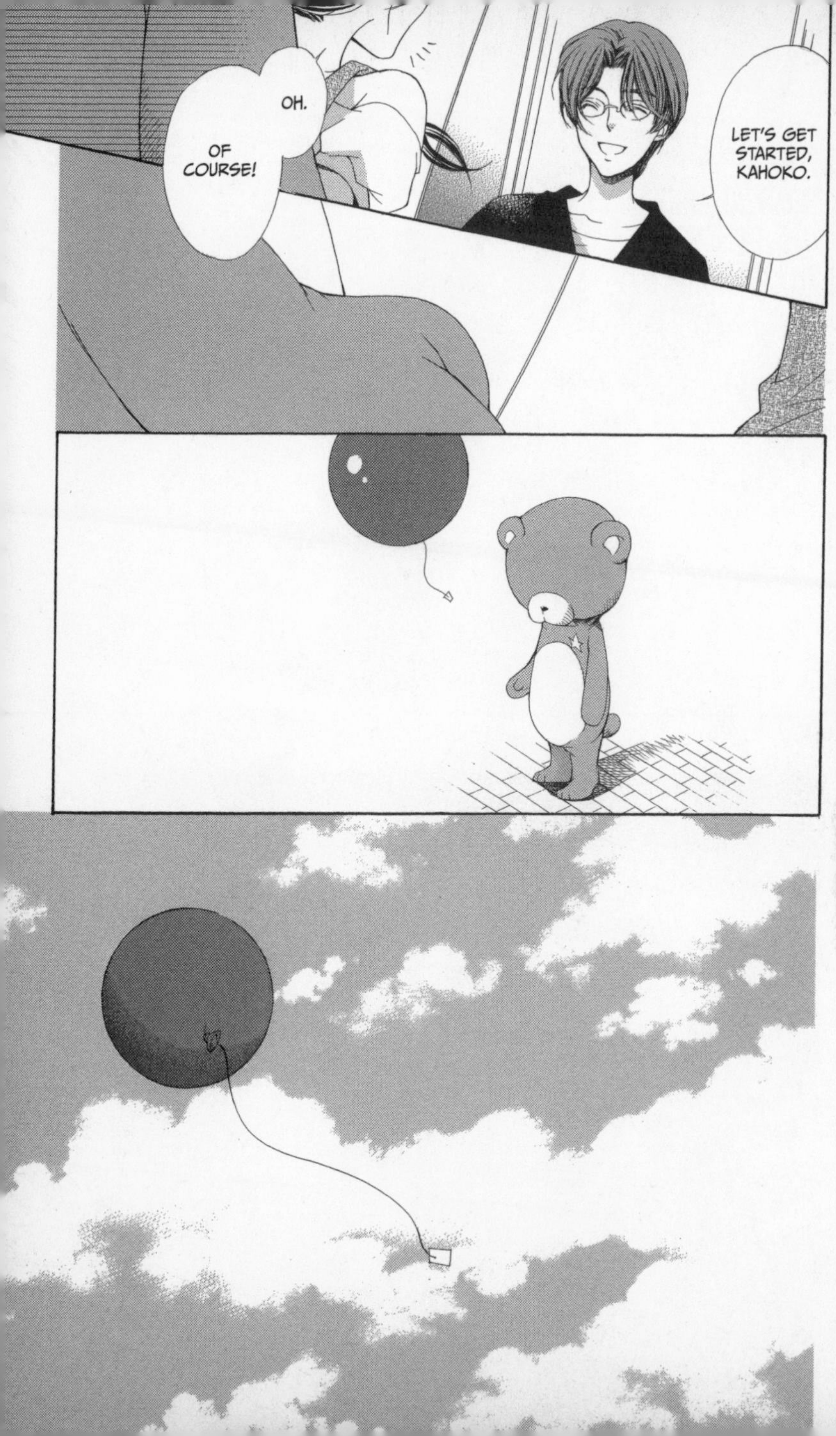
LET'S GET STARTED, KAHOKO.
OH.
OF COURSE!

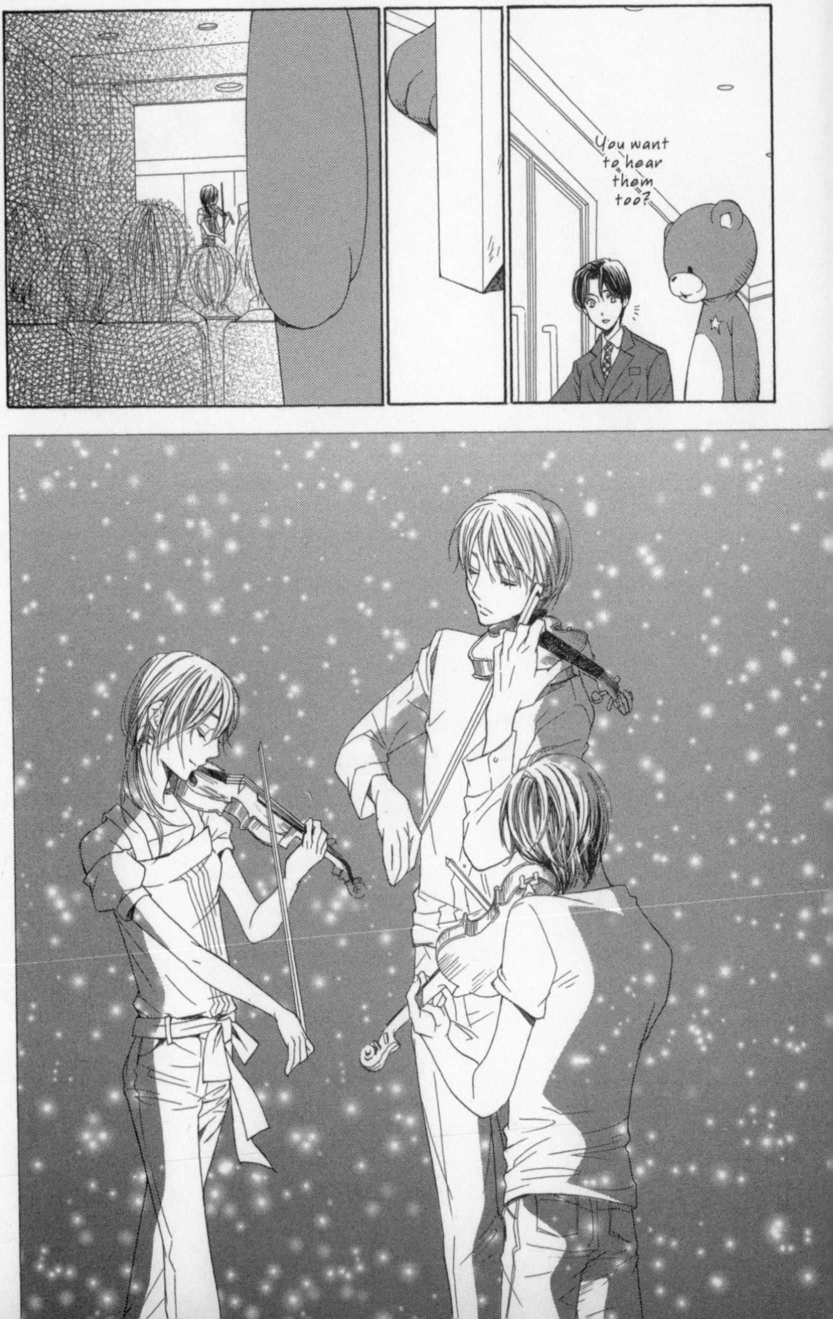
You want to hear them too?

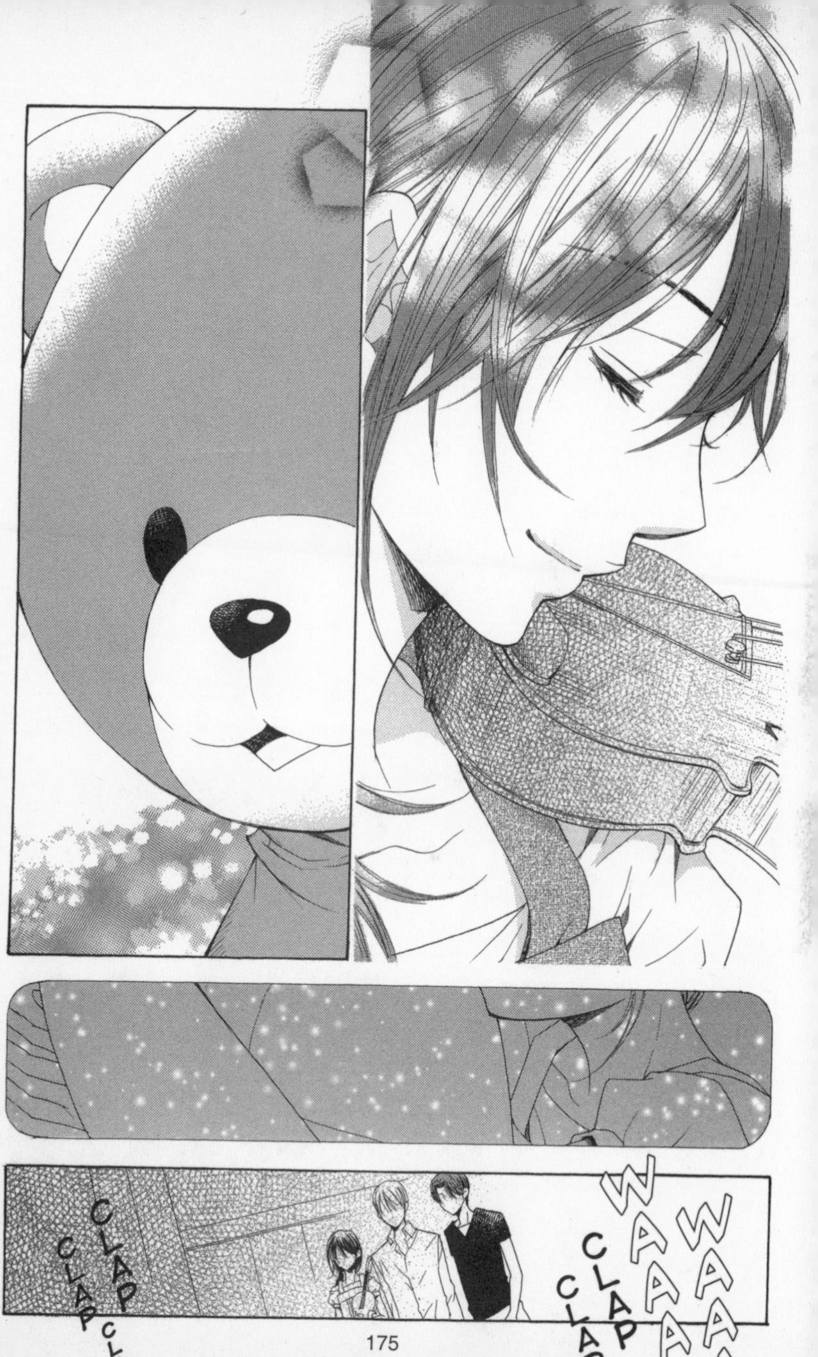
WAAAA
WAAAA
CLAP
CLAP
CLAP
CLAP
CLAP
CLAP

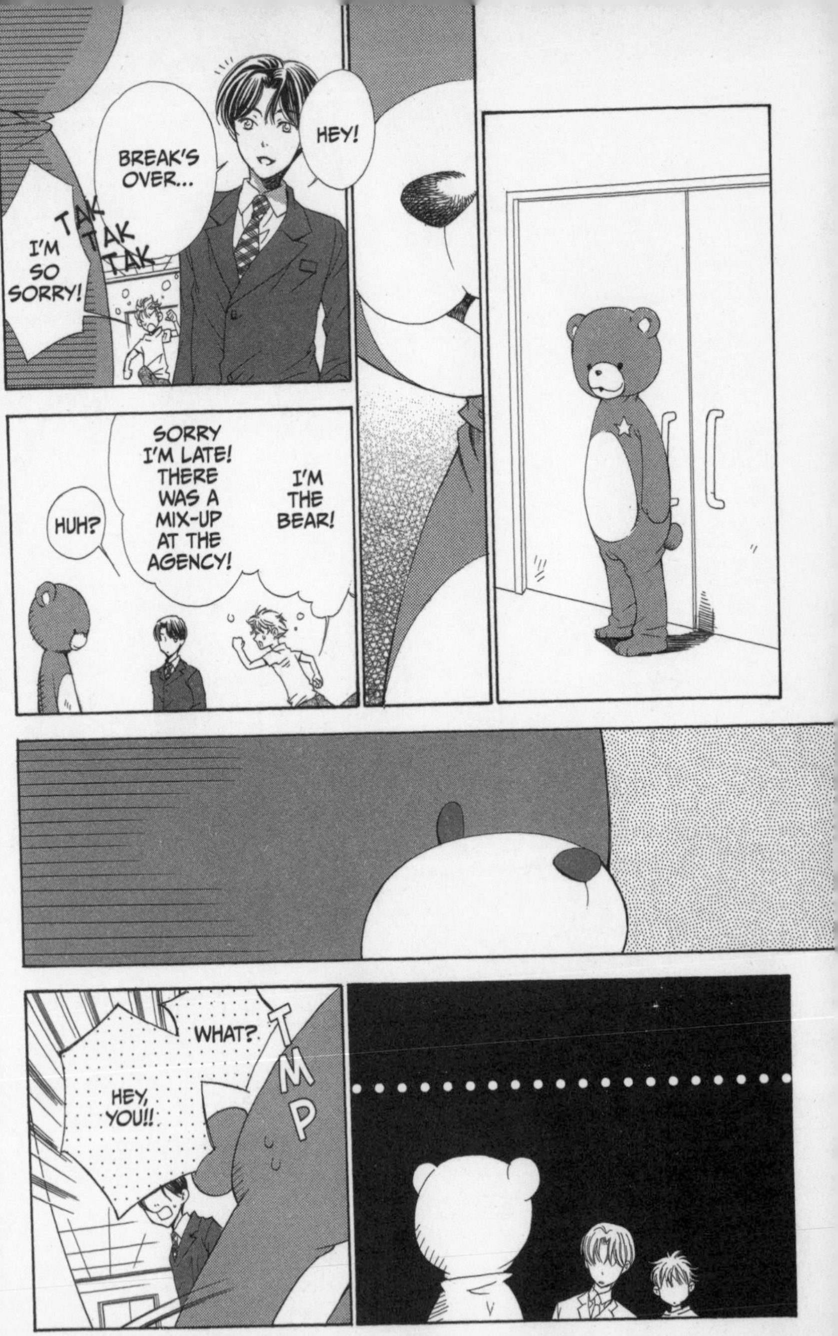
HEY!
BREAK'S OVER...
TAK TAK TAK
I'M SO SORRY!
I'M THE BEAR!
SORRY I'M LATE! THERE WAS A MIX-UP AT THE AGENCY!
HUH?
TMP
WHAT?
HEY, YOU!!

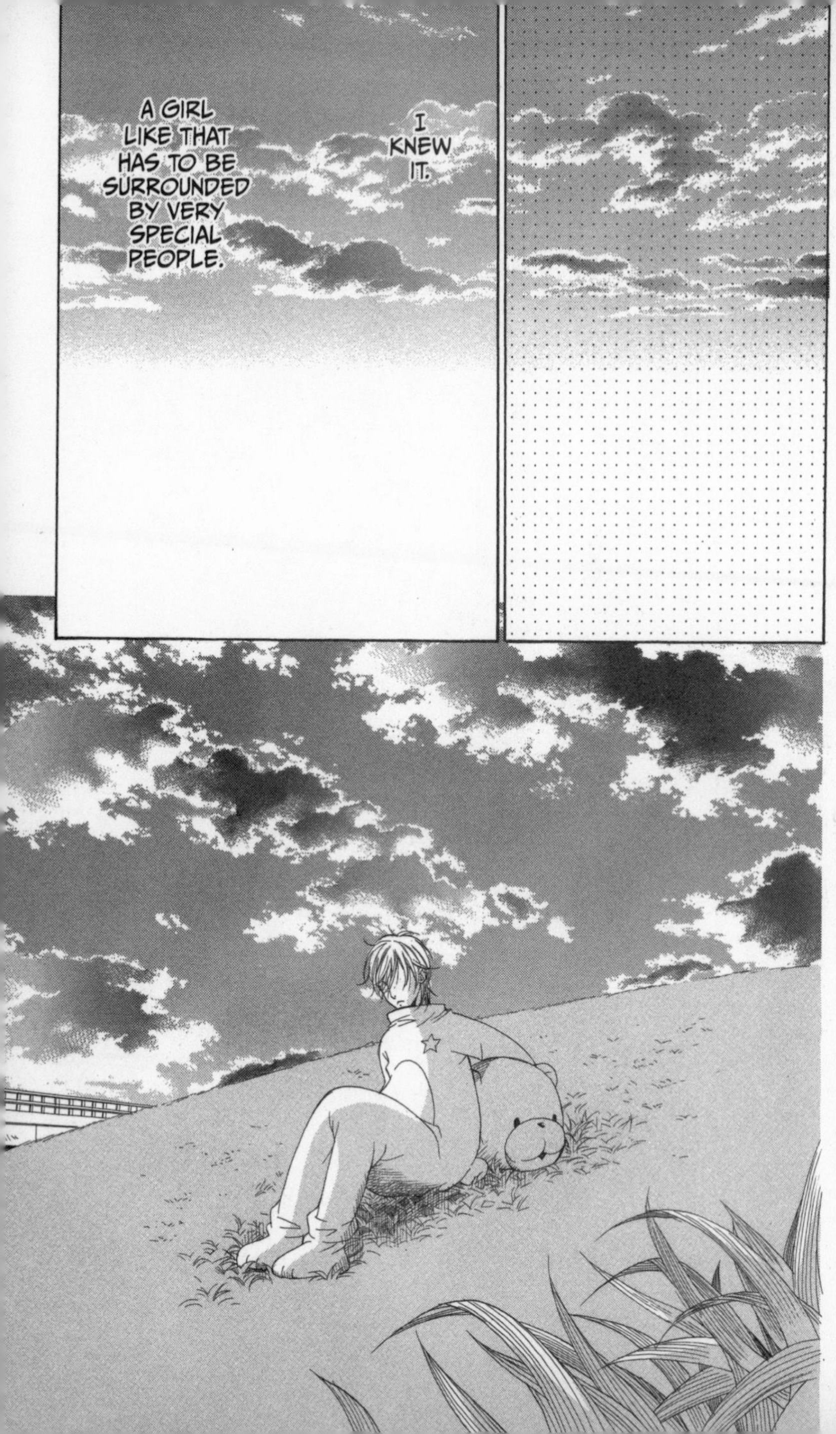
I KNEW IT.
A GIRL LIKE THAT HAS TO BE SURROUNDED BY VERY SPECIAL PEOPLE.

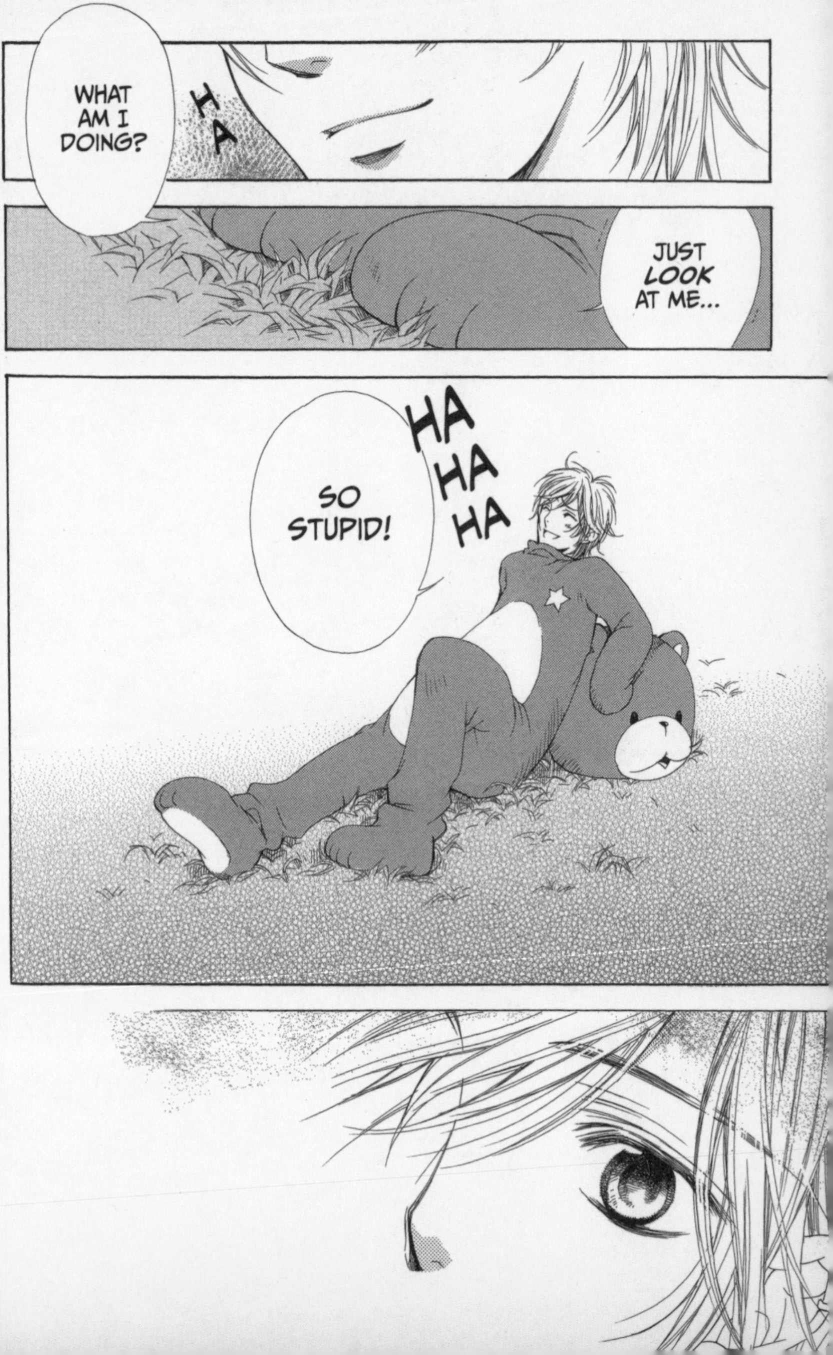
HA
WHAT AM I DOING?
JUST LOOK AT ME...
HA HA HA
SO STUPID!

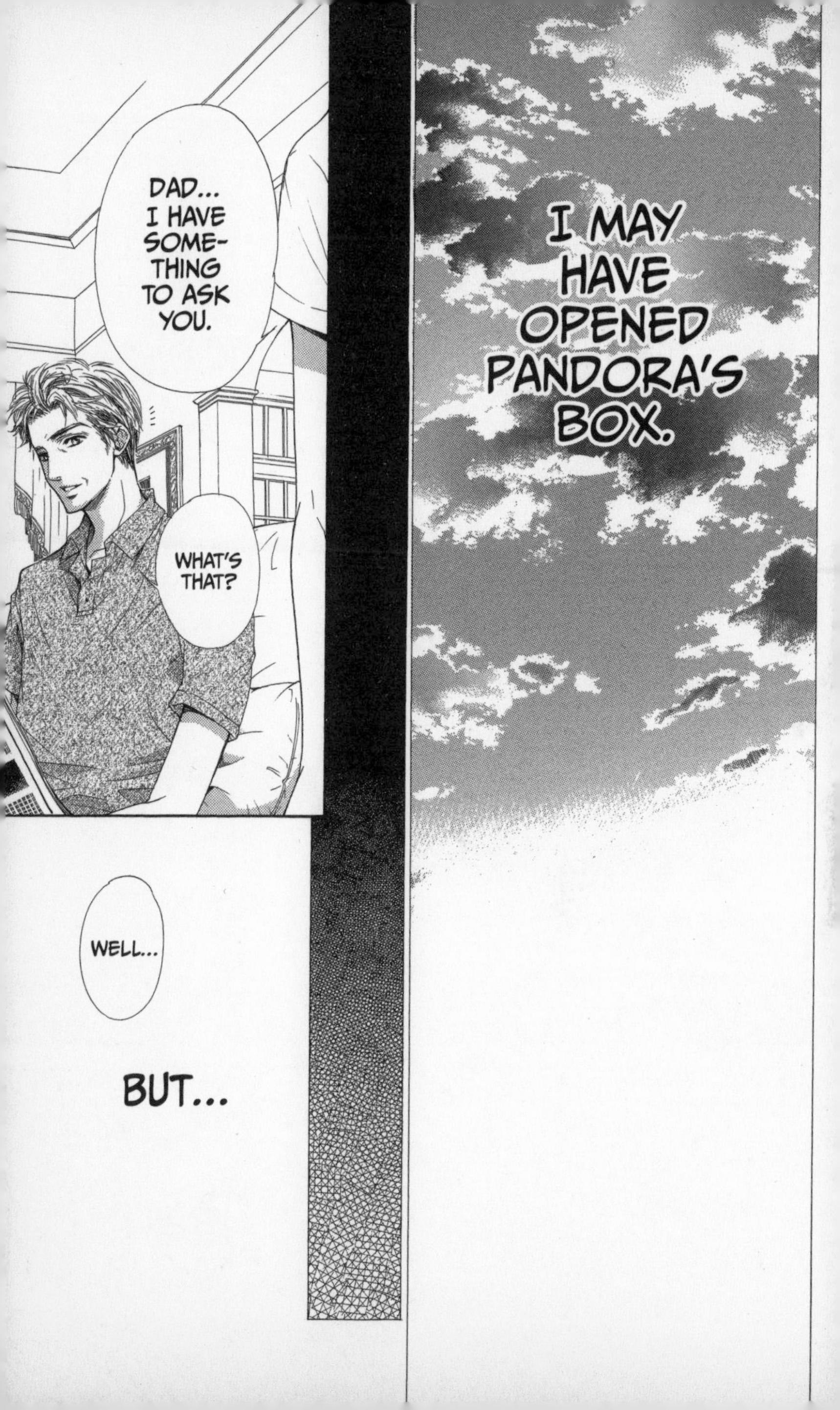
I MAY HAVE OPENED PANDORA'S BOX.
DAD... I HAVE SOME-THING TO ASK YOU.
WHAT'S THAT?
WELL...
BUT...

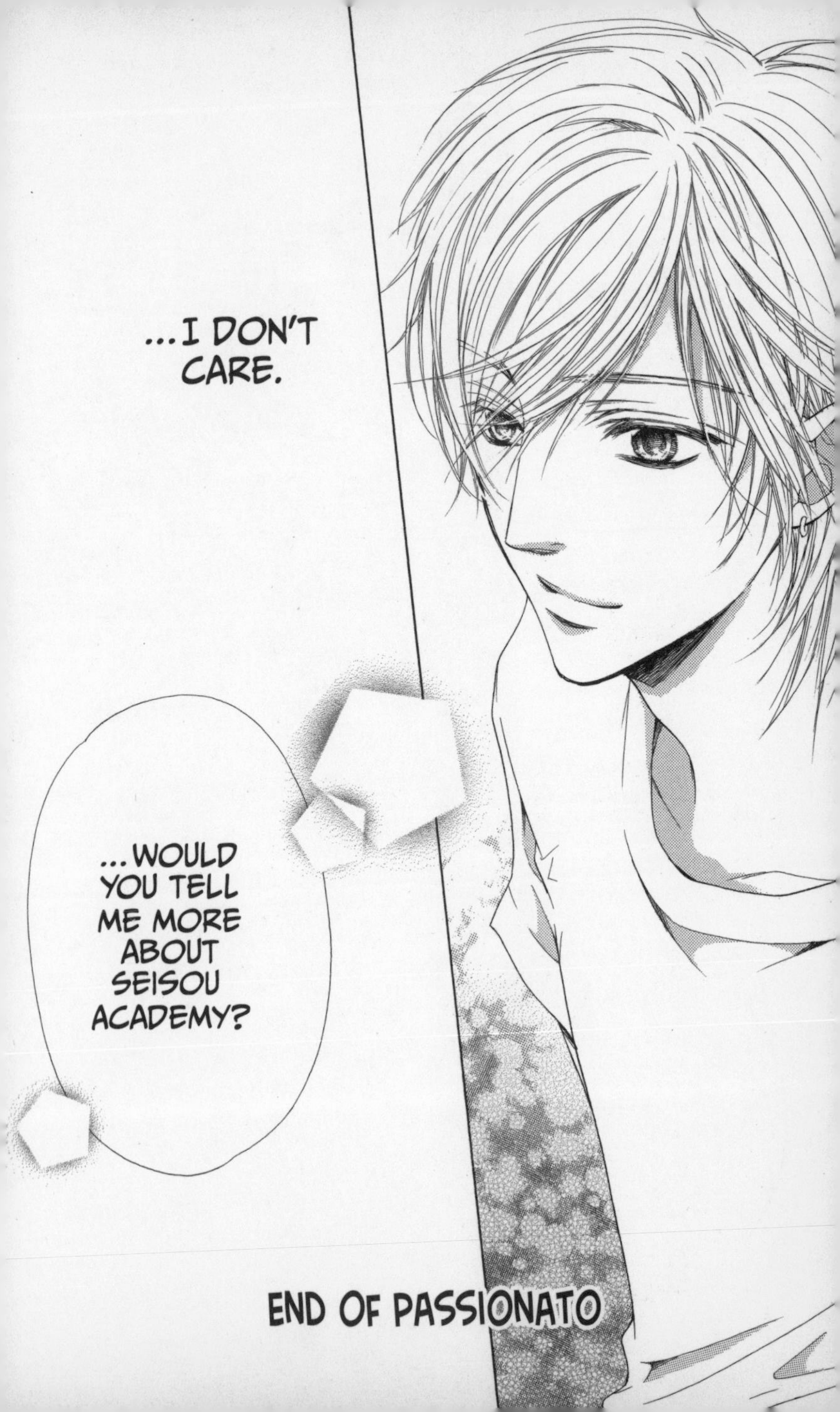
...I DON'T CARE.
...WOULD YOU TELL ME MORE ABOUT SEISOU ACADEMY?
END OF PASSIONATO

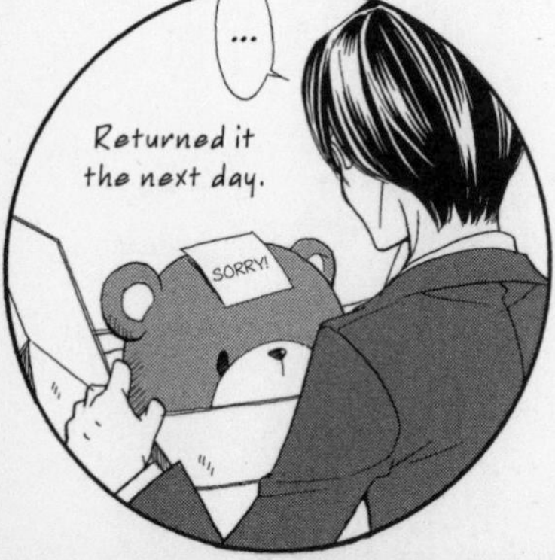
...
Returned it the next day.
SORRY!

Postscript ✿

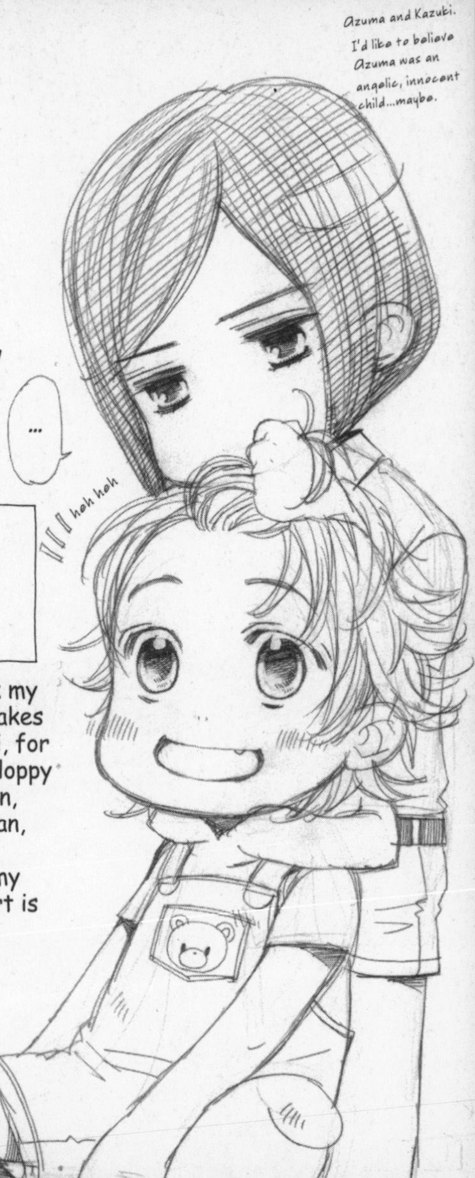

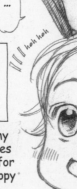

Azuma and Kazuki.
I'd like to believe Azuma was an angelic, innocent child...maybe.
...
heh heh

Dear readers,

Thank you so much for your continued support! The letters you send me are my prized possessions! ♡
I'm sorry I'm so slow to respond...but I do love to hear from you.

↓↓↓

VIZ Media, LLC
P.O. BOX 77010
San Francisco,
CA 94107

Also, I want to thank my editor, who always takes care of me...and Koei, for putting up with my sloppy rough drafts...Natsun, Midori, Aya, Shokotan, Himaya-san, etc., etc...And of course my mother...Your support is much appreciated!

Hope to see you all again in volume 12!

Until then,
Yuki Kure 2008

EXTRA

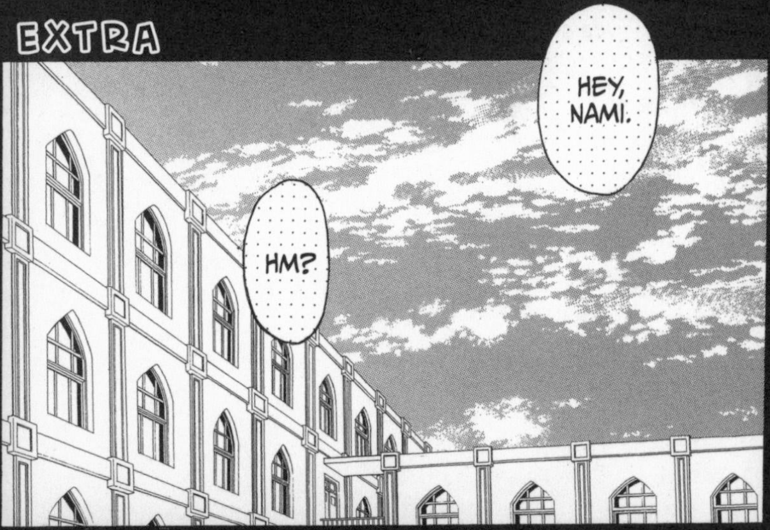
HEY, NAMI.
HM?

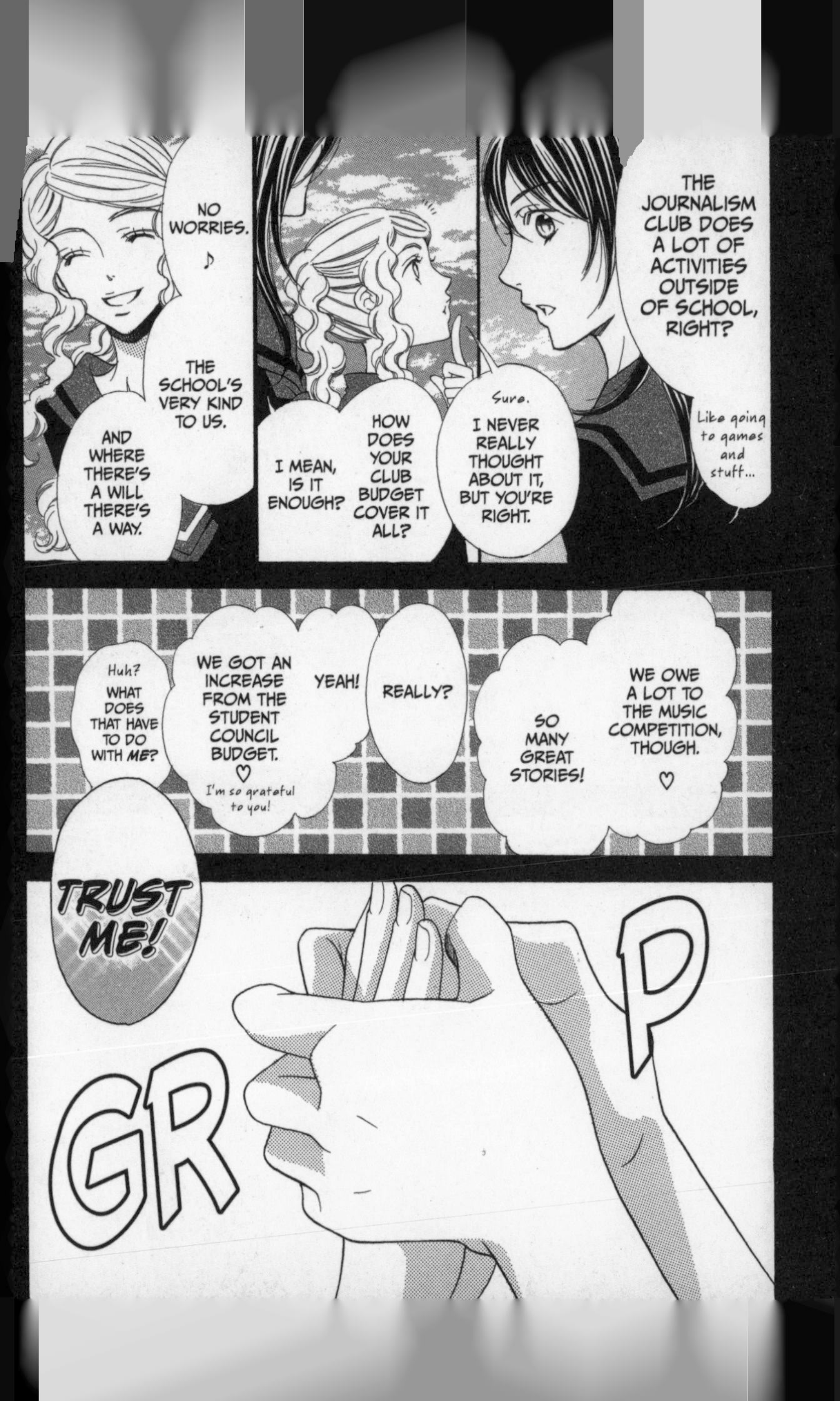
THE JOURNALISM CLUB DOES A LOT OF ACTIVITIES OUTSIDE OF SCHOOL, RIGHT?
Like going to games and stuff...
Sure.
I NEVER REALLY THOUGHT ABOUT IT, BUT YOU'RE RIGHT.
HOW DOES YOUR CLUB BUDGET COVER IT ALL?
I MEAN, IS IT ENOUGH?
NO WORRIES. ♪
THE SCHOOL'S VERY KIND TO US.
AND WHERE THERE'S A WILL THERE'S A WAY.
WE OWE A LOT TO THE MUSIC COMPETITION, THOUGH. ♡
SO MANY GREAT STORIES!
REALLY?
YEAH!
WE GOT AN INCREASE FROM THE STUDENT COUNCIL BUDGET. ♡
I'm so grateful to you!
Huh? WHAT DOES THAT HAVE TO DO WITH ME?
TRUST ME!
P
GR

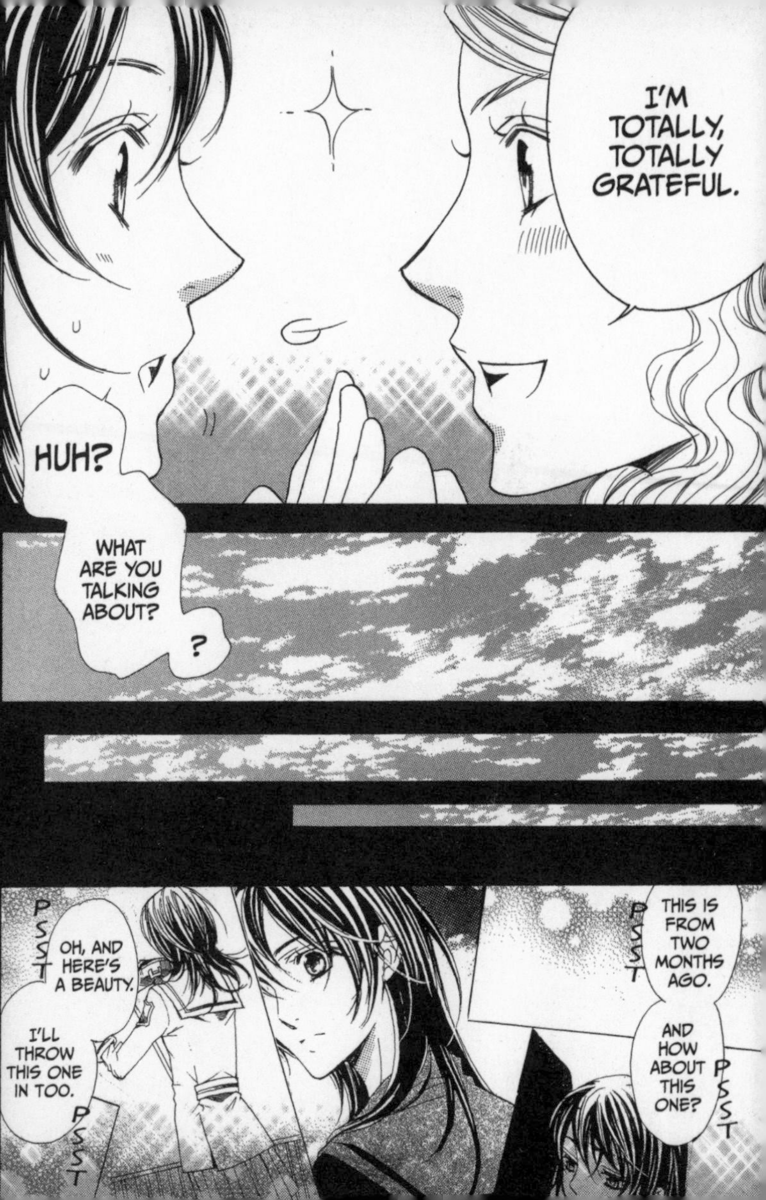
I'M TOTALLY, TOTALLY GRATEFUL.
HUH?
WHAT ARE YOU TALKING ABOUT?
?
PSST
THIS IS FROM TWO MONTHS AGO.
AND HOW ABOUT THIS ONE?
PSST
PSST
OH, AND HERE'S A BEAUTY.
I'LL THROW THIS ONE IN TOO.
PSST

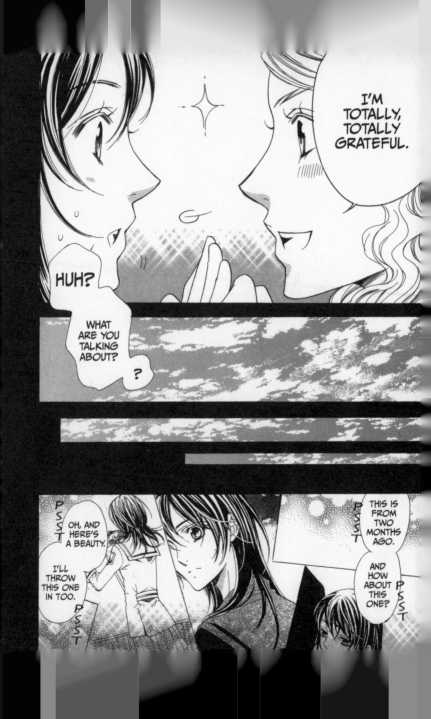

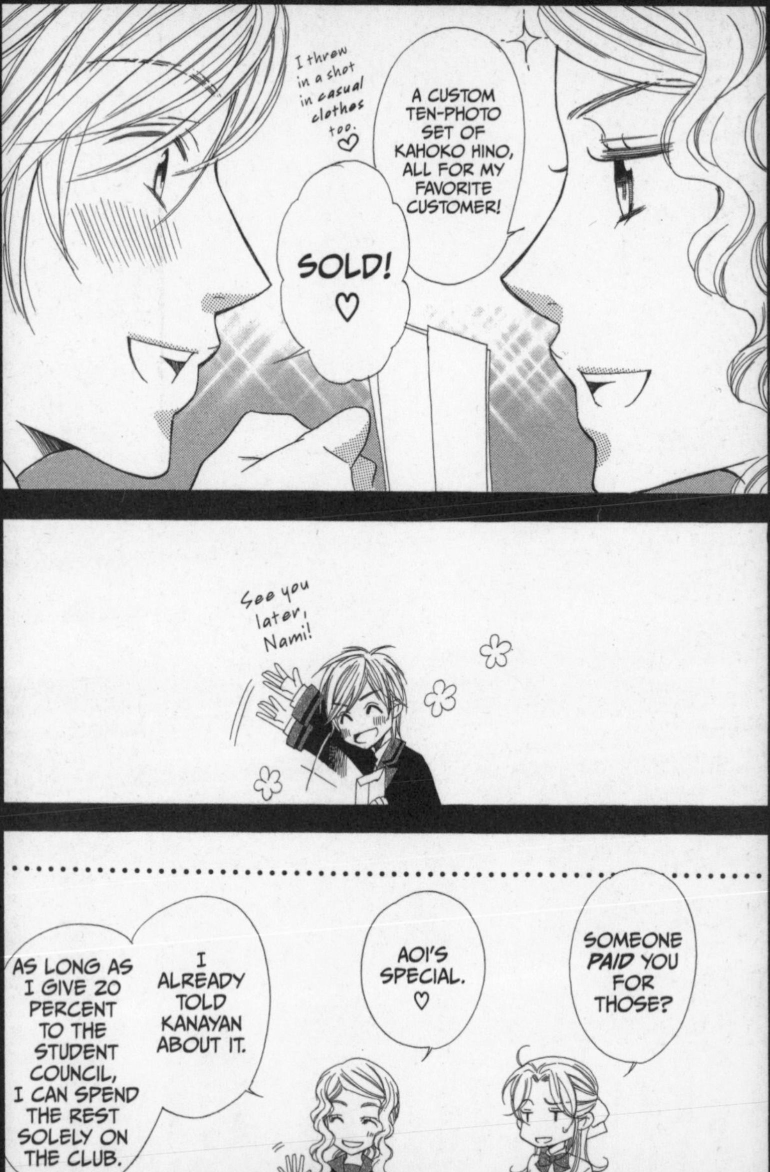
A CUSTOM TEN-PHOTO SET OF KAHOKO HINO, ALL FOR MY FAVORITE CUSTOMER!
I threw in a shot in casual clothes too. ♡
SOLD! ♡
See you later, Nami!
SOMEONE *PAID* YOU FOR THOSE?
AOI'S SPECIAL. ♡
I ALREADY TOLD KANAYAN ABOUT IT.
AS LONG AS I GIVE 20 PERCENT TO THE STUDENT COUNCIL, I CAN SPEND THE REST SOLELY ON THE CLUB.

The End

SPECIAL THANKS

M.Shiino
N.Sato
A.Kashima
S.Asahina
M.Hiyama
A.Uruno
_____
A.Izumi

La Corda d'Oro End Notes

You can appreciate music just by listening to it, but knowing the story behind a piece can help enhance your enjoyment. In that spirit, here is background information about some of the topics mentioned in *La Corda d'Oro*. Enjoy!

Page 79, Author's Note: 180 cm
About 5'11".

Page 81, panel 6: *Scherzo Tarantella*
As mentioned in volume 5, this fast, technically challenging piece by Henryk Wieniawski, based on a traditional Italian folk dance, is often chosen to show off a top musician's skills.

Page 115, Author's Note: LaLa
The magazine in which *La Corda d'Oro* appears in Japan.

Page 137: Passionato
In music terminology, *passionato* means "play with passion."

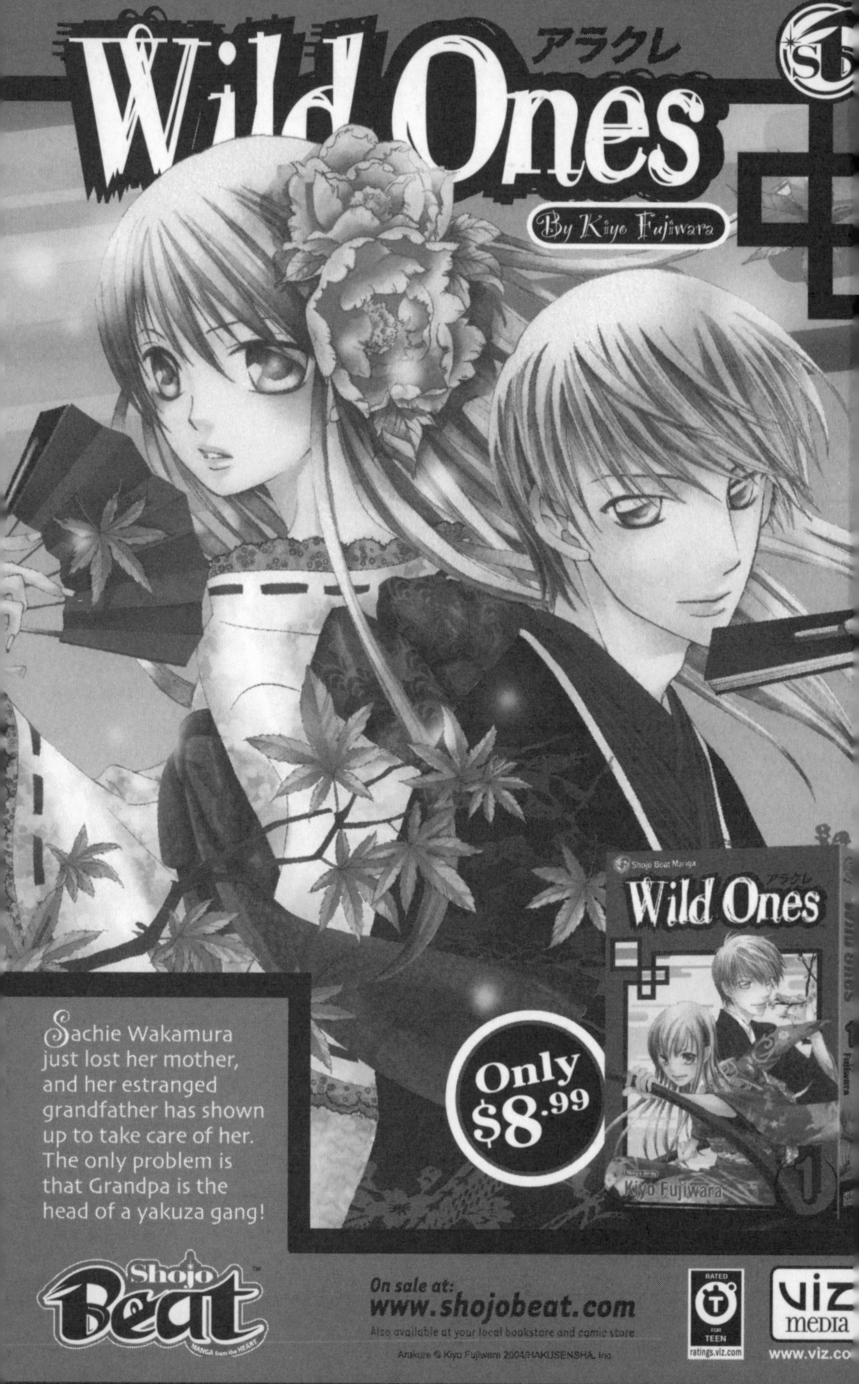
Wild Ones
アラクレ
By Kiyo Fujiwara
Shojo Beat Manga
Wild Ones
アラクレ
Kiyo Fujiwara
1
Only $8.99
Sachie Wakamura just lost her mother, and her estranged grandfather has shown up to take care of her. The only problem is that Grandpa is the head of a yakuza gang!
Shojo Beat
MANGA from the HEART
On sale at:
www.shojobeat.com
Also available at your local bookstore and comic store.
Arakure © Kiyo Fujiwara 2004/HAKUSENSHA, Inc.
RATED T FOR TEEN
ratings.viz.com
VIZ media
www.viz.co

Tell us what you think about Shojo Beat Manga!

Our survey is now available online. Go to:

shojobeat.com/mangasurvey

Help us make our product offerings better!